THE TWILIGHT SAINT

JESSICA PENOT

Warning

This book contains adult language and scenes. This story is meant only for adults as defined by the laws of the country where you made your purchase. Store your books carefully where they cannot be accessed by younger readers.

www.mascotbooks.com

The Twilight Saint

For more information, please contact:
Mascot Books
620 Herndon Parkway #320
Herndon, VA 20170
info@mascotbooks.com

Library of Congress Control Number: 2017910263

CPSIA Code: PBANG0218A
ISBN: 978-1-68401-352-4

Printed in the United States

JESSICA PENOT

THE
TWILIGHT
SAINT

"I have come to set the earth on fire,
and how I wish it were already blazing."

Luke 12:49-53

I

Last Rights

I walk the way of the storm. It is all I have ever known. In the haze of early childhood memories, there exists brief moments before the storm, but now it has consumed everything. Every piece of me has been lost, and all I can remember is fire and smoke and the remains of old dreams singed by death. Even as I sat high above the city, looking down on the magnificent beauty of my tribe, the smell of death lingered. Our tribe's city was alive, vibrant, and prosperous, but to me it was nothing.

I sat perched on top of the highest tower of the karash, looking down on what most people in our tribe would call the real world. I was a Xenderian. I was part of the most powerful tribe of its time. I was more than part of it; I was the sword that cut the path to its glory. I was a karake. I was born to fight for the glory of my people, but as I looked through the icy air, I felt dead inside. My scars were long, and my nightmares haunted my every moment.

The city I looked down on was a strange mixture of archaic and modern. Our glory had bought us favor with those who horded the power of technology and knowledge. Our wars had bought us electricity and medicine and electric vehicles that buzzed through our streets quietly portending future glory. Our brutality had given us links to worlds most tribes could only dream of.

Xender was the most brilliant city of its time. It was in the north, pressed up against the back of the world. North of us there was nothing but ancient mountains and glaciers, and south of us there were lush forests and dark rivers. Xender was buried in the Muet Mountains. It hid in a high placed valley, where the air was thin and crisp. It emerged from the snow like it was built from ice, like white was the only color we knew. From a distance, the city was invisible. It was covered in mountains and snow so deep that it was almost consumed by the snow in the winter. Even in the summer, the glaciers barely receded far enough to find our city. All of our buildings and architecture were constructed from marble that gleamed in the sunlight like a fallen dove. Our streets were made of white brick, and even the hovels of the poor that clung to the sides of the mountain in hungry desperation were made of a white washed wood.

Xender was a city of monuments and ideals. It was built on principles and ideals older than the mountains that embraced it. Those who lived there believed in two things: Zender was the only god and all people were born to create a better society. We were all born to a place. We were all born to inherit goodness and the greatness of our brilliant society.

I smoked my pipe, exhaling black smoke and staring out at my city. It was my city. I fought for it. I kept it.

"You never sleep, do you, Ailive?" Ieya's soft voice woke me from my trance. She sat down next to me, pulling my eyes from the electric utopia at my feet.

I shook my head.

"Me either," she whispered. She was shivering. She looked out over the city. Her eyes lingered on its beauty. "I wonder what it's like—to be one of them, to sleep without dreaming. To live like everyone else."

I shrugged.

"How long now?"

"Until what?"

"Until we die."

"Don't be so dramatic. You're always so excessive."

"They've entombed us here," Ieya whispered. Her voice was filled with such sorrow. She was always like that at night. Ieya had once been beautiful, but her beauty could only be perceived beneath deep scars and a permanent scowl. Her long blonde hair was tied up in a top knot just like the male karake. She dressed in the stark armor of a warrior.

"It's an honor to be here," I said coldly.

"You've changed."

"Of course. I've grown up. You haven't."

"I'm leaving."

I laughed. My voice was as bitter as the wind that cut through the mountains. "Where will you go?"

"I'm going to The University."

"How? The elders will never send you there. You aren't good enough."

"I'll slip on board. When the air ship comes, I'll stow away."

"Do what you want, but I think you'll end up tribeless and alone."

"You never spoke to me this way before. We used to be friends. There was a time you would've helped me." Ieya's voice was heavy with remorse. An ocean of regret divided us.

I shook my head sadly. "That died with Suun."

"There was nothing we could do."

"No. We did nothing. That is different form not being able to do anything."

I stood up and balanced on the narrow edge of the wall that surrounded the fortress like karash. I bowed to Ieya and walked away. I walked back to the tower and leapt down onto the roof and returned to the fortress. The karash was a fortress. Millennia ago, when the world was still chaos, the first Xenderians had built their city within the walls of the karash, but times had changed, and The University had given us a brilliant shield wall that glistened above us, protecting us from invasion. Our city had expanded under the security of that wall, and the karash had been abandoned by normal people. It had been left only to us. It had been left only to the karake, the ghosts, the warriors.

There were over a thousand of us. Although there were men that fought with us in war that lived normal lives, they were not soldiers. We were the soldiers. We alone walked the way of the storm. We lived our lives in its temple. We lived as its lover. We were artists, divinely inspired by Zender himself, practicing the ancient art. Many tribes had forgotten the art. They had been seduced by technology, guns, and easy paths to victory. Yet, we were unvanquished, and although we knew the new arts of war, we knew that the truth only came with the wind.

I walked through the enormous courtyard. The ground was covered in snow and black ice. The white carpet was punctuated by the occasional hint of red where some poor student had fallen during practice. My feet crunched in the snow, leaving my footprints as a reminder of where I had been. It was a long walk to the chapel at the center of the karash.

I entered the chapel and fell to my knees on the bloodstained stone. The huge statue of Zender grimaced down on me. I averted my eyes and stared at the long talons on his feet. I rose slowly, walking toward the stone image of my god and kissed his black feet. He looked down on me with angry eyes.

I lit incense for him and stood beside him, quietly praying.

"Let me be chosen, Zender," I whispered to him. "Please, let me fly away from here. Just for a few years. I swear I will return to you. I will cut down all those who would harm you. Just give me a few years, and I promise I will return. I want to go to The University. Please. Please. Please."

I kissed his feet again and looked up at his face. He was part man, part rwan. He was unmoved by my prayers. But what god is moved by the requests of mortals? We are the dust in their toes. It was our job to honor them.

The incense burnt my nose and clouded my eyes so that as my father entered the chamber, I barely saw him. He kneeled dutifully before Zender and lit a stick of incense before he walked over to me.

My father was a hard man. His face was made as much from stone as Zender's. He was not my real father. My real father had died years ago, but this man, whom I called father, had taken me from my mother and made me a karake. He had saved me from the disgrace of triblessness and made me part of something honorable.

I bowed to him, and he returned the gesture.

"It's good to see you at prayer," he said.

"Zender is kind to those who honor him, Father."

"Is he?"

"So they teach us."

"So they do. The prime minister has a job for you."

I nodded grimly.

"She will meet you at the long house tomorrow before noon; don't be late."

I bowed, and he walked away. I fell to my knees again and prayed.

I loved leaving the karash. I loved deserting its black stone and walking out onto the white marble of our city. I loved the smell of flowers that lingered in the air and the sound of children laughing over the soft whisper of the wind in the trees. The sun seemed brighter, warmer in the city. All around me men and women in colorful saris and tunics made their way to their jobs and lives. They went to the markets and bought silks and imported electronic gadgets that I would never touch. They lingered on street corners talking about their children and their families. I had no family, only my brother, whom I seldom saw.

I lingered on my journey to the longhouse. I walked through the park and listened to the prayer bells as the wind tossed them about. I watched the first flowers of spring poke their heads up from beneath the snow. I watched a mother teach her daughter how to kick a ball. I did all these things with suppressed joy. I kept my face hard, but my soul was light.

The longhouse was in the center of the city. It was the seat of our government. It was a simple structure of white marble. Tall, ornate columns surrounded the long building, giving it an elegance. I stood at the stone steps at the base of the longhouse and took off my shoes. I looked up and took a deep breath before I walked up past the columns and into the building. The longhouse was bustling with people coming from court or making some request to be filled by some government official. I told the guard who I was, and he looked down at me with trepidation. They all did. Karake were feared by all. We were the angels of death. No one saw anything but our red robes. Our faces were all the same. I accepted the irony in this. The Longhouse was a symbol of peace and freedom. Our people viewed it as representation of goodness, yet it was the longhouse that called me when I was needed. They would argue that our wars kept the peace. Our wars were fights for our freedom, but I knew death was death and my work was no more peaceful than any act of violence.

The prime minister had a large office at the end of the longhouse. I entered the room and bowed to her. She was talking to someone on her computer when I entered, and she smiled and ended her conversation before she rose to great me. She was an elegant woman. Her skin was as white as ivory. All our people were fair, but she seemed more like ice than woman. She had painted her lips red and her eyes were brushed with purple to match her elaborate, stunning sari. She must have been wrapped with over a mile of silk, embroidered with tiny flowers. Gold glistened in her ears and on her toes.

I stared at her in awe. In the karash, vanity was forbidden. I had never painted my face or worn silk. Her beauty was as foreign to me as the electronic toys children carried.

"Ailive Karake," she said softly.

"My lady," I answered humbly.

"I'm told that it was you that assassinated the Verdu king."

"Yes."

"That's quite a feat for one so young."

I smiled darkly. "It's my apparent youth that makes it so easy."

The prime minister frowned a little. "You've been honored many times by the high council and by the elders of the karash, yet you have not even gone through your last rights yet. Is that correct?"

"I proved myself in Verdu in more ways than assassination. I am the best assassin, and one of the best karake." I took no pride in this. Assassination was easier for me than for the others. No one expected me to be violent. I was pretty, and I looked far younger than I was. I was the snake in the grass. No one realized what I was until it was too late.

In my heart, I wished I could be more than this. I wanted to fight face-to-face, with honor, but I was a creature of duty, and I did as I was told no matter how I felt about it.

The prime minister nodded thoughtfully. She moved across the room and stood at the tall windows that looked out on the market place outside.

"I have a job for you. I want you to tell no one of it, not even your father."

"Of course. We are a silent people."

"An airship with University colors will be in the courtyard tomorrow morning at dusk. I want you to get on board. Your instructions will await you inside."

I nodded. The minister studied me sadly for a moment. "How did you become what you are?" she asked.

"My lady?"

"I don't mean to intrude, but it seems a tragedy that our people would let such a pretty girl be lost to the storm."

"I am honored to serve our people."

"Are you? Did you not want children? A husband? Did your mother give you over to this fate?"

"I know nothing of children, and my mother hated me. She wanted to cast me out, but my brother, Xander, saved me and took me to the temple."

"Why would he take you to the karash and not the church where the priestesses would have cared for you and educated you?"

"I was born for the storm, my lady. I was born to fight. The priestesses would have cast me out as well."

"Born to fight? You were a little girl. You can't be more than seventeen now. How old were you when you fought in Verdu?"

"I was fourteen, my lady." The Verdune War seemed like it was centuries ago. I felt like I was as old as the crones that sat knitting in the park. I had been a girl when I left for the war, but that girl was dead.

"I will have to talk to the elders about this. It just doesn't seem right."

"Don't. Don't talk to them. My mother was afraid of me. I broke my sister's arm. I was a violent, hateful child, and she left me to die, but my brother knew the truth. He told me all people have a place in Zender's tribe. We are Zender's chosen people. Zender forgets none of us, and he gave me over to the gods of war and fire and I am theirs now. I am where I belong." I spoke with a hint of bitterness. I was what I was, and no one could change that. Even the elders couldn't turn back time and make me something I wasn't.

The prime minister nodded. "Very well, little assassin. Be at the ship at dusk."

Karash was taken from the old word for "to dream." In the old days, those that slept in the fortress keep were said to dream of the future. They were seers and prophets. Zender spoke to men in those days, but it seemed to me that the karash had become a place haunted by its past. The future had faded. It drifted into shadow, and those of us who slept in the keep were tormented by dreams of what had been.

Ieya and I slept together in a room with a small window and a large bed. Rwans and birds were painted on the walls and a great fire roared at the foot of our bed. I knew that Ieya was dreaming. I heard her heavy breath. I woke up and looked down on her just before she sat up. Tears stained her cheeks, and her eyes were wide with terror.

"More dreams?" I asked.

"I saw Suun," Ieya said with sorrow.

I got out of bed and walked over the fire. I looked up at the walls. I didn't want to think about Suun. Thinking about her wouldn't change anything. What was done was done, and Suun was gone. I tried to focus on the walls of my room. They were hung with the weapons Ieya and I had mastered. There were guns and knives and swords. You always learned to shoot first. The sword came later. Only a master can kill with a sword.

"This time I tried to save her, but you weren't there."

"Don't talk about Suun. She's dead," I said gruffly.

"They held her down and tortured her. She was screaming. I can still hear her scream. I tried to save her, but you weren't there."

"It's an ironic dream, isn't it? Seeing as I was the one who wanted to help her and you stopped me." I tried to mask the anger in my voice, but some of the anger seeped out.

"I was afraid."

"You're a fool."

"It's easier for you. You know that don't you? They don't bother you, because you're strong. I'm not like you. They would have forgiven you if you had killed those boys, our friends, but I would have been executed. You're an asset. I'm not."

"That's the difference between you and I; you always think of the outcome. You think too much. That's why you are weak. Suun didn't have to die, but she did because you had to think about what would happen to us."

"If I could go back..."

"You can't go back."

"I miss her."

"We shouldn't have ever spoken with her to begin with. She was a Verdune. She was the enemy. We should have killed her to begin with. We betrayed our tribe by talking to her."

I closed my eyes. I could still see Suun. We had been young when we met her. We were children. Ieya and I had spent three years in the occupied Verdune city. We had grown up there. We had learned to fight, learned to kill. We had befriended Suun against our better judgment. She had shown us her world, her tribe. She took us to libraries and operas and taught us how to paint. We had seen the world through her eyes, but in the end, she had to die, like the other Verdune.

Ieya began to cry. She drew her knees up under her chin and curled up and sobbed. I looked at her coldly. Part of me wanted to comfort her, but that part was crushed by the greater part of me that saw only her weakness.

"It's always been so easy for you," she wept.

"I've worked just as hard as you."

The sun poked its lonely head up over the mountains and through the window. The sky bled bright orange. Dawn had come, and I had work to do. I didn't say goodbye to Ieya. I just put on my robes and walked down to the airship waiting for me in the snow. I had seen airships before. They came and went in the night. Taking and bringing trade goods to The

University. I had even traveled in a few of them before. I had traveled to far off lands to kill strangers in the dark. They were stunning devices. To me, they seemed like magic. They glided across the clouds the way boats glided across the water.

I stood at the door of the small black ship and looked hesitantly into its belly. This airship was nicer than our old airships. The Xenderians had maybe ten airships, and they all seemed old compared to the modern marvel that sat before me. A man dressed all in black emerged from the ship and glared at me. I had seen foreigners before. I had fought them, but Suun was the only foreigner I had ever spoken with. The man in front of me was different from any foreigner I had ever seen before.

He was tall and lanky. He had bright red hair and green eyes. His fair skin was dotted with odd pigmentations. He looked down on me with a cold cruelty that made my scowl even deeper. I didn't bow to him as I would have any equal. Instead, I pushed past him into the belly of the ship.

The ship was comfortable. Soft chairs had been attached to the floor and there were computer and television screens everyplace. The red-haired man followed me into the ship and sat down at some kind of control panel. I sat down behind him and said nothing.

I looked out the window carefully, deliberately hiding my awe. The world was spread out beneath us in miniature. The clouds pressed up against my window, and in a childish gesture I reached out, trying to grab one. I watched as the mountains passed away and we passed over large forests and rivers. I saw other tribes and their cities pass by us and then the forests thinned, giving way to grass land.

"You've never been on an airship," the man said.

"Never one as nice as this," I answered.

"I'm Myrd."

"I'm Ailive."

"I didn't expect you to be so young."

"Neither will they. They'll expect an assassin, but they never expect me," I said coldly.

Myrd smiled. "There are five people on the list. I'll set down as far away as I can. We aren't supposed to be associated with this, you understand?"

"You mean The University?" I asked.

"I mean us, and you don't need to know who. Just do your job and if you get caught…"

"I won't get caught."

"What makes you so confident?"

"Trust me."

Myrd handed me a sealed envelope, and I took it, opening it. It was written in Etrusan. I knew Etrusan, but only barely. It was the language of The University. It was the language of the ancient scholars that had built The University and saved knowledge from the chaos of anarchy. That's what they say, at least. Once there had been one country and one law, but war had divided it and, in the vacuum of anarchy, the scholars had built The University, and the tribes had created themselves.

The packet contained maps of the city and pictures of the people I was going to kill. I studied them carefully. Myrd handed me a drink.

"If you get caught, you must say nothing of me."

"I won't get caught."

"If you talk, we'll kill you and your family."

"I have no family."

Myrd handed me a pile of brightly colored clothing. I stared at it.

"Put it on. You'll blend in more in their attire," he said.

"Thanks," I said. "I'll wear what I'm wearing," I said indifferently. I didn't need his help. This job was like a well-rehearsed dance. I knew the steps by heart. I looked out the window. The grassland was gone, and there was only desert. Vast stretches of dirt punctuated only by rock. I stared out at the sun bleached landscape and noticed that the ship was landing. Myrd set the ship down in the middle of the desert. As far as I could see, there was nothing.

Myrd stepped off the ship with me and pointed west. "Go that way," he said. "The city is walled. You'll have to climb over. Meet me here in three hours. I'll leave if you're late."

The ship vanished in a cloud of dust, and I stood alone in the desert. I had my knife and a short sword and that was all. I breathed deeply and peeled off the top part of my robes. I was all but naked. I was covered only by a thin slip of fabric. Experience had taught me that most soldiers were men and that men were easily distracted by skin. My flesh was the only disguise I ever needed. I took my sword and knife and started my run to the city.

The sun had not yet risen in Hyra. It was dark, and I used the cover of night to approach the city walls. Hyra was large. In the north, there was only Xender. All the other tribes were small. They had no technology. They still lived in the dark ages. Hyra was different. I scaled the wall and passed through the shield. I sat atop the wall for a long time looking out at the city, studying its contours.

Hyra was even more advanced than our city. That scared me. We were the kings of the North, but the south had its own rulers. The streets shone a polished black in the moonlight. The moons didn't matter, however, because the city was lit from within. Every house, every structure, had electricity. Even the streets possessed their own lights. In Xender, only the wealthy could afford electricity, but in Hyra power was given to all. I grimaced as I jumped off the wall onto the well-lit streets.

I clung to the shadows as I navigated the streets of the labyrinthine city. It was hot, and my clothes were quickly saturated with sweat. I was used to the cold air, the wind of the Northern Mountains. The home I was looking for was in a tall building. It climbed upward and looked down on the rest of the city.

I walked in easily. The guard looked at me as if I was an alien, and I returned his astonished glare. I had never seen a Southerner before. His skin was black and he was tall, taller than I thought it was possible for men to be. I quickly muffled my shock at his appearance and walked toward him. He stared at me, blinded by my strangeness, and I slit his throat before he had even reached for his gun.

At that time, I had never seen an elevator, so I passed them by without notice and climbed the ten stories to the top of the building. The climb was easy for me. I had spent many mornings hiking in the high mountains and climbing over the scree that lead to the karash. I followed the instructions I was given and found the door to my target's apartment. The door was made of a soft wood. It shattered easily, and I stepped inside.

Two guards sat just inside the doorway to the luxurious apartment. They were both chatting quietly and not paying proper attention to their job. The both jumped when I walked in. They drew their guns reflexively, but they hesitated before they pulled the trigger. This hesitation was all I needed. I smiled at them, and they waited just long enough for me to slit both of their throats. The blood poured out of their necks in violent shades of alizarin crimson and stained the white carpet.

I walked through the apartment to the backroom where I had been told my target would be sleeping. I was careful to walk quietly. The carpet beneath my feet muffled the sound of my footsteps. I walked into the bedroom where the man I was supposed to kill laid wrapped in pleasant dreams.

I pushed the door open quietly and stood in the shadows, watching him breath. I had killed many, but the scene before me left me still. The man was lying in a large bed with his wife next to him and between them, was their infant daughter. I knew what I was supposed to do. I was supposed to kill them all. You can never leave witnesses. I should have slit their throats quietly and moved on, but I couldn't do it. My sword was in my hand, dripping blood onto the white carpet, but I stood still, unable to move. The baby's soft breath echoed in the darkness. The thought of silencing that breath filled me with dread.

It was the wife that opened her eyes as the first light of dawn spread out over the room. She yawned and looked up at me with black eyes. She was so dark. Her hair was thick. She was large. She was different. She stared at me quietly, and for a while we just looked at each other, but then her lips parted, and she whispered an almost inaudible plea.

She spoke in Hyran, and I couldn't understand her but I knew the heart of her words. I knew she was begging for the life of her daughter.

I responded as I was trained too. I killed her husband with a gesture. She should have screamed, but instead she grabbed her daughter and crawled away from me. There were tears in her eyes. I could almost hear my father screaming, "Kill them." I heard his voice urging me forward over the vast expanses of space, but the woman's eyes were desperate and her baby was perfect.

So I let my sword down and nodded to the weeping woman.

"Tell no one," I said in my stunted Etrusan. "If you speak of me, I'll come back for you."

The woman nodded. "Thank you. I promise. I'll never speak of you," she whispered in Etrusan so clear she must have been University trained.

I quietly stalked out of the room and finished my work. The others were easy. They died quietly, and no one who saw me lived. I climbed out of the city and put my robes back on. I tightened my topknot and painted my face with indifference. But despite my façade of apathy, I heard my father in my head: "You've failed. The storm will never touch you. You are a woman led by her heart."

I went back to the temple that morning and stood at Zender's feet. I pled his forgiveness for my mistake. Zender could be merciful. I didn't have long for my prayers. Time was precious. Our tribe always seemed to be balanced on a razor's edge. The sword kept us from annihilation. Outside our shield walls, the forces that would destroy us were constantly mounting and we had to be vigilant. We could never stop fighting.

Another war came and went. We won. We always won, and Ieya and I sat in the snow looking down on the rubble of the decimated city below us. My teeth chattered in the cold, and Ieya's face was splattered with blood.

"How long now?" Ieya asked.

"Until?" I asked.

"The ship comes from The University."

I lacked the strength to argue with her. "I don't know. Maybe three weeks."

"Three weeks," she said between clenched teeth.

"Yes."

"Do you think we're monsters?"

"What?"

"We killed all those people, and we don't even know why. Aren't we the devils from the scriptures? Aren't we the devils that come down at night and feed on the innocent?"

"I think you've gone mad. We're Zender's chosen people. We serve Zender. They are pagans. They aided the Verdune."

"We don't know that. We just do as we are told. What if they did nothing, and we just stole their marble?"

"That's absurd." Everything we had ever been taught went against what she was saying. Every teacher we ever had told us that we were good. We fought for Zender.

"We..."

I interrupted her. I stood up and walked away. I couldn't listen to anymore of her sedition. A group of the apprentice karake, who were also ready to take their last rites, stood on the edge of a cliff looking down. They were smoking pipes and laughing. Their breath froze in the air, but the pipe made them immune to the cold. I walked up beside them and Marcus, a man ten years my senior, gave me a jovial slap on the back. I was the youngest to take the last rites, and I stood out amongst my peers as much as I had stood out to the Hyrans. The group of men in their twenties looked at me as a cat regards a mouse.

"You did good today," Marcus said with a robust laugh.

Marcus inched close to me. Ieya and I were the only females they ever saw on a regular basis. "Did you see the way that girl's head exploded when I hit it with that club?" He laughed.

"I was too busy to study your conquests," I said coldly.

"It's always amazing the way people beg for their lives in that gibberish. They're too stupid to know we don't understand," Marcus said.

"Too stupid to understand," Xeres said.

"It was a good day for us. You did very well, Ailive. If it weren't for you, I would think all women were squealing weaklings."

"I'm glad you think highly of me."

"I've had Ieya ten times now, but we all know you'd be the last woman we ever had if we touched you. You bring honor to your gender," Marcus said.

I grimaced with disgust and looked back at Ieya shivering, alone in the cold. Marcus grabbed my breast and smiled. "Unless of course, you wanted me to touch you?" His invitation was as repugnant as he was. I grabbed his hand and bent it backward, snapping the bone of his arm like a dry twig. He squealed, and I smiled.

"I would rather cut off my legs than let you touch me, Marcus, and if you touch Ieya again, I'll kill you," I spat. The thought of Marcus defiling my friend made me wish he were the enemy. Ieya deserved better, and Marcus was nothing more than a pig driven by lust.

Xeres pushed Marcus aside and stood beside me with a cruel grin. He touched me, and I flinched. "Remember what side you are on, little Ailive," he said. I flinched. Xeres was one of the apprentice Karake that could stand up to me. He was the strongest of us.

"I walk the way of the storm."

Xeres punched me. I tried to dodge, but he was faster than me. I fell in the snow with a heavy thud. The blood poured out of my nose and onto the white snow. Xeres looked down on me. I thought he might kick me, but the group of young men seemed satisfied and left me in the snow.

I stood up and braced myself against the increasing blizzard. I walked away from the group. The wind howled and blasted me with a constant barrage of snow, but I pushed forward, driven only by my desire to escape the others of my kind. I didn't belong anywhere. I didn't even belong with my own kind. I was utterly alone, and I fled from all the emotions that accompanied that isolation. I finally found my way to a lonely precipice encased in ice. I sat down and lit my pipe. My shivering stopped, and I stared into the whiteness of the blizzard around me. The wind was angry that night, but I let it have me. I let it take me, and I prayed to Zender that it would consume me. I prayed that I might become the storm, indifferent and deadly.

I opened my eyes and saw a rwan. It stood before me as if Zender had answered my prayers. I had never seen a living rwan before, and it took me a moment to realize what I was seeing. It was a black beast, with long curved horns. Its eyes glowed an ominous red from beneath its sleek, obsidian flesh. It stood on four legs, with its claws clutching the ice. Its large wings were folded back, and its long tail twitched with demonic rage. It looked at me and opened its mouth into a deafening roar, exposing razor sharp teeth.

Tonight I die. As soon as I thought it, I knew I didn't care. There was nothing in the afterlife that could be any harder than what I had survived in life. So I stood up and walked toward the beast that was known as living death. I stood up and approached the beast that was Zender's own son, abandoned and tortured, left to torment Zender's human children. I reached out for it, and it regarded me with curiosity. I touched its flesh. It was smooth, like rock, and hot.

It looked at me one last time, and then it vanished. It vanished into the storm like a specter or a dream.

"Thank you," I said to Zender. "Thank you."

The last rites were always given on the first day of the gnawing, when the three sister moons aligned and the air grew thick with heat. The snow melted off the mountains, flooding the valleys and filling the lake at the edge of the city. The sky turned orange and violent red and for two weeks there was heat and light. There was no darkness, only gnawing. We were woken before dawn. Before the gnawing began. Before the heat and the flood. I was awoken and brought down to Zender's chapel like a sacrifice. I stood with the twenty men who would become master karake. Marcus was there and so was Xeres. I looked for Ieya, but couldn't find her. All of us were stripped down to our waists and painted red, and then we joined the parade. The parade was long. All of those who wanted to become masters of any trade joined us: doctors, engineers, brick layers, and farmers. They all progressed slowly through the city, naked and red.

We shivered until the first light of the gnawing painted the city in a violent orange and then our sweat cut rivers through the red paint, streaking us. Finally, we made it to the church. We stepped into the brilliant building of cool marble. It was surrounded by incense and offerings, and inside it was bright. The floors were covered in ornate rugs and the windows were all stained glass. Elaborate murals showing the glory of Zender filled the church. The priestesses stood at the altar, wrapped in white linen.

Zender is as nature is. He is all things. He is merciful and cruel. He brings darkness and light. So as darkness is to light, the karash is to the church. We of the karash celebrate Zender with death, and the priestesses of the temple celebrate him through kindness and charity, through prayer and love. No one but karake went to the karash, but the church was always filled with people praying for salvation.

We entered the church and knelt before the priestesses and one by one we were given the last rites.

"These are your last rites," the priestess said to me. "Once you have been given them you are free no more. Do you understand?"

I nodded.

"Once you are given them, you will always be karake. You may never leave. You may never choose another profession. There is no turning back."

I nodded again.

"Then rise, Ailive Karake." I rose and was anointed and began the long walk home. Before I left I saw my brother, Xander, kneeling before the priestess.

"Once you are given them you will always be a doctor. You may never leave. You may never choose another profession. There is no turning back," she said to him.

My brother nodded and then was anointed.

I didn't expect what happened next. Everyone knew the last rites that occurred in the church. Everyone knew the parade and the anointing. We had seen these things since we were children, but what was done in the temple, in the karash, was shrouded in secrecy. The first thing I remember is the cold stone of the chapel beneath my feet. We were herded into the chapel like swine ready for slaughter and then we were stripped naked. We remained silent. We dared not voice our terror. The elders laid us down face first on the cold stone and then the artists came. They came with knives and ink. For over twenty-four hours we lay on our faces and let those men cut into our backs and arms. They cut and then they ground ink into the weeping wounds, and we bit our tongues and prayed. They turned our bodies into living scripture painted with the words of the prophets. It covered us in the long elegant writing of the old ones, our founders, our fathers.

I don't know when, but at some point the others began to scream. Their courage failed, and their wails filled the temple with violent intensity. As the screams circled me, my father turned me over. He leaned down on me and pinned me to the ground. I looked up at him with fearful eyes. I saw one of the elders coming toward me with some kind of surgical instrument, and I felt woozy. My head began to spin. Two men pried my legs apart and when they cut my insides, I screamed until my throat went dry and there was no sound left in me. We had all been castrated.

I lost consciousness. Sometimes, I would wake up in a puddle of my own blood, and the pain would make me scream again. The other newly castrated karake healed and left. Their wounds were cleaned and bound and they healed, but my womb could neither be cleaned nor bound, so I bled. I saw death many times that week. I imagined I spoke with him. He came and sat beside me. He called my name. I dreamt. My dreams were so vivid they seemed real, and in my dreams I was five again, huddling in a corner, listening to my mother.

I was home, in our little house high on the mountain. The snow was thick on the ground and the wind was beating our humble, wooden house. We had lived high on the side of a mountain and the wind battered us with all its angry vengeance, but I could still hear my mother above its howl.

"I can't do it anymore," she wept.

Xander had answered her calmly, "She's been through a lot. Give her time. She'll get better."

"There are twelve of you. I can hardly make ends meet. I can't waste my energy on her cruelty."

"She isn't cruel. She's lost."

My mother's tears were as cruel as any karake. "She's a monster."

"Please." Xander was pleading with her.

"I can't."

"But she's mine," Xander cried. I had been Xander's. He had been the one who took care of me. He had been the one who held me at night when I cried.

"She beat your sister almost to death," my mother said coldly. "I can't afford any more hospital bills."

"Don't cast her out. Take her somewhere else. At least make sure she is safe."

"Who would have her?"

"Take her to the karash."

My mother laughed again. "It would be better to cast her out."

"Everyone has a place in the tribe. That's what the prophets say. Maybe the karash is Ailive's."

I couldn't see them, but I knew my mother hugged Xander. I knew that she leaned heavily into his boyish arms and found refuge in his precocious brilliance. I pulled my covers over my head and shivered.

Xander had gotten me up before anyone else. He had dressed me in my heaviest wool and handed me my only toy. It was a tiny stuffed cat. I clung to the thing as he carried me into the cold. I could hardly see my mother in front of us. Her tiny form was nothing but a huddled mass beneath her wool jacket. It was a long walk to the karash, and my mother didn't stop until she came to door of the enormous building. The karash stared down at us with its dark eyes. Its architecture was different from the rest of the city's. It sat high on the mountain, surrounded by old stone and mortar. The gates were open, guarded only by two huge, stone demons. The demons were Zender's minions and instruments of his vengeance. They stared out at us with fierce, black eyes. My mother shivered and drew back.

"You have to come with us," Xander whispered.

My mother only shook her head.

"It's perfectly safe," Xander said.

"It reeks of death in there," my mother said.

I walked ahead of them into through the thick walls and into the snow filled courtyard. I looked up at the looming towers of the karash. The courtyard was filled with boys and men running or kicking or doing strange dances in the swirling snow. They did not shiver or whimper or complain. I moved past the demons and into the light.

"See," Xander said. "Ailive isn't afraid."

My mother stepped toward me and pulled me into her arms. It had been a long time since she had touched me, and I leaned into her embrace like a desperate lover. The tears on her cheeks were cold against my skin.

"Forgive me," she whispered into my ear. "I'm weak."

I held her with all the strength in my body and I knew, in that moment, that the only monster I would ever fear was weakness.

My mother held my hand as we were led into the blackness of the fortress by a sullen soldier wrapped in a red cloak. I knew where they were leading me. They led me into the center chapel of the karash, the temple of fire. Grown men died there in the struggle to learn the path. Blood stained the stones beneath our feet. My mother tried to pass me off to Xander. She tugged at her long, silver hair and whimpered. Her gray eyes filled with tears as she made her flaccid excuses. She didn't want to enter the temple. She shook and trembled at the gateway. She stared up at the faces of rwans and the monsters that dwelt in the ice that was carved into the temple and turned to run, but I walked in. I walked over the hard stone and stood before the flame. Even then, I knew my place.

Xander and my mother followed me into the inner chapel of the karash and put me before the elders. I looked at the elders defiantly and spoke with a clarity that's rare for a five year-old. The man who was to be my father was the questioner at our inquisition.

"Why do you bring this child before us?" he asked my mother.

"Because she is wild and fierce and has clearly been born for you," my mother answered.

"She is young and female. She will have a hard time amongst us."

"You wouldn't say that if you knew her."

"She must pass the test."

A small puppy was brought into the room. The creature was a lump of fur. It was small and brown with long fur and blue eyes. It was sweet and soft. It cried into the emptiness for the warmth of its mother. My mother turned away, trying to leave the temple again. Xander held her. "You have to watch," he whispered into her ear.

My father gave me a large axe and pointed at the puppy. I looked up at the man who would be my father and then back at my mother. My mother stood in the doorway weeping and wiping her nose. My father stood above me with his arms folded in front of him. He looked down on me like a god. I couldn't imagine him submitting to weakness or fear. I couldn't imagine him letting me go because he was not strong enough or because he lacked will. I took the axe and dropped the stuffed cat I had been clinging to. The velvet animal fell into the filth as I moved toward the whimpering puppy. I had watched Xander kill the chickens for dinner more than a dozen times. I had watched how he had cut their heads off and plucked them. I had seen my father killed in front of me. I had seen things that I didn't want to remember. What was one small dog's life in a world of death?

I cut the dog in two without thought or remorse. The tiny dog fell to the ground, limp like the stuffed cat, into a puddle of its own blood. I was tired, and the only thing I could feel was the cold. I smiled up at my father in hope of approval, but I found none. He hit me, three times. I fell to the ground, clutching my cheek. With the irrational rage my mother so loathed, I lunged at my father and bit his hand as hard as I could. I hit him and kicked with all my tiny strength.

"We've seen enough," one of the elders said. "Are you willing to give your daughter over entirely to us? You'll never know her as yours again. She'll not look to you with love or affection. She'll be ours, and all she will know is the storm."

My mother nodded and left without looking back at me. I spit on the ground behind her as she left. My father took my hand and smiled down on me. For the first time in as long as I could remember, I felt safe. All of my fear melted away. I knew I had finally come home.

I awoke up alone in the temple and called Xander's name. I pleaded for him to come, but only Zender, my angry god, answered me. The others were all gone when Ieya came and sat down beside me.

"I ran away," she said. "I hid, but I saw what they did to you. I know you'll curse me later, but I had to find help."

Xander emerged from my pain soaked dream. He examined me gently. He gave me medicine, and the pain faded, and then I slept. I awoke, and the bleeding had ceased. There was a lingering pain, but the blood was gone. Xander was holding my head and Ieya was holding my hand.

"I'm so sorry," Xander said. "Zender forgive me."

I reached out and touched his tear stained cheek. I felt the moisture of his tears beneath my callused fingers. I wished I had the strength to hug him. "What sin could you possibly have committed?"

"I brought you here," he wept. "I didn't know it was like this."

"You did right." My voice was soft. I wanted to take away his guilt and sorrow. He was the only person I really loved. I smiled up at him sweetly.

"This is going to stop," he said with a vehement resolve. "The Prime Minister knows of this. She thinks that this is barbarous. We are a modern people now. This can't go on. It will stop."

"No," I whispered. "It's an honor to walk the way of the storm."

"You would have died if Ieya hadn't brought me."

"I would have died bringing honor to my tribe and my god."

"Your faith is blind, Ailive."

"Isn't all faith blind?"

They sat with me for a while, my only friends. I smiled and looked over at Ieya.

"Thank you," I said to her.

"I love you," Ieya said to me as she stroked my forehead. "You've saved my life so many times I can't count. You are my sister. I couldn't let them kill you."

"I wish I had done more to protect you…" Ieya stopped me. She put her finger over my lips and smiled. There was nothing I could say that she didn't already know. We had both done the best we could in terrible times.

"I hate them, you know?" she whispered.

"I know."

"I would kill them all if I could." Her voice was heavy with hate and hurt so deep it burned on her breath.

"I'm sorry for what they've done to you. I'm sorry for what they did to you."

We were silent. They had always done things to Ieya they never dared do to me. She was the only girl amongst violent men and that never ended well. I was strong enough to fight them off, but Ieya wasn't so lucky.

"Is this what you have faith in?" Xander asked.

"You can't blame the weakness of men on Zender."

"No, but this place can be burnt to the ground."

"Xander, you saved my life. This place saved my life."

We stopped talking. There was nothing more to say. They held me and Ieya cleaned me, but they had to leave before the elders came. They snuck away quietly, but they left me wrapped in warm wool and linen.

My father found me. "You live?" he said in surprise. It occurred to me, in my drug induced lucidity that this is why there had never been any women master karake. They never survived. The castration was something men could survive, but having an old man yank your uterus out with a hook isn't quite so simple.

"I live."

"Someone helped you?"

"Only Zender."

"Who brought the blankets?"

"I saw only angels."

The elders greeted me with pomp and ceremony as I exited the chapel. All twelve of the karake elders took turns presenting me with swords and robes, but it was my father's gift that meant the most to me. He had never been a kind man, but he stood at the end of the line that day beaming with pride in his disciple. He handed me a gilded sword and bowed to me.

"It's an honor to be your father. It's an honor to be part of shaping one of the most powerful warriors of her generation."

I bowed to him. I was happy. I had honored my father and my people.

He even leaned forward and kissed me on the forehead. I blushed, and he smiled.

I was a master karake and that very night the elders voted me to be one of the five karake to study at The University. I was bubbling over with warmth inside.

I was finally free.

II
The University

A lone bird flew over the marble walls of Xender the day I finally found my freedom. Fifty of us gathered in the last warmth of the gnawing moons. We stood at the edge of the city, in front of the church. I was alone that day. Although four other karake departed with me, I went alone. I knew I was not like them. There were other students with us, but you couldn't tell us apart. The engineers and the doctors and the karake all looked the same. We were all wrapped in heavy gray cotton that covered our tattoos. From a distance, we must have all looked like a strange cluster of phantoms.

Our long white hair was tied back. None of us wore topknots, and none of the women had their hair plaited. Our faces were varying degrees of white, and our eyes were either blue or gray. Without our clothes and jewelry and status, we were all the same. Small, frail- looking, and pale. We were part of the ice covered mountains or the white city. We were ghosts.

The airship that landed before us was not like any had seen before. It was like a small flying city. It was gilded and lined with gold and silver. We all stared up and waited, and an army of gray clad scholars emerged from the ship's belly. They could have been clones too. They were fat and ruddy. Although their hair and eyes came in different colors, their roundness marked them as scholars.

I followed the procession onto the ship and sat as far away from the crowd as I could. I pushed myself up against the back of the ship and hid. Xander found me.

"Ailive," he said with a warm smile.

Despite myself I grinned. "Xander," I said.

"You look better."

"Thanks to you."

"Thanks to Ieya."

"Is she all right?"

"I hope so. Who knows? She said she was going to try to hide on this ship. I pray she makes it."

"Me too. What'll happen to her if she doesn't make it?"

Xander put a comforting hand on my shoulder, and I drew back involuntarily. I was not accustomed to being touched, and the warmth of his hand felt odd. I shivered and looked at him. He was a small man, even for our people. He was short and thin. He looked like a strong wind would knock him down. His eyes were a strange clouded blue that made him appear distant. He had chiseled almost handsome features, and there was a calmness about him that spread through the room, inducing a strange quiet in those around him. He had cut his hair short, a style that had recently been imported from The University. Many of the more modern young men cut their hair now. I wasn't accustomed to it, but it suited him.

"You never ask about the family," he commented blandly.

"Do they ever ask about me?"

"Point well taken," he answered. "But that doesn't mean they don't care."

"Yes it does." There was nothing Xander could say that would make me believe they cared about me.

"Mother regrets what she did to you."

I laughed bitterly. "Don't," I said. "Don't. I really don't care."

"She says she's sorry."

I shook my head. "So you're going to be a doctor?"

"I am a doctor. I'm just going to be a better one."

"I'm sorry. I forget. Sometimes I forget I'm a full karake," I said in disbelief. "It all happened so fast."

"Did it? It seemed to take forever to me." His voice was heavy with fatigue.

I studied Xander's face. He seemed older in the light of airship. His face seemed warn and tired. "I guess to me, too. I don't know. I just can't believe we're going to The University. I've been waiting my entire life for this."

"Really? I've been an apprentice for a long time. I've watched people suffer and die, and there was nothing I could do. There are only three University trained doctors in the city and they're the only ones who can really... They can do miracles. I want to do miracles."

I smiled. "It's good to see you." It was good to know he was still the same Xander, fighting to save people the way he had saved me. It was comforting to know that he was the same good person he had always been.

"You too."

"What will you learn in The University? You seem quite proficient at your trade," he said coldly.

"I'll learn sociology, about the other tribes. I'll learn who our enemies are, and how they think. I'll learn linguistics. I'll learn more about explosives and bombs, and there is even a class taught by an older master on the art of the storm."

"I thought The University was supposed to immune to the politics of the world around it. I thought they would have nothing to do with war or war craft."

A sudden image of the Hyrans I had killed for The University passed before my eyes and vanished. I wished I could still believe that the University was the peaceful utopia we had been taught it was. The images bathed me in unwelcome knowledge that I tried to hide from my conscious mind. "I don't think they're as noble as people think," I whispered.

The University had been founded over five thousand years ago by several groups of tribeless who had banded together. By luck or fate, they had all been tribal elders with much great knowledge and had sworn off war. They had decided to pool all the tribes' knowledge into one place for the betterment of mankind. At first they had worked alone, writing books and experimenting. But as age crept up on them, they let others in, and their knowledge deepened. They built an amazing city with a science so advanced it seemed like magic to the outlying tribes. They discovered gunpowder, electricity, antibiotics, and created machines that could fly. The tribes grew to fear the ever-growing magical society and banded together to launch an assault on these men of learning. But these men were wise and offered the tribes a truce. The University would open its doors to all who wanted to learn as long as they were of age and willing to come without tribal colors and with the understanding that if they ever whispered a hint of their tribal allegiance, they would be cast out.

Since that time, technology, art, science, and culture had flourished under a hidden exchange of ideas. At The University, a master physician would learn more about chemistry and physics. They would grow in their understanding of anatomy and physiology. They would learn everything that was known in the world about their science, and they could choose to return to their tribe or stay at The University. A warrior would learn weapons that had just been built and skills that had never been seen in their own tribe. More important than this to me, everyone who went to The University could study all fields. We got a break from being what we had always been. I could walk the streets as a woman, and no one would see the blood in my eyes. I could read poetry and paint or learn to sing. I had four years to learn the knowledge of all tribes, and I embraced the idea of freedom.

At The University, everyone wore gray. Everyone had to cover any tattoos or markings that revealed their tribe, and everyone spoke Etrusan, the language of The University. Not everyone got to go to University; only the more advanced skills required this level of training. And even amongst these elite trades, only the best were allowed to go. Those of us on the airship were the best of our people. We were the strongest, the brightest, and the most adept at our trades.

I looked over at Xeres as I contemplated this.

"Is he one of your friends?" Xander asked, noticing my gaze.

"No. I don't care for him."

Xander studied the young man. "He's good looking, and he must be bright, if he's here."

"There is more to a man than looks and wit."

"Is there? Would Zender say so?"

"Probably not outright, but the prophets say the Zender values mercy."

"I've never seen that in any of his disciples."

"You sound like Ieya. She speaks heresy like it was her native tongue."

Xander shrugged. "It isn't just us. Our tribe is at a crossroads, I think. There are many of us, including the prime minister, that believe change is necessary. However, those devoted to a traditional notion of Zender will never change. The karash will never change, so what are we to do?"

"Why should we change? Zender favors us above all others. We are strong, and our people are free and happy. We have free trade and a thriving economy. We have equality amongst all. Why should we change?"

"Because times change and because Zender does value mercy." I shook my head and looked out the window. Beneath us, beneath the thin veil of clouds, the Muet Mountains gave way to forest. We passed over a large city and then over a small one. From the ship, they looked almost the same. Their shields glistened in the noonday sun. Only their size varied.

"Do you believe in faith, brother?" I asked.

"Very much so."

"I am a karake. I live my life in devotion to Zender and to the storm. You will marry and live a life in this world. I have been given over to prayer, the sword, and solitude. Every night I read the scriptures. I have had them cut onto my body. Every morning I pray in Zender's chapel. I have faith that what we do is right. This is my faith, and it is not subject to the whims of the times."

"Blind faith is a terrifying thing."

"Faith is the only thing that has kept me alive."

Xander nodded, and we were silent. We watched the landscape pass by us with interest. The forest thinned, and we passed over a large river and then there were rolling hills covered by soft, green grass. Trees poked their heads out, reaching for the sun. They were evergreens, and I could almost feel the cold breath of the north on my cheek. Xander put his hand on mine as he fell asleep, but I clung to consciousness until the day passed. Only as the stars awoke from their slumber, ending the gnawing, did I rest. Only as summer began and the sister moons parted did I allow my eyes to shut. My wounds still burned beneath my robe, but I could finally rest.

We landed at the upper docks at the top of the city. I woke up with a jolt as the jarring noise of the metal clamps locked the ship in place. We all shifted and grabbed our tiny bags. I looked out the window. Workers were already frantically unloading our cargo; the price of our admission was rice and marble. We paid well, and the boxes poured off the ship.

We exited the ship, and a swarm of young people in yellow poked us and prodded us and jabbed us with needles. They injected us with honey colored serums and forced to take pills we couldn't identify. When they were done, we were herded into a dark room.

We were greeted by several stodgy, old men and women in gray robes. The stodgy, old people led us to what we would later know as monorails. All of us stood dumbfounded. The city seemed to us to be from another world. It had been transplanted onto our ice-covered planet from some distant star or foggy future. We watched from the monorail with misty eyes, and finally I understood why so many left their tribes to stay at The University. The buildings were so tall they became lost in the clouds above them, and they were made entirely of glass. Even the air was artificial and unseasonably warm. The artificial atmosphere glistened in the sky above me. It almost looked like sky, but it was not. It hummed, keeping its occupants safe and forever warm.

Small circular vehicles drove across the roads and occasionally took to the sky. The people wore no tribal colors, no saris, or traditional attire. They all wore gray pants and dresses. There were no guards or warriors, only throngs of people carrying books and computers and other buzzing and humming devices that were lit from within. Our city had considered itself advanced for its few computers and electricity, but here people carried computers in their pockets and worked on the train.

The main educational buildings sprawled through the center of town. We were taken to the heart of this complex, where all the monorails met. I followed the men into the crowd and up into the clouds of the tallest building. We were all quietly shown into a huge lecture hall where seventy or eighty other youths in gray robes were gathered. One of the old men began to speak.

"You see around you many wonders," he said. "And you will see many more. This city never sleeps, but always dreams. You all come from tribes of varying levels of technology and understanding, but soon you will see the stars and wander on the moons. We give you this gift, and all we ask in exchange is that you never wear your tribal colors or show any tattoos or brandings that would label you. You speak only Etrusan. Forget your tribe's tongue. You will be housed with people from other tribes, and you are not to seek out your own tribe. You must do everything to promote peace here, and if you break this vow, you and all your tribesmen will be cast out. Your people will never learn our secrets or advance past your own tribal darkness. Take our gifts and enlighten your own kind."

So we were separated. I waved goodbye to Xander, and he blew me a kiss. I was pulled away by a plump young scholar who talked incessantly. We spent the rest of the evening signing up for classes, getting our books, and purchasing new clothing. The young woman took me to my apartment, gave me a map, and vanished.

My housing was in the back of the city by the walls. It was a small apartment, barely furnished, but filled with magic and wonders. There were machines that could produce food with the push of a button and devices which showed plays, news, and other moving pictures on colorful wall hangings. There was a blanket that heated itself and a box which produced music. In the corner, there was a room you could step into and be bathed in warm water and massage. The bed made itself, and there was a tiny little machine that buzzed around the floor picking up crumbs. I even had a computer in my room.

I spent the evening fiddling around with all the strange devices in my room. I made myself a mountain of food from parts of the world I had never even heard of. I turned on the device that showed plays on a colorful screen and watched it until I discovered it was called a television. I took a shower and gave myself a massage. Finally, I passed out in the huge bed. It was so soft I fell asleep as soon as I rest my head on the pillow.

Each class I went to made me feel like I had just awakened from a long sleep. There was so much I didn't know. In the karash, I had read only the scriptures. I learned only the sword. The moon was nothing but an orb in the sky. Humanity was capable of so much more than I had ever known, and I stood in awe of everything the world had accomplished. We had traveled to the stars, the moons, and had observed other peoples. We had traveled to the impassable icy north and south in ships that moved on ice. We had dove beneath the ice into the frigid seas and saw monsters so large they could eat rwans like the treats we fed children. Our world was round and had been around long before Zender or any gods. There were records in the ice of peoples long since dead and species of marvelous beauty.

I had been a child in the dark, and now I saw the light.

I lost myself in this light. I took classes on art, history, astronomy, and math. I read every book I could find and spent hours wandering through museums and galleries. I knew I was supposed to be learning missile design and engineering. I was supposed to learn war, but I took only one class that tied me to home.

I took only one class on the art of the storm.

My professor, Cahir, came from a tribe so far from us that he scarcely seemed human to me. He was much taller than any man I had ever seen, and his eyes were black. He had shaved off all of his hair. His skin was black like the flesh of rwan, and he moved with the grace of a cat. He was the most beautiful thing I had ever seen.

"What is the art of the storm?" he began. "What is the storm? You know it only as an urge to kill. This is what your tribes have taught you. You must kill and destroy those that worship different gods or follow different paths. This is not the path I will teach you. To worship the storm is to follow the wind no matter where it leads, regardless of ideology or tribe. It is to bring order to chaos. All of your tribes will die. All of your gods will be dust on the feet of another tribe. So it has always been. Where will you go then? Will you wander tribeless and lost? Or will you smell the water and ice on the wind and follow the path home?"

There were thirty people in the class, all men and boys, but we sat enraptured. Even Xeres looked like he was listening. Cahir took out a long, curved sword and held it in his hand. "A true warrior will only use one weapon. He will never touch a gun or arrow. He has no need for guns or explosives. The storm gives him all of the strength he needs. He will use only his own sword."

After class, I heard one of the students muttering to another classmate. "I thought this class would be interesting," he said. "But only a fool would forsake modern weaponry for a sword. I'm surprised they still teach this crap."

I turned on the boy. "Anyone can kill with a gun. Hell, a child can point and shoot. Good soldiers can kill with anything. That's why this is important. If you can kill with a sword, you can kill with anything."

The boy looked down on me. "I doubt you could kill with anything, little girl."

"I could kill you with a breath," I said defiantly.

The boy sat his books down, and looked at me, challenging me with his glance. I followed suit, smiling at him.

The boy was stronger than me and more than a foot taller than me, but he was slow and clumsy. He had clearly never been in a real fight and was reluctant to hurt me. It was easy for me to hurt him. I dodged his first punch and drove my finger into the soft tissue above his clavicle, breaking his airway. He fell to his knees gasping. I wanted to break his neck. I wanted to punch him until he lay unconscious on the floor. The desire to do these things was more reflexive than born of anger or rage. My training was part of me, like a second skin. I attacked without thinking and reacted before I even knew I was reacting. It was like I was in a trance.

The professor grabbed me and pulled me back. His arms around me yanked me out of my trance. I suddenly realized what I had done. I saw the boy on the floor in front of me and knew I had made a mistake. I went limp in Cahir's arms and let him pull me away.

I was standing in a brightly lit hallway surrounded by students and teachers, and everyone was staring at me. The neon lights flickered, and my audience waited. The boy on the floor gasped again, and I looked up at Cahir. His arms around me were like a vice. Every muscle in his body was taut and tight and in that moment, I lost my breath.

"This is not the way," Cahir said. "There is enough time to kill each other when you leave this place. You have but a brief moment to learn something higher."

The boy stood up, and he ran away into the crowd. Slowly, all those around us moved on and Cahir pulled me back into the classroom. "They'll throw you out for that," he said.

"I'm sorry. Where I'm from, it's considered honorable to fight those who insult you," I said.

"This isn't your home. If you want to stay here, you have to forget everything you were before."

I laughed bitterly. "That's not as easy as it sounds."

"I know you," he said. "I know where you have come from. I would not name your tribe, but I know what it is to be raised to kill. It's all you have. It's all you know, but you have been given this gift, this small reprieve from all that. You should embrace it."

I nodded. For some unknown reason, I felt tears burn in my eyes. I looked around me. The tall, high windows offered views the ground fifty stories below us. The people ran like ants to and from classes amidst the forest of epic buildings. Above us, there was no sky. There was only the surreal glow of the artificial atmosphere. I looked at him, his calm face and intense eyes, and I felt completely lost.

"I'll try to embrace this world," I whispered. "Fleeting though it may be."

Cahir taught us how to use the sword. All of us were adept warriors. We fought well, but he moved in ways that defied all laws of gravity and physics. He could be two places at once. He bent like water. He was a force of nature, and the sword was his arm. We practiced what he told us and wrote our homework down like greedy animals, hungry for knowledge. We had to read to learn and practice every night.

After my sixth class, I pulled him aside. "Is it magic?" I asked.

"There is no magic. The storm gives power to those that follow it."

"I want to thank you for this. I've had my hands dipped in blood since I was a girl. It's nice to know the storm also can bring a cool breeze."

He took my face in his hand. I was like a doll in the hands of a giant; I only came up to his waist. It was like I was twelve years old again, preparing for my first battle. "It's a sacrilege what some tribes do. You must be no more than a child now."

"I'm nineteen."

"You're like a child with fire in her eyes. You must find peace before you can feel the wind."

"I don't know what that means," I said in confusion. I knew nothing of peace. I thought it was an idea for poets and pretty girls with sweet lovers. It was not a concept that a karake should ever know.

He took my hand and led me to his office. He handed me a small blue book. "Don't practice like the others every night. You know how to fight and kill. I've seen you spar. You know how to move with the sword. I'll show you and you must practice what is in this book every night. You must find the peace in the wind and the calm of the rain."

He spent two hours with me. What he taught me was like a dance. It was a sword dance. We twisted and moved quietly, softly, and then finally, we sat with our eyes closed. We sat on the manicured green grass, beneath a twisted willow. Water sputtered out of a fountain a few feet away from us. Birds sang, and I could lose myself in the illusion of nature and peace, but our piece of grass was small, lost in an ocean of concrete and humanity. I couldn't shut out the noise. I couldn't turn off my senses.

"You must learn the art of the wind that comes before the storm," he said. "You must let go. We are trained never to sleep, to always be aware, but you need to find peace first."

He touched me. He put his hand on my shoulder. "The world never sleeps, but you must rest your mind, or it will consume you."

I tried again. I sat on the grass with him and let go. We sat together and closed our eyes and for a brief moment there was nothing, only his breathing and the gentle sounds of the world passing us by.

That moment lingered. I went to my classes and studied. I learned about the world, about our planet, Earth. I learned about the five key tribes. The Hyran, in the south, who were master engineers. They lived in peace and accepted immigration from the tribeless. They were manufacturers and artists, and they supplied The University and the world with most of their manufactured goods. There were the Notuans, great island scholars, so linked to The University they seemed like part of it. There were the Critons, a new tribe, who held vast expanses of farmland and had developed much of their own technology without the aid of The University. And in the far south, pressed up against the Southern Seas there were the Efferitas, a group of a savages about which nothing was known. The Xenderians were the last tribe. We defended The University. We supplied her with food and raw commodities. We were her sword, although none would ever say it.

I listened. I took notes. I watched the stars in astronomy. We spoke of the lunar colonies and I was interested, but in the back of my mind I felt the wind and heard the birds. I imagined that I carried them with me, and when I did this, a sense of calm spread through me. I understood what Cahir meant when he spoke of peace. He penetrated my every waking moment. I thought of him on the monorail as I rode to classes and in the evening when I read. I thought of him so much I wished I could shut my mind down and erase his face.

Every day I ran to his class. I skipped into the room and sat with bated breath awaiting his entrance. He entered. He spoke and there was nothing but him. Mercifully, he showed me unusual attention. He met with me after class almost every day. He taught me specifically, and he favored me alone.

"You know he just wants to fuck you," Xeres snarled after class.

"What?"

"You think you're so special. You think you're Zender's chosen. You've always been that way. You're so much better than us? But he just wants your pretty little cunny. That's the only gift you have that we don't. Perhaps he'll be the one to finally penetrate that sacred hole of yours, little Saint Ailive. Make you beg to be like an ordinary woman."

"I hate that. Don't call me that."

"What? Saint Ailive. That's what you are. Better than the rest of us, aren't you?"

I pushed him, and he laughed at me. "You don't scare me," he said.

He moved forward quickly, but I blocked his first blow and spun around to deliver a side kick to his groin. He moaned, but didn't lose any of his composure. He lunged again and I moved to block him, but he grabbed my throat with his other hand and lifted me off the ground. I struggled. Xeres had always been stronger than me, and I hated him for that as much as I hated him for anything.

He pulled me to him and kissed me and then he threw me down on the ground and kicked me. I tried to get up but he jumped on top of me, pinning my arms to the ground with his legs. I pulled my legs up over his shoulders and tried to pull him off of my, but he punched me so hard in my face I saw stars.

"You're no better than us," he said as he took out a knife. I tried to stand up, to run away, but he was too strong. There was nothing I could do. I lay back and glared at him with utter malice. A movement out of the corner of my eye told me that Cahir was standing behind us, watching us. I blushed. I hated to think that Cahir saw me so easily defeated. I tried to get me legs around his shoulders one last time.

I couldn't let Cahir see me like this, but Xeres pushed the knife so hard against my throat I felt it begin to break the skin. I snarled at Xeres. He wouldn't have beaten me so easily if he hadn't of taken me by surprise. I didn't expect him to attack me at the University. At the karash, I would have done better. I would have been prepared. Xeres leaned over and licked my cheek, pushing the knife even deeper into my flesh. Cahir pulled Xeres off of me. He pulled him off and threw him across the room. Xeres fell. He wasn't as big as he thought. Not compared to Cahir.

"Pack your bags. You leave tomorrow," Cahir said coolly.

"What?" Xeres said angrily.

"Violence is strictly prohibited here. You are to leave. I'll send security for you in the morning."

"She started it!" he yelled.

"It doesn't matter. You were the one with the knife."

"Fuck you. You're all a bunch of heathen scum. Faithless, godless; servants to your own pride!" Xeres spat on the ground in front of Cahir. "Your time will come like all the others."

Cahir picked me up and carried me back to the class. He washed my wounds and bandaged them. He didn't say anything. He worked quietly, and I watched him move. I watched his long fingers pick up the bandages. I watched the way his black eyes regarded me.

"Do you need to go to the hospital?" he asked when he was done.

I shook my head. I was so ashamed I didn't want anyone else to see my injuries.

"Why did he do this?" he asked.

"He enjoys hurting others."

"People like that shouldn't be allowed here."

"He's the best warrior of our generation. There aren't any others that can defeat me."

"You could be better."

"No. I'm small and a woman. I've already exceeded my expectations. He will always be the best karake."

"You have a gift that none of them have. You could be better. I could teach you."

I smiled, consumed with my own divine happiness. He didn't see my shame; he still thought I was worthy. I felt warm inside and my heart pounded in my chest. "I would love that."

From then on we spent our nights together. He taught and I listened. Every free moment he had he gave to me, and I took his time greedily.

I couldn't explain his kindness. He never showed any of the other students any favor, but every evening he would practice with me and every night I read the books of poetry he gave me. I was in awe of him. He was nothing like any of the boys or men I had met at the temple. When we were alone, he did not talk of war or fighting. He talked of poetry and history. He loved mythology and told me about all the gods of war and peace that had lived and died as the world aged. He could talk forever, losing himself in his own stories of ancient battles and perfect tribes.

He was an idealist. He dreamed of perfect worlds and perfect people. Most of all he wanted to end suffering and inequality. I sat at his feet and listened, like he was a god and I was his mortal follower. I believed everything he believed and loved everything he loved.

"What is it like, living here?" I asked Cahir.

"It's a complicated place," he answered. "I wouldn't live anyplace else."

"Where's your tribe? Do you miss them?"

He smiled. "Do you miss your tribe?"

"No."

"Why not?"

I shrugged. "It was lonely there. It was hard."

"The world is hard. Here we don't have to face the world. We deal only in ideas, most of the time. That's why I like it here."

"But you're a great warrior. Don't you miss the storm?"

His face seemed so wise. His skin was smooth. He had the aspect of youth, but his eyes showed age well beyond his appearance. "The storm finds me here, sometimes."

"How?"

He handed me my sword. "You have too many questions. This is a place for secrets. Look at us. We all wear gray. We can't talk of our past. No more questions."

He took up his sword, and I followed his motion. I grew lost in the movement. Swordplay to him was a dance. We never sparred. It was not about combat. He called our practice the dance.

He would look at me and say, "It's time to dance."

"There is only one truth," he said. "There is only one God and when we dance, we can feel him. He will guide us into the storm and teach us a magic more powerful than war or science, because he is the storm."

Cahir and I began to morph our nightly meditations with the sword-play until I found that I began to move like fluid. I was at peace. I still ran for hours in the morning, and my days were spent at study but in the evening there was always Cahir.

Long before our tribe emerged as a superpower, other tribes had grown and faded with the rippling of time. History was the same. Tribes rose out of the ashes. They conquered. They learned. They invented and grew and then they fell. The old walls of ancient cities were buried in glaciers and beneath the rising water. The ice rose and fell. The water rose and fell. Landscapes changed, and men lived and died fighting for transient glory.

The wars seemed far away for me. I fell in love with books and quiet. I fell in love with my evenings. Cahir would take me all over the city to practice. We would practice on the tops of buildings or in the park. We would dance by the lake or in the fountains. He said that we must move with nature to find the rhythm of the tempest. I always took all of his classes. The other masters never even knew my name, and he always found private time for me. We had been working together for over a year when I finally asked him the question that had lingered in my dreams for months. Despite all the time he and I spent together, I seldom spoke, and I trembled as the words passed my lips.

"Why me?" I asked. "I'm not blind. You never work with any of the other students outside of class. Why do you take all this time for me?"

He was such a strong speaker in class. He read the history of war like an orator and spoke the great epic poems like the poet laureate himself. But now he paused before speaking. He shrugged his shoulders. "We are all the same here. We came from blood and pain. Even here, there has been little solace. Maybe I take what solace I can find now. I enjoy watching you. I enjoy the intensity in you. The others, they waste their time with women, gambling, and the pipe. They fight and they lust on very fundamental levels. I know that when they go back to their tribes, they will be better warriors for this. But you are different, maybe because you are a woman. I don't know."

I began to cry. The little girl in me longed to leap into his arms and find the love I had never known. "Thank you," I whispered as I pushed the tears away.

He touched my cheek and quoted from Marius the Lesser's most famous epic, "We have never known love or pity. We are cold like the ice that blows from the north. Death is our only lover and genocide our only child."

I laughed coldly. "When I was a little girl, I was so happy to leave my mother; I thought I had found paradise at the temple. When we went to war, I knew that I had to die to be what they needed me to be. The living part of my heart had to die, so I died in my heart."

"When I first saw you, I knew what tribe you were from. Only one tribe would take a girl child into the storm, and I hated them even more for what I thought they had done to a beautiful woman. I thought it was such a waste. Now I see why they chose you. You are the perfect warrior. You are the only one who moves like a true master. If you progress, you'll be able to reject gravity and time. I can't regret any decision that has brought you to me."

When he kissed me, I forgot about Zender and my tribe. I felt the dead part of my heart warm and beat again. My entire body tingled with emotion and sensation that I didn't know the words to name. The past vanished and there was only the moment. The moment he touched me and I touched him I felt alive again. We spent that night together in his apartment in the clouds. I never wanted to come down.

In the morning, he and I slept in. He made me a breakfast of soup and fruit and kissed my hand.

"Have you ever seen a movie?" he asked.

"No. What's that?" I answered.

"It's our day of rest. Spend the day with me. Come see a movie with me."

He took me down to the part of the city that cut into the earth. It was beneath the rest of the city, in its catacombs. We went to a black building, surrounded by flashing lights and he bought two tickets. We watched a great war won and lost on a giant glowing screen. In the midst of this war, a young couple fell in love. They made love in the rubble of their dying city and escaped, just barely. We ate sticky sweet candies, and I watched in complete fascination.

"So, what do you think?" he asked.

"I never want to leave," I answered.

He took my hand, and we walked hand in hand down the street, like the people I used to watch in the markets. He took me to dinner and bought me gold earrings. I had never owned jewelry.

"You look stunning," he said.

"So do you," I answered.

"No. I'm just an old man chasing a pretty girl. You are the sun, and I'm just the insect that crawls in her light."

I laughed. "I'm the sun? Me?"

I spent the night with him again that night, and after he fell asleep, I crept out of bed and looked at myself in the mirror. I looked for what he saw in me. I was small and pale. I had fine features, and my eyes were bright blue. They weren't like the others in my tribe. They were brighter. I had a small scar on my cheek, and my hair was thin and lifeless. I couldn't see anything in myself that resembled a star. I had always known I had a pretty, girlish face, but I saw it as something plastic and cruel. I had never seen myself as anything light or beautiful. Cahir came up behind me. Sleep still hung in his eyes, and he looked at my image in the mirror.

"What're you doing?"

"We don't have mirrors at the karash."

"You've never seen yourself?"

"I've seen mirrors. I'm not from the Stone Age. I just never really looked. I never thought there was much to look at."

Cahir laughed and pulled me to him. "Every man who sees you turns to look at you. You are lovely."

I blushed. "I don't think so."

Cahir kissed me. "Come to bed."

I didn't go back to my own apartment. I stayed with Cahir. The year passed, and we spent every free moment together. Time seemed to stand still, and I thought our love would go on forever. From then on, we practiced at his apartment. We met as we always had and began with the dance. We danced with our swords. Steel on steel. Metal to metal. We danced. We sparred. We read the great epics, and then we made love. In the morning, we ran together. Our lives moved in unison, like we had always been together. It felt like everything before and after him was a shadow of life. I would lay in bed at night staring at his profile in the soft glow of the city lights. I would trace the scars on his body with my finger and wonder at his origins. My love. My life. Sometimes, he would watch me dance. He would stop and set down his sword and just watch. He would say that death was art. I was art.

I never wanted anything to change, but my past was filled with too many ghosts. Too many people. People move in and out of each other's lives like phantoms. Xander moved back into my life the night Cahir took me to see my second movie. Xander was there with a young girl. He was smiling and laughing happily. When he saw me, he ran to me and hugged me merrily.

"Ailive," he exclaimed. "You look extraordinary! By Zender, you are beautiful. Are you wearing make-up?"

I blushed and returned his embrace. He looked healthy and happy as well. "I almost forgot you were here," I said. "How are your studies?"

"Wonderful. I wish I could stay here forever. They can do anything here, short of bringing the dead back to life, and they are even working on that. Did you know the professors here live to be two hundred or more? It feels like I can never learn enough to take back to the tribe, but I'm definitely trying. At least I know how to synthesize a cure for the pox. That took two of our sisters, you know? How about you? Learning any new skills?"

I smiled. He fit in at The University. He wore a handsome gray suit, and his hair was cut almost to the skull. He was with a pretty girl with light hair and tan skin. She looked at me expectantly.

"I've learned more than I can say," I said looking up at Cahir. He smiled

44

down at me and then turned to my brother.

"I'm Cahir Gitypl," he said to Xander.

"I'm Xander Physician. Good to meet you." Xander looked at our linked hands and smiled again as he turned to me.

"You two are…you're— " He paused and made a strange hand gesture in his inability to communicate. "You two are…together?"

I nodded. Xander leaned over and kissed me. "So you're happy then?" There were tears in his eyes.

"Yes."

"Are you two in love?" he asked bluntly, making my face blush even more deeply. He looked at Cahir as if he was demanding an answer.

Cahir was unmoved by the demand. "I love Ailive with all my heart," he answered. "She's given me hope again."

I looked up at him. We had never spoken of love. Such words were foreign to me. I wouldn't have known how to express my love if I had meant to. I had taken the joy I could from my moments with him, but poetry and expression were impossible. He also seemed awkward in such expressions. They left him off balance.

Xander pulled me gruffly aside into the shadows behind the theater. "You should stay with him," he said.

"What?" I answered.

"You love him. He loves you. Where ever he is from they'll embrace you if you marry him. Stay with him."

"You're mad. I can't leave my tribe, my god, my people."

"You're happy. Look at you…you're beautiful. I've spent my entire life regretting what I did to you. Every time I see you, your bruises are darker, your scars burn brighter. That place, the karash, it's killing you. It's killing the little girl I love. Stay with him. You deserve happiness."

I broke free from him. I pulled away and wiped the tears from my eyes. I hadn't thought about the future. I had spent two years at The University, and I had spent one year with Cahir, but I had never thought about what was ahead. I had lived in the moment. I had thought only about him, the way I felt when I was with him, the way I felt when we danced, when we made love.

"You don't have much time here," he said. "Two years? Less? Don't go back."

"Why are you saying this? I don't understand. You're Xenderian. This is your tribe. Why would you say such sedition?" I was crying.

"I love you more than I love my tribe."

"You love me?" I suddenly felt dizzy, overwhelmed.

"Of course. You're my baby girl. I held you in my arms while you slept. You're my little sister."

"I thought you had forgotten about me." My voice was a whisper.

"No."

I embraced him. I pulled him to me, and we hugged in the shadows like secret lovers. He smiled and wiped the tears from my eyes. "Think about it?" he said. "At least consider it."

I nodded and smiled like a stupid child, and he took my hand and we went back to Cahir, who was making uncomfortable conversation with Xander's friend.

"Well, let me know what you decide," Xander said as he pulled his friend away.

He left Cahir and me alone and unable to articulate the impact of what had just been said. He took my hand and we walked through the park and for a long time we were silent.

"Why do you love me?" I asked.

"We all have our demons, Ailive. For a long time, I have been consumed by mine, but since I've known you they have been silent. You are my gentle breeze, my reminder that even in a world of violence and hatred, there are still those that fight out of faith."

"I'm nothing, you know? I'm just a karake. I don't even know how to translate what I am into Etrusan. A monk warrior maybe? I'm not much."

"I know what you are. You're a soldier. In your heart, you are the last follower of the storm. When you fight, you don't fight out of cruelty or rage. You surrender to the art; you become one with the storm. You are an artist and a prophet. You and I are the last of our kind. We are the last of our faith."

"I love you too, you know that?" I said.

"I don't know that. I don't think you do either. You are young. You see me as a symbol of greatness and comfort. I'm your teacher. But do you love me as a man? Who can say?"

"Of course I do."

"I'm not the great man you think I am. I was the weakest of my tribe. We were great, but small. In the end, we lost out to technology and modernization. We clung to the old ways. All my betters died when my tribe fell, I was left alone. I'm neither great nor glorious. I'm just an old man who lives in the past."

"I don't love you because you are great. I don't love you for your skill. I love you because you are kind to me and you listen to me when I talk. I love you because you read the great poets and you dream of a better future. I love you because you are an idealist and a warrior. I love you for what you are."

And so we made love again, but a shadow had passed between us. We knew I would have to go. We were reminded of the transient nature of our joy. I cried as he kissed me.

The more time I spent with Cahir, the more I noticed the oddness of his life. At first, I was so enamored with Cahir that I was oblivious to these things, but as my infatuation faded and grew to love, I noticed things I hadn't seen before. I would watch Cahir come and go. I would sit up and wait for him late at night and wonder if he hadn't been right. Maybe I didn't know him as a man. Maybe I didn't know him at all. I didn't dare ask him where he went or what he did, but some nights I would fall asleep next to him and wake up alone. He would vanish from classes and my life for days. I would go back to my apartment and read and study and wait. He would return with a kiss and a smile.

During my third year of studies, I had to stop taking classes with Cahir. I had learned all there was to learn academically with Cahir. I had taken all five of his courses. Our roles changed, and I was more compelled to go to my apartment to study. My classes were more rigorous and expectations were higher. I was writing a particularly lengthy paper when Cahir vanished for two weeks.

I felt his absence profoundly. Some nights I took my studies to his elegant apartment in the top portion of the city. I sat on his leather sofa and worked on my computer. I waited and prayed he would walk in. It was a night like that when he found me asleep, with my studies on my lap. I heard the door open, but I didn't move. I lay motionless watching him. He was in all black, in some kind of uniform. He had a gun belt and his sword was at his back. He had blood on his face. He walked up to me and placed his hand on my head.

"What are you studying?" he asked softly.

I sat up and looked at him. He was filthy and wounded. "I'm working on a paper about the tribeless populations."

"Oh, and what are your thoughts on the tribeless population?" His voice was soft, like he was lost in a trance.

"It seems like it is an unanswerable question. War ruins tribes and leave people tribeless. The tribeless wander, raid, kill, steal—do what they have to do to survive. Those that find them kill them or enslave them. If they settle and try to build a new city, they are weak and vulnerable and easily decimated by other tribeless. There seems to be no answer."

There was a vacant look in Cahir's eyes, as if he wasn't really seeing me at all. "There's an answer," he said.

"What?" I asked.

"Earth has to be cleansed."

"Cleansed?"

"They all have to settle down or die."

"I thought The University and its inhabitants advocated peace."

"The tribeless are the cancer of this world. Until we root them out, we will continue to decay," Cahir hissed these words. In the dark, stained in blood, his face changed, and I almost didn't recognize him.

"Who would initiate such a grand scheme?" I asked.

He smiled, as if woken from his slumber. "Never mind. I'm sorry to wake you. I need to rest now. I have council in the morning."

"You're on the council?"

"Yes."

"I didn't know you were involved in politics."

He smiled and touched my face before he vanished into the shower. The water went on, and I didn't follow him. I packed up my books and went home. In my sleep deprived state, I wondered if I really knew anything about him.

By the end of my third year at The University, I had grown completely accustomed to my life. I studied and worked and spent all my spare time with Cahir. We had developed a relationship dedicated to the protection to the ideals of The University. We never spoke of the past, only of the present. We were the perfect University citizens. We spoke of history and global politics. We debated about trade agreements and tribelessness and the benefits of the lunar colonies. We danced, we ate, but we didn't speak of what had been or what would be. So even as my stay at The University reached its inevitable end, we went on in blissful ignorance.

"We should go to Notua," Cahir said. It was early in the morning. The perfidious sun shone brightly in the windows. It was the gnawing, somewhere outside the false atmosphere the sky was painted orange and red, but inside The University the gnawing didn't exist.

I woke up and looked at him. He was nude, sprawled out on the bed.

"Why?" I asked.

I stood up and stretched and looked out the window.

"Because Notua is beautiful during the gnawing, and it's nice to travel."

"I don't know. I have to finish up my dissertation on the symbiotic relationship between The University and the core tribes. I also have that stupid project on personal cloaking devices I have to do."

"You can take your work with you."

I looked out over The University. Its beauty never ceased to amaze me. "I don't want to leave," I said.

Cahir stood up behind me and put his hands on my shoulders. He kissed my neck. "Why?"

"I don't have much time left," I whispered.

There was an uncomfortable silence. We both stared out the window, holding each other. The fake sun shone in its full intensity. Clouds flickered and passed over the too-blue sky.

"How much longer?" he asked.

"This is my last year."

Cahir nodded. "You could stay."

"If I were another woman, I could. But I am what I am and I must return."

"Because you promised your god?"

"I am my tribe. I have to do my duty."

Cahir pulled me into his arms and kissed me all over my face. They were soft kisses, slow and sweet. I looked into his dark eyes and tried to divine what might live within him. I tried to imagine his antecedents. I thought if I looked hard enough, I might understand him.

"The storm could find you here." His voice was a caress. "You could stay, and I could show you new paths to the storm."

I shook my head. "I love it here. I love my studies. I love you, but this isn't where I belong. Every night I study, we dance, and I fall asleep in your arms and I know that this can't last. I have to go home. I promised Z—my god I would return to him."

"Gods understand when promises must be broken."

"Not my god."

"Well then, my little rwan, I guess we must make every moment count."

The last year I studied strategy and tactics. I learned how to plan battles and how to lead men. This was taught under the façade of history, but it was practical. We learned about all the old wars. We studied the maneuvers that won wars and those that were fatal. We learned about the advantages of blitzkrieg and how to attack cities with shield walls. We wrote papers on how the lost tribes could have avoided decimation.

The year went by in the blink of an eye. A whisper and it was gone.

Time is elusive. A moment can go on forever, but years can go by in your sleep. The mind plays tricks on us. It creates history. And so, for me, my year was only a few days of warmth. It was a series of brief kisses that have been lost in the fog.

I remember that last day like a painting. Like paint on rock. I went to my apartment and put everything I had bought or been given at The University in a large box. I filled it with lovely gray silk dresses and soft gray pants. I filled it with all my gold bobbles and ornaments that Cahir had chosen for me. I put the small computer I had purchased to complete my work on in the box, and I sealed it. I drug the heavy thing through the city and onto the monorail. I pulled it upward to Cahir's flat at the top of the city, and I left it there. I left it in a corner behind a plant.

"You look different," Cahir said as he studied me. I was different. I had taken off all my makeup and jewelry. I had tied my hair up in a topknot. I had put on the same simple gray robes I had arrived in.

"I know," I said as I wedged my box in the corner.

"Why are you doing that?" he asked.

"I don't need these things anymore. I thought you could keep them for me, in case I ever come back."

"You might come back?"

"You never know what the wind brings."

"Now, if you want to stay, I can find you a position. I can help you stay, but once you leave, I have no power."

"Why?"

"What would bring you back?"

I shrugged. I was unwilling to say what I had been thinking. I blushed. I was afraid to say what I had been thinking or even why I had thought it. I knew that it didn't make sense. I would never be back. My tribe was strong, and Zender protected us, but even in the artificial world of The University, I thought I could smell something in the air. There was a whisper of wind that drifted in through the ventilation shafts and whispered of wars to come. I shook my head. I had to be imagining things.

"Don't be a coward. Say it."

"I'm just being silly," I said with a shrug.

"I've know you for a long time now, and you are never silly."

"Sometimes I am influenced by the whims of imagination, just like everyone else."

"So what silliness and whim of imagination drove you to leave your things with me? What could happen to bring you back to me?"

"If my tribe fell."

"And if you're tribe fell, you would become tribeless. We don't take tribeless here. It would take a decision from the council to grant you entry."

"It doesn't matter. I won't come back. I just want you to keep it for me."

"I'll keep it. And I have something for you."

Cahir walked across the room and handed me a large bundle. I took it in my arms and felt the weight. It was neither heavy nor light. It sat in my arms as if it was meant to be there. I unwrapped the gift slowly, revealing the precious object beneath. I sat down and laid my hand on the hilt of the sword. It was carved in ebony. It was carved with symbols I couldn't read and engraved with pictures that showed lightning and storms, tornadoes and hurricanes bending trees. The blade was long and narrow; it curved slightly at the end. It was a thing of rare beauty.

Cahir took out his own sword. It was the inversed mirror image of mine, gleaming white. He held it out toward me, challenging me. I rose and bowed and the dance began. I had evolved. I knew it and felt it with every move. We moved in unison. I moved as quickly as he and as metal hit metal our motions became one. I struck, and he blocked and then he attacked me. He would move with the air and then he would be behind me and I would turn and face him and metal would hit metal again.

He jumped and kicked me with his left leg, and I fell. He had me. He always had me in the end, but then he gave me his hand and pulled me to my feet.

"My father made them. Long ago. He gave one to each of my brothers and one to me. I give this one to you, because you are a great warrior like my brother. You have his gift for the storm. His strength. You deserve a sword that is worthy of you."

"Thank you."

He walked me to the docks. The ship was waiting. All my peers were already on board. It was a strange morning. The atmosphere that surrounded the city opened up to allow the ships to come and go and the fog outside was so thick that it drifted in through the portal covering us in a blanket of clouds. I turned and walked toward the ship, but when I looked back Cahir was gone, lost in the fog.

III
The End of the World

My father embraced me warmly as I got off the ship. "It's good to have you back, Daughter," he said.

I bowed slightly and said, "It's good to see you."

"Times have grown complicated, and we have hopes that you will be ready to leave again in a few weeks."

"I serve Zender," I answered.

"We would like to test you."

Despite myself, I flushed with joy. They wanted me to be an elder karake. I was young, and I was a woman. I would be the first of my kind. Pride spread over me like a warm bath, but I was a pragmatic being.

"Why? You haven't seen me in four years. My skills could have faded, and I could be fat and slovenly."

My father only laughed. "I know you better than that."

"Even so, what's the rush?"

"We've been involved in a long conflict with a tribe to the south and despite our victory, our troops are depleted, and we have lost many of our officers."

"I see." The city looked the same. In fact, years of war had only served to make it more crowded and larger, seeping up onto the mountains and spreading out into the other low lying valleys.

Yet, the city looked pale in the evening light. It looked squat and white, a geometric mass of columns and white marble. I looked back at my father. He looked small. His face was pinched with stress and time. I nodded. I would do what I had to do in a world I no longer wanted to be part of, because it was my tribe.

Worst of all was the temple. The karash smelled foul, and the men within it seemed like brutes and grunts. They swaggered about with their swords and guns, but they moved clumsily. They depended on force. I was welcomed back with open arms. But all they talked about was war. It was to be an epic battle between good and evil, again. Our enemies were monsters. They were the enemies of peace. Peace. Freedom. The same words over and over again to explain war.

I was taken to the elder karake the night I arrived home. They met me beneath the karash, in the old catacombs. I had never seen the catacombs. I expected a dungeon. I expected it to be filled with more grimacing demons of war, but I found that beneath the karash, the heart of our temple was firmly planted in the modern world. The room was filled with huge computer screens and maps of the world and tracking systems that seemed to following the movements of different groups of tribeless and raiders. I looked around in amazement, but kept my mouth shut.

Bezytere was our leader. He was the oldest of the karake. He planned every battle we ever fought. He decided who got the last rites and when. He was our king, but we all called him Father Bezytere. I bowed to him as he approached me.

I was still in University gray. I had my new sword at my back. I must have looked strange bowing in the artificial light of the computer.

"Ailive Karake," he said my name. "Your father has always spoken highly of you."

"Thank you, sir," I said.

"We would like you to join us here."

I looked around. There were only fifteen elders, including my father. The men in the room were older, seasoned warriors. They had painted the world in blood. They had trained students and apprentices and lived life by the sword alone. My mouth went dry.

"I am honored, sir, but I don't understand."

"We would be a foolish people if we didn't bring the best into the ranks of the best."

"I'm sorry, sir."

"May I?" Father Bezytere pointed to my sword, and I handed it to him. He took it and held it like it was his religion. He thrust it into the air and smiled. "It's a beautiful thing. I envy you." He handed it back to me, and I clutched it until my hand bled.

"Cahir says you are the best pupil he has ever taught."

"You know him."

The old man laughed. His eyes crinkled with mirth. "There is one thing every man in this room has in common. Do you know what that is?"

I shook my head.

"We all trained with Cahir. He chose us all. He took us aside after class and taught us the true art of the storm, as we attempt to teach it here. To be here, you must be one of his chosen."

I looked up at Father Bezytere and then over to my father. Father Bezytere was at least sixty, and my father was well into his forties. Cahir looked no older than forty. I must have looked confused because everyone laughed.

"Cahir even taught the elders that initiated me," Father Bezytere said. "He takes the serum. They all take it there. It prolongs life. It's a gift they will never share with the rest of the world."

I felt a little nauseous. My head spun, and I had to put my hand on the wall to catch myself. I hadn't known Cahir at all. The only man I'd ever loved had been a stranger. Father Bezytere took a gold sash out of his pocket and wrapped it around my waist. I stood up, and I was an elder. We spent the night in that room looking at maps and charts and talking about eminent risk and danger.

In the morning, I went to the chapel and two young boys were given to the karash. I was their mother. I looked at the grubby creatures I had inherited and saw myself. I saw rage and abandonment. I gave them their robes and told them to bathe. They were mine. I sent them to classes and taught them to fight. When they were in classes, I worked. I met with the council and prime minister, and we discussed the state of the tribe and the need for withdrawal from our engagements in the south. We were stretched too thin.

I went to bed that night with a bad taste in my mouth. I lay in my large bed, but I found no sleep. I knew something was wrong. I felt them coming in the tips of my toes: the distant sound of an army marching ever closer. I sat up. There was a strange hiss in the wind. I got out of bed and walked down the hall in my nightgown. I clutched my sword in my hand.

"What are you doing?" my father asked.

"I heard something," I whispered.

"What?"

"I think I heard an army."

My father laughed. "It's our army."

I shook my head. "No."

"It's in your head."

"No."

"You're a good soldier. Too good to act like a hysterical woman."

"I'm no hysterical woman. Something is coming," I said assertively. I squared off against my father and met his eyes boldly. Something terrible was coming. I knew it as well as I knew the sword. This wasn't some vague intuition or the whisperings of my imagination.

"Then you are too good to act like a fool."

"I've never been a fool. You should know that better than anyone." My voice became as angry as his.

"Well, then you are too good to lie because I can tell you that no army could make through the Muet Mountains and to Xender unnoticed. It is impossible. Even if they could, they would never breach our walls."

"I speak only the truth."

"You should sleep now. You're a woman. It's not good for you to wander the halls of this temple, filled only with men, dressed like that."

"I don't fear them."

"It isn't you I'm worried about."

I resigned. I went to be, but the thunder boiled in the sky above me and the whispering wind had become a deafening storm. It was as if a real storm were blowing the roves from the houses outside the karash, a wind that would peal the flesh from my bones. I had to close my eyes to focus. Something was coming. The weeks past and my knowledge of impending doom only became worse with each passing day.

I never slept. I couldn't sleep with the boys at the foot of my bed doing whatever it was that young boys did. I lay in my bed rigid and acutely aware of their every motion. I would get up when I heard them fall asleep. I would get up and wander the karash, watching and waiting for the inevitable. There was something wicked in my bones, like the wind itself was corrupted.

I was up wandering the halls at night when I heard the scream of one of my students. I ran back to my room and stood and looked down on my apprentice clutching the dead body of my student. The boy was soaked in sweat and vomit.

"He said he felt ill," my apprentice said. "I thought he was trying to get out of work. I didn't know!" The boy helped me carry his brother to the incinerator, and we disposed of his remains by feeding it to Zender's fire. I put a hand on the boy's shoulder, but he did not weep.

I stayed in my room for the rest of the evening. I woke up to the sound of my apprentice moaning in desperation. I sat up and pulled him off of his cot and into my bed. I held the boy I had hardly known in my arms and put cold compresses on his forehead. I called for a doctor. He cried out, and I cleaned up his vomit. Finally, he looked up at me with blood-shot eyes and said, "I want my mommy."

"She's coming," I lied. "She's coming to take you home."

He vomited again, and in the morning I carried his remains to Zender's fire. Fifteen other boys and men were fed to the fire that morning, and the fires had never burnt so bright.

The plague came to our city like death's finger. The karash was littered with the bodies of dead boys, and the city was filled with the sick. I knew that this plague was what I had felt in the wind.

I went to Xander. He was working in the hospital. His face was lined with the creases of fatigue and anxiety.

"How are you, brother?" I asked.

Xander's smile was small and strained. He was standing over the body of a young girl, examining it. He shrugged. "I can't figure this out," he said desperately.

"You look tired."

"We all are. We can't rest with this thing looming over us. Over five thousand have died. How is that even possible? We've used every antiviral and antibiotic known to man and we can't seem to do anything." He seemed to be teetering on the verge of tears. I put my arm around him, to steady him.

"Maybe it isn't a disease?" I asked.

"What else would it be? They get fevers, and then they die. It's such a short course. There is hardly time to bring them to the hospital before they die."

I closed my eyes, and everything suddenly came together in my mind. The storm that had been coming, my premonitions of war, the deaths all made sense.

"Have them stop drinking the water," I yelled. "Tell the people only to drink bottled water."

"You think it's in the water? Why?"

"You'll think I'm crazy."

"How can I think anything is crazy when we have lost five thousand people in less than a week?"

"Something's coming. We are going to be attacked, and our attackers have poisoned the water."

Xander laughed. "What? Who would attack us? How could they?"

"We have many enemies."

"How could they touch us? Our tribe is second only to The University. We have the largest standing army in the world, and as far as the water is concerned, we have a very advanced water purification and testing system. There is no way they could poison the water, even if they wanted to."

"Just look into it, please, Xander."

"Okay, but if you suspect an attack, you should talk to Father Bezytere or Mavicho. He's in charge of that sort of thing. Isn't he you guardian? You should be able to convince him to do something."

"You should get some sleep, Xander. Killing yourself won't help these people."

Xander looked down at the girl he had been examining. He put his face on her cheek, and I watched as the tears fell from him onto her. His voice became a whisper. "How can I sleep when children are suffering? How can I rest when such things as this are allowed to happen. Where is Zender?"

I kissed him and walked away. I walked down the long hall filled with the sick and dead and climbed back up to the karash. I went back to my father's room and knocked on his door for the last time.

He came out in his night clothes and looked at me with terrifying gray eyes. "What is it?" he demanded.

"I think our water has been poisoned," I said.

"Go to bed, Ailive," he hissed.

"Our water has been poisoned. That's why so many people are dying!" I yelled. I was tired of debating with him.

"This paranoia doesn't suit you. No one could poison our water supply. All of our water goes through the water treatment plant. There is no way."

"We are going to be attacked! Your stupid pride will kill us all. Not tribe is invulnerable, not even ours."

"Go to bed, Ailive." He was so condescending I wanted to punch him.

"Why make me a master if you don't respect me enough to listen to me?"

"Why? Because the longhouse says we are unjust to women, that is why. You may be strong, but you are a woman, and you never would have been a master if that sniveling brother of yours hadn't made it political. Your behavior over the last few weeks has only proven me right. Women haven't got the constitution for war. You are a weak, emotional fool."

"Please, listen to me," I said desperately. I didn't care about his insults or his judgments. I had to save our tribe. I had to do something. I felt utterly powerless.

"Okay. You want me to listen. Tell me why you think such things. I need proof. I can't go before the council and tell them that one person thinks we should cut off our entire water supply. You give me proof, and I will listen."

"I have no proof."

"Then go to bed!"

But I couldn't sleep. So I wandered the karash. Every night I would sit on the karash walls listening. Every night I heard them. Every night I knew they grew closer. So when they came, I was sitting on the walls of the temple in my nightgown, with my sword in my hand. They came quietly in the night—without honor. They had poisoned our water, and by the time they came, more than half the tribe was dead. They did not fight like soldiers or warriors. They poisoned us. Children died in their beds with vomit in their mouths. They were coward, but they won before the first shots were fired. The surviving women and children ran to the caves to hide.

Four tribes swept in unison down upon us, pummeling us with bombs and machine gun fire. My father ran out into the courtyard, his armor dangling from his nightclothes. He had a look of someone who expected to wake from a dream. He looked at me, but said nothing. We both moved at the same time. We woke all those we could. We organized them, and we attacked the savage hordes that had descended upon the sleeping civilians of our tribe.

It was a massacre. They killed children in their beds. The city was awash with blood. We were too late to stop it. We hadn't been prepared. They had gotten past our guards and security cameras. They had studied us. I pointed to my men, even Xeres stood beside me, and we attacked the army from behind. We were better than them, but we were outnumbered, tired, and unprepared. My men fell, one by one under a barrage of machine gun fire.

Xeres and I hid behind a large wall, while the enemy fired what seemed like a ceaseless stream of bullets at us. Xeres looked at me with a strange smile and handed me a black box.

"I'm sorry," he said.

"What?" I yelled above the chaos around us.

"I'm sorry for what I did to you at the University. I dishonored you. Take this."

"What is it?" I asked.

"I stole it from Cahir before I left. I was mad."

"What is it?"

"It's a cloaking device."

"You use it."

"No. You're better than me now. You stand a better chance. I'll distract them. You use it. You put it on like a belt and push the button. That's all. You'll become almost invisible."

I nodded and put the belt on. Xeres gave me a brief bow before he ran out into the arms of the enemy. Every gun fired on him at once, and I moved toward them quietly. I cut them down while Xeres bled to death in the mud. Cahir's sword was deadly. It cut through them like butter. They were stunned at first, but they recovered quickly and began blindingly firing into all the space they could find. I killed many, but there were too many. I felt the first bullet penetrate my side, and I flinched. I flinched and continued hacking, but the second bullet pierced my chest and I fell. I fell and the cloaking device cracked. I looked up at the man who had shot me. He had lovely green eyes. The green eyes of the Verdu. He caught me as I fell and looked at me.

"I am Greenlef of the Verdu. Your people killed my wife and children. Behind me are other men whose wives you have butchered from other tribes you have laid waste too. Before you die, know that justice has been served," he said in the melodic Verdu tongue.

He dropped me, and I lay in the dust for a long time, breathing and waiting for death. But only the breeze came, covering me in the scent of evergreen and rhododendron. I opened my eyes and watched the warriors slaughter everyone who could walk toward them in their steady progression toward the cave that sheltered our women, children, doctors, priests, and officials.

In the middle of bedlam, I felt the calm Cahir had given me. I felt the mud beneath me and the gentle breeze that caressed my cheek. I opened my eyes and looked up at the clouds. They gathered, dark and strong, portending some strange future. They gathered, and the water came, wetting my cheeks with lost emotion and forgotten dreams, and I stood up. I stood up, and the wind pushed me forward.

I moved as if propelled by nature herself and the elemental forces that guided me gave me the speed of the storm. I became the storm incarnate. Where I walked, there was thunder and I moved with the clouds. I descended upon the warriors of our enemies like a hurricane and danced across their bodies before they could even see my face. My sword was part of me, and I was one with the wind. I killed them all and stood before the cave looking down on my beautiful city.

When I opened the door, the men shot at me, but I dodged the bullets easily, and there was a hushed awe in the cave as everyone stared up at me. I stood silhouetted in the light, covered in blood, held aloft by the wind. Weeping turned to silence. Fear turned to awe.

Xander rushed toward me and embraced me, kissing my face. He ran into the city with his team of doctors and medics, and they immediately began to attempt to heal all that still breathed. Women moved through the rubble searching for their sons and brothers, and the elders went to sit in the burnt husk that was the longhouse and talk. Nothing remained of the city, and the water would be tainted for a long time. The tribe had been reduced to a few hundred, mostly women and children. It was clear that we were to become tribeless.

When the work was done, Xander disappeared into the mountains. I watched him climb. Darkness settled over the city and I went home, to the karash. There was little left of my fortress. Most of the walls had fallen, and the rest were badly burnt. The bodies of the youngest students lay on the floors. I climbed over old stone and pieces of the wall until I came to the chapel. I looked up at Zender. He had fallen. He was nothing but a head surrounded by rubble.

"Ailive," my father, Mavicho, said from the shadows.

"Father," I answered coolly.

"That little shit Ieya betrayed us!" he cursed.

"Ieya?"

"She knew the city and the karash, and she sold them all our secrets. They paid her. They paid her, and she betrayed us and ran off with them."

"She betrayed us?"

"She turned off the shield. She gave them access to the water table."

"I'm sorry to hear this," I said. I couldn't bring myself to be angry at Ieya. What she had done was unspeakable, but what had been done to her was also unspeakable. Monsters make monsters, and the world burns in their shadows.

"I'm going to hunt her down and kill her. Will you come with me?"

I shook my head and looked at my dead god. "No, my duty to Zender is done." My world was dead, and I was relieved. I would never have to fight for Zender again.

Mavicho looked at the dead god and then disappeared. I watched him leave and then collected what I could from the rubble. I salvaged little. A couple of guns and a knife. It was a short hike down to the long house. The statue of Zender had fallen there too. When the statue had fallen, it had crushed a crowd of people. Blood stained the old god's face and hands.

I watched the sun set and stars emerge, and I waited. The sound of thunder in the distance was moving away from me. A cloud floated over the mountains and into the distance. When the sun returned, so did Xander. I knew before he spoke that everything was going to change. I knew that heaven and earth had collided and that somewhere along the way Zender had died. Xander called a meeting in the longhouse. I watched the elders talk. They called to me to join them, but I shook my head. I waited for the tribe's decision. I no longer cared. My work was done. I had saved those that could be saved.

I sat on Zender's head. It had fallen off his megalithic statue and had rolled down the mountain into the center of the city. All around it were bodies and ashes. The marble still remained, but the life was gone. There were only a few hundred left, sitting at Xander's feet, listening to him speak with an animated passion. I lit my pipe and watched him. The wind tickled my face, and birds sang in the distance. The gentle breeze gathered the ashes of the dead and carried them away. There was a sweetness to the wind. It was a spring breeze, and it held the scent of lavender.

Xander found me there. He came and stood in the shadow of Zender's head, looking up at me. "Will you come with us?" he asked.

"I don't think so," I answered.

"I had a vision," he said. He seemed like an ant. "This has to end. We have been chosen to create a new life. We have been chosen to create a new world, a world without war, a world without bloodshed."

"Chosen by who?"

"God."

"What God?"

"The only God."

I laughed. "Well I'm sitting on his broken head. I don't think he's fit to choose anyone."

"Zender is not God."

"Really. He's the only god I've ever known."

"Come with me. Ailive, please, we need you. I need you." I shook my head.

He kept talking, but I couldn't listen. I couldn't hear anything. After my brother had told me about his visions and his new god, I went back to the temple. I pieced together my life in the crumbling ruins of Zender's torso. Finally, I was free. I was free of all my duties to gods or tribes. I didn't owe anyone anything, and I wasn't about to take on any new gods.

I took off my filthy gown and put on soft gray robes made out of saris and silk. I took only my sword, the sword my Cahir had given me, and I left the city forever. I didn't know my way, but I hoped I would find it. I looked up toward heaven and prayed to the wind to carry me home, to my love and the wind answered. It answered with a gift I never expected. It sent me a friend.

The rwan that landed in front of me stared at me with angry eyes. It lunged at me, as if it was going to devour me, but I didn't flinch. I only put my hand out and pressed it to the beast's hot skin. It flinched. It flinched, and I fell. We both felt it, like an earthquake. I had seen through his eyes. I had understood him, and he had understood me. He was an elemental being, and he heard my voice. We were the same, the rwan and I. He was the forces of earth and fire, and I was the wind.

We sat in the earth together, my monster and I, and I stroked his skin. He wanted me. I felt it. He wanted the understanding I gave him, so he carried me. He took to the skies and carried me, and I prayed that he was carrying me toward Cahir.

IV

The Savage Plains

This world is vast and varied. It's a boundless cornucopia of endless diversity and color which few shall ever know. We are so bound. So limited by tribe and language and culture and all those things that tie us to one idea of what life should be. I began my voyage with no knowledge of the vastness of humanity. Even in The University, we saw only the world within The University. The scholars might travel to other worlds and distant stars. They would study the oceans and the ice caps, but few had voyaged to the tribal cities. Few had tasted their cuisine or learned their languages. They were too afraid.

My monster and I wandered the landscape of our world for many months. We traveled away from my home, away from The University, away from Verdu, to the distant south, which I knew nothing of. We wandered through the painted night skies, which caught the solar radiation in brilliant purples and green, and under the lavender day skies. We journeyed over vast plains of endless grass and into a land which was warm and lush. I took off my robes, and the rwan and I moved into a heat so thick I felt I could cut it with a knife. I wore only my slip of an undergarment and my long pants, and still the sweat dripped off me. We voyaged past ancient cities, ruined and forgotten. Old marble and decaying statues dotted the deserted landscape. All around us were the remnants of forgotten tribes, erased by those more powerful than themselves. The rwan led me, and I followed. Sometimes he would let me ride him into the cool skies, but such breaks were fleeting, and the beast was fickle. We passed small towns and strange cities, but the rwan pulled me on. He pulled me on, and I followed, knowing that he was driven by his own motive. I followed knowing he brought me no closer to Cahir.

I followed because the rwan had possessed me. His visions had become mine, and his longings had overwhelmed me. My will was lost in sorrow, regret, and confusion. My tribe had died, and I had been happy. My brother had called to me, and I had abandoned him. My confusion overwhelmed me. I wanted Cahir but I couldn't find him, so I took the path of least resistance and followed the only guide I had.

The creature's muscular body and black horns pressed relentlessly forward until we came to what I thought had to be the edge of the earth. The place where the land gave way and there was only water, vast and dark, eternally crashing against jagged rocks. Finally the rwan stopped and let me slip onto his back. He flew high above the crested waves and then dove down again, deep into the water. I held my breath. Again he flew up, until he found a small opening in the side of the cliffs by the water. There he landed. There he rested his head on his claws and closed his burning eyes in what I knew had to be sleep. I lay down next to him, touching his smooth, warm skin. The creature snorted and smoke billowed out of its nostrils. For a moment, I thought I heard him. Not words, but feelings and images older than words drifted out of him and into me, like a mosaic, or an old picture book.

The images washed over me like a warm bath. I saw the rwan's life in my mind's eye, and I didn't understand. He had lived in a time before The University, before tribes, when the world was ruled by a different society, older than time. Pictures of the rwan's ancient world flooded my senses. I drew my hand away, and the images faded. The beast opened his eyes again and looked at me. My antediluvian friend. His bifurcated tongue darted in and out of his mouth in a serpentine gesture. I fell back onto his belly and into a deep sleep.

I don't know how long we slept. When I awoke, I was surrounded by children, scraggly, skinny, filthy, little children that looked like they had seen the fires of eternity twice and crawled their way out on blood encrusted finger nails. They stared at me with their saucer like eyes. When they realized I was awake, they jumped backward in unison. I stood up slowly and stretched, examining my surroundings.

The cave was much larger than I had thought. In the waning evening light, I saw that there were a myriad of tunnels which twisted off in various directions. The light caught the crystal growths on the edge of these tunnels and refracted it, so that the twilight shone with unprecedented brilliance. The children were clutching tools for fishing or gathering in their hands: small baskets, bowls, shovels, and fishing rods. The children looked so different from any race I knew. They were tall and dark, like my Cahir. Their hair was thick and braided, and their features were sharp. Their eyes drew back, and their limbs seemed preternaturally long to me.

A voice from one of the tunnels made the children jump. Bedlam followed, and the children disappeared into various tunnels with a cacophony of speech I couldn't understand. When they reappeared, they were followed by two dozen poorly dressed women. Some of them were clutching babies and others also carried tools. These women were large, much taller than I, and I could tell that they did not even consider me. It was the rwan that made them move back.

I could tell by looking at the women that they were tribeless. They were hiding in the caves, looking for sanctuary in a cruel world.

There are many ways to explain magic, but at the time, I knew only the wind and the storm, and I knew that it was these forces which had changed me. They had changed me after I had been shot. They had brought me back and shaped me in their image, so I was no longer simply a woman. So as the women spoke, in their desperate, panicked speech, I began to comprehend.

"Who are you? What is that!? What do you want?" the women were yelling.

I raised my hand and all the talking stopped. "I'm no one," I responded. "I'm a traveler. I'm lost. I'm only looking for shelter and rest for a few days."

A pudgy woman stepped forward. Her features were finer than the others and her hair was longer. I couldn't tell her age, but she seemed older. She limped when she walked. "You can't stay here," she said.

"What's your name?" I asked.

"Dania," she responded curtly.

"I'm Ailive and like you, I'm tribeless. I wander alone, as I know you have. I'll be no burden to you. My friend is tired, and he likes this spot. Do you want to try to convince him to find a new spot?"

Dania looked at the rwan and shook her head. "You can stay," she muttered. "But it's dark now and we must work, so stay out of our way."

There was a loud exclamation of joy from the children, and they all rushed forward to meet me. "To work!" Dania yelled and the children scattered out the mouth of the cave and down to the beach below.

The women moved slowly passed me, eyeing me angrily as they went. I sat at the mouth of the cave watching the women and children work in the dark. They scattered out over the treacherous rocks gathering bits of seaweed and oysters. They waded into the water and speared fish. Some of the children played and every once in a while, laughter would drift up over the sound of the waves. The moons dappled the black water with light, and the sky looked down on them benevolently.

The small group stayed out late into the night. I watched them. They seemed so foreign to me, not only because they were from a distant land, but because I had never been part of a family.

I smiled as the children joined hands and sang. They danced in a circle and fell in the sand. The women sang as they worked. Even in the darkest of places, these people had found a shadow of joy I had never known. I sat, with my back pressed up against the rwan, and wondered at the miraculous tapestry of life.

Finally, they came back. They picked up their heavy baskets and moved into the caves as the first moon fell on the horizon. The children rubbed their sleepy eyes, and the women carried the littler ones on their hips. I followed them into their stone labyrinth. I followed them to their home. The women tucked the children into their beds. The beds had been brought from some other place, before they had been tribeless. They seemed warm and clean. They all lived in one large room. An underwater river flowed past their kitchen and they had decorated the large cavern with all that was left of their lives.

Dania saw me loitering in the shadows and barked at me, "We told you to stay in the opening. We didn't tell you to come in. You aren't wanted!"

"I'm only curious," I responded.

Another smaller woman stepped forward. She was covered in scars worse than my own, and she was missing a few fingers. "Let her alone, Dania. What harm can she do? She's only one woman. A tiny woman. You could pick her up and break her in half. My daughter could break her in half." The woman waved to me and smiled. "Come in. Come in. You look hungry. Eat something. It isn't much, but you looked starved." I followed the woman in and took her bowl, filled with steaming seaweed and shrimp. The bowl was made of the most sublime crystal, inlaid with pictures of tiny animals, but it contained the most vile concoction I had ever tasted. I ate it with gratitude and sat down by the fire with the other women.

The women sat sewing and talking. The kind woman looked at me and smiled again. "I'm Salome," she said. "We were Hyran. Our city was two miles from here. Do you know it?"

I nodded. "I'm lost, but I know Hyra. I've been traveling for a long time now."

"You've been traveling alone, and you haven't been picked up? A pretty, little thing like you? Times must be getting better," Dania said.

"I travel with the rwan. No one will bother me."

"Ha!" Dania snorted. "People have been catching and selling those things for years. They are sorry protection. So, what tribe are you?"

"I was Xenderian, but not anymore. I'm nothing now."

Salome put her hand on my shoulder. "Don't say that. You'll always be Xenderian. They may kill your people. They may burn your home. But you are always you. They can't take that."

I shook my head. "No. I have no tribe." I had left my tribe when I left my brother.

Dania grunted. "The mighty have fallen," she said. "You're Xenderian? The most powerful tribe in the world? Ha! I remember when your priestesses came to our city telling us to embrace Zender or burn forever. We took them in and listened. We listened and sent them off. We were so afraid we'd be attacked because we didn't convert. Not that it matters now. Everyone was afraid of you. I guess not anymore."

"Not anymore," I said.

"Be kind," Salome said. "She's just a girl. She didn't have anything to do with the atrocities of the Xenderian. Don't you remember what it felt like? Has it been so long? How long ago did you lose your tribe, Ailive?"

"It's been two months," I answered.

"Good," Dania said. "Your people sent an assassin to kill my husband. Your people took advantage of our good nature. They put us at a disadvantage so when the Efferitas came, they slaughtered us." Salome grew angry. "Stop! This girl is an innocent!"

"I'm not," I whispered. A wave of guilt washed over me.

"Don't let her get to you. You can't carry the burdens of an entire tribe."

"I could have killed your husband," I said to Dania. "I've killed many. I never asked why. I only went as they sent me."

"You?" Salome laughed. "You can't be more than eighteen. You couldn't hurt a fly."

I stood up and removed my robe exposing my shoulders and back. My entire upper torso was painted with the tattoos of a soldier. "I walk the way of the storm," I said. "I take responsibility for my tribe because I could have been the one who killed your husband. I've killed many men asleep in their beds just because I was told too. It's who I am. It's who I was. I'm sorry."

"We should kill her!" Dania hissed.

"You couldn't if you wanted to," I responded.

"Like hell I couldn't!" Dania lunged clumsily toward me. I moved back allowing her to fall on the floor. She cursed.

"I don't want to hurt you," I said.

"How can you do these things?" Salome asked.

"I've been killing since I was twelve, and I've been fighting since I was five. It's all I've ever known."

"Your people are monsters. Who does that to a child?"

"Maybe I'm the monster, but I don't want to hurt you. I just want to listen. Just for a while. I want to understand. Tell me about your tribe. Tell me what happened." I needed to know what had happened to her people to understand what I had done. I had killed her tribe. I was the thief in the night that had carried the decimation of her people in my arm like a child. I was the lone assassin who had killed Dania's husband, and I hated myself for that.

"We will tell you nothing," Dania said.

For some reason Salome smiled. She moved closer to me and began to speak into the fire. "I believe in the fates," she said. "Dania has always been a skeptic, but I still believe and I believe that the fates must have brought you to us. I was born into a poor house on the outskirts of our city. We were a prosperous tribe. We considered ourselves very progressive. Some of the scholars from The University even came to teach our youth. We took in the tribeless. We allowed the worship of many gods. We believed that the fates favored those that took care of others. But all of this was kept in a delicate balance. We had trouble with crime, and we had an army of ambassadors in constant negations with other tribes."

Salome sighed and threw a piece of wood on the fire. "My family was tribeless. My mother's tribe was decimated by the Xenderians. We were taken in. We were poor, but we felt that we were safe and that was a lot for the tribeless. My mother was a cleaning lady, and my father worked at a factory that produced the tiny chips that make computers work. I went to The University. I became an engineer, and I designed bombs. It was a good job. I was happy. I took care of my family. I married a wonderful man, also an engineer. I had two beautiful boys."

"We all saw the trouble coming. We refused a contract with the Xenderians. After that, it didn't take long for the Efferitas to smell fresh blood. They sent four ambassadors claiming that we were occupying their croplands. We stood our ground; it was all they needed. They swept down on us like locusts."

"I watched it all. They killed every man and boy that stayed to fight and took all the women for slaves. They found me and beat me and left me for dead. For a long time I wished I had died. For all of us here, it has been hard to find the will to continue, but we want our children to survive so we are strong. That was four years ago. Now we hide, coming out only at night. During the day the Efferitas watch. They scour the earth and sweep up the tribeless for slaves. We won't be slaves."

"Death first," a pale woman to her right muttered.

"I was in the senate," Dania said. "I was there when your people came and demanded our services. My husband was too. An elder named Mavicho came and said that if we did not supply what they needed, they couldn't support us. My husband stood up to him in the senate, and he was dead by morning. The next day this Mavicho told us they would no longer protect us."

"He was my father," I said sadly.

"Who?" Salome asked.

"Mavicho was my father."

Silence filled the cave. The women stared at me like I was demon straight up from eternity. Like I had come to devour their souls while they slept. "I'll leave when the sun sets," I whispered. "Thank you. Thank you for your stories. They have meant more to me than you know."

I went back to my rwan. My mind swarmed with thoughts I couldn't silence. Guilt overcame me. My entire life I had been taught the rest of the world were godless heathens and monsters, but we had been the monsters. I was a monster. Slowly, everything I had believed in had dissolved in front of me. My god was dead. My tribe were assassins and murderers. I was tribeless. I was dust, and the wind only spoke to me in my dreams.

When I awoke, the women and children had already left and were out on the beach. The rwan was awake, and I knew that it was hungry. It was time for us to go. We left the cave, and I waved to Salome. She returned the gesture.

I climbed up over the hill that led away from the sea. On the grassy spot above the hill, a handful of children were dancing in the moonlight and singing old songs. In the distance, not too far away, I saw riders. The children were unaware of the men watching them, but their breath carried on the wind. I grabbed the children and pushed them toward the cave, shouting at Salome, but it was too late. The riders were gone and more would come.

"What are you doing?" Dania yelled.

"I saw riders!" I yelled. "They saw the children."

"What riders? What did they look like?" Salome asked.

"Their heads were wrapped. They were dark skinned, and they rode large horses."

"Efferitas," Salome whispered. "We need to leave now."

"And go where?" Dania asked. "We'll be picked off by raiders if we leave this place."

"We'll be Efferitas' slaves if we stay!" Salome screamed.

"Let me go," I said.

"Better to live a slave. I'm not going to take these children on a death march," Dania said.

"Better to die free!" Salome yelled.

"I'll go and take care of this," I said again. "I owe you that. For what my father did. For what I did."

"I'm old," Dania said. "I would die. I've seen the end and back, but I'm not going to take my babies to be devoured by scavengers."

"Listen to me," I said. "I will go."

"Go and do what?" Dania asked.

"I'll kill whatever comes over the hill."

Dania laughed. "You're crazy."

"Do you know that when my tribe was massacred, they killed everyone standing? I alone survived facing an army. When I was done, there was only me."

"Don't be ludicrous," Salome responded.

"What do you have to lose? Barricade yourself in. I'll go out. What loss is it to you if I die?"

"It'll be like killing two birds with one stone. We'll kill a Xenderian and maybe a few Efferitas. I support it. Run up to the hill, imbecile, and die," Dania hissed.

Dania limped into the cavern pulling her children with her. All of the other women and children followed her. Only Salome remained.

"Why would you die for us?" Salome asked.

I shook my head. "I'm tired of fighting for the wrong reasons. I'm tired of killing people in their sleep and obeying simply because I'm told to. The storm brought me here. You don't deserve to die or worse. If I die fighting for you, I'll have died fighting for something I believe in."

"What do you believe in?"

"The storm."

"Do you really believe you can do this?" she said.

"I know I can."

"I'll go with you."

"No. You'll only be an impediment."

"I'm a mother. I'll fight for my children. Women are like lions when they need to be."

"A lion would die in this battle. Go in with the others. Your children need you alive."

So I mounted the rwan, and he and I flew out over the sea and back to the verdant slopes of the hills above. He flew high, carrying me into the clouds and then sank low landing softly on the grass. He almost looked like he smiled at me as he sat on the grass.

I touched his shoulder with my hand. He turned his massive head and faced me. His deep, red eyes burnt with a sullen rage I had never seen in anything before. Like a god had been caged behind his flaming skull, waiting for the moment to break free.

He stood up and flexed his chilling claws. Slowly, he bellowed out a sound I had never before. He opened his mouth and a ghastly roar exploded from his jaws followed by billows of smoke. He took to the air as I saw the riders returning over the horizon. He swooped down upon them like a bird of prey, picking up men and dropping them onto the jagged rocks by the sea. Cacophony followed with bursts of gunfire and desperate screams. All eyes tilted upward.

I sat in the grass for a while with the evening light glistening on my lap. I listened to the sounds of the ocean over the screams and the whisper of the wind over the damp grass. All around me, tiny insects crept and crawled. The clouds moved, and the sun danced in and out of them. The first moon had just risen over the horizon, painting the sky in shades of blood red and orange. I rose slowly, taking my sword from its sheath and sauntered toward the hysterical men.

It was a long time before anyone saw me. Everyone was too preoccupied with my rwan. I raised my sword, and the men fell before me like blades of grass before a gardener. They didn't see or hear me and still their friends aimed their guns toward the heavens, shooting mindlessly at what couldn't be killed. Finally, a regal looking man in a gold gilded robe turned to face me. Our eyes met, and he surveyed the carnage at my feet. I moved steadily toward him, killing everything that came between us. I heard him yelling something in his native tongue, and then the riders all turned to face me. Still the rwan descended on them, but they all lunged for me.

And then I heard nothing. I could no longer hear their language or the beating of the sea. The deafening roar of the rwan was lost in the screams of the wind. It was like I was standing at the edge of a tornado watching it wipe the earth clean. When the noise dissipated, vultures cried above me, and all around me there was only blood and the dead.

The regal man was kneeling before me, covered in mud. He shook violently. There was fear in his eyes. He was no real soldier. He was not even worth the energy it would take to kill him. He gazed up at me with the most startling green eyes, like the grass beneath us, and I smiled. He was beautiful.

"Please," he begged. "Let me live." I hated the Efferitas' language the moment it slid from his vile tongue. I spoke, and its vile, throaty sounds spat forth from my mouth like old vomit.

"Why?"

He stammered. His body shook. I think he began to weep. He was a coward, a pitiful coward. He shook his head back and forth. "There are more coming!" he said.

"More riders?"

"No. They have diggers and workers. We were told there was a group of tribeless holed up in some caves or something here. Some of our riders saw some children by the ocean. We only came to dig them out."

"I'm one of those tribeless, and I'm not going to let you have them. Are there soldiers with your excavation equipment?"

"A few. You would kill them easily."

I raised my sword. I wanted nothing more than to hack the revolting coward in two. But he raised his hand and yelled, "Wait!"

I stopped, raising an eyebrow. He lay on the ground breathing heavily. The light fragmented over his body as the sun set and the second moon rose, half shadowed, over the cool plains. The stars peppered the sky, and the man lay trembling at their feet.

"What now?" I asked.

"You can't just kill us all!" he yelled over his sobs.

"Why not?"

The rwan moved through the remains of the men on the battle field, grazing on their limbs. He was covered in blood and seemed sated by the slaughter. He roared again, and the man began to cry harder.

"Because they will keep coming. We are many. We have more than a million soldiers, and all are men that have a taste for war. They won't stop. Please, they'll keep coming and the more men you kill, the angrier they will get. We would have just taken your tribeless band as slaves, but if they are tried for war crimes they'll be skinned alive! You have children with you. Do you want them skinned alive?"

I lowered my sword. "What do you propose?"

"I think that," he stammered. "I think that if I could take just a few of you as slaves, I could say that you were well armed, and all my men were killed. I can take a few children and say that we killed all your men. I could say that you were all dead except these five? Five would work. These five slaves I've taken."

"I won't give you any children."

"Just one. Just one. We executed the rest, for war crimes. We crucified them, and they were devoured by a hungry rwan."

"You can have me and only me."

78

"Not you."

"Why not?"

"Because you're…you're…what are you?"

"I'm the storm."

"I don't know what that means."

"Neither do I."

"You're dangerous. I mean, if I take you with me, you might kill me or kill whoever I sell you to or kill everyone in the city you can and I can't do that. I may be a coward, but I can't risk my people."

"Then you'll have to die." I cut off his finger slowly.

He screamed and wept like a little girl. "Please! Please! Give me someone old and feeble. Someone you don't like. I'll take anyone. Don't do this!"

"You'll take me," I said as I pierced his shoulder with my sword. His blood dripped down the sword's blade and over my hand.

He nodded. Spit dripped out of his mouth and snot dripped down into that same weeping hole. His face was plastered with sweat, and he had urinated on himself. A wretched mixture of odors rose up from him and the corpses around us. I wanted to kill the man, but some small part of me believed him. I knew that if I killed him, all of the Hyran would be killed.

I was one woman, and I was a killer. I had killed fathers and mothers and children. I had spent my life lost in death. I had this one chance to save life, and it seemed like a small sacrifice. I grabbed the man by his hair and punched him. I would have to take him with me to the cave so he would not escape. I would have to explain everything to Salome before I left, so she would know they were safe.

I looked at my friend, my rwan, still feasting on the dead, and he met my eyes. He understood me without speaking. He moved in and grabbed the blubbering fool and carried him to the cave. I followed them slowly, drinking in the sanguineous evening scene. The sky turned alizarin crimson as the third moon rose over the battlefield. The blood disappeared under the red light and then the light softened and all faded to black. Only the stars and the moons' steady glow remained.

I told Salome what had happened. The women seemed afraid of us. They stood back, in the shadows watching us. The rwan dropped the coward at my feet, and he stood up, clutching his injured hand.

"I promise you we will not come back!" he shouted. "I will tell them you're all dead and that several rwans have taken over this area as their territory."

"Thank you," Salome whispered.

"My friend, my rwan, will stay with you awhile longer, until I need him again. He'll keep you safe. Take care of him. Invite him in your cave. Make sure he is fed and safe."

Salome put her hand on the beast. "I promise. I'll never forget this kindness."

I shook my head and wiped the blood from my forehead. "It was nothing. I owe you more than this…" I stopped. I closed my eyes seeing the faces of the Hyran I had killed. I had aided in their decimation and, in my heart, I knew it hadn't been my father who had killed Dania's husband. It had been me. "I'm not a good person, Salome. This is a small thing in comparison to the debt I owe."

Salome only kissed me. "I thank the fate that brought you to us," she whispered.

So the Efferitas man and I walked over horizon to where his horse waited for him. He had regained a little of his composure. He cleaned and dressed his weeping wounds. He took off his soiled robes and rewrapped his hair. He wiped his face and hands.

"You understand that I'm taking you back as a slave?" he said. "I must ride and you must walk behind me with your hands bound. You must wear a collar and I will pull you by a leash. You're pretty. Do you know what they do with pretty slaves? Are you sure this is what you want?"

"I believe that this is what I must do," I responded. I placed my sword on the ground and offered him my hands. "Bind me. I will be as placid as a cow."

He shuddered as he tied me. His eyes were still wide with fear. He placed a rope around my neck and took my sword.

"Lady," he said. "I don't understand why one such as you, one who is surely possessed by the gods, would give herself up for a handful of women and children. I beg you to reconsider."

"I owe them this."

It was a long walk to Efferitas. We walked over lush plains and passed tepid streams. There were a plethora of small cities, walled up and flying the Efferitas' flag, along the way. Dark people with frightened eyes stared out at us on our journey. The landscape changed, and the plains became more and more desolate until there was nothing but wild, dead looking grass. The sun bleached the flat landscape, giving it the appearance of a wasteland.

We camped on the wasteland under the moons. My captor had lost a lot of blood and had begun to lose his color. His body was limp in his saddle. We stopped, and I gave him some of the water we had left.

"Take off your shirt," I said.

He looked up at me with distrust. "I don't think so."

"Your wound needs fresh wrappings, and it should be cleaned."

"No."

"Your pride will kill you."

"You'll kill me."

"If I wanted you dead, you'd be dead."

He reluctantly shed his shirt, revealing the soft body of an aristocrat. Without all his robes, he looked young. He was barely a man. I studied him and frowned when I realized he was my age or younger. I cleaned his wounds gently, and he grunted in pain. He looked down at the earth while I cared for him. I cleaned and dressed his wounds and put out his sleeping bag.

"Why are you doing this?" he asked.

"I'm your slave now. Isn't this what slaves do?"

His eyes narrowed. "What manner of creature are you?" he asked.

"I don't know," I answered.

"What were you doing with those Hyran women? Why do you care about them?"

I looked up at the stars above me. The air was hot and dry. It was different from Xender. "I don't care for them, but I'm trying to make amends for past sins," I said. "And I don't think they should die only because they are tribeless."

He smiled a strange smile that revealed some passion in his green eyes. "I agree."

"How long until we get to your home?"

"Another day's ride and we'll be there. They'll not be kind to you. They may kill you."

"I don't mind dying."

"What's your name?"

"Ailive."

"I'm Hotem."

We slept beside each other in an ocean of nothing. I listened to his desperate breaths as he struggled to find a place without pain. In the morning, I helped him into his saddle, and we moved onward over the plains and away from the ocean. Every once in a while a small mouse or rodent would watch us walk by, but the walk was long and marked only by the absence of scenery.

Finally, we reached a jungle of corn and wheat which we navigated quickly. Hotem waved at slaves and farmers as we wandered the infinite croplands. It was more than two days before I saw the city; it was on the other side of an enormous river. The city was strategically placed between two long rivers. Between these serpents, the city stretched out in both directions as far as the eye could see. Before we entered the city, he stopped his horse and looked back at me. His face was creased with fear and worry.

"I ask you one last time to reconsider and if you will not, I ask you one humble favor," he said.

"I won't, so ask."

"When you realize you can't live as a slave, promise me you'll only kill the men that stand in your way, no women or children."

"Why should I make such a promise to a man who hunts disowned women and children?"

"They are only tribeless. There are women and children of honor within these walls."

"The only difference between the tribeless and you is a single battle, and from what I've seen of you on the battle field, that fight is not far away. You'll live up to our bargain, and if I ever learn anything has happened to those women and children, I will come for you. It doesn't matter if it's your fault or not. They're now your responsibility."

The Efferitas had a beautiful city. The people were wrapped in heavy linens cast in vibrant colors. The walls were painted with bright collages and the floors were covered with intricate mosaics. Filth and dirt intermingled with the scents of jasmine and rich spices. Children ran barefoot through narrow alleys. Ancient building jutted out at strange angles. All manner of animals roamed the streets. Men pulled rickety rickshaws up and down the tangled roads. There was no order, no plan, only a pandemonium of motion and color that blinded me.

The most notable oddity about the Efferitas' city was its complete lack of modern technology. In our city, the old had juxtaposed with the new. Archaic marble libraries had glowing neon signs and computers were prominently displayed in the homes of the wealthy. Electric lines covered the landscape and the hum of mopeds overlapped the steady thud of horses' hooves. In Efferitas, there was none of this. There was no sign of any modernization anywhere.

We wandered in and out of alleys and dark streets until we came to the center of the city. The Efferitas were a people of water and sand, for beyond the rivers and croplands in every direction there was nothing but desert and savage plains.

The madness diminished in the center of the city. The chaotic assortment of unplanned buildings and roads gave way to a large circular road which surrounded a series of beautiful buildings with a domed architecture I had never seen before. These buildings stretched out for acres, surrounded by colorful tents and huts.

Hotem dismounted as we entered the circle and handed his horse to a slave. We walked through the palace grounds until we reached the largest, most ornate buildings in the circle. The walls were painted in swirls and brightly colored patterns. Banners hung from the walls and ceiling. The building was so enshrouded in colorful fabrics that we felt like we were entering a tent. Hotem pulled me through a labyrinth of long hallways past a series of enormous rooms. We walked over brilliant mosaics into a waiting room filled with richly robed men. The men stared at us with angry eyes, and Hotem stared back with all the confidence of a king. We were quickly escorted into a large chamber where a man sitting on a throne was talking with a group of turbaned men.

The king stood up as we entered. Hotem bowed deeply.

"Get up, Get up," the king said impatiently. "Where are your men? What happened?" The king was a middle aged man with a heavy beard and thick belly. He was wrapped in bright robes and wore many gold chains and jewels. His green eyes shimmered beneath his thick, black eyebrows. His forehead was painted with several red letters and so were his naked arms. The vibrancy of the color that enshrouded the king brought attention to the darkness of his skin and the green of his eyes. They almost glowed in the eerie light of the throne room, pining Hotem to the ground with the intensity of his gaze.

"Sire," Hotem said. "Things went very poorly."

The king got down from his throne and stood in front of us. "What do you mean poorly? Are you completely incompetent? I sent you to capture a handful of tribeless women and children. How badly could it have gone?"

"My Lord, there was a group of Xenderian soldiers amongst the group. We were completely unprepared for them. They cut us down, but our men fought bravely and took the entire group with them. The only one remaining was this girl, who stands behind me."

"I find it impossible to believe that a group of Hyran tribeless would be guarded by Xenderian soldiers. It was the Xenderians who were critical in the Hyran destruction. They ordered it! They came to us with a treaty. And all our intelligence indicates that all of the Xenderian soldiers were killed. Only a handful of religious fanatics remain and all have given up the sword." The king slapped Hotem. "Why am I cursed with a blithering idiot of a liar for a son?"

"Sir," Prince Hotem replied. "I only report what I saw. Look at this girl. She is clearly Xenderian. Look at her coloring. The way she is tattooed. What else would she be? I don't know how or why they were there, but the remaining Xenderian were with the Hyran tribeless in those caves. I wouldn't lie to you, father."

The king pulled my shirt off roughly and looked at my tattoos. He walked around me studying the elaborate mural that covered the better part of my upper torso. I met his eyes boldly and stood, unwavering in front of the court full of men.

"She's definitely Xenderian," he said. "But I don't know what to make of her. I went to Xender once, once I was very young. We were contemplating a raid on one of their trade caravans. I spent two weeks studying them. We decided the raid wasn't worth the risk. Their women were a bold breed, allowed to work and live like men, but I never saw anything like this. Only their soldiers used these markings."

One of the king's advisors stepped forward, a grizzled old man that looked like he had seen the bad end of a battle axe. "She must be a soldier," the man barked. "We should kill her."

"That's absurd," the prince said. "How could this little bird of a woman be a soldier? I saw her there, and she never fought. She just stood amidst all the chaos, like she is now. I thought maybe she was stupid." Clearly the prince was at his best in court. All his trembling and cowardice had vanished. He stood tall and proud. He lied without flinching and spoke with a conviction that almost convinced me of his lies.

The grizzled old man shook his head. "Some tribes use women soldiers. Heretics have no morality. The Xenderian let women work and live as men. Why shouldn't they let them die as men? Ordinary women aren't branded like this."

"Well, why don't we ask her," the prince retorted.

"A slave never speaks in the presence of a king," the man responded. "Let alone a woman slave."

"Let her speak," the king said. "The king is law and I say that it's necessary. So girl? What are you? What are these markings?"

"I'm Xenderian," I responded coolly. "I was a priestess. These are the marks of Zender."

"You see," the prince said. "She's nothing. We should sell her like we would any other slave."

The king paused again and returned to his chair. His forehead creased with thought. The room became heavy with the weight of the man's thought. The blue moon hovered at the horizon, slowly drawing in the evening and seeping its strange wavering light on the poorly lit room. Slaves drifted in, lighting candles and lamps.

"I think I'll keep her," the king announced.

"I don't think that's wise," the prince said. "She's a heretic priestess. She would bring bad luck on our house."

He wanted me gone. Beneath all his bravado, I could still smell the prince's fear. He wanted me as far away from him as he could.

"No, and I'll not argue this point. I want her here. She can work in the kitchens."

"You'll see to that," he said pointing to a man wrapped in gray in the corner. The man stepped forward and pulled me away by the rope that was wrapped around my neck. I heard the heated discussion continuing in the king's chamber. They were arguing about the caves, but their voices faded as I was pulled further and further into the back of the palace. I followed without fear. It didn't matter where I went. I was tribeless. I was a monster. I deserved nothing more than to be a slave.

Finally, the fine mosaic covered floors gave way to dirt and stone. The smell of incense faded, and new odors took over. The smell of fire and food and waste filled my nose. All around me slaves shuffled to and fro, laden with the burdens of their work. They all bore a large brand on their necks that marked them as the king's thralls. Some wore multiple brands, as if they had many owners over the course of their lives. All were dressed in gray wool and most had no shoes.

The slave who pulled me took me to a large man in rough red tunic with hair was wrapped in a stained turban and a dirty beard. The slave handed me over to the man, who ran his hands coarsely over my body. "Did the king say where he wanted her?" he asked.

"He said the kitchens."

The man stripped me to my undergarments and took my clothes. For a moment, I forgot myself and reached out for them. The man slapped me, and I punched him in the face. The action was more reflexive than intentional. I hadn't meant to hit him. He fell on the ground with a hard thud and then he pulled himself back up to his feet. He cursed me and punched me. I fell to the ground and felt the cold stone beneath my back. His fists dug into my flesh, bruising me. The pain was nothing. It was nothing compared to the pain of the karash, so I lay on the ground and took the beating and prayed to whatever god was out there that I was saving the women in the cave.

"What asshole sent us this bitch?" the man asked as he kicked me.

"Probably that idiot Hotem," another slave handler said. "That boy will be the death of us."

The man shrugged and threw me over onto the table. He strapped me down and branded me. The pain was just a pinch for me. A reminder of old battles. I thought of Cahir. I thought of his hands on me, and then the slave handler picked me up and tossed me onto the ground.

"Crian!" he bellowed.

A small red haired woman crept out of the kitchen. She was hunched over and her hands were bent with age. Her skin was thick and tough like old leather, and her eyes were forever looking down. There was a twinkle of something that resembled beauty beneath all the age and abuse, but it was faded and long forgotten. She kneeled before the brutish handler.

"This one's new. She's for the kitchens. Show her the ropes," he said.

Crian was an uncommonly kind woman. The other slaves quickly tired of my ineptitude. They thought I was lazy and useless, but Crian guided me through everything. I knew nothing of cooking or any other menial work. Crian showed me how to build and feed the fires, how to regulate the temperature within the hellish ovens. All the food was made from scratch. We killed the birds, plucked their feathers, and butchered them.

We cut the wood for the ovens. We ground the grain for the bread.

We all slept in the same cellar room. We each had a pillow and a blanket and a bit of straw to sleep on. Strange green birds slept on the straw next to us, and the room was full of noises and smells. Children cried in hunger. Men and women moaned in their copulation. The slaves that did the night work shuffled in and out, fetching things for the nobles upstairs. There was snoring and farting and pissing and shitting, and in the morning I felt as if I hadn't slept more than two hours. War seemed easy.

The work never stopped. We cooked and cleaned and cooked again. I passed several months this way. I never left the kitchen or the sleeping quarters. I ate only stale bread and drank only water. I bathed in the evening and put on fresh clothes and went to bed.

The other slaves didn't talk to me. They moved around me like some sort of irritating tick. I never caught on to the work of the kitchen. I could never move as fast as the others, and they hated me for it.

"Don't worry," Crian crooned in an accent so heavy it danced across the words. "It will get better. You'll learn."

"Were you always a slave?" I asked her.

"We cannot speak of such things," she said in a fearful whisper.

"How long have you been here?"

"Since I was your age."

"It seems almost unbearable here."

"I have no choice. I don't believe in suicide, so I live and I work."

"I had a choice," I said sadly.

"How can you have a choice?"

"There is always a choice." I lay back in the straw and pulled the blanket over me.

"Little girl," Crian whispered. "Once a very long time ago, I had a daughter. A beautiful girl, like you. They took her from me and sold her to a brothel. There are no choices here."

"What's her name? What does she look like?" Anger overcame and images of Ieya filled my mind.

Tears filled the old woman's eyes. She buried her face in her hands. "It doesn't matter."

"Tell me," I insisted.

"Her name was Mia. She had thick, curly red hair and eyes like the rwan's skin. She was spirited and beautiful and that's why the king took her. He called her to his chambers and when he tired of her, he sold her. That's all we are. We are cattle. If you have a choice, you should run now, because it won't be long before you are summoned by someone. You are too pretty to be left long down here."

"Someday, when it's time for me to go again, when my friends are safe, I'll find your daughter and free her."

"We should sleep now," Crian said as she lay down. "The third moon has risen and tomorrow will be long."

I felt warm next to her. She felt like a mother was supposed to feel. Warm. Safe. Loving. My real mother had never felt that way. She had always been too busy for me. There had been no long night talks or sweet kisses to assuage my nightmares. Crian put her arms around me, and I fell asleep in her arms.

So I became content as a slave. The work was hard, and I never saw the sun or the moons. The wind never touched my cheeks, and the sweet grass was far gone, but I had Crian, my mother, who I could tell anything. She stroked my hair and kissed my scars. I became her daughter, the daughter she had lost, and she became my mother, the mother who had cast me out.

I wanted to stay with her forever, in our little nook under the stairs. I wanted to lie in that straw and tell her stories. There was a safety in it. There would be no killing, and we would not be killed. Nothing was expected of me. I could just lose myself in the monotony of the moment. The clockwork of the daily chores. Get up. Get clean. Get dressed. Cook. Clean. Eat your crust of bread. Cook. Clean. Eat your crust of bread. Cook. Clean. Eat a meat stew and then down to the straw to lie in the flickering light of the fire, surrounded by the stench of the other thralls. There was no fear. No apprehension. No tension. No wind. Only the sound of humanity fluttering around me.

Hannah was the only other slave who talked to me regularly. She was five years younger than I, but she was much smarter than I in all the ways that counted. I was attempting to pluck a bird for lunch when she snuck up behind me and grabbed my hands.

"You have to twist as you pull," she said. She sat down next to me and began plucking, and I followed her advice.

"That's better," she said. The fire flickered, catching her soft features. "What's it like up there?" she asked hesitantly.

"Up where?"

"Upstairs. I've never been anywhere but here."

I shrugged. "It's large. It goes on forever. It's filled with people and colors and sweet foods and blue skies. There are vast expanses of water and ice so large you cannot see their ends and oceans of people so large you can't even imagine their number."

Hannah smiled. "Do the people look like you?"

"No. They come in all sizes and colors."

"My mother says that if I'm good I'll go to market in a few years. Maybe I'll be bought by some nice merchant and used as a house slave. I could travel then. See the world."

"It isn't that bad here," I said.

"It's hot and dark, but my family is here."

"What are those bruises from?" I asked without thinking.

"I'm Jayden's pet," she said. Jayden was one of the slave keepers. His job was to keep us all in line.

"Pet?" I asked stupidly.

"Yes. You know, he takes me when he pleases."

I still didn't understand. "Takes you where?"

"He has sex with me."

"Oh." I suddenly felt flat. Cold. "I'm sorry."

She shrugged. "My mother says it will help me. He likes me most of the time, and if I'm good to him, he'll send me to market when he's done with me."

I put my hand on the girl's shoulder. She was only a baby. I wished I could set them all free. Take them away some place pretty, but I couldn't imagine the place where they would be welcome even if I did fight to set them free.

Hannah left, and I finished my work. Crian came to help me lay the birds out on plates for the house slaves to take upstairs. "You shouldn't talk to her like that," Crian said.

"What do you mean?" I asked.

"Don't fill her head with dreams of other people and places. It'll do her no good. She'll never leave this place. She has to learn to be happy here," Crian said.

"I just thought she might…"

"Don't think and if you do think, don't talk about it. You and I have nothing to lose, but that girl could move up. She could get out of these kitchens. If she starts questioning her place or wanting more than she should, she'll get nothing."

I nodded and cast a shadowy glance at Jayden in the corner. He was an ugly man who was missing one eye. He was filthy and his long hair glistened with grease and funk.

Hannah came to see me again and again over the following days. I tried to avoid talking to her, but she liked me. She helped me learn to spice the cabbage or butter the birds. She taught me how to put the sauce on the fat cakes to make them sweet, and she showed me how to arrange things so they were more pleasing to the eye.

"You aren't as stupid as they say," she said. "You just need to be taught."

"I had never cooked before I came here," I said.

"Were you rich? Did you have slaves?"

"No. I just never cooked."

"How did you eat?"

"I don't know. We had these meals that came in bags that we bought at stores. No one cooked where I came from. We ate at restaurants, and we ate meals in bags."

"Really. My mother says you lie. She says the world you tell me about only exists in your head. She says you are crazy."

"It's possible," I answered. "It would be easier that way."

"Jayden hasn't taken me in four days. He's taking Sarah now. Mother says he's going to recommend me for market soon."

I nodded and gave her faint smile. She walked away, and I continued with my work. It was late when I found Hannah again. I had walked down to the cellars to gather roots for breakfast, and I found Hannah tied up in the dirt. She was crying.

"What are you doing here?" I yelled. I began to untie her.

"No! No!" she yelled. "He'll kill me if you untie me. Just leave. Just go."

"I won't leave you. Tell me what is going on."

Hannah shook her head. "Please go. He'll kill us both."

"If you want me to go, tell me what is going on."

"I made a mistake," she wept. "If mother knew, she would beat me."

"What mistake?"

"I asked Jayden if I could go to market now, since he was done with me. I told him I wanted to see the world and said I had pleased him well and had earned my place. He got so mad. I've never seen him like that. He dragged me down here and said that I had not pleased him. He said I was nothing, and I would never see the light and then he left me."

I untied Hannah while she screamed and fought. "I'm not leaving you here," I said.

"No," she protested. "He'll kill us."

I laughed. "No, I don't think so."

I sat with Hannah for a long time. She wept, and I held her. The room was dark and smelled of mold and earth. Being trapped there felt like being buried alive. Finally, Jayden came with a group of drunk guards. They stumbled in the dark and cursed and laughed. I moved back, into the shadows and let the men descend on Hannah. She squealed as they moved toward her, but I only smiled.

I didn't kill Jayden. I pulled on his shoulder, dislocating it, and causing him an exquisite amount of pain. He screamed, and the others attacked me. It was easy for me to break their legs. They were drunk, and it was dark. They fell and squirmed in the mud like worms seeking solace. I laughed with a sadistic pleasure as I stepped on Jayden's groin. "I could kill you," I hissed as he wept. I wanted him to hurt for what he did to Hannah. I wanted him to hurt for all the cruelty he showered on those that were helpless to stop him.

"Please," he begged.

"I'll let you live under one condition," I said.

"What?"

"Take care of Hannah. Make sure she ends up someplace nice. Someplace safe."

"I will. I promise," he said.

"If you break your promise, I'll find you, and I will castrate you and leave you to bleed to death. Do you understand? Ask the prince what I can do. I'm the one that took his finger. I'll do worse to you if you hurt her again or if you betray me. Do you understand?"

"Yes! Yes! Just please stop."

I did stop, and Hannah fell into my arms. She wept and kissed me and thanked me and praised me. In the morning, Jayden and his friends were found beaten almost to death in the root cellar. They claimed they had been attacked by starving thieves. Jayden also said that Hannah had saved them with her cunning and suggested she be made into a house slave as a reward. Hannah vanished into the upper levels of the world.

The other slaves warmed up to me. Hannah's mother whispered about what I had done for Hannah, and the other slaves stuck close to me. They came to me with their problems and looked to me for help. I did what I could, but it was never enough. However, for many, there was joy in just imagining that some small victory had been won, even once, for slaves.

The others also began to enjoy my company. Maybe it was because I had become a good listener. I soaked their stories up. They talked while we worked in the evenings. Their stories varied. Some had been captured and enslaved. They were still loyal to their own fallen tribes. Others had been tribeless their entire lives and admitted to liking the security of slavery more than the constant fear of tribelessness. There were many who had been born slaves. They had been raised in the kitchens or in the fields, working. They had grown up at their mother's hems playing, and then when they were old enough, they had taken on the burden themselves.

In the end, maybe slavery wasn't so different from normal life as my life in the karash was. Travesties were committed, but maybe not so many as

I had seen before. Children flourished around us. People fell in love and got married and made love in the straw. Slaves had certain rights. They had the right to stay with their wife or husband. They had the right to stay with their children until the child turned thirteen. Children didn't have to work until they were eight. They worked hard for nothing, but so do many others. Being a slave was the closest I had been to real people and real life.

I watched mothers and children and husbands and wives. I saw friendships blossom and fade. I listened to gossip about nothing important. Lady so-and-so did this and that and a plethora of other things that didn't matter at all. The men left to work in the fields on the other side of the river. The women complained about the danger inherent in this work. Outside the city walls, outside of the shelter provided by the twin rivers, the slaves were vulnerable to raiders and tribeless. Sometimes men didn't come back, and wailing filled the nights.

We didn't measure time like other people. There were no calendars, no counting the years. We counted the moving moons, and the changing seasons. I had been a slave through the rains and the harvest and well into the snows when my summons came. Crian wept when I left. The old woman shook as she brushed my hair and passed me off to a clean woman slave: a lady's slave, well-dressed and pretty. Her feet were bare, and she wore a look of utter serenity.

I followed her up from the kitchens back into the palace. We wandered under the great banners and through a great room filled with plants and birds that opened to the sky above us. We passed through the arched doorways of the garden room and into a room filled with tiles and long pools filled with steaming hot water. The room was empty. Candles were lit, and their flames flickered in the gentle breeze that came from the adjacent atrium. It had been a long time since I smelled the wind.

The slave took my clothes off and bathed me. She plaited my hair in a plethora of tiny braids and wrapped ribbons around each braid. She painted my forehead blue and put blue beneath my eyes. I was wrapped in a fine, silk dress, and a heavy ribbon was used to bind my waist so tightly I could hardly breathe. It stretched from beneath my breasts to just below my hips, and it felt more like a torture device then an article of clothing.

My hands and feet were painted, and I was escorted to a large empty bedroom. The room itself was sublime, beautiful and intricate. Bas-reliefs covered the walls in elaborate depictions of ancient battles and gods. The floor was covered in a brilliant mosaic celebrating the harvest. The ceiling was on fire with depictions of rwans and sea beasts the likes of which I had never seen. I sat down on the bed and stared in awe at the possibility within mankind.

"Do as you are told," the woman said as she left. "It's easier if you pretend you are somewhere else."

She shut the door and left me alone beside the roaring fire. I wandered through the room looking at the paintings and the statues. I smiled as I touched the huge depiction of the rwan, thinking of my friend. Finally, I grew tired and stretched out on the large comfortable bed. Fatigue spread out over me, and I drifted off into sleep. I heard him coming long before he opened the door. His footsteps were heavy and awkward. Clumsy. I knew them well. He opened the door and sat down on the bed beside me.

"I didn't expect you, prince," I whispered.

The prince sat beside me quietly. He wasn't looking at me. His eyes were fixed on the fire. "It isn't what you think," he said. "It's my right to use the slaves as I wish, but I haven't and never will do that."

"Why not? Too afraid they might bite you?"

"I'm not like my father. I respect my people and our gods. I believe that the way must be followed as it always has, but I also believe that sometimes a little change doesn't hurt things."

"Will you change the world when you are king?" I asked sarcastically.

"I may not be king," he answered earnestly.

"Why not?"

"My father doesn't respect me. He thinks I'm a fool and a coward."

I laughed. I rolled over on the bed and laughed like a little girl. Waves of humor washed over me like a long lost friend. Finally, I sat up, almost choking on my own tears. "Well, Zender forbid!" I exclaimed. "You, a coward? No."

"Your sarcasm isn't appreciated," the prince said with a sullen grimace.

"You are an enormous baby! I've seen children fight with more courage than you!" I exclaimed. "Your father is right. You're no king. You urinated on yourself when you faced me on the battle field. I had always heard the Efferitas were savages, but maybe you have some wisdom after all, at least your father does."

"Enough! I know I'm no warrior. I have never had a taste for killing. If I had been born in another tribe, I would have gone to The University. But I was born here, and I know my place. I know more than you think. I need you to teach me. You are the greatest warrior I have ever heard of, and I would be a fool not to try to learn from you."

"I will not teach you!" I said with utter disdain.

"You would rather work in the kitchens? In the smoldering heat? Never seeing the sky? Never smelling the wind? The gnawing is coming. Would you miss that? The sky will catch fire, and everyone will dance under it, except for you. You and the others in the kitchens."

"I've been through plenty of gnawings. I wouldn't teach you for a lifetime of gnawings and brilliant summers. You are the pathetic." In Xender, someone like him wouldn't have even dared ask me for such a thing. It would have been an insult to both of us.

"Please," he said. "As a favor. I need to lead my people. Look at me. If I come to power, I can make life better here. The way is strong here. People follow tradition and the gods before sense, but I can inch in and help my people. I know it can be different, that not all tribes live like this. But I cannot do anything if I'm not king. You pretend to be indifferent, but I know you care."

His words moved me. I was touched by his passion and zeal, and I found myself moving closer to him. He looked at me with such honesty.

I saw something in his eyes that reminded me of Xander. It reminded me of the way Xander had spoken of medicine and healing and making our tribe a better place before Xender had fallen, before he had found his new god. I found myself wanting to help him.

"Even if I did, your people would mock you and disdain you for studying under a female slave."

"That's the beauty of it. I've never taken a slave before. My father says I'm not a real man. If I see you every night, if we study every night, it will look like you are my concubine. I will be seen as developing a man's tastes. You are beautiful, and no one will think we are doing anything different than what we say. Every night, you can teach me."

"I can teach you to fight, but I can't strip away your fear. I can't make you a hero."

"Start with the sword then, and we'll go from there."

I shrugged and examined Prince Hotem. He was a soft man, plump with wealth and food. He attempted to hide his extra girth by wrapping it in layers of heavily embroidered silk. He wore his hair tied back loosely in a heavy turban, like all the other men, exposing his eyes. His dark skin and hair gave way to the most distinctive green eyes I had ever seen. Beneath them I thought I saw something. Something more than the coward I had watched on the battlefield. Something I lacked the intuition to identify.

"I want the woman slave Crian brought up from the kitchens and kept as a house slave, and I want her daughter, Mia, who was sold to a brothel, brought back to her. Only under these conditions will I help you."

"It isn't uncommon for concubines to have attendants. I could give you the two women as your attendants. You would share a small room in the attic slave quarters. Not much, but better than the kitchens."

"I'll help you become a king."

He and I began our work quietly. Hotem was a quick-witted man, and although he lacked the brute force of many of his cohorts, he was agile and fast. He knew many of the rudimentaries and had much training, but he lacked details. The Efferitas, it seemed, relied almost entirely on brute force, rage, and surprise to overcome their enemies. They had stolen all of their technology, so they had guns and canons, but they could produce nothing on their own. They had a shield, to protect their city from aerial bombardment, but there was a strict religious ban against any open, common use of technology. It was viewed as unnatural and against the will of the gods.

It was clear that Hotem had potential, but it had been squelched by his small size. For an Efferitas, he was small. I began his training by playing to his strengths. We went through the simple steps of the dance as Cahir had first taught me. I showed him how to move with the wind. I told him to ignore force and focus on the movement itself. Hotem was thrilled. He was overjoyed to discover that he wasn't the utter waste of time his former teachers had told him he was, and I was happy to share the dance with someone else again.

The next day Crian and her daughter, Mia, were moved into the upper chambers of the palace as my handmaidens. We had a small room, filled with a bed and two cots. It was in the attic, as all the main house slaves rooms were. It was hot and windowless, but it was private. As Mia entered the room, she fell onto Crian's lap crying. I don't know how long the women wept. It seemed like days, but may have been only moments. I stood like a voyeur, watching them, wondering at the nature of such emotion.

Finally, Crian looked up at me with her cheeks smeared with tears and soot. "How did you do this?" she exclaimed. "It's never done."

I looked at Crian's daughter. Her face was broken, and her body sagged with hopeless sorrow. She had the look of something that had already died. Her face was painted to be pleasing, and her body was still wrapped in a prostitute's robes. As I watched her with her face on her mother's lap, I realized it was already too late for the poor girl. Years in the brothel had killed her. The soul in her was dead. Only shadows and flesh remained.

"The Prince owes me a favor," I said.

"The Prince owes a slave a favor?" Crian asked incredulously.

"More than one," I responded.

"Thank you. Thank you. Thank you," Crian muttered as she kissed her daughter's hair.

Mia stood up on shaky legs and moved slowly to the cot. "What now?" she whispered.

"I'm the prince's new concubine," I said. Mia laughed bitterly. "You are to make sure I'm kept. Feed me. Clean me. Make me pretty. That's it. I think mostly we are just supposed to stay in the attic until I'm called. I don't know the traditions or the rules here."

"Ailive, Oh, Ailive," Crian said. "This will be only a short reprieve.

All men tire of their concubines, and then they are sold. And then we will be sold."

"No," I responded. "We are safe. The prince owes me a favor."

"But how?"

"I'll tell you my story if you tell me yours. Where do you come from Crian?"

"I suppose they can't hurt us now. I want you to know, my Mia, my beloved Mia, that we are more than slaves. My people live on the islands in the North Sea. We lived very close to The University, so we subsisted mostly on trade and commerce. We had existed for almost a thousand years with no need of war. All of our children went to The University and most of them became doctors or philosophers. I was a well-respected astronomer." Crian paused and took a deep breath. She looked off into the distance, and I thought I saw tears gathering in her eyes.

"I had just gotten married when the Efferitas came. My husband and I were alone on our wedding island. That was our way. We didn't even see them coming. They killed my Jemmy and took me. I was given to the king, and since I was ugly, I was put in the kitchens. I was lucky in only one way. Jemmy left me one gift; he left me with Mia in belly."

"It sounds like heaven," I said.

"What?"

"Your home."

"It was."

So I told her my story. I told her about all of my journeys and battles.

I described the streets of my home and the texture of the sky beneath the mountains. All the while, Mia lay on her cot, staring vacantly at the ceiling. Crian stroked her hair, and after a while we fell asleep.

Crian dressed me the next day. She bathed me and painted my body.

She helped me with my hair and makeup. Finally she wrapped me in my robes and bound my waist. It took three hours for me to dress, and when I was done I could hardly walk or breathe. Mia put on the soft gray robes of a house slave and escorted me silently back to Hotem's chambers.

Hotem locked the door behind me and closed the curtains. He handed me my sword. I laughed when I saw it. I grabbed it from him and felt its weight in my hands. It was dirty, but it was mine. I pushed the blade to my lips and kissed it.

"You saved it?" I whispered. "Thank you."

"It's a beautiful sword. We have nothing like it."

"It was a gift," I said. I ran my hand along the blade and tried to conjure an image of Cahir in my mind. The University seemed so far away and long ago. Cahir's image was wrapped in a fog and so were my emotions for him. I thought I could almost smell him in the sword.

"I am happy to return it to you." He smiled gently at me. His green eyes lit up when he was happy, and kindness shone through them.

"There are no words. Thank you."

"I'm not a monster."

"I know."

"Let me see your sword," I said. He handed me a large, straight bladed sword. I could hardly lift it. The handle was encrusted with jewels, but it felt more like a sledge hammer than a sword.

"How hard would it be for you to have another sword made?" I asked distastefully.

Hotem frowned. "I could never fight with a tiny blade like yours," he said.

"Yes, you could. You are bigger than me, and you can handle a larger weapon, but this…" I didn't bother to hide my sneer as I resisted the urge to let the awkward thing clatter to the ground. "This is an awkward weapon with no grace. It will only hinder you."

This time, Hotem's frown was for the sword. "What should I have done to it?"

Hotem's words were more a relief than having the overgrown axe taken from my hand. "Just have it sharpened and have the blade narrowed so it's lighter. You need to be able to move with the sword."

"I'll have it done in the morning."

That night we practiced with his clumsy sword, and when we were done we ran together. We ran while the world slept. He panted and gasped for air. We stopped and started, but he was determined and followed my orders.

The next day he came with his new sword, and I taught him to meditate as Cahir had taught me. We stayed up all night, and I taught him to dance. It felt strange, dancing with someone else, but Hotem mirrored my every move. As the first light shimmered through the windows, Hotem and I stood holding our swords in an exhausted delirium.

"We should sleep," he said.

"I know," I said.

"We should sleep together, so it will look like we have been intimate. The slaves will assume we exhausted each other with…passion and leave us alone to sleep a little."

I nodded and took off my robes. He and I lay next to each other in our shifts for a while. We were both uncomfortable, but eventually fatigue overtook us, and we surrendered. When we awoke our breakfast was laid out on the table, and we ate. Hotem smiled at me over his eggs, and I smiled back.

"One of our great philosophers said that the gods give us what we need. They bring salvation on the wind when we least expect it."

"I've always believed that salvation comes with the wind," I said. "It comes with the storm."

"You are my salvation," he said with a smile.

"I'm glad to help you." I smiled back at him.

"When I'm king, I will free all of the slaves."

"I hope you do."

"I'll bring peace to the land, and there will be no more raiding or attacking. We'll send our children to University, and we will come out of the dark ages."

I put my hand on his. "I truly hope you do."

And so our life fell into this rhythm. I enjoyed teaching. Hotem was an eager student and a diligent worker. He always did all his homework and listened to me like I was a high professor at The University. He thinned out. The fat that lined his torso and face gave way to lean muscle and tight sinews. He became quicker and lighter on his feet. I had him running every morning, and every evening he stretched and danced with me.

He was kind to me. He gave me books to read and took Crian, Mia, and I out to the roofs in secret to see the waning lights of the gnawing. The four of us stood in the dark shadows, before the eclipsed sun and watched the light vibrate off sky.

"They teach us that the great mother fashioned the world out of fire, and the gnawing is our reminder of this," Hotem said. "But I'm a heretic at heart. I've never believed this. I always wonder what causes the gnawing."

Crian pointed her crooked finger to the heavens. "Our world rotates around the sun, and the moons rotate around our world. But they do not have circular orbits. They move in odd egg shapes around each other. Once a year, during the gnawing, the world bends inward toward the sun at the same time our outer moon moves away. Solar radiation is bounced off our atmosphere at the same time the outer moon blocks the sun. It's the beginning of the warm days, when the world is closest to the sun."

"I don't understand," Hotem said.

"We live in a vast and infinite universe, and our world is just a speck of dust in space. Our sun is one of countless suns. Each star in the heavens is just another sun. Our world rotates around the sun as our moons rotate around our world. The light from our sun catches off of the particles in the air and created the gnawing. Does this make more sense?"

Hotem looked up toward the sky with an indescribable longing. "Each star is another sun, and each sun has a world like ours rotating around it? There must be countless races of men out there."

"No," Crian said. "Each sun is the center of what we call a solar system. There are eight planets in our solar system. The University has its citizens living on one moon. As far as we know, there are no other planets in all the solar systems in the universe with life on them. The worlds that rotate around those stars you see every night are nothing like our world. Some are made only of gas or fire. Some are so cold that if you walked on them you would instantly freeze; none have air that we could breathe. Despite the apparent vastness of space, we are very alone."

"Have you been to The University?"

"I spent ten years there when I was a girl. I studied the stars."

"My people believe that The University promotes heresy, tribelessness, and the worship of false gods."

"How?" Crian asked.

"Our priests believe that to contradict nature is to contradict the gods' will. Medicine, engineering, all of these things contradict the gods' will. The University asks that men and women are treated equally. If the gods had wanted men and women to be equal, they would have been made the same. Therefore, again, this is a path toward heresy. We live according to our nature. We plant, we grow, we reap, we hunt, we mate, and we fight because it's our nature. It's the will of the gods. To fight this will would be to fight the gods, therefore it would be heresy."

"Strangely logical," Crian said. "I never thought you would make sense."

"We have many brilliant philosophers and poets."

I looked out over the Efferitas' city. It was radiant in the gnawing light. The colors from the sky dripped down upon the city like old wax, blending and burning together over the ancient architecture. The light painted the two rivers on either side of the city making it into a surreal rainbow and between the two rivers, men and women adorned the landscape in their colorful robes and head wraps. Trees lined the streets, bright with the newly blooming flowers and flowers sprung out of the earth along the banks.

Hotem pointed to a large building in the distance. "That's our library. I've written five volumes of poetry. They are all there. It's the greatest library in the world."

"But if you don't share it with others, if you don't send anyone to The University, and you don't send copies of your books to The University, it will all be lost when your city dies," I said.

"Efferitas will never die. The gods fight with us. They always have. We have no real technology. Nothing to match the marvels of other races. We have only our swords and our wits and still nations fall before us. We were fashioned by the gods to be the sword of the gods. We will never fall."

"Such poetry is found in the language of every nation. My own people, long ago, thought Zender himself had given us dominion over the infidels. We were supposed to bring light to the darkness, but gods die and nations fall."

"Not Efferitas. Someday we will rule the world." Hotem spoke with pride.

"I would like to hear your poetry," I said because I didn't want to argue with him. No one believes their nation will fall or their world will change, until it does.

"I would be honored. We should go now."

The gnawing faded. The lights dimmed and the moons shifted. The sun grew bright, and the slaves returned to the fields on the other side of the rivers. They worked endless hours beneath the scorching sun and slept beneath the moons. From our rooftops, we watched the men wilt away in the relentless sun of high summer. Crian shook her head, and Mia sat in the dirt.

"Hubris is the death of all tribes," Crian said.

"What?" I asked.

"When a tribe forgets that it can be swept away, when pride bloats it, then the end is near."

Hotem and I worked on the roof beneath the sun. It scorched my paper-white skin and turned his as black as the winter sky. His green eyes shone out with preternatural strength beneath his black flesh, and I watched as I created a king. He stopped stumbling and moved with fluidity. He blocked my blows and struck out with skill and grace and slowly, we began to dance. We danced at night under the glistening stars. We danced until fatigue pressed down upon us, and the slaves collapsed where they stood.

"What are they?" Hotem asked me.

"What?"

"The stars. The suns."

"What do your philosophers and priests say they are?"

"The souls of the dead looking down on us."

"They are gas and fire. Explosions."

"Have you been there? Have you left this world and seen the moons and planets?"

"No. I didn't study such things, but Crian has. She's been to all the moons. I think she lived on one for a few months."

"When I'm king, all people will go to The University. All people will know these things."

"Isn't that against nature?" I asked. I knew that he wanted these things, but I also thought he didn't realize how difficult it would be to change his entire nation's thoughts on the subject. I could still remember standing in the karash trying to convince, one man, my father, that a woman could know the truth of the future. People don't change their minds easily.

"If nature created a strong king with the desire to make such things so, it must be the will of the gods. After all, kings are the chosen of the gods. Kings are gods."

"Fair enough."

The planting season ended, and the sun crept away. The days shortened, and the cool wind brought the returning rains. The rains bled down upon the fields, and life sprang forth from every piece of soil. The slaves rested, and the nobles prepared for raiding season. Young men from every section of life dusted off their swords and prepared to pillage and burn and capture new slaves. They would steal guns and technology. They would push back the Efferitas' lines and crush any tribeless that had gained foothold in their territory. It was time to scour the landscape.

Hotem came and went. He went on all his father's campaigns and some he led. I saw less and less of him, but more and more he returned with new skills and new strength. He practiced when he was away, and while he was gone, Crian, Mia, and I read his strangely hypnotic poetry. His words were so sweet they should have been written by a scholar. We sat in our attic reading and telling stories until I was sure Crian was my mother and Mia was my sister.

And then Hotem would come back, and I would be summoned, and we would dance again. His strength deepened as his father aged. A year passed, and he and I watched another gnawing. We watched the planting come and then the rain, and finally I knew that he did not fear me any longer. When we fought, he did not cringe. He did not hesitate. He had killed men. I saw it in his eyes. I had fashioned him into a killer, and in doing so, I had killed the artist.

"You are gone longer and longer now," I said to him one night.

He lowered his sword and studied my face. "Do you miss me?"

I smiled. "You have become a good friend. Yes, I miss you."

He smiled back at me. "I miss you too. But the world is crumbling around us, and we have to fight. All of the colonies are in upheaval. We've had to squash rebellions and push out large scale invasions of tribeless. These are difficult times."

"Aren't all times difficult?" I asked. I had never known simple times, and I was inclined to believe that they didn't exist.

"Yes, but things have become more complicated."

"You're doing better out there? Are you doing well as a soldier?" I ignored him because I couldn't imagine how one time could be more complicated than another. His times didn't matter to me, but I wanted to know how my student was doing. I imagined he was doing much better.

"I'm earning a reputation as a leader."

"Good," I said with pride.

"I may stay here for a while now. The rains are coming and things have calmed down."

"Good," I said happily. Although I was proud of Hotem as his teacher, I missed him deeply when he was gone. He had become a good friend. I enjoyed listening to him talk about his impossible dreams and his brilliant ideas. His idealism filled me with hope and showed me a part of the world

I hadn't known of. It showed me a part of the world with kindness where war and death weren't the only things that mattered.

He raised his sword, and we continued our dance until we fell asleep next to each other in our lavish bed. I leaned into him as we slept and felt his breath on my hair. I smiled as I drifted off to sleep, and I dreamt of a utopian world without tribelessness or slavery. Where war was forgotten and I could sit in the sun and let my sword rest.

For a long time the rains kept us inside. Hotem and I spent more and more of our time together until I knew he was forsaking his duties to be with me. Sometimes we didn't dance. We sat on the bed talking about politics. We spoke of the rise and fall of tribes and the expansion of Efferitas' influence. He showed me pictures of their growing territory, and we discussed which tribes posed the most threat. He spoke of his father's failing health. I found myself enraptured by our conversations, by his candid nature and his empathy. Sometimes, I even spoke of myself, of Cahir or of The University. I told him about the Hyran women, and he listened with large concerned eyes.

"We are raised to think of the tribeless as the living dead. They are nothing, ghosts too weak to fight or live. I've tried to make myself believe it, because the alternative is too horrible, that we kill helpless women and children. But listening to you talk about the Hyran, about yourself, I know we are wrong. Our way has to stop." Hotem spoke with such violent conviction that I put my hand on his.

Sometimes we would talk of nothing at all. We would talk of his sisters or his father's wives. He would tell me about his education, and how he would sneak into the libraries of other tribes and steal books. I told him about The University, and he listened hungrily. I had never spent so much time talking to anyone in my life, even Cahir.

Something else entered into our conversations. Something I didn't recognize at first. There was a large group of tribeless banding together under the flag of a new god. Everywhere they went, these tribeless gained new followers. Sometimes people even left the safety of their tribe to follow this god. This scared Hotem's father more than anything. The leader of this band of religious zealots had been a doctor. The rain pounded outside as Hotem spoke to me of the prophet.

"Xander," I whispered as Hotem told me of this new prophet.

"How do you know his name?" Hotem asked.

"He was of my tribe. He was of my blood."

The rain fell on, and I knew that a storm was coming. I wondered what storm awaited me.

It was during the worst storm I had ever witnessed that the queen called me to her chambers. Outside, slaves secured levies and beat back the twin rivers with sandbags and stones. The poor, whose houses were closest to the rivers, lost everything. People died, and still the rain came. Inside the palace, incense was burnt to pay homage to the gods, to beg mercy.

The queen sat on her own kind of throne in the women's chambers.

She was wrapped in layers of jewel encrusted silk and bound with belt of pure gold. With her painted face, long nails and braided, ribbonwrapped hair piled into an odd sculpture on the top of her head, she looked as if she could barely move.

"Slave," she said. "Kings may not speak to your kind. You are forgotten by the gods and thus, forgotten by kings. So the loathsome task of dealing with your kind is left to me. You know that you are slave?"

I lowered myself to the floor. Laying down face first on the floor beneath her feet. "Yes, my lady," I said.

"You have been condemned by the gods. I remind you of this because it has come to my attention that my son has taken to spending a significant quantity of his time with you. At first, we were happy. My son has not had many women. He seemed…uninterested. He has become a man befitting a king. He should be married soon and produce an heir of his own. But now we are left with what to do with you. You are nothing but a bit of phlegm to be disposed of. But how? When the prince enjoys your company so much?"

"We must somehow make you abhorrent to him. Upon careful consideration, I have decided to give you to the guards to use. You will be scared and ruined. He will no longer want you."

I smiled as I stood up, meeting the queen's eyes. This one gesture created some kind of social earthquake within the queen's chambers. Gasps swallowed the silence of the room. The queen herself shuddered, disgust and loathing coating her serene mask. She stood up, like a statue rising. All of the fabric that encased her moaned and sighed as she moved across the cold mosaic floor. "Kill her," she hissed.

Her guards stepped forward. I watched them with anticipation. Their blood was cold on my hands before they had even began to move.

I hadn't realized how much I had missed the motion. The quick hiss of death. The sudden smell of blood lingering in the air mixed with the scented candles. I held my sword like a lover and crouched down low, slicing the guards first at the knees and then at their throats. They toppled and fell like broken dolls.

I smiled. It had been too long. The wind blew in through an open window.

It was time for me to go. I could smell it in the air, heavy with rain. The storm outside called to me.

The queen stood in her long red robes. A puddle of blood bathed her carefully painted feet, but still her face wore a mask of disdain. I smiled at her.

"I think, my lady," I said. "That you are right. Your son should marry a queen, and I should go. I will tell him of my departure, and I will leave tomorrow."

"What are you?" she asked.

"I walk the way of the storm," I answered.

V
The Prophet's Camp

E
tiquette no longer mattered. I walked through the halls of the great palace painted with blood. My brilliant gown was soiled beyond repair, and my hair had been torn out of its pink ribbons. The paint on my hands smeared, and my gown tore. I ripped the binding from my waist and strutted proudly toward the conference room where the great lords discussed politics and economy. Men attempted to stop me. They lunged at me with guns and swords, but I had forgotten nothing. I moved like fog or smoke flying through the air and across the room. Behind me, there was a trail of blood and death.

I flung open the door to the conference room and a stunned silence encased it. Only Hotem stepped forward. He looked at the cacophony behind me and laughed. Our eyes met, and he reached out for me, stroking my blood-stained cheek. Thunder shook the palace and lightning streaked the sky, but in the conference room there was only silence. Slowly, Hotem took me by the arm and led me away. He led me back to our room, the room where we had started.

"I didn't think you would last this long. I guess I should thank you for your mercy."

"It's time for me to go. I hope the nature of my departure has not cost you your kingdom."

"My father is dead. I'm a god now and nothing can take that away."

I knelt before him. "You will be a good king. It was an honor to serve you."

"You should never kneel in front of me. You are my superior and always will be. My twilight goddess." His words were soft, but his eyes were hard. "Stay with me. Be my queen."

I stayed on my knees. I stayed beneath him, but I met his eyes and studied the man he had become. "I can't, my lord. It's time for me to find a friend I left behind."

"I'll bring her here. I need you."

"No. You've become a worthy king. I wouldn't have thought it when I met you by the sea. You kneeled before me and begged, but now I kneel before you. I have taught you all I know."

He fell to his knees beside me, taking my hands in his own. "I love you. I want you to be my wife. You are my fire, my storm, my reason for being."

"I can't be a bride. I can't be a queen. I'm a killer. I'm nothing. You want something that doesn't exist. You deserve a queen who can bear you sons."

"You're wrong. One of our greatest poets said that women are all things that men can never be. Women are gentle and kind, warm and soft. The carry with them the light of hope. The light of life. The light of eternity. I see that in you. You are the kindest woman I have ever known."

My laugh was dry and bitter. "I have laid waste to thousands. I have enjoyed disemboweling those that would challenge me. What mercy do you see in my eyes?"

"You gave up your life, your freedom, to save a group of tribeless women and children you hardly knew. You could have asked anything from me, and all you asked was for the life of two slaves. No one on this world cared for these people but you. You save those who need it the most. You are the heart of mercy."

"Thank you," I said. I put my lips against his and then stood up. "But I must go." I walked away from him, and I didn't dare to look back. I didn't dare turn and look at the green eyes of my poet king. I was nothing. I was a monster, and Hotem deserved so much more. I blinked back tears and left in the storm.

I thought only of Hotem as I left. I thought of those brief moments we had shared. I couldn't stay with him. I wasn't a queen. I belonged with the only man who understood my nature. I belonged with Cahir.

Hotem was generous to me. He gave me five horses, laden with supplies. He also gave me Crian and Mia. I heard him speaking to an assembly of people as we rode away. His voice was loud and clear, full of confidence and conviction. "This is a sign from the gods!" he yelled. "We would be foolish to ignore it. The gods have spoken through that tiny girl. They have said that slavery is an abomination…"

His voice lingered in the air as we wandered away from the palace. The city seemed even larger upon our departure. It seemed like a labyrinth of infinite proportions. We rode well into the evening until we came to the edge of the city and then we crossed back over the river and found ourselves lost in an ocean of maize. We wandered through these goliath crops until we came upon the plains, vacant and endless. Mia sunk into her saddle, already exhausted from a voyage that had not even begun. We camped in the maize, hidden and safe.

It took us several days to make it back to the caverns where I had left the rwan. Mia slowed our progress. She slumped over in her saddle, unable to carry herself. She didn't speak, but her body was limp and resigned. Crian sung to Mia, urging her on. She did everything she could for her, but Crian was old, and she was slow enough without Mia's burden.

When we finally made it to the caverns, we found them deserted. I searched the caves thoroughly and found no sign of violence. The Hyran had packed many of their belongings and had left everything in order. It was clear that they had chosen to leave. I wandered the beaches for a long time, searching for their tracks. What I found was an army of footprints and the remnants of a massive camp. The Hyran women had joined an enormous group.

We slept in the cave and followed the tracks left by the nomads in the morning. At first, I was afraid we would never catch them. I feared that we were too slow to keep up with another group, but they were traveling even more slowly than we did. They made camp frequently and stayed for long periods of time, following the coast.

The landscape along the southern sea was dotted with tiny villages bearing the Efferitas' flag. Everywhere we went were the signs of Efferitas' expansion. The nomads stopped at all of these conquered villages, and their numbers grew after every stop.

As we traveled, it became clear that the Efferitas had conquered everything south of the great plains. Every village we passed, every town, every city, bore the Efferitas' flag. The cities that did not fly the flag had been reduced to rubble.

At The University, Crian had studied geography more thoroughly than I had. She had vague memories of direction and could tell me which way would lead to her home and which back to The University.

"Will you take us home?" she whispered to me one night.

"I don't know the way. I'm lost. I'm just trying to find the Hyran, and I'm hoping one of them will know how to get back to The University."

"I know the way. I know that if we follow this coast it will take us to Notua and from there it is easy to get to The University."

"Of course, I'll take you home," I said with a sad smile.

"Thank you, my little angel. Thank you!" she said passionately.

"I have a friend to find first," I said.

"A friend?"

"I don't know why, but I feel lost without him. Like he's taken part of me, and I can't really rest until I've given it back."

"What manner of friend is this?"

"He's a monster."

"A rwan?" Crian sounded incredulous.

I nodded.

"They are soul stealers."

"What?" I asked in confusion.

"Soul stealers. I've never seen it done, but our histories record incidences of rwans taking the very life from people. They take their will to live. Sometimes they even carry them away."

"I've never heard of such a thing."

"We are an old tribe. Our memory is long."

"Sounds like a fairy tale to me," I said.

After a week of walking, Mia lay down on the sandy beach and shut her eyes. She pushed her face into the earth and gave up. I can't say if any real illness plagued her or if her soul had just worn too thin to move forward, but I picked her up and propped her in front of me on my horse, and we rode on.

In the end, it was not we who found the rwan and the Hyran, but the rwan that found us. We had camped early, long before dusk, and I was gathering firewood while Crian rested. Five heavily armed men on horseback approached us.

Raiders.

They were fair skinned, from the north, and they spoke a language I had never heard. I raised my hand to greet them, but they charged without hesitation. I was briefly taken aback, lost in surprise. The rwan swooped down from above us and carried one of the raiders away as I drew my sword. It didn't take long for the raiders to die, and then I looked up.

It's possible that he had been with us all along. He could have been following us, flying in our shadows. But as he landed, I knew he had been waiting impatiently for my return. I embraced him and as he looked at me with his glassy eyes somehow I heard his accusations, his questions.

"Forgive me," I whispered as I stroked his skin. "My absence was necessary."

The silence around me took form. It became light in color. It swirled around me creating sound. I heard my ancient friend. I didn't know how or why, but my connection with the rwan deepened. He had a voice, and I felt his pain. "I'm lost. Take me home," he said with the deepest sorrow.

I smiled and kissed his brow. "I will find your home," I answered. He and I walked slowly over the grassy hills to the beach. He lay down, and I curled up next to him like I had before. I was safe and warm. I lay awake by the light of the twinkling fire for a long time. There was so much to do. So many places to go. Time cramped up on me and the vastness of the distance before me seemed to make my journey impossible.

I had to make sure the Hyran women were safe. I had to take Crian and Mia home, and I had to find the rwan's home. And when all this was done, when I had crossed the world twice and wandered to the farthest reaches of the land, then I would go back to The University. I would find my Cahir. I would leave the wind and the smoke and the storm behind me.

I looked over at Mia and Crian. Crian held her baby, as always, and I had to wonder if Mia would make it home. I fell asleep and dreamt of Cahir. I dreamt of his dark skin and dark eyes. I dreamt of his eyes, smoldering burnt umber filled with pain and desire. The memories hurt and filled me with a desperate longing.

The rwan and I left before the last moon set. We went ahead and looked for the Hyran. We moved quickly and found the smoldering remains of their recently evacuated camp. That day we rode hard. I pushed Crian and Mia, and we rode well into evening. As the stars rose, I saw the smoke of the campfires in the distance. Mia and Crian did not see the lights in the distance, so I told them it was time to camp, and I helped them settle in for the night. I waited until I knew the two women were sleeping and snuck away into the evening light. I did not want to risk getting them hurt in an unknown camp.

The camp was like a moving city. Tents sprawled out over the plains, consuming everything I could see. I didn't even know where to begin, so I asked the first person I saw.

My gift remained, and I picked up the strange clicking tongue of the tiny redheaded man like I had been born to it. "I'm looking for a handful of Hyran tribeless that were living in the cliffs by the sea. Have you seen them?" I asked.

"Ask the prophet," the man said as she shuffled away.

I wandered through the camp, asking the same question, and I always got the same answer. Finally, I changed my question. I asked for the prophet. I found the prophet on a hill, surrounded by a mass of people. He spoke clearly in Xenderian, and everyone understood him. All races and tribes knew, as if by magic, what he was saying. He spoke of peace and kindness. He said that God was tired of war and slavery. He said that God loved most those that had nothing. I smiled and sat down on the sand.

When the prophet was done, I went to him. He laughed and embraced me. "I knew you would come back to me," he said.

"I'm glad to see you, Xander!" I exclaimed. "I have spent many sleepless nights worrying about you."

"God protects me."

"You are amazing. You've created a tribe out of nothing but dust and the conviction of your will."

"We aren't a tribe or an army."

"What are you?"

"We are the city of heaven."

"The city of heaven?" I laughed a little. I looked at the mass of tribeless people before me and saw only lambs going to the slaughter. "You should leave this place and find some nice piece of land to build that city. You have enough people here to start a tribe. You could create safety for these people."

"God is the only safety these people need."

"The Efferitas know about you. It won't be long before they send soldiers for you."

"They already have. Sister, let's not waste words on argument. I'm just happy you are here. Tell me what it is I can do for you?"

I smiled and hugged him again. "I'm sorry, Xander. I'm tired. My journey has been long. I didn't mean to start an argument. It's good to see you."

"It's good to see you. My greatest regret has always been that I didn't bring you with me."

"We all have regrets. If you aren't building a city, where are you going?"

I asked out of pure curiosity. Xander was a mystery to me. His devotion to this new god left me muddled and confused. It wasn't consistent with the Xander I had known before. It wasn't consistent with the Xander who had once told me that blind faith was dangerous.

"We're wandering. We're gathering believers and spreading the word of God."

I shook my head. Xander had always been a particularly lucid man. He had been meticulous in the details of his life. His eyes had changed. They had become distant and foggy, overwhelmed by something I couldn't place. His hair had grown long, and he had a beard. His white tunic was dirty, and his feet were bare.

"You've changed," I whispered.

"So have you." He put his hand on my shoulder. "You should stay with us. Put down your sword. Help me. Help me change the world."

"I don't believe in your God. All gods fall."

"What are you looking for here, if not God? Tell me why you've come."

"I'm looking for a group of women I think may be with you. I just want to make sure they are all right."

"The Hyran women from the cave? They spoke of you, sister. They're fine. Their tents are over there." He pointed to a small tree which shaded a handful of tents.

"Thank you, brother. May I ask one more favor?"

"Anything."

"I'm traveling with two women. They're both ill and tired. I want to take them home, but I don't think they'll make it. Could you spare a few men to help me bring them back here and give us shelter for a few days until they heal?"

"Go see the Hyran, and then I will go with you to see your friends."

"We'll need more than two people to carry them back."

"I promise they will be cared for."

I nodded and went to seek the Hyran. They were exactly where my brother said they would be. They were sitting in a circle around a cooling coil, making strange statues out of clay. Their children were playing in the shadows, and the women laughed giddily as they worked.

"Ailive!" Salome cried as I approached them. "You're alive!"

Salome embraced me. "I thought you would be dead by now. God must be with you! Have you come to follow the prophet?"

"No. I just wanted to make sure you were all right. When I saw the cave was abandoned, I wasn't sure what had happened to you."

"There aren't enough words to thank you for what you did for us. You must be one of the chosen to offer your life for a group of tribeless."

"You aren't tribeless anymore?"

"No! We're part of the city of heaven. We're believers, part of the greatest tribe to ever walk the world," Salome exclaimed.

"I see that. I'm just glad you are safe."

"Safer than we have been since the sacking of Hyran."

"What're you making?"

"Sculptures of the rwan; God's creature."

"Really." I was tired of gods. I was tired of the capricious nature of religion. One moment the rwan was a devil, the next an angel. I didn't even want to ask why the rwan had become a holy beast. In truth, I preferred the Efferitas to this bunch of sticky sweet disciples. I preferred their honesty and brutality.

"It was the rwan, the very rwan you sent to protect us, that drove the Efferitas' raiders away when they came for the city of heaven. The king sent a small garrison to kill us, and the rwan swooped down from heaven, devouring them. He is a sacred animal."

"Something like that," I whispered remembering the vision I had been given by the rwan. I saw his icy home in my mind's eye and his brutal birth. The rwan was a predator, an elemental monster. He was my kin, and I was glad that they worshipped him.

"I have to go now," I said.

"The prophet has said that you and the rwan are one. You are instruments of God," a voice from behind me said. I turned to see Dania sitting in the dirt behind me. Her face glowed a luminous blue in the light of the cooling coil. "You think you have free will, but such things are illusions. We will see you again soon," Dania said. She looked different. Her scars were gone and so were all of her old wounds.

"Maybe," I answered.

"Belief is irrelevant. Only what is matters," Dania muttered.

Dania seemed to have been lost in the same sickness that had taken my brother. Her eyes were clouded and distant. It was as if they were someplace else altogether. I backed away from the Hyran women slowly. "I'm glad you are safe," I muttered as I stumbled away.

I became lost again. It was an uncomfortable and unfamiliar landscape for me. Thousands of people had accumulated at Xander's feet, and there was no uniformity. They did not wear the white robes of priests. They did not speak the same language. All of them wore their native garb and spoke their native tongue. Women in saris wandered past women in pant suits, and they brushed up against women in long Efferitas' gowns.

As I crested a hill, throngs of people came out over the horizon. Villagers whose true tribal name had been erased by Efferitas' occupation came in clusters. Some came just to listen, others came to stay, with their tents and possessions strapped to mutas or wagons. Above all of this, Xander sat tranquilly on the hill in the white tunics of our tribe.

"Will you help me get my friends now?" I asked.

"Of course."

It took a long time to walk through the camp. Everywhere we went Xander stopped and talked with people. He introduced me to everyone we met. He hugged people and kissed them. He held their babies and blessed their children. People threw flowers at his feet and kneeled down as he passed them. The rwan walked behind us, and he was treated with fear and reverence. People threw flowers at him and then backed away in terror. I felt like I was back in Xender and had just returned from a victorious battle.

We left the camp and walked quickly to where I left Mia and Crian. Crian was awake and tending the fire. She hugged me tightly when I arrived. There were tears in her eyes. "I thought you had abandoned us," she wept.

"No, I only went to get help."

Crian studied my brother with scrutinous eyes. "You brought another slave?" she said. "At least he is strong. Welcome."

Xander ignored Crian. He walked quickly to Mia. "Your daughter is dying," he said in perfect Efferitas. "She will not live through the night."

He knelt down by the sleeping girl and put his hands on her. He kissed her forehead and stroked her hair. "No one should be used like this," he whispered. "Let God bear the burden of your memories."

Mia opened her eyes and looked up at the prophet. A shadow passed over the sun, and when the sun again became bright, the girl's scars were gone. "I had a strange dream," she said.

"It's over now," Xander said. He took her hand and pulled her to her feet. She smiled brightly and looked at me.

"Who are you?" she asked me.

I didn't know what to say. Crian put her hands over her mouth and wept. "What is it, Mamma?" Mia asked.

"Nothing, I just thought, I thought you were ill. But you are better now!" Crian sobbed.

Mia broke free from Xander's grasp and went to her mother. Mia held her mother up and embraced her at the same time. "You are tired. Let me help you," Mia said.

I didn't know what to make of my brother. I was overwhelmed by a series of intense emotions that fluttered in my head making it impossible for me to interpret them. I knew I loved Xander. I couldn't change that, but I didn't understand this new Xander. His faith angered me, and his apparent healing ability left me utterly bewildered. There had to be a rational explanation, but I couldn't find it.

When we had lost our tribe, something had changed in both Xander and me. I couldn't explain how, why, or by what means, but we had both been given gifts. I knew Xander would explain these gifts simply. He would say his God had given them to us. Perhaps that would explain his miraculous power to heal, but why had he given me an equally miraculous power to kill, to hear the wind and move with the elements? It was irrational nonsense. I closed my eyes. It would come to me in time.

We walked back to the camp in good spirits. Age had melted away from Crian, and Mia had become an extraordinarily beautiful girl. Heads turned when she walked and men stumbled. That night we pitched our own small tent in the center of the camp. Mia and Crian sat up late talking. Crian tried to explain the holes in Mia's memory without telling her too much.

The sun set was particularly extraordinary, painted with brilliant alizarin crimsons and violent topaz blues. All eyes turned to the sky in wonder and awe. The ocean stilled, and the colors of the sky caught in the water.

"What is it?" I asked Crian.

"It's the Adura, the southern fire. The atmosphere thins in the south sometimes and in the evening when the planets axis tilts the south closer to the sun, there is a reaction between the thinning atmosphere and the sun. It can only be seen safely from here. I sat here once before with a team from The University. We went out on a little boat as far as we could and gathered data. We were so afraid we would be captured by Efferitas' raiders or a whale shark would jump out of the water and devour us. It was the adventure of a lifetime." Crian's eyes grew misty. She smiled and dried her eyes.

I wanted to say something to comfort her, to take away the years of slavery and abuse, but my tongue was dry. All I could do was smile dumbly at her and watch the sunset.

"When we get home, back to the islands," Mia said. "Can I go to The University?"

"When we go home, you can go anywhere and do anything. You will never be bound by anything again. You can skate on the ice of the Ocean Froid or dive with the plesiosaurs in Forest Verde. Anything you want my love, you can have." Crian put her hand on her daughter's. A wave of jealously passed over me. I looked at my own hand. Her real daughter had been returned to her; there was no longer any need for me. I would be alone again soon. I had lost Hotem, and I would lose Crian. I would be left to drift in the wind with my monster, and the thought of it left me feeling empty and cold.

Mia curled up in her mother's lap. "I think," Mia said after a while, "that it will just be nice to be home. It will be nice to sit by the water and rest. I would like to learn to read."

Crian's face creased in anxiety for a moment and then the creases smoothed out again. "Of course, my darling, that will be the first thing you will learn."

I put my hand on the rwan, and he crept closer to me. I wanted to go home. I wanted to find my way back to the only person who had ever held my hand. I closed my eyes, and I almost saw him.

Cahir.

I wondered if he still remembered me. If in dreams, we ever crossed paths. I should have returned to him when Xender fell. Now I couldn't leave. I had to finish what I had started. But those I had saved had already left me.

I left our little camp and went to find Xander. I wandered the beach for a long time staring at the strangely stagnant sea. The water was so still. A light breeze kissed my cheek pushing my long hair out of my face. I leaned into the breeze, and I felt something stir in me, a memory of battles fought years ago on distant shores. But now there was only the stillness and queer water. The third moon peeked her tiny head over the water, bathing it in a periwinkle blue. The sky darkened, and the three moons glowed above me, illuminating the world in a cool, peaceful light.

I wandered the white beaches until I came to a large tent made of white linen. It was humble, but sturdy, and I entered the tent knowing it had to be Xander's. Everything inside the tent was equally as austere. Xander was dinning on the ground with a handful of his followers. There was a stack of blankets and pillows in the corner and not very much else to add to the comfort of his abode. They were eating fish and some stale bread. Salome sat on his right side and my youngest brother, Mark, sat on his left. Ieya sat beside Mark. All around him were peoples of all colors and sizes and tribes. They all spoke Xenderian, but many of them spoke it with noticeable difficulty.

Salome saw me enter and immediately cleared a place for me. I was served and began to eat. I smiled at Mark, and he smiled back. I had never really known Mark. He had been a baby when I left, and although we were connected by blood, there was little else between us. Ieya looked away from me, as if she wanted to pretend I didn't exist.

The small group spoke of many things. They spoke of the long journey behind them and of what they had ahead of them. They talked of God and of new prayers and how they had seen God in the setting sun or the heard him in the song of a stray bird.

"This is just the beginning," Dania was saying very loudly so everyone heard. "We are God's chosen people, and we will gather up his people and make them his again. We will be like a tsunami, and we shall wash the earth clean."

"No," Mark disagreed. "Dania, you are too passionate. God is not a God of such rebirths. He calls to those who would come willingly. We will be patient and those that need God will come to us."

"Xander," Dania said, leaning toward him. "How can God be so passive? Does he not want us to save all of his people?"

"The people must save themselves," Salome said softly.

"Just like the Hyran saved themselves?" Dania responded bitterly.

"Salome says you are a hero," finally, my brother said to me.

"Salome is kind. I only fight when I'm called to. I have no noble ambitions," I answered.

"Who calls you to fight?" Xander asked.

"I walk the way of the storm. The wind tells me where to go."

"And where does the wind send you now?"

"I have friends to care for and then it calls me home, to The University," I said firmly.

"The University is home?" Xander asked softly.

"It's the only place I have ever known peace. That's the closest thing to home I can think of." My words were quiet and empty. Xander and I both knew that the University wasn't my home.

"There are no storms there. They control the weather inside the dome. It's always seventy degrees and sunny. I thought you walked the way of the storm?"

"I'm tired, brother," I said wearily.

"God can help you find rest."

"No thank you. I've had enough of gods," I said bitterly.

"What are you looking for there?"

"Just comfort and quiet. The same things we all seek."

"You have no one there."

"I know what you want, and I won't stay with you. I don't believe in your God."

"Then stay for me. I'm your family."

"I have someone waiting for me at The University."

"The man I saw you with?"

"Yes."

"Do you really think he'll have waited all this time for you?"

"I don't care. Even if he hasn't, I'm not staying with you!" I snapped.

Xander stood up and cut his arm. The blood dripped down the length of his white arm and delicately fell off his fingers, pooling at his feet. It stained his white robes and his white feet. He walked slowly toward me and placed his thumb on my forehead drawing a line on it in his blood.

"You are Caeimoni, sister. You are sacred to God. He has gifted you with the ability to speak in tongues and with the power of the storm. I anoint you in blood in his name."

I stood up and pushed him down. He fell into his own blood, and became matted with a thick paste of blood and sand. He lay at my feet looking up at me with his petulant blue eyes. They almost glowed in the ocean of his white flesh and hair. He was so like me. I hadn't seen another Xenderian in years. He smiled up at me, and I kicked him. He flinched, but did not cry out. I wanted him to stop smiling and leave me be. I couldn't be part of his mad religion, and I resented being force to be part of his god. Gods died and betrayed, and I would have no part of any religion.

I looked at the group of people around the table. They all looked up at me placidly. They did nothing to protect their prophet. They didn't seem to notice.

"What's wrong with you people?" I yelled, and I ran out of his tent. His blood still dripped down my forehead. I ran through the white sand, tripping and falling in my desperation and waded out into the tepid sea. The water surrounded me like a warm bath. I heard people screaming at me from shore. Their shouts became hysterical in tone, but I kept going until the water came up to my chest.

I turned and looked back at the crowd that had gathered to watch me. They were all screaming, but none of them moved into the water. I looked down through the diaphanous surface of the smooth water and saw a mass of writhing serpents. I turned around, staring back at the beach. Crian was screaming something at me. My brother was there. The beasts were getting closer to me. I couldn't fight them. Fear penetrated my limbs with a dull tingling and then spread up to my lungs. I looked down again. A black eye, stared up at me, contemplating me.

I looked down at the monster and drew a deep breath. I pushed myself beneath the surface of the hot water. I would not become a slave to fear. I pulled myself down as deep as I could go. I scrubbed the blood off my face with sand and saltwater until there was nothing but burnt skin and tears. I had to get the blood off of me. I wouldn't become one of my brother's vacant-eyed chosen. I couldn't be a slave to any god.

I can't say which serpent pulled me down. I think it was the big one. It wrapped its body around me and dragged me into the deep. My breath burned as it ran out. Desperation overwhelmed me, and panic consumed me. I kicked and struggled in futile dismay. The serpent that lay on the ocean floor waiting for me was enormous. Its jaws were like iron traps lined with ferocious teeth. Its black eyes stared out through the blue water like the devil's, but I didn't care. The only thing I could think about was breathing. I couldn't breathe. I opened my mouth to scream, and the water flooded my lungs.

When I awoke, I was still submerged. For a moment, I fought again. I kicked viciously in an attempt to ascend and then I became aware of an exquisite pain in my back. I arched my back and looked around. The large serpent had me in her coils. She gazed at me with her black eyes and pulled me closer. I reached out in desperation, and my hand fell on her flesh. It was cool and smooth, covered in hard scales. Her skin drew back beneath my touch, and I felt a moment of profound clarity, like I had felt with the rwan. Images floated before my clouded eyes.

I saw through the serpent queen's eyes. Her memories were weak, foggy, and wrapped in violent, indefinable emotion. There was no color or sequence, only brief scenes of life. She was the queen, and all the smaller serpents around her were her offspring. They brought her prey, and she impaled them, giving them air, keeping them alive.

She liked to eat live food.

Nothing else lived here, in the south sea by the coast. They devoured anything that fell into water. The serpents survived by going into the deep ocean, where larger and more dangerous creatures lurked in the eternal night of the deepest, coldest abyss. Many of her young didn't return. Her emotions swarmed me, encasing me in a tomb. Hunger, fear, hate, and the desire to protect her young were all she knew.

I removed my hand, and the beast regarded me. She had felt it too. She had seen glimpses of me. Pictures of a world beyond her comprehension. She removed the stinger she had planted in my back that was feeding me air, and I felt myself drowning again. I was swept away as quickly as I had been pulled down. Thousands of serpents pulled me back and threw me on the beach.

I lay with my face buried in the sand. I couldn't move. The pain in my back was too intense for any voluntary motion. I gripped the sand with my hands, trying to memorize its texture. I pushed my face into the sand trying to drown out the pain. Voices echoed around me, the lingering sweat of the crowd stinging my nose.

I couldn't bring myself to face them.

I was like a child who believes that if they can't see something, it isn't real—lost and alone.

I hated every one of my brother's followers.

I knew my brother's hand on my back. I knew his smell. The pain faded, but I lay there a little longer, hoping that people would get bored and walk away. My wound was gone. He had healed me, but the pain remained in my mind. I had chosen the serpent over him.

Finally, I rolled over and faced the crowd of my brother's faithful. They stared at me with their glazed eyes and vacant expressions. I wanted to draw my sword and kill them all. I wanted to wipe all their simple faith and hopeless passivism off the face of the earth, but I only stood up and walked back to my tent. I crawled inside and tucked myself deeply into my sleeping bag and wept. I hadn't cried in years. I had survived lost love, near death, the decimation of my people, slavery, and exile, but I couldn't bear Xander's touch. It was like fire on my skin, and his blood had made me feel like a ravished child.

I had planned on leaving in the morning. The only thing I wanted in the world was to escape, but as I slid away, I saw riders on the horizon. I smiled. A cool wind had come from the north, rich with the scent of rain and dust, Efferitas' raiders. They were not really Efferitas. Few were. They were a desert people from a primitive tribe. Their eyes were black as soot and so was their skin. They had been conquered by the Efferitas.

Hotem had explained the brilliance of his people to me once. Their power base was simple. They conquered all the little tribes in the south and then they offered them a choice, enslavement or servitude. Those that accepted were occupied by a Efferitas' governor and gave forty percent of all their product to the Efferitas. In exchange, they could be somewhat free, and they gained raiding rights. It prevented slaves from escaping. It prevented large scale invasions from the north, and it gave the Efferitas' access to technologies they would never have developed on their own. They inherited all the wealth and power of all the tribes of the southern deserts and coasts.

The riders that approached us were a vanquished people. They had sacrificed their own gods and traditions for safety. They lived like Efferitas' people lived, despite their infinite loathing of the Efferitas. Their rage seeped out of their pours. I saw it in the way they clutched their guns. They had come for my brother's people.

I smiled and wandered slowly toward the large band of men. I drew my sword with giddy anticipation. The sun rose behind them, and I moved to attack, but my motion was cut short by Xander's approach. The wind stopped, and the air grew still and stagnant. The sun glistened off the white sand, temporarily blinding me. I swayed backward, avoiding the hand he meant to put on my shoulder.

"No, sister," he said. "These men are our brothers. We can't harm them."

"You fool!" I spat. "They have come to kill you!"

"They don't know why they have come. They only know that they are thirsty, and I shall bring them drink."

I put my sword back in its sheath and backed away from Xander. The riders came in a fury of dust and stamping hooves. They clutched their guns to their chest with as much passion as Xander clutched his God. The heat smeared them in sweat and antagonized the state of their emotions. They rode up to my brother at full speed, and I was sure they were going to trample him, but they stopped.

Their leader yelled in wretched Efferitas, "I'm going to kill you! You should run for your pitiful life!" He fired his gun in the air. Xander did not flinch. He walked toward the man and placed a hand on his leg.

"You're tired," he said. "It has been a long journey. Come with me, and I will give you rest."

A cacophony of emotions danced off the man's face. Anger melted to ridicule and confusion and then sorrow transfigured his face into something human. The sorrow built up and faded, and he placed his hand on Xander's.

"You are the prophet," he said.

Xander did not answer in Efferitas. He switched tongues and responded in an old dialect, almost forgotten by its conquered people. He spoke in the raiders' true tongue, the tongue of their fathers. "I am," he said.

"They told us to kill you on sight," the raider responded.

"But you won't kill me. Come and eat with us."

I watched a hundred men dismount their war horses. I watched them put their guns in the sand and walk with Xander toward the hill. They stripped off the garments of the Efferitas and sat in loin cloths on the mountain. They ate and as evening settled again over the land the entire camp came to sit at the foot of the mountain and hear my brother speak. The things he said were simple, like stories a mother might tell a child, but their content was revolutionary.

He smiled as he spoke. "We have all known suffering. We are prisoners on a world ruled by tyrants and monsters. We have watched our families murdered and our children starve. God spoke to me on the mountain after my tribe was decimated. He came to me and told me that it was time for the world to change. He said it was time for us to lay down our guns and our swords. These tools can only contribute to our own demise. Those that take up these weapons will watch their own people die by the same means." Xander paused and looked down at the sand beneath him. He drew a deep breath and then looked up again.

"Death only makes more death. Hatred only brings more hatred. We must make it our mission to free this world of these things. All tribes are equal. All who come here are welcomed by God. God forgives all sins to those that lay down their swords and embrace him." Xander spoke on, and I listened.

I listened to Xander for a long time. I sat and listened to his stories and his commandments. He spoke beautifully. He had always been a poet. The anger I had felt for him faded with the sun, and I realized that he was helping these people. He was guiding the lost toward a better place. In the morning, some of the raiders rode home and some stayed. The next morning more people came from the raiders' tribe. They sat on the hill and listened to Xander speak. People came and went. Some brought their possessions and some brought nothing at all, but when the camp was finally ready to move again, we had accumulated over a hundred new followers.

I tried to leave that camp innumerable times. It seems like that's all I ever did. I wandered the camp like a sleepwalker during the nights and spent the days packing. But there was always some reason to stay. The only reason to go was my pride. More people joined the caravan every day. We would stop. The raiders would come and then people would pour out of the villages. Sometimes I would go with Xander to one of the villages. If no one came, he went to them. We moved steadily north along the coast and watched the desert change form. The blasted sands by the tepid ocean turned to a burnt red rock, covered with green cacti. The ocean changed as well. The water licked the shore delicately, perpetually moving, promising rain that would never come.

It made more sense to stay with Xander. No matter how desolate the landscape, no matter how barren the land, he could always find food and water. I would wander all day searching for meat, and when I returned, there was always plenty to eat and drink. He was going the same direction as we were and staying with him provided sanctuary. So we stayed with him for months, creeping northwest along the coast. We traversed the outer rim of the Efferitas' land, and we saw every aspect of their culture and world. I became accustomed to my brother's rituals. The followers called themselves the Caeimoni, an old word from a dead tribe. The word for sacred. Every morning and every night they went down to the water and sat, with their legs crossed. They prayed under the light of the single morning moon. They prayed only in Xenderian. They prayed only in the dead language of our lost people. It became the language of God, the language of a God of peace born from of a god of war. They burnt palms and sang songs. It was the beginning of a new way of life.

In the evening I caught my last glimpse of the Efferitas I had known as a slave. In the outlying villages, we saw only hunger, poverty, cruelty, and desperation. In the city, I had seen a collage of beauty and wonder expertly intertwined with cruelty. The Efferitas were a people of possibilities. They held the capacity for brilliance, but their tyranny eclipsed their potential. The last night of summer, Myhanna came. She came bearing all the glory of the Efferitas with her. Her livery included over one-hundred slaves wrapped in white. On their backs, they bore a small structure that looked like a miniature castle. In the heat of the fading sun, the slaves looked like dying dogs floundering for life. The building must have been fifteen tons, but the men carried it because they had no choice.

A man on horseback, a higher slave, came to our caravan and asked to speak with Xander. After a brief conversation, I was summoned. Xander, Salome, and I walked alone into the desert. A true Efferitas lady had emerged from her portable castle and sat beneath a massive umbrella on a bed of pillows. Her hair was braided and wrapped in an intricate overlay of ribbons. Her eyes shone out a brilliant blue, like the turbulent sea before her, and beneath her eyes were puddles of blue paint. Her waist was bound in thick flat ribbons embroidered with eagles and falcons. Her bare feet were painted with lovely vines and flowers.

I would have known this lady anywhere. I had never met her, nor had I seen her up close, but the slaves had whispered her name as they whispered the queen's name. I had seen her paintings in the halls of the palace. She was one of the highest born aristocrats, and poets spoke of her beauty the was priests spoke of their gods. Myhanna was everything I expected her to be.

"You do not know me, I'm Myhanna, second born to the throne," Myhanna said slowly. "I would have never demeaned myself to talk to you when the Great King ruled, but now things have changed." She made a dismissive motion to one of the slaves, and pillows were brought for us to sit on.

"I was to marry Hotem. I was to be a Queen. It's my right by the gods."

"Congratulations," I said dismissively.

"Do you know why I'm here, unclean one? Do you know why I'm wandering the desert amongst these villages of unclean savages seeking a caravan of tribeless, godless, slaves?"

"I can't imagine, but I guess it has something to do with me."

"Hotem sent me," she hissed with rage and contempt. "To give you this." She waved and a slave brought me a small glass bird.

I looked at it. It was sublimely beautiful, expertly crafted. It was made of glass and beaded with gems. I had no idea what to say. "Thanks," fell out of my mouth with all the grace of a pregnant whale.

"You don't even know what it means, do you?" she scoffed. "You will never be anything but a whore. Never. A murderous, savage whore."

"Is that it? Are we done? This has been pleasant, but I think I'm done with you." I rose and began to walk away.

"He wants you to marry him," she said.

I looked at the tiny bird and smiled. Warm memories of Hotem flooded over me. The poet king who wanted to be a warrior. I placed the bird in the folds of my sari, next to my heart. I turned to face Myhanna.

"Myhanna," I whispered. She drew back, but I held her face in my hands. "He is your king, not mine. I'm no man's bride."

Myhanna looked up at me with confusion and disgust. Finally, some hidden emotion, carefully covered by makeup and etiquette arose from a deep slumber in her breast. "You do not want Hotem?" she asked in a teary awe.

"No. He is too good for me. I'm nothing. I don't deserve your king. I'm barren as the desert wind. I'll live and die by the sword."

"It's true?" she asked touching my sword. "You're a warrior?"

"Yes."

"How can a woman be a warrior?"

"A woman can be anything, if she is willing to fight for it. You can be a queen if that's what you want."

Myhanna and I sat next to each other for a long time, contemplating each other. The stars erupted from the sky, and a cool breeze turned the desert into an oasis. "I don't understand," she whispered.

Xander sat beside us on his pillow, waiting. Finally, he spoke. "You should come and join us for the evening. Your journey has been hard. Your men are tired. Bring your people and dine with us."

"They are only slaves. They can't dine with us."

"At God's table there are no slaves, only men and women."

"The things you say are profanation. You could be killed for them."

"We aren't of your tribe. We aren't subject to your laws."

"The old king would have mowed you down for even existing. This isn't the way."

"Do you believe the way is right?"

"What I believe is irrelevant."

"No. It's all that matters here. In the sight of God. On this deserted shore. The way is washed away and there is only you and I. I'm asking you if you believe in the way of your people."

Small tears gathered at the corners of Myhanna's eyes. Her eyes drifted back to the darkened ocean. She shook her head. "It's not my place to question the way. The way has always been."

"Nothing has always been, except God. You aren't happy." Xander's hand rested on the would-be queen's shoulder, and the tears emptied out of her eyes like rain on stone.

"Come with us," Xander whispered.

"I cannot."

"Let go of everything you've been taught to believe and learn for yourself. Come with us and find peace." Xander had a gift. I had been blind to it before. But in the light of the rising moons, it shone out of his face like he was the moon. He reached into Myhanna's soul and pulled out all of her longing and sorrow. He took her hand and pulled her someplace she had never dared to go before. Xander had always been a healer. He had even saved me, all those years ago. How could I hate a man who brought so much happiness?

"We'll dine with you," Myhanna answered.

At first, Myhanna sat stiffly staring down on the Caeimoni, but slowly her pretensions melted away. She listened to Salome and Xander speak. She smiled as the mosaic of different types of music filled the air with an odd harmony. Myhanna took off the ribbons that bound her waist and sat in her silk shift on the sand. Her slaves sat beside her, and the sound of laughter and merriment rose through the camp. People sang in a multitude of languages that all melted into one voice. Myhanna even danced.

I went to bed long before anyone else had retired. I crept into my tent and watched the rwan leave for its nightly hunt. I lay awake in my bed clutching the tiny bird at my heart. I took it out and looked at it for a long time.

Hotem. I couldn't imagine why he had loved me. There was nothing in me that resembled the beautiful princess that danced outside. I pushed in on the bird's head and it bent, releasing a tiny piece of paper.

A small poem was written on the paper. I breathed deeply and read Hotem's poetry. They were brilliant words that should have been written for a more perfect woman. I put the paper back and put the bird back by my heart. I knew why Cahir had loved me, and I knew why I loved him. We were the same, he and I. He looked at me, and he saw the same elemental forces that drove him. I was his own art perfected.

I was lying on my bed brooding when Myhanna pushed her way into my tent. She sat down on the foot of my bed. Her braids had come loose, and her hair fell in long black curls along the sides of her face. "Please," she whispered. "Don't tell anyone about this."

"Who would I tell?" I answered.

"You might change your mind. You might go back. I would be shot for this."

"Why not stay? Everyone else does." She seemed like she would fit in with all of Xander's starry eyed followers.

"I can't. Maybe I'll stay for a few days longer, but I can't stay." She spoke with regret.

"Why not?"

"You wouldn't understand. To be noble. To be royalty is to own duty. My family would be dishonored by me. They would be cast out."

"I'm learning," I said harshly.

"I've freed the slaves. They won't talk. I'll say they abandoned me to follow the prophet. Xander's offered me a horse and carriage to return in."

"You'll be killed by raiders."

"No. I'm a goddess here. Anyone who touched me would be skinned alive. A few of my slaves have agreed to return with me. I won't be alone."

"Why did you free the slaves?" I still found it hard to believe Xander could change someone so quickly.

"I don't know. It just seemed wrong. Maybe it always has. I've always been afraid to speak. I'm a woman, and it's not my place. The way has no place for my voice. I've always followed our way. I just accepted the way as right because it was. When I thought about it, I knew that it was wrong."

"It was Xander. He clears the eyes."

"What is he? Is he a man? A God? A prophet?"

I shrugged. "He's just a man. He was a doctor."

"How can you be here if you don't believe he is more than that? Some people here say he's God made flesh."

"Some people here used to worship gods with five heads and wings. What kind of compliment is it that they think Xander is a god?" I said with a wicked grin.

"I think he speaks God's wisdom. I think he is holy. You're right. He clears the eyes. He changes everything. I was lost. Every day for me was a struggle. I hated myself. I wanted to be queen because I wanted to be something. I wanted to be anything. Just something more than a baby-making monster that lives and dies in the bedchamber. I wanted to read the great books, like Hotem, like a queen."

"You don't need Hotem for that. You don't need to get married. Go home. Tell Hotem how you feel. He'll help you find your voice. He's a good man."

The wine had loosened her tongue and her wits. All the years of obeying mores vanished in an instant. She spoke her mind like she had never done anything else. "Why won't you marry Hotem? You're nothing. You're a slave. How can you say no? Don't you want to be free? Don't you want to know the world like only a queen can?"

"I'm free. I've seen the world. I've wandered the world's back on my bare feet. I've flown through the sky on the rwan's back. How could I go back to that city? Even Hotem is a prisoner there."

"He is king."

"He is king, but he can't leave. He can't do the only thing he's ever wanted to. He can't go to The University."

"He wants that?"

"It's all he's ever wanted."

"They'll kill him eventually."

"Who?"

"The priests. The nobles. He's changing too much too fast. They hate him. His father was called the king of heaven. He has been made a god. The only thing that keeps Hotem alive is his success in his military campaigns."

"He's a good warrior?"

"They say that no man alive fights with his skill."

I smiled. "Good," I whispered. "Why do you want to marry him if they are going to kill him? Won't they kill you too?"

Her expression changed, and she looked down at her hands. "No, that's not our way."

I raised an eyebrow. She was smarter than she appeared. "Tell me about your way. I'm ignorant." My tone became more hostile.

"When the king is overthrown, the queen takes his place until she can remarry. Men can fall. They are corruptible, even as gods, and gods that turn bad become demons. Women are not corruptible. They are the mothers. It's the queen's place to name the next king."

"You bitch," I hissed. "Do you want Hotem to die?"

She shook her head. "No. I want to help him. If he married, he would be seen as less of a radical. Right now, he's doing everything he can to uproot all of our ways. He wants to change everything. He wants to marry a slave! If he married me, he would be seen as a traditional man with some modern views. He is a strong military commander; if he had a good wife of noble birth and many heirs, all the rest could be overlooked. I could save him."

"Why in hell did he send you to woo me? Was he blind to your intentions?"

"No. I think he wanted to be away from me. He was tired of the pressure. Things have been difficult since his coronation, and I'm just another pressure. They have already attempted to assassinate him. He's a very agile man, however, and he dodged the bullet."

I leaned back into the mountain of pillows on my bed roll. I studied her. She was looking around my tent with a mixture of apprehension and disgust. She studied the dirty floors and junky sleeping bag. Her eyes rolled off the filthy spot where the rwan slept beside me and then moved back upward to the dome of my oversized home. I had bought it from a group of Northerners who had used it to house their livestock during the winter. Myhanna seemed to be searching for something, looking for answers.

"I know," I said. "My tent isn't much. But I'm only a slave, right?"

"Why do you stay here? You don't believe what Xander says. You show nothing but disdain for the people here. Why stay?" she asked.

"He's my brother," I said.

"Who?"

"Xander."

Her expression changed. Before, I had been beneath her. I was a nothing. I was a slave who had seduced the king in her bedchamber. Suddenly, I was transformed. I became some epic piece in a divine puzzle, the lost sister of a god who was waiting for her moment to bloom. I had seen the look in a thousand faces. The faces of a thousand true believers.

"I think I need to take a walk," Myhanna said. "I need some time to clear my head."

I walked out of the tent with her and watched her move through the camp. She walked slowly, studying everyone she passed. I turned my face to the morning moon, the last moon to fall in the morning.

Soon the desert would fade to high grass and prairie and the barren Efferitas' landscape would give way to a world crowded with cities and tribes. I would leave Hotem and his people behind forever.

He would be hers, and this made me weep.

I left camp to look for my only friend. I didn't know where the rwan flew at night. I wandered over dunes and rough sand until I found him lying on the highest dune. I paused and studied him with awe and wonder. His black skin shone in the moonlight like it was giving the light, not catching it. The red that cracked beneath his flesh illuminated the sky around him. He seemed more like a monument than a living thing.

I sat beside him, and together we looked down upon a tiny Efferitas colony. He snorted, and I placed my hand on his hot flesh.

Rage. It burned through every part of my body. I looked out at these dreams and saw a landscape painted with blood. I lingered in his dream, in his secret world. He descended upon every person he had seen with equal zeal, devouring them, except me. For me, his dreams were like ice. He wanted to take me home with him. He wanted me to be his.

I couldn't understand the root of his desire, only the desire. I couldn't understand his indiscriminate bloodlust any more than I understood his desire to keep me. I couldn't tell if he wanted me as a pet, or a friend, or a mother. I could only feel his desire to keep me, and I knew that the only reason he hadn't killed everyone in camp had been because I hadn't wanted him to.

Such dreams clouded my eyes that night with such a ferocious intensity that sometimes I'm still blinded by them. In his dreams, the rwan took me home, to his icy castle, to his fiery mountain. There was no will be or has been, there is only what is.

Ancient beings smoldered in their caverns waiting for time to give them back what humanity had taken. They sat on their mountains, watching and waiting for my friend. He was the father, the creator.

I took my hand off his back. The creator. He looked at me. He had dreamt my dreams. He had seen my heart. The sun rose over the blistering dunes, and he carried me back to our ragged tent. We slept together as we always had. I pushed my face on his leg and dreamt my own dreams. They were tormented by images of impossible wars and genocide. I awoke sweating and crying. I pushed my way out of the sweltering tent and looked out onto the horizon.

I smelt it long before I saw it. I felt it in my bones, deep down like a wound that never heals. A storm was coming, a storm to peel the dust off the dead.

We packed up camp that day. The desert disappeared, and long grass spread out over gentle rolling hills. Strange deer and elk appeared on the landscape. Rodents ran in and out of elaborate burrows. Birds dotted the sky. It was finally time for us to part ways. He planned on traveling east along the river into the mountains. Crian's home was north off the coast by The University.

Xander and I dined alone that night. He never gave anyone the honor of a private audience. He had said, in one of many of his prophetic speeches that God had sent him for everyone. For him to show favoritism would mean God showed favoritism, and God loved everyone without preference.

"Don't leave," he pleaded.

"Why? You have a legion of people who worship you like a god. What could you possibly want from your atheist sister?"

"When you are gone, there is nothing left of home. Mark is Xenderian, and he should remind me of home, but he only wears Caeimoni clothes now and never speaks of anything but God and salvation. Ieya is all but mute. She says she's taken a vow of silence to atone for her sins." He suddenly sounded so sad.

I laughed. "Doesn't that make you happy?"

"It is as the Lord would have it."

"Isn't that what you want?"

"It's what God wants. But I'm a man, and although I can never say this to anyone but you, sometimes I feel lonely and lost."

"You feel lost?" I asked in disbelief.

"Not like you think. I just feel like I miss the way things used to be. I miss Mom's kitchen and the smell of her breads. I miss the mountains and the cool crisp air. I miss our people and our home."

"Me too. I never thought I'd say this, but I miss that cold temple. I felt like I had a purpose there. Everything made sense. I knew who I was and where I was going. I was so certain what I fought for was right."

"Stay with me. Be my balance. In a world of disciples, you could be my friend," Xander pleaded.

"No. It wouldn't work. Your God and your people won't let you have a relationship with me. I'm a monster." I shook my head and spoke firmly.

"Ailive, I know you've done questionable things, but you're one of God's children."

"I'm a killer. I always have been, even when I was a little girl."

"It wasn't your fault."

"I live for the storm. That's why the rwan and I stay together. Because we are creatures of fire."

"When are you going to let go?"

"What do you mean?" I asked quietly.

"No matter how many people you kill. No matter how many wars you fight, you can't change the past."

"I don't know what you are talking about," I said hesitantly.

"You don't remember?" Xander seemed amazed.

"What?"

"Do you remember Father? Do you remember when we were a family?"

"No."

"Didn't I ever tell you about when father was alive, and he was a merchant?"

"No."

"When we were young, our father was a merchant. We went on a trading expedition to Montai. Raiders shouldn't have been a problem, but the tribeless can be desperate. You don't remember any of this?"

"No." I felt an overwhelming sense of loss crawl up from my toes and into my stomach. My mouth went dry, and my heart pounded in my chest. Images that had laid dormant in my mind for years resurfaced, and I gasped for air.

"We were attacked by a group of men. They killed Father. Slit his throat in front of you and raped mother. You were brave. I'll never forget you. You got a gun and tried to shoot one of the men who was raping Mother, but you were too small to work the thing. They beat you and stole everything."

"I don't remember any of this," I lied as the memories bubbled up from the deepest part of my unconscious mind.

"No one is born a killer, Ailive. Killers are made."

"What was I like before this?" As I said this, I hoped that I wasn't the monster I thought I was. I hoped I wasn't a born killer.

"You were a sweet little girl. You were my favorite."

I closed my eyes, pushing tears away. I remembered feeling helpless and powerless. I remembered feeling like there was nothing I could do. I had felt so weak. I had wanted to save my parents but I couldn't. I hated the memory of such tremendous weakness. I couldn't save my mother and anger had filled me like fire.

Everything changed. I had always thought that I had been born with the storm in my heart, without conscience. Born to fight and die. But I had been a little girl, like any other.

I could have been a woman, like any other.

"It doesn't change anything," I lied.

"Doesn't it?"

"I have to take Crian and Mia home. I have to take the rwan home. What I could have been is irrelevant. This is what I am, and I don't belong with you."

He put his hand on my shoulder, and I turned to him. His eyes were so blue, like the sky before the gnawing. I could have drown in them. "Please," he said. "Stay." His eyes spoke more than he could. He was pleading for our lives. He was pleading for something I would never have understood or believed.

"I can't."

VI
The Islands at the Edge of the World

O ur journey was pleasant. The landscape became hospitable and comfortable. Strange limestone monoliths jutted out of the ground, like monuments. Tall grass and pastel flowers leaned up against these geological oddities, finding shelter in their shade. Small streams and rivers innervated the earth, feeding it. The heat left us. Clouds sheltered us from the oppressive sun. Sometimes it rained. We leaned back in our saddles, letting the rain fall into our open mouths.

We had been traveling for many weeks when we finally stopped and camped in some old ruins about half way to Notua.

I'm never as strong as I think I am. I have fought fiercely, but luck and the winds have brought me as many victories as my own skill. That night I would have slept through a hurricane, curled up in my sleeping bag with the pounding surf singing me to sleep, but my friend, the rwan, never slept. Its red eyes scorched the landscape with its watchful hunting.

It heard them coming and let out an enormous wail, sending all of us out of our beds. It sounded like thunder crashing over a screaming child. The rwan beat its wings, and rocks scattered around our camp. I stood up and watched the beast take flight. He disappeared over the horizon, and I was left with a queasy uneasy feeling.

They were right next to us when I finally had the presence of mind to draw my sword. I crouched down and watched them walk into our camp. There were at least twenty of them, heavily armed, led by a small woman with black hair and white skin. They all dressed the same in some kind of tight green body suit.

Crian and Mia were hiding somewhere behind me. The woman called out into the night, "Come out! I know you are there. You should come out, or it will be much worse."

I summed the war party up quickly. I could tell that the four soldiers that had surrounded us were less prepared. They moved clumsily, and I could smell the fear drifting off them like a heavy cologne. They were breathing heavily, and they gripped their guns so tightly their knuckles were turning white. The leader was different. I could tell that before she spoke or moved. She moved silently, gracefully, with the deadly grace of someone trained in the art of the storm.

I attacked the four soldiers before I addressed the leader. I turned so quickly they didn't even see me move. I ducked behind them and hid myself in the shadows before they had time to figure out what was going on. For a dreadful moment, the night exploded with gunfire. The noise was deafening, but I slid behind the first soldier and slit his throat. The second soldier panicked and fired more wildly into the night, shooting one of her comrades. While she was shooting, I slit her throat. Silence retook the night, and the gunfire stopped. I was behind the final soldier and I put the knife to his throat. The leader pointed her gun at me. "Let my sergeant go," she said. "Or we will torture you when we catch you."

I laughed. "That's assuming you catch me."

"You are alone and armed only with a sword. How could we not catch you?"

"I walk the way of the storm. A sword is all I need."

"Ha. That mentality is a relic of dead tribes, wiped out by their own fidelity to false gods. This is your last chance, let my sergeant go."

Her bearing showed her to be a more than proficient soldier. For a moment, I hesitated. I knew that she alone might prove to be a challenge, but she was carrying an automatic weapon and that gave her a distinct advantage.

I moved quickly. I slit the throat of the woman in my arms and leapt into the shadows hamstringing the three men on my right. Gun fire exploded around me, deafening me, silencing the ocean. I slid through the dirt and crawled under another man, cutting him in half before he saw me. The wind began to howl and I breathed in, moving with the breeze. I cut five men in half and stood, facing the woman. She smiled as she put her gun to my forehead.

"It's almost a shame to kill you. A thing of beauty like you should be kept in a museum. But you just killed my friends, and I'm a vengeful woman."

I dodged the bullet and bent backward moving to her right. She dropped to the ground, somersaulting as she fired her gun. I flipped backward, dancing around her bullets.

The gun shots stopped. She was reloading. I leapt, but she rolled over, missing the blade of my sword. In one quick motion, she kicked the sword from my hand and jumped on top me pounding my face with her bare hands.

For what seemed like forever, we rolled around in the dirt, exchanging blows, but luck aided me and a sharp rock cut her knee. She screamed and in her momentary disorientation, I was able to jab my thumb into her right eye and then into the soft neural tissue beneath.

I leaned up and bit out her jugular. Her blood filled my mouth, and I spat in disgust.

She fell limply on top of me like a broken doll. I pushed her body off of me.

I stood in the dark for a long time, staring at her ravaged body. I couldn't remember the last time I had felt my own blood in mouth. Now her blood mingled with my own. My arm was broken.

I smiled. Cahir had trained her. I recognized the way she carried herself.

I was almost home. I walked up over the hill a ways and made sure there were no others. They had left their land rovers at the base of the hill, to conceal their approach. I burnt all of the vehicles except one.

We abandoned our horses there and set them free. We drove along the desolate beach, avoiding any signs of civilization. The sparse grass grew thicker, and the trees became dense and tightly packed. The undergrowth spread out like a net beneath the dark green canopy and provided shade and privacy.

We were able to ride in the car for a while, but the terrain changed, and we were forced to abandon the fleeting luxuries of technology. We saw less and less of my friend. Days would pass without sight of him, but occasionally the sun would glint off the mountains, and I would see his face glaring down at me in impatience.

Crian hummed to herself as she made camp. "About ten miles that way," she said pointing north along the coast. "Is a little village with high walls. They are the Ferrymen. They guard the gates to our home."

Crian sighed deeply and wiped the tears from her eyes. "I never thought I'd see home again." The old woman bent in half, sobbing into her calloused hands.

The gates to Notua were not what I imagined. The village was a collection of enormous houses, made of pink brick and sea shells and built along the shoreline. The houses were surrounded by an enormous wall, high and thick, allowing only fleeting glimpses of the buildings within. All the boats were chained to the docks and apparently unreachable without swimming an impossible distance or entering the gates to the Ferrymen's village.

Crian walked up to the gate and banged on the door. The door was surprisingly small, white-washed and surrounded by flowers.

A small, red-haired woman wearing a piece of elaborate silk wrapped around her top answered the door. "Strangers aren't welcome here."

"I'm Crian D'Artua. This is my home."

"Crian D'Artua. I think I've heard of your family. Well, come in then." She signaled us in with an impatient waving of her hand.

I gasped as I entered the door, and then my gasp melted into a smile.

The village was composed of small stone paths that wove through a mass of elaborate gardens, orchards, and vineyards. Right in front of the door, there was a beautiful stone castle, made of what looked like sand and shells. Men and women worked in the gardens while children sat on benches reading books.

"There've been bad times lately," the red-haired woman said. "Lots of raiders and tribeless have been coming this way seeking sanctuary or trying to breech our walls."

"Really?" Crian said.

"Yes," the lady said. "I'm Morrow D'ferry. Let's go in and look up your papers."

We went into the castle. The interior had sleek, marble floors and clean white walls. We went into a large room filled with computer terminals and things I couldn't identify. Morrow sat down and started typing.

"You are Crian," she said after a while. "Abducted and enslaved by the Efferitas twenty-five years ago."

Morrow looked up at Crian in amazement. "You survived the Efferitas?" she asked.

Quite suddenly, she stood up and embraced Crian fiercely. "Welcome home. It is always good to see survivors. Do you mind if I send your family a memo that you are all right and returning home? Would you like to hear about your family?"

"Very much."

Morrow returned to the computer and looked at its glowing screen. "Your husband died in the raid, but you know that. Your sister keeps your estate with her husband and son. Her daughter has married and has two sons of her own and has moved to her husband's estate on Chiurn. Her son is married and has a daughter. Your sister is now the dean of the lyceum and has done quite well for your family."

Crian was crying again. Her tears dissipated and melted into a kind of hysterical laughter. Morrow stood up and embraced Crian again. "They will be happy to see you," she said. "I'm sure the parties will last all week. I'll send her a memo so she knows to meet you at the dock."

She typed a few more words and then turned to Mia. "I hope that you have a family that will be as overjoyed to find you safe," she said. "What is your name?"

Crian answered for her. "She is Mia D'Artua. She is my daughter, of pure Notuan blood, born in slavery. There will be no record of her."

"Well we have to change that," Morrow said. Morrow bustled around. She drew some of Mia's blood and analyzed it, proudly announcing that she was of pure blood. She took her picture and fingerprints. She typed on the computer for what seemed like forever, and then she took more pictures. Finally, she smiled and pointed at the screen. "There you are, now. A citizen of Notua."

"And how about you," she happily asked me. "Are you another daughter born in slavery?"

"No," I said. "I'm nothing."

Her smile vanished, and her forehead creased. "Oh, I see. I'm sorry. You speak such perfect Notuan. I assumed you were one of us." She stood up and walked away from the computer. "You're tribeless?"

"I'm nothing," I said again.

"I need just a minute," she said. She pulled Crian into another room. I couldn't hear what they were saying. It didn't matter. I knew what they were saying without hearing them and so did Mia. Mia put her hand on my shoulder.

"I owe you everything," she said. "I'm no more Notuan than you. I don't know this place. If you ask me to, I'll stay with you. You're my sister."

"No. Go home. I'm okay. Really." I put my hand on her shoulder. She was soft. There was very little muscle on her shoulder. Only soft flesh and hard memories.

"I'm afraid," she whispered. "I don't know this place. They expect something of me. I know it, and I don't think I can be what they want.

Did you see what she just did on that glowing thing?"

"It's a computer," I said.

"What?"

"The glowing thing. It's a computer. Once you understand this world, it won't be so overwhelming. You'll have your mother, and she'll have you."

She shook her head. "I don't know," she whispered. With Mia and

Crian, we had always spoken Efferitas. It had never occurred to me that she couldn't speak Notuan fluently. I had begun to take language for granted.

Morrow and Crian emerged from their sheltered corner reluctantly. Crian couldn't meet my eyes. "Our people have very strict laws," Morrow said. "We are one of the oldest tribes on this planet, and all of our longevity is based on a principle of adherence to our laws and protection of our own."

"I understand," I said calmly. I had never intended on staying. Notua was not my place any more than Xander's caravan of prophets had been.

"You are tribeless, and it's forbidden for us to take in the tribeless."

"I understand," I repeated patiently.

"Your people are no more. You are tribeless, and even if this weren't the case, our people had no allegiances with the Xenderians."

"I understand," I said again.

"Forgive me," Crian whispered. "I wanted you to stay here with us. I wanted you to live as my daughter, but I can't change the law." Crian threw her arms around me and hugged me. "You have been like a daughter to me. When there was only darkness in my life, when I had given up all hope, you came and brought me light."

"I only went the way the wind blew. What I did was nothing. You deserve your home. Don't feel bad for me. I couldn't stay here. The wind still blows, and I have to go with it."

"If you ever need help, come to this place and the Ferrymen will call me. I will always do whatever I can to help you," Crian said as she kissed my cheek. "Are you sure you will be all right out there?"

"You know me. Do you think there is any need to worry?"

"No."

I walked out of the castle and into the streets of the city, admiring its architecture and gardens. Behind the castle, there was a lovely market filled with beautiful objects of art and rare fruits and jewels. People bustled through a long chain of small tents, seated on the beach. I stood in the sand, watching my only friends sail home.

I turned and looked at the city and realized that there were as many people in gray speaking Etrusan as there were Notuans. It was clear that many University citizens came to vacation or trade with the Notuans. All around me were signs for hotels and different shops which catered to The University tourists and traders and businessmen.

Morrow came and found me. She stood for a while with me watching the boat disappear over the horizon.

"You are a good woman," she said. "They would have stayed with you if you had asked them to and you knew it. Now you are alone."

"I've always been alone."

"You should buy some achas to go with your wrap. Those pants look ridiculous."

I turned and smiled at Morrow. "I can't wear short pants. Legs are the first thing to go in battle. You fall. You get hit. The scars build up. My legs are nothing but scars and tattoos."

Morrow looked away at the blank horizon and the fading sun. "The gnawing begins tomorrow. It's a good time to travel. Most tribes have some holiday or ritual associated with the gnawing. It will be cool, and the sun will be hidden."

"But after the gnawing comes high summer, and that's not a good time to travel," I said without thinking.

"Where are you going?"

"I have another friend I have to take home."

"His people won't want you either."

"No. I have my own people to find. I've waited a long time to find my own people."

Morrow shook her head in concern. "Do you need supplies? You can have anything you want from the market. You're a good person. If it were up to me, I would let you in."

"I know, but even if you did, I wouldn't stay. This isn't my home."

"You want to be tribeless?" she said in disbelief.

"I want to be free," I answered honestly.

"Such words are only the imaginings of children and innocents. There is no freedom. Only the cages we choose for ourselves."

"Thank you, Morrow."

I was allowed to stay with the Ferrymen for several days, and I was tired, so I accepted a hotel room. I was uncomfortable being there, but I needed the rest, and I greatly enjoyed the creature comforts that had been lost to me since I last slept in my own bed.

I left after a few days. Morrow was happy to see me go. As I wandered through the blossoming, fragrant hills that surrounded the Ferryman's city, I was consumed by the sudden isolation of my own existence. I knew I should feel free. I should feel alive and excited at the sudden possibilities that lie before me. But instead I felt, for the first time, truly tribeless. I walked with my eyes desperately tilted upward, searching for my lost companion, searching for my last friend.

But he never came. He had vanished over some distant spot on the horizon. He had gone home to what he needed and left me with no place else to go. So I followed the well-worn road between Notua and The University. It was the only other place I could think of going.

VII

The Ancient Ruins of K'ylanjiro

The days spread out before me like blank sheets of paper. I walked all day and well into the night. Sometimes I ran. There was no point in stopping. I couldn't sleep, so I walked. Occasionally, I looked upward, praying for the return of my friend, but such motion was wasted.

It was a pleasant time to travel. The gnawing was fainter in the Northern regions, but the colors still painted the sky like melting watercolors, and the air was cool and fresh. The landscape took on the hues of the sky, making the mountains around me shimmer in pale blues and soft pinks. Sometimes I wished I was an artist so I could capture some piece of the beauty of the world to keep and hold.

The road between Notua and The University was paved. It went through tunnels and under rivers, never swerving or bending. I had never seen anything like it. The bridges seemed to float over the water, with nothing to suspend them, and the tunnels looked as if they had been cut by giants. Everything around the road was untouched. Only the road was man-made.

I walked for two days without making camp. I wanted to get Notua behind me. On the second night, I made a rough camp at the base of an enormous tree. It was cold, and I built a big fire. I ate some of the food the Notuans gave me and pulled my jacket up over my shoulders. I made myself some tea and fell asleep looking at the stars.

My dreams were terrible that night. I saw a pale man wrapped in black. He was a great leader, vicious and relentless. He was building something, something monstrous, something beautiful. When it was done, he was hailed as a god.

Time stood still. I saw the man again. The man was dying or changing. His tribe was dying. Their world was freezing, fading around them. Their screams howled through me, even when I woke up.

I dusted the dream from my eyes and looked around me. He had come back. Finally, he had come back. The rwan sat above me, looking down on me like some ancient relic, long forgotten. He looked like stone. I smiled. I wasn't alone anymore. I embraced the stone demon before the remnants of the dream had completely faded.

The beast backed away from me, and I regained some of my composure. I was suddenly twelve years old again, standing before the Verdu king with a knife in my hand. The monster stood up and stretched its huge wings. It stretched its front limbs like a cat and yawned, baring its massive ivory teeth. I touched him, and I knew what he wanted.

I obeyed him and crawled onto his back. He sprang into the air with one momentous push of his wings. It was wonderful to feel the cool air pulling my hair way from my face, to lay my face on his back and just be carried. I couldn't remember many moments in my life when I had relaxed or rested, but when I was riding the rwan, I was freed of the burden of my labor. There was nothing I should be doing or wanted to be doing. I could just be.

We landed on the icy slopes of some distant, unknown glacier. I had no idea where we were, but I knew we had to be very far to the north. We walked about one hundred feet until the remnants of the glacier stood before us in the form of a terrifying looking icefall. The rwan crept beneath the icefall until he found a deep crevasse. I crawled on his back, and we went down, beneath the glacier, into the ice.

When we found level ground, I walked again. It was a strange cave, carved by lava out of ice. A tiny crack in the earth seeped magma, melting a portion of the glacier. I followed the rwan into the glacier until the ice opened up into a gargantuan cavern.

I froze in my tracks.

Before me stood the largest city I had ever seen. It was nothing but black rock and ice, but my imagination could rebuild it, full of splendor and light. The glacier it was buried in was at least a half a million years old, if not older, but the city was modern. The tall skyscrapers and strange art testified to the technology of the city's inhabitants.

I had not studied much history, but I knew that The University had designed the first cars and computers a couple thousand years ago. I knew that this city, this city encased in ice, was impossible. I sat down on a black rock and just stared.

The rwans slowly stepped out of the shadows of their collapsed city. There were thousands of them. They swooped down from the sky above me to perch on the distant volcano, filling the room and letting out one long tormented wail. My friend went to follow the females and create more young, and I was left alone in the rubble surrounded by a thousand ancient demons.

I should have been afraid, but I felt only curiosity. The scholar in me was left wondering at the beauty of the place and longing to know its antecedents. I wandered in and out of old buildings looking for some clue to the secret of the place. I dusted off reliefs and studied old statues. I looked for any little bit of writing, but found that everything had been encased in volcanic rock. The city had been preserved by a massive volcanic eruption.

But the city made no sense. I couldn't reconcile the brilliance of the architecture with the ice that surrounded it. Enormous domes were held aloft by nothing. The buildings were stacked against each other forming strangely geometric arcs. Tall lean building of black glass stretched up so high that the tops of the buildings were imbedded in the ice. Beautiful stone churches were filled with colored glass and marble floors.

None of it made sense. The city was so old it shouldn't have existed. The ice it was entombed in was at least three hundred thousand years old.

Finally, I laid down on one of the stone beds and stared at a basrelief of the planets on the ceiling above me. A small rwan sat outside the room, staring at me her smoldering eyes. I fell asleep staring at her, lost in my own curiosity.

My friend sat beside me when I awoke. I smiled up at him, my only friend. He looked down at me with some kind of strange desperation, and I knew it was time for me to learn why he had needed me. He had not stayed with me for so long because he loved me. I had always known there was something. I had always known that I was just a pawn to him.

I crawled forward and placed my hands on his face. He leaned into my embrace and a flood of images washed me away.

I was the man I had seen before in other dreams, dark and petulant. I had lived my entire life in New York. The city only a part of a great nation. My name was Jason Byant. I had been born into a powerful family that had great ambitions for me. My father was the president, the most powerful man in the world.

All my life I had struggled to impress him. My father had wanted me to be a politician. He had wanted me to follow in his footsteps, but I had greater visions than my father, and he had never understood that. I had visions of ending war and famine and disease. There could be no true happiness in the world until all of these things were eradicated.

I had told my mother this, and she had laughed. She had called me a child and told me that everyone wanted to end these things, but that it was immature to believe it was possible.

I didn't think so.

I decided that the answer lie in creating a perfect person who could be the perfect warrior: resistant to disease and famine. Once I had designed these people, all other races would be eradicated.

War would end. Hunger would end. Disease would end.

Just as my laboratory assistants began to abandon me and my money run thin, it happened. I found way to change and shape the nature of humanity itself, to make us better.

My plan worked. It was wonderful, people who had been sick got better, people who had been mad, suddenly saw clearly. The elderly grew young. The young grew strong. Years passed and over the course of thirty or forty years, we began to realize that our lives might be prolonged indefinitely.

We were gods amongst men. Our nation became the world, and there was nothing we could do that failed. I was praised throughout my nation and hailed as a god and savior. My father called me the most brilliant man in history. There was no hunger or disease or war.

There was only us and our slowly changing bodies.

Over time, the side effects of my alteration became more and more apparent.

Women conceived rarely, and when they did have children, they were all female. We were all beginning to show some definite physical deformities. It was too late. We became monsters, losing our ability to speak.

As time passed, we forgot what we were. Only in fleeting dreams, we saw ourselves as we were, but those dreams came and went only leaving us with the relentless drive to see it all end. We were consumed by sorrow and loneliness and dreams on impossible suicides. We craved some end to the relentless passage of time.

But then I found a girl. I found a strange girl who was just a little more than human, and she heard me. She knew me, and I knew that if I could just bring her back, she would teach us to speak again. She would allow us to speak just one last time and in exchange for that I would give her anything she asked. To be able to speak with my wife one last time…

When I awoke, I was in the center of the city surrounded by the glowing eyes of the rwans. I sat up and looked at Jason. I was afraid to touch him, afraid I would be sucked back into his world of infinite silence and hopeless hunger. I pulled my legs up against my body and sobbed into the snow. For Jason, for our endless history of violence and desperation.

We would never change.

Jason's people had been more advanced than ours, and still they had fought and eventually created their own demise.

I just wanted to find a warm bed.

But what we want doesn't matter, so I wiped my tears away and did what Jason asked of me. I touched them. I touched all of his people. I became their voice. I stayed in the strange, warm city in the center of the ancient glacier for over a year. Over that year I became a thousand dead people begging for forgiveness. I was an empty vessel for them to fill up and pour out over and over again until I had nothing left to give.

Jason was always there. He slept with me at night, whispering his secrets to me in my dreams until I knew him better than I knew myself. He was self-absorbed and egomaniacal. He was a monster not because he was a rwan, but because he was a man.

Finally, I placed my hand on his face and told him that I could do no more. My soul was stretched thin, thinner than it had been by anything that had come before. That city changed me. It took away my hope.

When Jason finally dropped me at the gates of The University, I had nothing left to give Cahir or anyone else.

Jason left me alone at the gates with a whisper and a promise. "What you have given us is priceless," he said. "We can feel you now, and if you ever need us, we are your slaves."

I bowed my head to him and watched him disappear into the snow.

VIII
Home

"What do you want?" the gatekeeper asked me through a small hole in the gate.

"I was told that I would make a good professor here. I have come to apply for a position," I answered.

The man laughed. I looked up at the impenetrable walls that surrounded The University. All roads lead here, but I was having great difficulty gaining entrance.

"Who told you to be a professor?" the man asked.

"Professor Cahir."

"It's going to take more than that to get you in here."

"I have many skills and much knowledge to offer the scholars."

"Everyone has a story. Everyone has skill. We have enough brains in here. We don't need any more. Go away."

The window shut. I banged on the door until my fist went numb. The man opened the window again. "We aren't taking new professors."

"I'm a friend of Cahir's. He'll want to see me."

"I don't know Cahir, but I know tribeless scum. We don't want your kind here."

"Can't you just get him? Can't I talk to him?"

"Wait here," he said coldly.

He disappeared and came back after an hour. The door finally opened, and I was put in a small cell that was built into the wall itself. I sat in petulant anticipation for another two hours.

Finally a chubby, low level bureaucrat came shuffling in the room and sat down in a chair as far from me as she could get. She didn't tell me her name or even waste time with the kind of standard salutations that people used when they were trying to be polite.

"We are sorry for the tribeless problem," she said without making eye contact. "But we have our own problems here. We have far too many people and far too many scholars."

"I was good friends with Cahir," I interrupted.

"That doesn't matter," she said. "We just don't have a place for you. You should leave."

"I'm a master swordsman, and Cahir himself invited me here. You would be stupid to toss my skills aside like I'm a tribeless nothing."

"But you are tribeless, aren't you? We know you are a master and that you know Cahir. You wouldn't have even been let in if you didn't have these attributes. You'd be sitting in the mud outside the wall, but here you are, and I'm telling you that we've done all we can for you."

"Listen to me!" I said in frustration.

"I'm sorry," she insisted. "I've done all I can."

"But!" I exclaimed.

"I'm sorry," she said, cutting me off again. She was a pushy little thing.

Finally, stood up and grabbed the poor bureaucrat by the throat.

"Listen," I hissed. "I may not make it in here legally, but if I don't get my chance to make in here, I'll scale these walls and find you and then I will skin you alive and eat your flesh while you scream."

Despite my threats, I was still taken to a dark room in a shabby building to be interrogated by a series of bureaucrats and policemen. It was in this interrogation room that I first met Sulen, an old man with a constant grimace. He wore a disturbingly tight, gray bodysuit that showed his bizarrely muscled body. He hunched over, making himself shorter and looked at me with bloodshot, gray eyes.

"You know," he said with a thick accent. "If we took in every tribeless whore who claimed to have some knowledge, we would become a refugee camp. I know you scared the gatekeepers into letting you in, but you aren't going to scare me."

"You would be a fool to let me go," I said.

"Why?"

"Because I know the way of the storm. I can teach, and many come here to learn how to fight. You teach many things, but you know that all the tribes really care about is keeping themselves safe. All they really care about is learning to fight. The rest is fluff. Keep me here, and I will be the most dedicated professor at The University."

"What made you think you could just come here and be admitted? New professors are only admitted by invitation alone."

Sulen sat down and lit a pipe. He twisted the hair of his long gray mustache into a fine point and looked at a piece of paper on the table in front of him.

My tongue was glued to the roof of my mouth. I had no answer for him.

"You're going to have to leave," he said. "You know that. The only reason you made it through the gates is because you said Cahir's name. It's my job to keep this sanctuary, this temple of knowledge in a landscape of war, safe. Cahir is an important person here, but if you think that fucking a professor here gains you entrance, you are wrong."

"I don't think you should let me in because Cahir and I were lovers. I think you should let me in because I have traveled the world, and I have seen things that your scholars can only dream about."

Sulen laughed. "Our scholars have vivid imaginations and wickedly intricate dreams."

"I know the origin of rwans. I've seen the palace of the Efferitas, and I have swam with the serpents of the southern seas. I can speak every language, fluently and I have, alone, killed over a thousand men in a single day. I'm offering my services. You can turn me away. I'll leave, but it would be a tragedy to sacrifice so much knowledge on some irrelevant point."

Sulen considered me. He looked me up and down, and then he

changed languages. He switched from Etrusan to his native tongue. His voice wavered as he spoke, as if he hadn't used his language in a very long time. "Even if I agree to let you in, others will fight to have you thrown out. If you understand what I'm saying, maybe you have a chance. If you don't, you are a liar and useless."

"Why would so many fight to throw me out?" I asked in his language.

The old man smiled. He changed languages again. This time he switched to Notuan. His fluency in Notuan was shaky, and he stuttered and stammered over the words. "There has been a population explosion here, and there are now more people than jobs. We are expanding the city walls to accommodate new people and students, but all of our charity has to stop. We've always had some room for refugees, but we're getting fewer students and thus, less food. We can't take care of everyone anymore."

"I'm sorry," I whispered in Notuan.

"You have a gift. Your grasp of language is exceptional," he said in Etrusan.

"It is," I said. "I've been traveling for a long time. I need to rest. I could help here."

"I believe you."

He handed me a stack of papers. I flipped through the ominous pile before me and flinched. "These are the applications for admission to our professorial program. I will give you my approval for admission, but passing through security is a minor hurtle. If you really want to stay here, you have weeks of fighting and filling out of forms ahead of you. If you have any place else you could go, I would consider it. I'll be honest; I don't think they'll let you in. We are sending our children out into the world. We have nothing to offer newcomers."

"I want to try."

"Understood. But you must understand that we have many come to our gates with amazing skills and knowledge. They don't even make it through the doors. You have made it further than most, and those that make it past this point have done things like design new types of energy or come up with cures to cancer."

"How did Cahir become a professor? How did he make it through?"

Sulen only smiled. "The University is a maze of secrets that can't be spoken."

"I want to try. If I fail, I'll be no worse off than I am now."

Sulen shrugged and left the room. I spent an hour filling out forms and pacing before a short, fat, pallid woman with short black hair came in. She wanted my life story. I gave it to her quietly, omitting the parts that were not my secrets to hand out. It was the things that I could tell her and couldn't explain that bothered her the most. She was infuriated by my ability to speak many languages. She wanted me to attribute it to some deep understanding of philology or some sort translating device I had designed or inherited. Finally, she stacked up her papers and scuttled out of the room.

The security officers took me to a large barren prison cell. They let me take my papers and gave me pen. I spent the rest of the evening filling out the endless forms Sulen had given me and fell asleep with the pencil tucked behind my ear.

I woke up early the next morning and finished my paperwork before I was interviewed by another series of pale, fat men and women. Late the next day, I wondered if I should have taken Sulen's advice. I was tired and the endless series of inane questions wore on me like a screwworm burrowing into my flesh.

By the time the next little, fat person came for me, I would have killed to get out of that cell, and I was seriously considering killing that little fat man and leaving The University forever. I had just decided I was done with the entire process when Cahir walked in.

I stood up and smiled, but his face showed me no warmth. He was as I had remembered him, tall and lean. His black eyes stared at me with a wicked intensity, and he was dressed in a light armor, as if for battle.

He walked toward me and handed me a long, straight sword. I took the weapon and gazed into Cahir's eyes.

"You say you are worthy of being a professor here. That you have skills you could pass on. If this is true, you should be able to fight me," Cahir said as he drew his sword.

I said nothing, but waited for him to make the first move. He raised his sword above his head and struck at me with ferocious power. I moved quickly to the side and crouched down, holding my sword beneath me.

We were not dancing. He would kill me if he could. I know I should have felt some kind of pain, but I felt only the warm tingles of lust and desire like a hot drink burning through my insides.

This is where it had begun for me. This had been how I had fallen in love.

He was brilliant. Every motion he made was art. I swung at him, and he caught my feeble motion slicing through my shirt and cutting my arm. Blood dripped onto the white floor beneath our bare feet.

"You've improved," Cahir said as he sliced at my abdomen and missed.

"There've been many battles since our last dance," I answered.

I dropped to the ground and spun myself around slicing the skin from his shin. He flinched and blood soaked his clothes. I took three steps back and waited with my sword slightly lowered. He set his sword down and took off his shirt, revealing deep scars over muscle.

"Long ago," he said. "My people fought naked. They said that any fool could fight with armor, but that only gods could fight with nothing."

"Is that why your people died?"

"My people died because of fate. Your people were eradicated because they were proud and blind."

"You always had something pithy to say, didn't you, Cahir?"

"That's why you loved me."

"No," I said. I moved like the wind, like smoke, and before he even knew I had struck him hard in the back. "This is why I loved you. I loved the dance."

Cahir groaned and fell to the ground with a heavy thud. I kicked him as hard as I could and stepped back, allowing him to get up. Cahir stood up and threw himself on top of me. He pinned me to the ground, and I lay beneath him, basking in the warmth of his body. It had been so long since I had been touched by a man, I wanted him to do far more than pin me to the ground.

"You're better with the sword than I am. The storm favors you, and your skill is beyond measure, but you must be twenty times better than me to defeat me, because you're small and weak and if I ever catch you," he said as he drove his knee into my abdomen. "I can kill you easily."

He let me up and nodded to some unseen camera above him. The doors opened, and he picked up his sword and shirt. "If you make it," he said. "I'll find you."

Seeing Cahir, fighting with him, reminded me of why I had wanted to return to The University. Memories flooded over me like a warm bath. All the long nights of dancing with Cahir came back to me. I would wait for him. I would endure days of interrogation to return to his arms.

I was returned to the small dark interrogation room and yet another plump, pale woman came to talk to me. Her name was Lia, and she smiled at me. None of the others had smiled at me.

"The inquisition board sent me your paperwork," she said. "I despise the inquisition board, and I'm sure you share this sentiment after spending a few days with them."

I smiled back at her.

"I try not to get involved," she said. "But your story is nothing short of miraculous. I'm Lia Brown. I'm a rwan biologist. You say they were genetically engineered by a tribe from antiquity? I have a million questions for you and would love to work with you to gain your professorship, if the inquisition board admits you."

I felt a little guilty. I had lied to them about the rwans. I had not told them the entire story. I had not told them they had once been people. I felt like I was betraying some trust between Jason and myself in doing that. "Thank you," I muttered.

Lia and I talked for a long time. She seemed enraptured and excited by every answer I gave her. Everything I told her reinforced something she had long known had to be true about the rwans. It was clear that she loved her work, that she was fascinated by every aspect of the rwan.

"I've written six texts on rwan behavior," she said. "I traveled to the northern glaciers, searching for their nesting grounds."

"They do reproduce," I said. "But there is only one male, and most of their young die. The rwans are immortal, but sometimes one goes to sleep and never wakes up. I'm not sure if it dies or if it just loses the will to go through the motions of life."

"How long did you live at their nesting grounds?" she asked.

"One year," I said.

"Why did you stay that long? How did you get there? Why did you go?" She asked her questions rapidly. She seemed utterly amazed.

"I'm not sure," I said. My stay with the rwans was a muddle in my brain, and I was fairly sure no one would believe or understand the relationship I had with them.

"I don't understand." She seemed baffled by my failure to answer her.

"For a long time I just wandered, and my wanderings took me there. The rwans liked me, so I stayed."

"If you are invited to stay, we can go back there together."

"I don't think the rwans would welcome you," I said. I could almost see them tearing her limbs off, looking at her like a plump little meal I had brought them as a special treat. They would offer her no mercy.

"We'll need to go back. In order to stay here, you have to get published, and I think that you could definitely pull a serious dissertation out of this. You would win a lot of prestige. Anyhow, I think I have more than enough information to write my report. Thank you for your time and I hope the rest of the inquisition goes well for you." She extended her hand to me, and we shook hands before she departed.

In the morning, I was interviewed by several historians who listened to my stories about the ancient city beneath the ice. They made it quite clear that they wouldn't fully believe anything I had said until they saw the city with their own eyes. I gave them all the data I could on its location, but half hoped they never found it. I was fairly sure they couldn't find it without someone to guide them.

After the historians left, a small man came in to speak with me. He was lean, with an angular face and slightly slanted eyes. His skin was fair, like his hair, and he moved with an athletic grace the others had lacked entirely. He set up a small camera on the desk in front of me and laid out a stack of papers and began to take notes.

"You lived amongst the Efferitas?" he asked.

"Yes."

"For how long?"

"Almost three years, I think."

"You know the language?"

"Yes."

"Well, we know almost nothing about the Efferitas. We know that they have mastered a blitzkrieg fighting technique that has made them almost invincible and a few minor cultural notes, but that's all. I guess my first question would be about their government. Do they have a monarchy?"

I thought of Hotem, sitting on his father's throne with Myhanna beside him. I wondered if he had been able to change his people.

"What's your name?" I asked the little man.

"Jacob Yluq," he answered hesitantly.

"I'm tired of this. If you want information from me, you should admit me."

"How can we tell if you are useful if you don't demonstrate your knowledge?"

I shrugged. "Why keep me if I've already given you everything you wanted?"

"I can't recommend your admittance in my report if you don't show me some proof of your expertise. No one leaves the Efferitas. I might be prone to think you were lying."

"The others may admit me. I'm tired."

Jacob leaned forward and smiled slyly. "The others have no power. No one cares about rwans or history. No one will let you in so you can help those people."

I leaned over and pointed to the brand on my neck. "The Efferitas brand their slaves. This is the brand given to the king's slaves. Is that proof enough?"

He shook his head. "These are strange times. The University isn't what it used to be. It was founded on so many beautiful ideas that have been muddied by unfortunate realities."

The next week was the longest of my life. They left me in that cell with no company or entertainment. Hours felt like days and days felt like years, but at the end of my stay in purgatory, I was granted admission to the professorial program at The University. I was taken before the board of the inquisition and an ancient looking woman with thick glasses told me I was lucky I knew so much about the Efferitas. She said The University had a keen interest in their emerging global power and that my knowledge of this alone had granted me passage.

Thus, when I was released, it was Jacob Yluq that met me at the doors. He smiled warmly at me and took my hand. "Welcome," he said. He was well dressed and looked very prestigious in his suit and long coat. He appeared genuinely delighted to see me.

"I've volunteered to be you advisor. You will have to meet with me every day, and we will work on a good dissertation for you to earn your professorship. I know you want to teach fighting techniques, but we think you would be better in sociology. Your gift in languages and your knowledge of war would make you an excellent diplomat."

"I've never done anything but fight," I said.

"Just because that's all you have done, doesn't mean that's all you can do."

"I wouldn't even know where to begin or how to live a life without the sword."

"You could still teach a class or two in technique, but your gifts would be wasted doing what Cahir does."

"What about Lia? She wanted me to help her with her research on the rwans."

"The University has more of an interest in your experience with the Efferitas."

"Maybe I can work with you and help her a little on the side?"

Jacob smiled broadly and put his hand on my shoulder. "You don't want to overwork yourself. Now let's go find you someplace to live."

My new apartment was in the center of the city and was nowhere near as nice as my student housing had been. It was dusty and old, but comfortable. I settled in happily and then went for a walk to get to know my surrounding better. I should have expected Cahir. He had been waiting for me in my arm chair, sitting with his long legs extended, reading an enormous book.

I dropped my bags and ran to him. We made love with a violent intensity that broke the armchair.

"I didn't think you'd come back," he said, as we lay on the filthy carpet.

"I've been trying for a very long time," I whispered.

"You shouldn't have left," he said as he kissed my neck.

"Such is life," I said coldly.

He rolled over and looked at me, tracing the contours of my body with his finger. "Are you even the girl I fell in love with, or has the world so much altered you?"

"That's a strange question," I said.

He kissed my back. "You seem different."

"I am different, but I've crossed the world over to come back to you. Isn't that enough?" I asked incredulously.

"Clever girl, using such words against me. You are going to be a sociologist now? You and I will be in different worlds."

"How so?"

"I'm a Southerner. I teach the loathed, but necessary, arts of war. I'll always be considered part of the bottom of the food chain. But you? You will ascend to the top of this pile of shit."

"I don't think so. I didn't even know it meant anything to be a sociologist. I just thought they were a bunch of stodgy, old people studying dead cultures. Why would that be a path to power?"

We hadn't moved, but the distance between us had grown exponentially. The passion vanished with a tangible proof. I leaned toward him, reaching out for his hand, searching for something I had lost for no reason

I could understand, but he was cold.

"What have I done?" I pleaded. "I just wanted to be with you."

"You haven't done anything," he said as he leaned forward and kissed me. "I should go. I have a long day in front of me." He kissed me again and left me sitting alone and totally dumbfounded. I had no idea what had just happened between us.

I found my way to Jacob's office. Jacob was rooting through a stack of books on the Efferitas on the floor. Jacob and I spent hours signing up for classes and discussing my future. We laid out a plan for my career at The University. He said I would end up spending some time with the philologists and wildlife biologists, but my primary course of study would be sociology.

Finally, we spent the remainder of the day talking about the Efferitas. It was dark by the time I left and I knew my work had just begun. Jacob and I spent hours poring over the details of the few garments and artifacts I had carried with me.

"Are all cultures treated with such vehement interrogation?" I finally asked. "Or is there something special about the Efferitas?"

Jacob turned away from his computer to face me. "No. The Efferitas are a great mystery to us. They are also the most powerful tribe in the world."

"For years we have survived in a delicate balance. There have always been three tribes which have been the most powerful and pivotal to us. The Notuans send us food and supplies and we give them unlimited access to our libraries and universities. For the last five or six centuries the second pivotal tribe has been the Xenderians and the third was the Hyran. They provide us with food and resources we lack and their military power shields us. Do you understand?"

"I think so."

"The Xenderians were a powerful military complex. No one ever dreamed of invading them. They conquered peoples and subjugated them to their laws and their gods and eventually were able to create more resources, which they shared with us. We trained their people and they provided us with protection and supplies.

"The third tribe was the Hyran. When the Hyran fell, we immediately turned to the Critons, who have come to significant global power, as a replacement source of our manufacturing core. Negotiations commenced and we were hopeful, but when the Xenderians fell, we found ourselves naked."

"In the midst of all of this, the Efferitas have been proliferating, against all reason. They have no technology, no skills. They don't communicate with other tribes. They issue ultimatums, and then, they invade. Every tribe they invade, falls. And then we never hear from them again. Any kind of treaty made with the Efferitas would be the saving grace of The University, and the man who brokered such a treaty, would be guaranteed a position on the high council."

He finished his lecture and studied my face, waiting for a reaction. He spoke like every other professor, with a didactic coolness that made emotion impossible to discern, but I knew he wanted me to react with some kind of emotion. I had none to offer. Everything he had told me, I had already suspected and what I hadn't expected was no surprise.

"Is that all?" I asked.

Jacob laughed. "That's it," he responded.

"I don't know if I can help you. The Efferitas are bound by their way. They don't change. They think technology is a tool of the devil," I said with a shrug.

"I don't expect change to occur overnight. I have time and I have you, which is more than anyone else. I've dedicated my life to the Efferitas and learned less about them then I have in the last month with you."

"There are some things I will never tell you."

"I know. You had a personal relationship with the king. I'm not asking you to violate trust, only to create new trusts."

"There is someone else who could help you," I said hopefully.

"Who?" he said reluctantly. It was as if he didn't believe me.

"When I was a slave, I worked with a Notuan girl, Mia, who had been born and raised as a slave in the palace. She was the concubine of the old king for a time. I know she wants to study at The University. You could bring her here, and we could work together. Maybe, we can find a way to negotiate your treaty," I said with a grin.

"Thank you," he said.

"That's why I'm here."

"Do you still see Cahir?" he asked with something that might have been malice.

"Not recently. Why?" I lied.

"Your relationship may cause problems."

"Why?"

Jacob shrugged despondently. "Why don't you go home? Take some time off. You start classes next week. You'll be busy. We have time."

"Thank you," I said. I left quickly and walked directly to Cahir's apartment. I hadn't really thought about him. I had been so lost in my work that everything had vanished. Suddenly, all I wanted was to see him again, and I began to wonder why he hadn't tried to find me. I wondered if he still cared for me at all.

I found Cahir at home, watching the television. I could never get used to this device. It felt too much like there were strange people in my home. He greeted me coolly, with a brief hug and a nod.

"You haven't called or come to see me," I said.

"Neither have you," he responded.

"I didn't know if you wanted to see me."

"Neither did I."

"Why wouldn't I want to see you? I came here for you!" I exclaimed.

"Did you?" he asked coldly.

"Of course." I wrapped my arms around him.

He melted in my arms. He wrapped his arms around me and gave in to my embrace. His lips found mine, and I ran my hand down his back.

"I did go by your apartment," he said breathlessly. "Three times. You're never there. You're always working."

"I'm sorry. I just would never have been let in if it hadn't been for Jacob and I feel like I owe him something."

We made love again, and I spent the next few days with Cahir. We danced again, like we had before, and we remembered what we had been. When I left to go back to work and study, he kissed me gently and whispered, "I love you."

He had to work too. He had to go back to his days clutching his sword and dancing for those who would never understand the art.

It was hard for me to keep up with time without the seasons. There were no gnawings, no rainy seasons. There was only the perfect still air, subtly fragranced with food and flesh. Time passed, and Mia finally arrived. Jacob found a place for her in my building, and I couldn't have been happier.

I hadn't realized how much time had passed since I left Mia. She had cut her hair short like all Notuan women, and she wore a gray silk wrap. She had also grown round and soft, and that softness somewhat faded her beauty.

"Thank you for this," she said. "They told me I wouldn't be ready to go to The University for years." There was sorrow in her voice.

I took her upstairs and showed her around her new room, which looked exactly like mine except the statue in the corner of her room was of a different god. Mia spent a long time studying the insect-like god in the corner of her room before she sat down in her musty armchair. She had brought several boxes of things with her and a multitude of suitcases covered the floor.

"This place is strange," she said with a sigh.

"I like it," I said. "How was your journey?"

"Not much of a journey really. It only took three hours. We flew," she said. "How did you do it? How did you get me in here?"

"What do you mean?"

"I've been at the lyceum for two years now and all I've heard is that I'm not smart enough to go to The University. The only thing I'll ever be good for is teaching children their letters and numbers. Not that I mind that. I like children. But I never thought I'd see this temple to human greatness."

"But Crian said you would go to The University. Crian said you could do anything you wanted when you got home."

"My mother wants the world for me. She always has, but she isn't always realistic. They treated me like I was special. That's what they called it. I didn't have any real skills or knowledge. I was so grateful when I got the letter from Jacob requesting my help I could have exploded."

We sat for a long time in her apartment, talking and telling stories. I helped her put her things away. She had boxes of pictures and little plants. She had even brought a few chairs and a table. She put a lovely silk blanket over her bed and tapestries on the walls, so that when I left her apartment was as different from mine and she was from me.

Time faded the pain of my prior life. For a long time, when I closed my eyes, I could only see the rwans, their cries, their lost souls. But these images began to disappear and when I slept, I saw friends and studies. I saw dances in the dark in the arms of my silent lover.

I was done with war, all that was left of the storm were my nightly dances with Cahir. The wind in my life was gone, and I grew lost in books. I liked books.

Jacob finished writing his book, and I finished my dissertation. Years of work were finally achieved. I hadn't realized how many secrets there were until I began to finish my work toward my professorship. I had been kept in a happy bubble as a student. But I had to emerge. I had to face the real world.

"You only have a few months left," Jacob said.

"Yes," I answered.

"My department will offer you a position as a full professor. You will be able to afford a better apartment and a better life."

"I'm happy where I am."

"Good. Good," Jacob said. "Because there will be other offers."

"What other offers?" I asked.

"Some other people may offer you work. They'll try to offer you more than us," he said.

Jacob shifted in his seat. He hadn't changed in the years I had known him. He had grown a little heavier and a little richer with the success of our department, but he was still the same cautious and reserved man. He never told me more than he had to.

"Really," I said. "Do you want to tell me in advance who I should be watching for or do you just want them to surprise me? I don't like surprises."

"The philology department. The wildlife biology department. The security department."

"Why the philology department? I can't teach language. I don't really even understand it. I just talk and it comes out."

Jacob met my eyes with an intensity that was uncommon for him. Usually, he tried to diminish the importance of everything. "They've been wanting you for a long time. The only reason I got you is because I'm on the council and I have some political sway. Sociology always wins, but this time, not by much."

"You little shit. Why haven't you told me any of this before? I had a choice. I could have done something else?" I yelled angrily.

"Fifteen years ago, a project was initiated in collaboration between the bioengineering department and the philology department. They designed a bacteria that was supposed to somehow restructure the functioning of the language centers of the brain. You and your brother were both infected with all the other students that year. Nothing happened."

"The project was abandoned until you appeared. Apparently the bacteria only worked on a few Xenderians. They want to study you and create more of you."

"I'm no lab rat!"

"No, you are not."

I sat down in my chair and buried my face in my hands. I had never believed in Xander's god, but I had believed in Xander. I had believed in his magic and his power and I had believed that I was a part of that.

A memory of the storm awakened the violence and rage in me and I stood up, throwing a chair across the room.

"Who am I? What am I?" I screamed and I ran. I ran for the first time in years, and it hurt. All the fat in my body jiggled and my lungs burnt, but I couldn't stop. I ran until I collapsed and then I sat in the dark watching the shadows crawl over my feet.

Mia found me in the dark and lonely night and sat down next to me in the dirt. "Jacob told me what happened," she said.

"All that time we were with Xander," I said. "We were linked by this miracle. He said it was God working through us. I never believed in it, but it was ours."

"There is more to you and Xander than some ability to speak a lot of languages and you know it."

"What if everything else is just some feat of modern science as well?"

"How does that change anything? All that matters is how it's helping people build a better life for themselves. Do you think I care if my salvation came from a lab rat or a god? All that matters is that I'm not a slave."

I put my head on Mia's shoulder. "Thank you."

"Xander and you carried me out of hell. I remember everything. I prayed every day to die and sometimes it still hurts. I don't care what you call it. You are my angel of mercy." Mia was crying.

I leaned over and kissed her cheek.

"It's a terrible world," she whispered. "I thank whatever god or devil fashioned anyone who can save us."

We walked home together holding each other's hands.

Perhaps I was not meant for peace and my attempts to grasp at it were inevitably doomed. As we walked home, several large, low-class looking men emerged from the shadows. One of the larger men punched me in the face before I had time to react.

I had become plump and sated, and I had forgotten what fear was. The blow knocked me to the ground. As I lay there, the men began kicking me in the ribs and each kick awoke the beast that slept in me.

With a quick kick, I leapt to my feet. One of the men grabbed me in some pathetic attempt to restrain me. Through new eyes, I saw the men tearing at Mia's clothes, and I knew they would kill us. For a moment, I just stared.

I grabbed the man's arm and twisted it, snapping it like a dry twig and then I turned and drove my fist through his chest. He screamed like a woman.

I killed him just to shut him up.

The men that were holding Mia froze. Several ran, fading into the shadows like rats or bad dreams. A large, pale man drew a gun and pointed it at my head. I lunged at him as he pulled the trigger and slid beneath the bullet in time to punch him in the groin. He fell on top of me and I jabbed my finger into his subclavian notch, flipped him over, and strangled him.

When it was over, I heard only the slow beating of my heart. The instinct to kill came without thought, like blinking or breathing, but as the moment faded I knew I had made a terrible mistake.

I turned around to find Mia dressing herself behind me. She was calm. It was as if nothing had happened.

"Are you all right?" I whispered.

"No," she said. "Do you have any idea what you have done?"

"What would you have had me do? Let them rape you?"

"No. Do you have to kill everyone you fight? They'll exile you or kill you."

"Quiet," I hissed. "We need to get out of here." I pulled her away from the bloody mess I had left on the sidewalk. I didn't really know where I was running, but I knew I had to get away from the scene of the crime. Finally, we collapsed in another dark alley and sat there in silence.

"It's such a small thing." Mia began to cry.

"What are you blubbering about?" I said.

"I love you," she whispered. "You are my sister. You are my friend. You are all I have. You are my safe place! What will I do without you?"

"What?" I asked in incredulous stupidity.

"Do you have any idea how many times I tried to kill myself? But you always come to save me. You saved me in Efferitas, and you saved me Notua. Who will save me when you are gone?"

"I'm not going anywhere," I said in my most comforting tone.

"But you killed those men!" she yelled.

"They were going to kill us. It was self-defense," I said dismissively.

"No one will believe that. We have no proof. It's their word against ours."

"I should have killed them all," I hissed.

Mia rolled her eyes at me. "No," she said with a hint of mockery. "That would have made it worse."

"I know what to do," I said.

Mia and I walked across the entire University and back that night and our voyage ended where my journey had begun. It ended with Cahir. We stood on Cahir's doorsteps filthy and torn, and he let us in without question. I didn't know how to address Cahir anymore. We never talked. We said vague pleasantries and occasional sweet nothings, but we never really talked, and I think I had forgotten how.

"I'm in trouble," I said as I lowered my eyes. I couldn't meet his eyes and ask for his help. I couldn't tell him what I had done and watch the expression on his face. I didn't want him to know what a savage I really was.

"What happened?" he asked as he studied us.

Mia sensed my apprehension and she spoke for me. "We were in the sidelines, and we were attacked by five men. They were going to kill us. Ailive killed them."

"What were you doing in the sidelines?" Cahir asked calmly.

Mia had no answer. She had only followed me, and my answer sounded stupid and childish. "I was running," I said.

Cahir lifted up my chin so he could see my eyes. "I'm sorry if so much has come between us that you can't even look at me," he said. "I love you. I will always help you."

It was so easy for him. I had been so blind. He was more than I had ever known. He pushed one button and made one call, and it was over. He smiled and took me in his arms. "The bodies will be incinerated and the evidence will disappear."

"How?" I asked. I looked up into his black eyes and began to understand the nature of silence between us.

"I'm on the security council."

Out of the corner of my eye, I saw Mia inching toward the door. "I have to go," she said.

"Stay," I pleaded. But she left me alone with him and what Cahir and I did that night had nothing to do with love.

IX
In the Council of the Gods

I walked into the heart of the city with fear and trepidation. The council building was a feat of engineering, beautiful and vast. It was composed of two spiraling helixes wrapped around a conical core that stretched upward forever. Jacob and I rode in an enormous glass lift into the stratosphere at the top of the council building to meet with the gods of The University.

They sat at the top of the world in a room made of glass. As a professor, I had become qualified to be Jacob's assistant, and he wanted me with him at council, but every fiber of my being wanted to run away.

I was unprepared for the extent of Jacob's verbosity.

"We are at a pivotal point in our history," he began. "Our way of life is changing. The tribeless are everywhere. Raiders kill students on their way to The University. Tribes refuse our services. The biggest factor contributing to our current predicament is the spread of the southern barbarians called the Efferitas. That's what my bill is about."

"The Efferitas now control one third of the inhabitable world. They are the most efficient killing machine we have yet seen. They attack without warning. They come at night. They crawl over city walls with a vastness of numbers and ferocity of attack that leaves cities terrified. People are afraid to fight back and every city they invade, they absorb, increasing their strength and territory. Any army invading them would have to make it through miles of hostile, colonized wasteland to even start an attack on the city."

"Creating an allegiance with the Efferitas is the key to a resolution of our current predicament."

After he was done, the right side of the room exploded with applause. I looked to the left of the room, to the progressive side of the room. Cahir was there, glaring intensely at the podium. The moderator stepped forward and asked if there were any other commentators or rebuttals for the current proposal.

Cahir quickly stepped forward. He looked different. He wore a crisp suit, like everyone else. He stood in front of the podium and took a deep breath. I had no idea what Cahir was going to say.

"The professor would have us believe that his proposal is an easy thing, an easy remedy for a complex problem. He himself said that the contributors to the current dilemma are innumerable. In this aspect alone, he is completely correct. I do not say that there is one solution to the problems of our time, but I do say that there is one remedy for most of the problems of our time. I'm not offering you a solution that may fall apart, that's dependent on the whims of a barbarian king. I'm offering you a solution that's feasible and executable right now."

"The tribeless must be either be forced into some kind of settled tribe that contributes to the economy of the world, or they must be eradicated. How many other tribes have fallen at the hands of tribeless over the last ten years? Five. Over five million people dead or lost because of the growing tribeless population."

"I'm not asking you to vote for violence, I'm asking you to vote against mindless passivism. Do not vote for a proposal that will waste years on futile negotiations with savages. Consider the options. If we signed a treaty with the Critons, they would supply us with students and supplies. In return, we would supply them with military advice and munitions. In one year, working together, the tribeless would be gone, and we could return to our prior way of life."

A small woman next to me stood up. "You are talking about genocide. That's unacceptable."

"No. I'm talking about relocation. The tribeless have become a threat to our entire world. Right now there is a group of almost a million tribeless moving from the deserts of the Efferitas toward The University lead by a religious extremist. That many people could invade even us."

"Don't be ridiculous!" someone said.

"I'm on the security council. We are not invincible. The Xenderians had far better security than us, and they were invaded. They had over ten thousand trained soldiers in their temple. Look, we even have one of them here. She will testify that they were helpless before the hordes."

All eyes turned to me and as I met Cahir's eyes, I realized what I was. Cahir was pointing directly at me. I didn't have to respond. I could have sat there and left Cahir to wallow in his unsubstantiated statement, but I stood up and spoke.

"We were invaded, and my people were destroyed by several bands of unified tribeless," I said. "There is nothing left of my city."

I sat down, but everyone kept looking at me for a long time, as if they were waiting for me to say more. I had nothing else to say. My heart was pounding in my ears, and I was sweating. I didn't hear anything else that was said.

I ran out of the room when the session ended. I didn't even know if Jacob's bill had been passed. I ran back to my office and sat behind all of my books and important looking papers. I sat there in my smooth gray suit, with my hair tied back in a neat knot. I placed my hands on my large mahogany desk and stared out the window at the world below me.

I heard Jacob come in and sit down, but I didn't turn to face him. "You are a tool," he yelled in impotent rage. "You know that. You've let him turn you into a tool. I thought that after years of study and education you would learn to think, but you aren't a thinking creature!"

"Be quiet," I hissed. "You're using me too. Aren't I just a tool to your greatness? At least he loved me before all of this."

"Yes. You've always been a tool, but I had hopes. I wanted more for you. I thought that with enough education you could learn to think for yourself."

"You just want me to believe what you believe," I said dismissively.

"No. I just want you to believe in something. I wanted you to learn to think and believe on your own, to fight for something great, but instead you backed an animal that wants to kill homeless people."

"I told the truth in council," I said passionately. "But I don't support Cahir. I love him. I will always love him, but my brother is tribeless, and I can't support Cahir. I don't entirely support you either."

"We passed the bill," Jacob said angrily. "Will you be going with me? Or will you be staying with him?"

"Jacob, I have always been loyal to you. I've always helped you in any way I could. I told the truth in council. That's all. I stand with you."

"This is important, Ailive. We can't fail. The journey we take decides our entire lives."

"I won't let you down," I promised.

"We must use all means at our disposal to get the king to sign our treaty."

"Of course."

"It'll take a couple months to get things together."

"I'll be with you in all of your preparations."

Jacob put his hand on my shoulder, and I took the long ride home to Cahir. The city lights were dimming. The false moon still slept. I was getting old. I had turned forty and had begun taking the sweet fruity cocktails that all the professors took to stop the chromosomal fraying that contributed to aging. I looked young, but I felt my age profoundly that night.

I arrived at his apartment before he did and sat down on his sofa. I turned on the television. Cahir always watched the news. I was barraged by large glowing men and women speaking coldly about the tragedies of peoples around the world.

Cahir turned off the television and sat down next to me. "I'm sorry," he said.

I put my hand on his leg. "We don't really know each other, you and I. There was no reason for me not to expect that. Perhaps it was my failing, if I had known you, I would have known what to expect."

"It wasn't fair of me to put you on the spot," he said apologetically.

"You were planning on doing that?" I asked indignantly.

"Yes," he answered evenly.

"How old are you, Cahir? How long ago did your tribe die?"

"I'm two hundred thirty-four years old."

"How did you come here? Who are you?" I asked crossly.

He looked at me with his scorching black eyes. "I've been afraid to talk to you for so long. Afraid that if you knew we were enemies, you would leave me. I don't even know where to start. I don't know which path to take to make you love me again."

"We aren't enemies."

"You are with Jacob. You are his creature. He took you from me."

"No. We aren't enemies," I said as I moved toward him. I kissed his face, covering him with my passion. "Jacob and you fight for the same cause. You just fight in different ways. You both want the hard times to end. You want the people of The University to be happy and prosper. You just disagree on the details."

Cahir scoffed. "I think we would even disagree on who the people are. Jacob doesn't believe that anyone but scholars are human. He's an elitist."

"But you still want the same thing. You want this place to be like it was."

He knelt down before me and put his head in my lap. I felt the tears burn in my eyes like a flood, like that moment before birth when your water breaks free. I touched his head. I held him and waited for our storm to end. It was strange to me, to watch a man who had been a pillar of strength lay himself at my feet. Strength is more than hard looks and cold stares, and I knew that Cahir would always be the strongest man I had ever met.

"Tell me," I whispered into his ear.

"Jacob took you from me," he said again. "He told me that the only reason you were here was because you had been cast out by a queen. He said you loved only one man, and it was not me. You loved some king. I wasn't supposed to see you, but I had to."

"I came here for you," I answered fervently.

"He showed me your entry documents. You wrote about the Efferitas' king."

"He was my friend."

"That's not what the papers said."

"Cahir, I wouldn't lie to you," I told him vehemently.

"I've been here at The University for two centuries. I've watched the world change through glass eyes. I've been with women, and they were all the same. The women here are all the same. They read books and talk about politics, art, science. They never shut up. They buy pretty things and paint their faces. You were different. You were like a light in the dark. I had a wife once, and children. They were all killed. I thought I died that day, but you brought me back to life. You're like my other half. I look in your eyes and I see the same storm that built me."

"You had a wife?" I asked.

"A long time ago," he said with a subtle smile. "I can hardly remember what she looked like anymore. She was pretty, small, like you. We had four boys. They were strong boys, good boys."

"What happened to them?"

He shook his head. "I don't talk about it."

"When I was very young, I watched my best friend murdered. She was being tortured, and I turned and ran away because someone told me to run. I left her to die because I was a coward and a fool, because I followed when I should have led. What could you tell me that would be more terrible than that?"

He touched my face. He kissed my cheek. "We were attacked by the Xenderians, by your people. Your people were cruel, but they did not kill my family. They turned our city into an extension of their own, but I couldn't handle it. I said I wouldn't be a slave to another tribe. I fought the tribal elders, and when no one would listen I took my family out of the city walls, to find a better life. It was only a few days. There were over a hundred men in the tribeless band that found us. I fought, but it wasn't enough. What they did to my family was indescribable. I hadn't known humans to be capable of such things."

I did the only the thing I could do. I kissed him. There were no words.

There was nothing for me to say.

"I died there. You were the one who brought me back."

"Yes," I said. "You've always been the only one. There have been no others, ever."

We held each other for a long time. For years, we had each been locked in a coffin of fear created by forces I had not understood. Now the veil had been lifted.

He told me about his voyage to The University, about his wife and children and their deaths. I told him about the Hyran and Hotem. I told him about my brother and the rwans. Love was like a well I thought I could drown in. Being lost in such an emotion was like dying; it left me breathless and trembling and afraid.

"Join us," he said. "I don't want you to leave Jacob. Come sit on the security council with us. It would do the conservatives good to have one of their own on our council, and it would give you a chance to travel and work your way up."

"Jacob wants me to be the ambassador to the Efferitas," I said.

"You can do both," he said. "It'll only mean more money for you. Not that it matters; you'll be elected chief councilor, and you'll still live in that creepy little apartment."

"You don't like that apartment?" I asked dubiously.

"No," he said with a smile. "I hate it. It's a vestige of the old scholars that the conservatives want preserved for posterity. We are a city without gods, and their buildings should be knocked down to create a new world without gods or elites."

"You're an idealist," I said, as I propped my head up on his chest.

"I am," he said.

"What is The Left Hand of Light?"

"Where did you hear that?"

"You mentioned it in council."

"It's a group of mercenaries that help tribes fight the tribeless."

"What tribe are they from?"

"They are from tribes that have been destroyed by the tribeless."

"Then aren't they tribeless?"

"No. Being tribeless is a choice. The tribeless could settle down, build, make themselves into a tribe, but instead they choose to wander, raid, kill. The Left Hand of Light has chosen to fight those forces."

"I like my apartment," I said again, ignoring him.

"I know. You're a sociologist. You like history."

"I just think it's pretty."

"I think you're a little crazy," he teased.

"You have no idea," I responded with a smile. "I'll join your council. You've piqued my curiosity. Also, Jacob said something last night that really made me reconsider my prior...behaviors...I want to try something new."

"What did Jacob say?"

"He said I wasn't capable of thinking for myself. He said I was only a tool."

"He should be careful what he asks for. I have always been terrified of the day you learned to think for yourself. I think the heavens would shudder."

By the time I left for Efferitas, I probably knew more than anyone alive about the subtleties and intricacies of tribal politics, life, and warfare. As Jacob, Mia, and I boarded the well prepared airship to travel to the Efferitas, I felt like I had evolved into an entirely different creature. I wasn't sure how Hotem would react to me. I was a forty-five year old woman. I was a scholar, and my temper had been calmed by years of study and by a realization of the consequences of my actions. The girl I had been was gone. I didn't look much older, the elixir I drank every morning erased all signs of age, but I felt much older than any of those around me.

Travel by airship was very comfortable. The ship had luxurious accommodations that offered us every possible amenity. My suite was huge and filled with all of my books and papers. It would only take us a little more than thirty-six hours to sail through the clouds to the Efferitas' city. I was nervous. My soft bed did nothing to ease my tension or help me sleep any better.

The night before we arrived, Jacob laid out our notebooks one last time. "We need to review the plans again," he said. He was nervous, and he hadn't slept. "So we land in the water at the dock of the royal palace tomorrow at dawn."

"I'll go out first," I said. I had been over the plan so many times I felt like I had done it already. "I'll wear my IA uniform, so I can carry my sword without seeming aggressive, but it will allow me to fight if an armed confrontation is necessary."

"Once contact has been made," Mia said. "Jacob and I will exit the ship, and we will request a meeting with the king, entirely banking on his former fondness for Ailive."

I laughed. "If not, we'll meet with whoever they send."

"Listen," Jacob said very seriously. "We all have to be prepared to do whatever is necessary. The future rides on this treaty. If we have to wait for months to see the king, we will. If we have to beg, we will. I need your promises that you will give everything needed."

"Jacob," I said. "We are tired, and we've made this promise a thousand times. I need to sleep if I'm going to be using my pitiful womanly wiles to seduce a treaty out of people tomorrow. So can we call it a night?"

"Don't do this to me," Jacob said.

"We will do whatever we have to," Mia promised.

"We have to be prepared for the worst," Jacob said. "They could open fire at us. We could be subject to an extended battle before negotiations commence. We all need to be psychologically ready for whatever happens."

I put my hand on Jacob's back. "I'm ready for anything," I said.

None of us slept that night, despite our fatigue. We all lay awake in our beds awaiting the moment that had been fifteen years in the making. Our thoughts ran circles around our heads as we measured all the possible outcomes of our first encounters with the Efferitas. There was so much at stake, and all we could do was wait and think.

We docked without incident, and I stepped out of the ship into the blinding light of the real sun. The real sun was always overwhelming after the fake sun of The University. I shielded my eyes. I drew my sword as a large group of guards encircled me.

I was ready to fight, but when the entire army fell to their knees before me I became completely confused. In my wildest dreams, in our most extreme planning, we had never imagined this. In the end, I asked to see Hotem.

The guards ran to get him.

Jacob and Mia came out, and we all stood around for a while waiting.

"That went well," Jacob muttered.

"Did it?" I answered.

"You must have been more important here than you described," Jacob said.

"No. I really was a slave. I have no idea what's going on."

Mia looked at Jacob and nodded in agreement with me.

Finally, Myhanna came. She looked nothing like she had before. She wore a long, embroidered, white gown, and her hair was wrapped in a white veil. She came to me and knelt before me and then rose to embrace me.

"I never expected you to return to us," she said.

"Myhanna," I said. It was all I could think to say. She looked so different wrapped in white. Her loose white dress was embroidered with rwans and images of the desert. She wore no makeup. She didn't look like a queen.

Jacob stepped forward. "I'm Jacob Yluq," he said in very stiff, uncomfortable Efferitas. "We have come from The University to offer a treaty between our peoples."

Myhanna smiled benevolently at him. "All are welcome here," she said.

Things have changed.

Even the palace grounds had changed. In the middle of courtyard there was an enormous new building. It was strange, and it took me a while to decide how I felt about it. It was built entirely of stone, and it rose above every other building in the city. It crept upward, as if part of the earth. Moss had been planted on the towers and vines covered the stone work. Trees grew from the top of the building and ornate stone statues stood in the artificial arbor on top cathedral. Buried in the stone walls were brilliant, colored glass windows that shone in the morning sun like gemstones.

"You have come to see King Hotem?" Myhanna asked Jacob.

"We are honored to be received by you, my lady," he said with a deep bow. "And would be exalted to meet with his majesty."

Myhanna nodded. "The king is not available at present, but I will review your requests and send word to him."

I can't explain why my heart sunk. I knew that Myhanna would be queen. I knew that we would see her and speak with her. I had no feelings for Hotem but friendship, but I hadn't known how excited I had been to see Hotem again until I realized that I may not see him at all.

It was almost more than I could bear.

The palace walls had been hung with large tapestries of Xander preaching in the desert. There were infinite tapestries of the Jason. They were everywhere, done in a strange symmetric style that made him more dazzling and more horrific. And as we approached Myhanna's audience room, there was a large tapestry of me. I felt dizzy. What the hell was going on? The girl in the tapestry was me, but was not me. She was a tiny, pale, pixie-like thing wrapped in long, intricate red robes. Her long, silver hair was blowing in the wind. She had a sword in each hand, and the dead lay at her feet. She was beautiful and serene and a halo hung high over her head.

Myhanna saw me staring at the tapestry and said, "It is of you saving the Hyran."

"I think I was wearing some sort of filthy, gray tunic the day I saved the Hyran," I said bitterly.

As we entered the queen's chamber, we were surrounded by priestesses in long white robes. "You converted the entire city?" I asked in disbelief.

"No. It wasn't that easy," Myhanna said. "Hotem received me and listened to me. Hotem was always an idealist, and he liked what I told him about what Xander preached. He invited Xander to the city. Xander came with his army of Caeimoni, and they spread throughout the city. The

Caeimoni stayed here for four years. Xander is a commanding speaker and all who heard him were easily swayed. The nobles thought that much of what he said was similar to our way and many embraced this new God.

"Three years ago Hotem declared Caeimoni to be the official religion of the Efferitas. Construction was almost complete on the temple and churches had formed all over the city. That same day, Hotem said that God had sent him a vision and that the slaves would be freed. Now the priests and priestesses work to help the poor and education is improving. We have built a number of schools. We have also sent missionaries to all of the colonies to convert them."

I shook my head. "Where's Xander now?" I asked.

"He's heading north," she said. "God spoke to him and told him he must go speak to those in the northern cities."

"The northern tribes won't have it," I said. "They are old tribes; most of them have given up organized religion. They believe in technology, and they fear the tribeless. Xander will seem like just another tribeless mad-man to them."

"No. God has told him that the fight for the world will be won in the north," Myhanna said.

"God told him this?" I asked sarcastically.

"God never lies," Myhanna said.

Jacob stepped forward, interrupting me. "My lady," he said. "We are overjoyed that your society has had this great epiphany, and we hope that we can help lead you down the path of higher learning. A moment ago, I heard you speaking of schools and improved education. We have come from The University, the heart of learning, with a treaty which, if you sign it, will offer you a multitude of the most brilliant teachers in the world."

"You want to send us teachers?" Myhanna asked.

"Yes, we do. We want to send you teachers and books and we want to help you build schools and improve the education of your people."

"What do you want in return?" she asked cautiously.

"We want to work with you to make a better world," Jacob said.

"How would we help you accomplish that?"

"You would help supply our people with food and manufactured goods."

She smiled. "I'll read your treaty, and we will discuss it tomorrow. But before you leave, I will say one thing. We'll not sign a treaty with any people or group who will not let us send missionaries to their people."

"The University doesn't support any organized religion or tribal affiliation within its walls. We could never allow your priests or priestesses to preach in our walls."

"We'll take your teachers only if you take our priests. Think on it and we will discuss the rest after I have read the treaty. Do you need lodging tonight?"

"No. We'll stay on our ship," Jacob responded coolly.

"Ailive, will you do us the honor of staying with us tonight? It would be a great honor for us."

"I don't think I can. I need to discuss things with Jacob."

"Of course, but it would be an inspirational for my people to have one of the saints in their church. We have not been in the presence of a living saint since Xander's departure."

"A what? What am I?" I asked irritably.

"You are the patron saint of the storm," she said with reverence.

"What? What does that mean?" I asked in bewilderment.

Jacob leaned over and whispered in my ear. "May I speak with you for a minute?"

Jacob excused us very diplomatically and pulled me into the hall where we stood beneath the giant tapestry of me that was not me and whispered in the shadows. "You should do this," Jacob whispered.

"Do what? Let myself be worshipped like some kind of god? I don't think that would be right."

"We need this. You know how important this is. You know what is at stake. The council will never accept their missionaries in The University. We need to offer them something else."

"Jacob. Jacob. I can't do this. It isn't right," I said desperately.

"Be their saint. Be their goddess. How can they say no to a request from a goddess?"

"You are a duplicitous son of bitch," I said indignantly.

"Sometimes you have to sacrifice what you believe in for the greater good. The progressives will win the vote if we don't make this happen. The council will sign a treaty that will lead to the eradication of the tribeless. Do you want to see that happen? We need to do anything at our disposal to make this treaty work, even if that means you pretending to be God himself."

I nodded, and we returned to Myhanna's chamber. I had to spend the night with the crazy Caeimoni and Hotem's wife. I would have rather gone back to Jason and let the rwan's devour my soul in their desperate hunger.

Mia took my hand in hers when we walked into the room. She kissed my cheek and whispered, "I'm sorry."

I had never been so grateful for Mia in my life. She alone saw how hard it was for me to spend the night in that place.

Mia whispered to me with such sweet breath, "None of this matters," she said. "We are slaves and dust. If you need to, run away and I will follow you."

"I'll stay," I said to Mia.

Mia and Jacob left quietly. They returned to the safe world within the airship to eat dinner and take baths and read books and discuss the treaty with the other professors that had traveled with us. They went back to the normal world, where everything could be calculated and logic made balance.

Myhanna smiled at me with her goddess-like grin and put her arm around me carrying me away to a world of faith and fire where the mind was devoured by unanswerable questions and brutal passions.

She and I walked across the palace grounds together. The gardens were the same, sublimely manicured. The slaves were gone, but there were still armies of servants. They fluttered about taking care of their wealthy masters.

The courtyard was filled with men and women clad in white, but it wasn't until we reached the temple that the Caeimoni engulfed me, falling to their knees and touching my feet. I cringed. I pulled away, but then I looked out at the people around me. I looked into what was actually a small crowd of devoted followers, and I saw the faces of the slaves I had worked with in the kitchens. I saw the face of my little friend. I stopped walking. I stopped cringing. I looked at the face of that girl. She was pretty and smiling. She glowed in the shadow of that cathedral. I reached out to her, and she took my hand.

"Hannah," I said. "Do you remember me?"

"My lady?" she said in awe.

"Do you remember me? You used to help me in the kitchens. We were slaves."

She smiled more deeply and she stood up. "How could I forget you? How could any of us forget you? You saved me."

"You were my friend. What I did was nothing."

"What you did gave us all hope when we had nothing to hope for."

"Are you happy now? Is this better?"

She nodded. "My mother has a little house now, not much, but it's hers, and my brother cooks in a restaurant. We aren't rich, but we are free and our lives are our own."

"Come with me," I said. "Show me your temple."

So Hannah took my hand and gave me the tour of the great Cathedral. It was the first and would be the greatest church ever built for the Caeimoni. It took us over an hour to walk through it. Myhanna just walked with us, but Hannah told me its history. She told me about Xander and about Hotem.

She told me about the people I loved like they were gods or angels and I smiled and looked at the enormous statues of the gods I knew and had walked with, had danced with, had loved. I sat through the prayers and the strange rituals. I lit candles at my brother's feet and listened to people call Myhanna, Popess. No one called her Myhanna. No one called her queen. She was the Popess.

Hannah left. She went home to the monastery where the priests and priestesses slept in soft white beds under stained glass windows, to pray and eat white bread and drink water and dream of a god of perpetual love.

Myhanna walked me into one of the main royal chambers where I was undressed by four quiet servants and fed the finest food. The chamber looked like the one Hotem and I used to spend our nights together again.

I smiled and let myself be consumed by warm memories. I fell asleep dreaming of my youth, and I woke up to Hotem's face.

I don't think he meant to wake me, but I had walked the way of the storm for too long to sleep through his footsteps. I opened my eyes just enough to see his shadow standing over me. I watched him watching me for a long time and finally I said his name.

"I didn't think you had the time to receive ambassadors," I whispered from the edge of a dream. I opened my eyes fully and looked at him. It was dark and very late at night. He was much older. He had lines around his eyes and around his forehead. A long scar cut jaggedly down his cheek.

"Myhanna sent word that you were here," he said.

"The Popess didn't make it seem like we were important enough for you."

"I'm sorry. I shouldn't have come into your room like this. I just didn't believe it. I had to see you with my own eyes. You haven't aged a day. You look the same."

"Don't seem so amazed. It's no miracle. Some of the doctors at The University designed a serum which prevents aging."

"I've spent many years wondering what happened to you. I tried to see you fighting some great war to free the tribeless in my mind." He sat down.

"I don't fight much anymore," I said.

"So I see."

I leaned over and pulled him to me. I hugged him like a daughter who had found her lost parents. "I'll get you dirty," he said.

"Please," I said. "Don't let Myhanna convince you I'm a goddess. I'm still Ailive. We've gotten dirty together before. What are you doing here? Won't Myhanna get mad?"

"I'm still king. Things have changed here. Myhanna's strength increases every day, but I'm still king, and my word is still law." I touched the scar on his cheek. Age suited him. It cut away the boyish softness of his youth and gave him a wisdom that made him handsome. He looked like a king. "Things have changed here more than I expected," I said.

"Myhanna and her prophet did that. I had little to do with it."

"You haven't converted?"

"No. I made my kingdom Caeimoni because it suited my purposes. I wanted to free the slaves. I wanted to educate and serve the poor. Your brother's religion advocated all the things I wanted."

"I was afraid you would be as crazy as Xander. I'm so glad to find you as you were."

He laughed. "You're a saint, you know?"

"I know. How did that happen?"

"You're a legend. You saved your people, and God sent the wind to speed your sword. You killed an entire army, alone. You saved the Hyran with only the word of God to protect you. You walk with the rwan. You speak in tongues and now, I will be hearing that you are immortal and un-aging."

I shrugged. "My supervisor would have me use this legend to forge a treaty with you."

"Is that really why you are here?"

"Yes," I whispered.

"I was hoping you were here for me," he said softly.

"How could I be? You have your queen," I said woefully.

"I have never had a queen."

"Myhanna."

"Myhanna is the Popess. She's celibate."

"I thought that you were married."

"No. I'm a priest king. I'm celibate as well." At that he smiled a little. "At least in title."

I wanted to cry. In a moment of weakness, I reached out to him. I let my hand settle on his leg and leaned in toward him, feeling the warmth of his breath on my lips. He leaned into me, his chest hot against mine. His heart pounded against my chest. My breath was caught in my lungs, and I closed my eyes trying to shut out the rush of emotion that flooded over me. I had missed him so much it hurt and seeing him again reminded me of everything I tried to push down and pretend I didn't feel. I felt his hand on the back of my head, pulling me closer.

Our lips touched, for a whisper of a moment, and I longed for more.

I pulled back, remembering who I was, remembering Cahir and what I had to do.

For a long time, he and I sat hypnotized by what might have been. He was still holding my hand and his pulse against my palm. His breath echoed in the stillness. My cheeks burned crimson red and I couldn't take my eyes from his. I wanted to lean forward and kiss him again, but I couldn't.

"I'm sorry," I whispered, and he let go of my hand.

"Why are you here?" he asked coldly.

"I'm a professor now," I said finally. "We are here to try to negotiate a treaty with you. I'm not going to insult you with diplomacy or art; we're desperate. The University is collapsing and if you do not sign this treaty, the University may fall. Its people will starve and the light of knowledge in the world will fade like a dying star."

Hotem stood up. I saw the tears in his eyes from where I sat. He shook his head and moved into the shadows. "Myhanna won't have it. She won't condone any action that will not further the spread of the Caeimoni faith."

"You are king; surely you can do something?"

"No. We have all converted, and we must follow this new God's law now."

He disappeared. We didn't see him again during our trip. I went to the morning prayer service with Myhanna and then we began negotiations. It was useless. There was nothing that would change Myhanna's mind. It didn't matter that I was a saint. Our attempts at forging an alliance with the Efferitas were futile, and we went home empty handed.

I told Jacob most of what happened and the only thing Jacob said was, "You should have fucked the king. He would have helped us if you had fucked him."

X
The Left Hand of Light

Councilman Grieg must have been more than five hundred years old. Even with daily doses of the serum, he looked like an animated corpse. "Councilman Yluq has been wasting our precious time," he said in an ominous voice. "We gave him two years, and he came back with nothing. Meanwhile, we have had to force over ten thousand citizens to immigrate to the lunar colonies. Councilman Yluq has brought about our downfall!"

Cahir stood up. "There's no point in making accusations. What's done is done. We must react to this by looking to the only answer to our problem. Everywhere you look the tribeless are growing in number. Tribe after tribe is falling, adding to the increasing numbers of hungry, desolate wanderers. We must form an alliance with the Criton. We must force the tribeless to relocate or disappear."

Jacob stood up. He overcame his shame and willed himself to move. "We can't do this," he said. "The University has stood for millennia. It was born on a simple premise, written into our constitution. We are not of this world. We do not involve ourselves in the wars outside these walls. This is why we have endured. My failure is my own, but do not strip our great estate of her glory because one man failed you."

Jacob walked down to floor. He stood in front of everyone and made his one final plea. I watched, transfixed by his passion and his love. He spoke with utter vehemence. His voice grew loud and his hands shook as they gripped the podium. "What are the tribeless? We keep talking about them like they are disease. They are terrorists. They are raiders. But they are none of these things. There are tribeless terrorists and tribeless raiders, but to destroy an entire people because of the folly of a few of their numbers is nonsense."

Jacob stepped out from behind the podium and looked around the room. "The tribeless used to be our brothers and our sisters. They used to be our allies, and now that they have fallen, we discard them like old paper. Who is this preacher? Everyone is speaking of him like he portends the end of the world, but did you know he studied here? He spent eight years here training to be a doctor. He earned the highest marks in his class. He was a Xenderian. He was our ally. His sister sits beside me every day. The only thing that divides the tribeless from the rest of us is one war, one battle, one night."

Cahir attacked like a savage dog. "Tribelessness is a choice!" he yelled. "Everyday groups of people, destroyed by wars, band together to try to form new cities, new tribes, new lives. The tribeless make this impossible. They prey on the weak and the small, and this preacher is the worst of them. He picks up the lost and convinces them that God has told him to unfold the very pillars of society. What happens when he gets here?" Cahir raised his hands to emphasize his point. His fingers spread as his voice reached a crescendo, and I knew we had lost.

That long council session marked our demise. I looked over and saw Jacob practically hiding in his chair. He would lose his position on the council during the next election.

I walked home with him and he said very little. What was to be said? I knew he blamed me. "I think it's time for you to find a new position," he said as I walked away.

"What?" I asked.

"You have a stack of offers. You can find another place. There's nothing left for you to do here. It's time for you to move on, Ailive."

"Jacob," I said, placing my hand on his arm. "I've always been with you. I'll stay with you until the end. I believe in you."

Jacob offered me a hint of a smile. "We are disgraced. Tomorrow, my department will be stripped of all of its resources, and I will become a glorified librarian waiting for his council term to expire. Why don't you go with your lover? There is power there."

"I've never wanted power. You know that. I want to stay with you and Mia."

Jacob only shook his head. "I'll have to give up most of my staff as well. Wouldn't you rather resign than have me fire Mia?"

"I'll go, but if you ever need me. You have a friend in me, always," I said.

Jacob hugged me in an uncharacteristically friendly gesture. "Good luck, old friend. May you find peace."

"Peace with you too," I said as we parted. I took the long way home. I wandered through the dark parts of the city. I watched children run over the dark streets and into their tiny apartments and wondered at what life lived inside the walls of the city. When I got home, I lay at the feet of my apartment's god and said a silent prayer to whatever powers there were to protect Jacob from the world.

So time passed, and there was a subtle shift in power. I went on more and more missions for the IA. Our work became less secretive and was hailed as work for a better tomorrow. What we had always done suddenly became public and legal. The IA was the same; it only seemed new to the world outside. We were mostly fighting to save tiny tribes from oblivion. Cahir and I were fighting for a future Jacob had lacked the insight to see.

The gnawing had just begun when Cahir and I went alone to the Criton city to help resolve an internal conflict in the west of their city.

We didn't discuss what the conflict was or how we would resolve it. We rarely did. Sulen just told us to help them.

Cahir and I traveled by airship and arrived at the gates of the city under the cover of night. I recognized the city and its location immediately. I had killed several soldiers on the coast not too far from the city. We were escorted into the sleeping city by several black clad guards and taken to the heart of the city where a small cluster of armed men slept in the burnt ruins of a large shopping area.

The men rallied when they saw us. They stood up and more men and women crept out of hiding places in the shadows to follow us. Their leader, he called himself the general, looked tired. His face was blackened with dirt and sweat. Cahir kneeled before the man, and I followed Cahir's lead.

Cahir spoke perfect Criton. "How may we be of service, sir?" he said.

The general snorted and stared vacantly at the rubble beyond the barricades. "It should be obvious," he said bitterly.

Cahir stood up, looming over the general. "I like clarity, and we aren't good with assumptions, so why don't you explain it to me."

"You want clarity?" the general asked bitterly and lit his pipe. "A group of our people rebelled several weeks ago. The rebellion was put down quickly, and martial law was declared, but the citizens revolted, demanding satisfaction for what they called military atrocities."

The general exhaled and the smoke from his pipe curled up in front of his eyes. "Half the military went to the other side, and we were able to hire a few members of the Left Hand of Light to help us, but things have been going downhill. We have more and more deserters every night. Our president has been in an underground bunker for weeks. We have all out anarchy here, and it was all started by a group of filthy tribeless." He spat on the ground as he said tribeless.

"How did tribeless start this?" I asked.

"Some fuckin' preacher came through this way. We had over a hundred people leave to follow the crazy man, but that wasn't the problem. The ones that stayed behind started trying to convert the entire city. We had to put them down. It's been chaos ever since then."

"What do you need from us?" Cahir asked.

"I was hoping you would help us negotiate with their leader. The Left Hand of Light says you are the best negotiators."

"When you say negotiate, what, exactly do you mean by that?" Cahir asked. "Off the record."

"I mean, if you could help us kill the bastards it would be wonderful."

"We can do that, but I want to clarify our situation here. We don't usually help negotiate internal conflicts. We help those that are under direct assault. Civil war is a sticky business, and right and wrong is not always as clear as it could be. If we help you reestablish order in your city, we expect your future support of The University."

The general snorted and looked out into the darkness on the other side of the barricade. "We're all on the same side here. We'll support you, and we can work together to go after the bastards that started this. We've all had hard times. Working together will benefit us all."

"Do you want us to kill them all? Or are there some you want to save? What do you want us to ask for once we begin negotiations?"

"What the hell do you think? We want those crazies out there dead. All of them." He pointed violently to the shadows behind a large barricade. "You can try to save those that put down their weapons. But we won't mourn the dead."

"It doesn't sound like they are going to put down their weapons," I said.

"Well they bloody well have to!" the general screeched.

I shrugged and looked at Cahir. I didn't care about the fate of crazy generals or those who followed them. I would have turned around and went right back to The University. As far as I was concerned, this battle had nothing to do with us. "We should go," I whispered into Cahir's ear.

"No," he hissed. He turned toward the general again and said, "Is the Left Hand of Light still here?"

"Yes," he said and pointed to a small room in the distance. "They wanted to see you."

"We'll be back to talk with you again later," Cahir said politely. He dragged me into the dark, toward the small band of mercenaries he so respected.

"What the hell?" I yelled. "This is none of our business, Cahir, and there is nothing we can do here. I know The University is seeking an alliance with these people, but we can't take sides in a civil war. This has nothing to do with us."

"If the Criton fall because of the influence of the tribeless, this will be the third major tribe to fall in the last century. There will be more tribeless than citizens. We have to resolve this situation!" Cahir bellowed.

"We can't support this man. He's clearly crazy. For all we know the people on the other side of that barricade are nothing but a bunch of women and children."

"It doesn't matter. We have to draw a line, and this is that line."

"A line for what? What do you think we are fighting here?" I argued.

"We are fighting the preacher and his influence. We are fighting the spread of a belief system that undermines the whole of society. We are fighting for the survival of the world as we know it."

"Oh please, don't get lofty on me. I'm not the council," I said indignantly.

"Then we are fighting to support our new allies and the biggest source of uranium on the west coast."

"Cahir," I said softly, in an attempt to subdue the escalating fight. "I don't like this place. There's something bad here."

"What does that mean? What does bad mean?" he yelled.

"I don't know. I just don't feel like we should stay here," I said in a whisper.

"I'm not backing out of one of the most important negotiations of my life because you have a feeling. Just keep your mouth shut."

The Left Hand of Light was the most polished groups of assassins I had ever seen. They all wore black Kevlar armor beneath their light black robes. Even at rest, they sat with their swords at their backs and their guns at their sides. Every man in that room looked up at me with remorseless, cold eyes, eyes that were attentive and constantly alert.

They were the eyes of predators. It was like walking back into the karash. These men were born to kill.

The Cahir of my youth died in that room. The man who had lay in bed with me talking about the art of the storm and the beauty of the dance with soft words and subtle caresses faded away as he joined that group of reptilian carnivores. His cause was turning him into everything I had hated about Xender.

"Ailive!" A voice from behind me woke me from my trance, and I turned to face the risen dead.

"Machovi," I said with a subtle smile. "I thought the tribeless must have taken you."

My father embraced me. "It'll take more than a few tribeless to kill me," he said. He looked old and worn. His face was wrinkled and scarred, and his blue eyes shone out at me with untold rage.

"Did you find what you were chasing?" I asked. I knew he hadn't, but I didn't know what else to say.

"I hunted down one traitor and killed him, but it was that bitch Ieya who did most of the damage. She's with that fuckin' preacher."

"Yes. I saw her. She doesn't talk anymore," I said gently.

"You've been inside the camp?" he said with a cruel smile.

I nodded.

"We'll have to talk. After we've cleaned up this mess, we have our sights set on that rabble."

"Rabble? Those are our people."

"Ailive, I brought you up to be smarter than that. They stopped being our people the moment they became tribeless."

"Those are our people. You should be fighting for them," I cried.

"Like you did, pretty warrior? From where I stand, you abandoned them just as much as I did. You're here with us, aren't you?"

I sat down as far away from Machovi as possible. We glared at each other as Cahir and the other members of the Light talked. I stopped listening. I didn't really care. So there would be a tribeless revolution. Maybe that would suit The University better than the current situation.

I excused myself and walked back into the crumbling ruins of the city. I wandered past the guards and crept quietly through the rubble over the barricades. I wanted to see what I was fighting with my own eyes. I wanted to see what had inspired such loathing and disgust. I wandered just far enough to see what the general had done to inspire rebellion.

All my life I had known war, but I had never seen anything like what I saw there. All around me were mountains of bodies that were half burnt. There were women and babies and men all piled up and burnt alive. The mountains of dead were so tall I couldn't even begin to imagine how many had been killed. The very ground I walked on was thick with the ashes of the dead.

I covered my mouth and nose to escape the repugnant odor of burnt and rotting flesh. I moved passed the mountain and saw women, laid out with swords shoved into their genitals and men mutilated beyond the recognition of humanity. I saw pregnant women that had their babies ripped from their wombs. I, who had killed many, bent over and retched on the blood-soaked pavement.

I sat there, bunched up, for a very long time. I stood up and was profoundly aware of the breeze on my back. It was a real wind, and above me there were real stars. There was no artificial atmosphere to shelter me from heaven's wrath. Heat lightning danced in the distance. The humidity was so thick I could taste it, and the black clouds danced with light on the horizon.

I turned around and saw a little girl digging through the bodies. I grabbed her and pulled her away from that terrible visage of human accomplishment. "What are you doing here?" I yelled.

"I can't find my mother," she said. Her voice was calm. Her face was clean. She had survived.

"What happened here?" I asked.

"The soldiers came and killed all the Caeimoni," she said.

"The soldiers did this? Your government did this?" I asked stupidly.

"The general didn't want us to pray," the girl said.

"He did this to stop you from praying?" I asked with hysterical rage. The anger felt like the heat lightning I had seen on the horizon. It lit up and painted me with fury.

The little girl only nodded before she kicked me and disappeared under the mountain of wasted flesh. The blood beneath my flesh began to tingle. The wind swept through the city picking up particles of dust that stuck to my face and flesh.

Somewhere in the distance, the thunder roared closer.

I walked back slowly and sat on the edge of the soldiers' stronghold, staring down at them like a rwan stalking its prey. The storm was coming. All the thought and reason that had bound me for so long drifted away like the smoke from a dead fire.

Some sins deserved vengeance.

It was Mavicho that woke me from my stupor. He placed his hand on my shoulder and pulled me away from the rest of the group. I followed him, because I was curious and because he had been my father.

"You have done well for yourself," he said.

"Yes," I responded.

"You haven't aged a day. You're just as pretty as when I last saw you, fighting for your life at Zender's feet."

"What do you want?"

He leaned over and kissed me. He kissed me in a way that left no ambiguity as to what he wanted. I laughed. My laughter mingled with tears as I slapped him. He only smiled. "Little girl," he whispered. "I watched you grow up. I watched you change from an angry girl into a brutal monster. I made you what you are. You owe me." He put his hand on my breast and pushed me down on the ground.

"Did you do that?" I asked as he rooted around beneath my clothes. "Did you make that pile of bodies out there?"

"I killed those that needed to die. That's what we taught you to do. That's what you always did. Don't act like you haven't killed babies." He pulled my shirt off and for a moment I lay there, letting him do what he wanted.

I felt the cold rain on my face and remembered the long line of atrocities I had committed because someone had told me to. I had never done anything like what I had just seen.

I saw red like Jason. Red like all the rwans. I snapped my father's neck like a chicken's and descended on the rest of the camp like I was the storm.

I saw nothing. I felt nothing, only blood and flesh and bone and tearing. There was nothing else. Nothing else mattered.

"Ailive!" Cahir's voice sounded so distant.

"Ailive, stop!" I turned and saw him, covered in mud and screaming my name. He looked desperate. I stopped, and the red faded. I stood up and dropped the heart that I had just torn from some poor boy's chest.

"What have you done?" he screamed.

I looked up at the clouds above me and let the rain pour over me. I became suddenly aware that I was naked, that Machovi had taken my clothes off before I had killed him. I looked down at my body covered in blood and mud. My hair was matted and all around me were the torn and tattered bodies of the men that had awoken me from my slumber.

I had killed them with my hands. I had left my sword behind with my clothes.

Cahir hit me. I couldn't even feel the pain. I couldn't feel anything. "What have you done!" he screamed again. "Why? What were you thinking?"

I laughed. "They deserved to die."

"Who are you to decide that?"

"I'm the twilight saint. I'm the saint of shadow and vengeance."

"What the hell does that mean?"

"I walk the way of the storm. You taught me that. I listen to the wind and follow it without loyalty to tribe or ideology. You don't walk the way of the storm. You've given it up for politics and power."

"You're crazy!"

"No. I've finally woken up. Just beyond that barricade lie the bodies of at least five hundred thousand people tortured to death by those you would have The University support. And support for what? A little bit of grain? A little bit of stability? I say let it all fall down, because nothing is worth that."

"What are they? Who are they over that hill? What is so terrible? We are talking about the fate of The University. It is the only stronghold of knowledge in a cruel and barbaric world and you would sacrifice that for a handful of people. It's worth everything."

"Cahir, I know you. You've spent years hiding from me and pretending to be different, but I know you. You're a father who is still seeking vengeance for his lost family. You want to kill the tribeless because you think they killed your family. But the people that killed your family died two hundred years ago. They are nothing but dust and bones, and killing these people will accomplish nothing."

"We are going to have to answer for this when we return."

"You didn't have anything to do with this," I said softly. "I did it."

Cahir shook his head and handed me a jacket. "You're shivering. We should get out of the rain."

I wrapped myself in his jacket, feeling suddenly very vulnerable. "You didn't do this," I said again.

"I didn't stop you."

"Why didn't you?"

Cahir walked me to shelter, and I followed him. He took me inside and washed the blood off of me. He found me clothes, and I put on the garb of the Left Hand of Light. "Why didn't you stop me?" I asked again. The rain outside stopped, and sunlight filtered in through the broken glass.

"You're right. I don't walk the way of the storm, and most of the time I know I shouldn't. You are the storm for me. You always have been. In all my life, I have never met another to rival me, but you are a master. I wanted to see how far you could go."

I leaned into the warmth of his embrace and wept. He kissed my tears away, and we made love on the clothes of dead men. It was brief and desperate. When it was over, he held me so tight I could hardly breathe.

"We should go," I said. "The general's enemies will realize that the soldiers are dead soon. We should go before they find us."

We slid out of the city quietly, leaving no footprints behind. We made it to the airship and got in with no idea where to go. "What now?" I asked.

"I'm going to the Left Hand of Light, and then I'm going to return to The University," he said. "I'm going to organize support and argue to gain backing for my original plan. I'm going to raise an army. This has to stop. These people have to be stopped. The tribeless are turning our world into nothing."

I shook my head. "Please don't. You aren't one of them. You aren't one of the Light. You're an artist, not a monster. You're a scholar. You're a professor. Stay with me. We'll find a place."

"I have to see this through. I have to end this. The world can't live like this anymore, constantly teetering on the edge of oblivion. The violence has to end."

"Why is it that men like you always say that the only way to stop the violence is with more violence? Only war can bring peace. I've heard that crap all my life. If we want to preserve freedom, all we have to do is kill these people. It's a lie."

"No. You're just reciting Jacob's nonsense. Order is required for peace, and the lawless must either conform and be relocated and settle down or they must be wiped away. If this doesn't happen, there will never be order, and there will never be peace."

"You're wrong."

"Don't be Jacob's puppet. He's let you go."

"I'm speaking now, not Jacob. I won't be anyone's puppet again. I have my own path to travel, and I've rested too long."

"Where are you going to go? You just killed the tribe we needed most. The University won't have you back."

"Back to my people. Back to Xander."

Cahir scoffed. "If you go out there with that crazy preacher surrounded by nothing but babies and flowers, you'll die."

I smiled. "No. I think I may find rebirth."

"Come with me," he said.

"I think our paths diverge here." I leaned over and kissed him. His scent was so familiar. It was the smell of comfort and warmth. It was the smell of years of happiness in a world of peace and prosperity. A world without storms or hunger. I missed it before I had even left it, before our lips had even parted. He reached out and grabbed my hand, holding me so tightly I thought I might lose circulation.

"Don't go," he said again.

"What choice do I have? I can't go with you to hunt down and kill my own brother. I can't follow you to join people that would do what I saw done in there." I pointed violently back at the city.

"They aren't all like that. That was a mistake. Sometimes men lose control. It was a mistake. I promise you it won't be like that."

"What about Xander? What about the prophet? What will you do to him?"

Cahir grabbed my arm and looked at me in the eyes. He was begging. "I love you," he said.

"What about Xander?"

"Ailive, this has to end. All of this has to end. There has to be some order, some law in the world."

"You're going to hunt him down and kill him?"

"Come back with me."

"I've actually helped you, haven't I? Now you can go back to the council and re-propose your solution to tribelessness, and they'll listen. You'll point here and say, 'look what the prophet's followers caused.'"

I stopped for a moment and looked back at the smoldering city. "Don't do this," I said. "I'll go back with you. I'll face charges for this. Just let this vision of yours go, and we can go back and everything can be like it was."

He shook his head. "I can't let go," he said. "I can't just walk away. This is too important."

He leaned toward me putting his head against mine, smashing his body against me. His pulse raced beneath his clothes. His tears were salty on my tongue. "Please," he whispered. "Stand behind me. You and I could change the world."

"No," I whispered. All I wanted was him. All I wanted was to go back with him and live my life in quiet.

"You wouldn't have to face charges for this. It was the prophet's followers that did this."

"That's a lie," I could barely hear myself.

"The truth is relative."

"I can't do this." My heart burned in my chest.

"I love you," he said again.

For a moment, I hesitated. I leaned into him. I let his warmth pass through me. I thought about just staying on the airship with him and going home. I conjured images of my dark apartment with its strange gods and my soft bed. Mia was waiting for me, but the images vanished with one thought, Xander.

One last kiss. One last taste of what I had crossed the world to find, and he left me alone, in the dust, listening to the roar of his mechanical bird soaring above me. He left me with nothing but my sword and a dead man's clothes.

XI
The Great War

Xander sat in a great white tent. It was raining, but that didn't stop his followers. Thousands sat around him, entranced with his every word. He looked up and saw me in the crowd, and his monologue stopped. He smiled and stood up. Everyone watched him with anticipation.

"I think that's enough for tonight," he said and he walked down out of his tent to meet me. "You're back," he said, and he threw his arms around me.

"I'm back," I said. He hugged me again, and I put my head on his shoulder. I fell into his embrace like a broken doll.

"It's all right," he said as he stroked my hair. "It's all right." I wrapped my arms around him and wept. I sobbed, and he pulled me through the crowd into his the tent that he slept in. We sat together, and he held me while I wept. He didn't say anything, and I didn't have to tell him anything. It was as if he just knew. He knew my suffering before I even entered the camp. He didn't have to do anything. He just held me.

"I don't want to do this anymore," I wept.

"Do what?" he asked.

"I just want peace. I want to be loved. I don't want to fight or change the world. I just want it all to go away."

"I want that too. That's what we all want, but what can we do? We are slaves to God's will. It's not our place to fight his will, and he has not sent me to bring peace, but rather division."

"I don't believe in God."

"It doesn't matter. You are still a slave to his will, and you aren't meant to have peace."

"I hate you," I said. I pulled away from him and wiped the tears from my face.

"You hate what you have lost because of me. You hate what you know you must do, but you don't hate me."

"How could I hate you?" I said. "I'm here now. What should I do?"

"Salome will take you to your tent, and you should rest."

I nodded. "Xander, I have a tent here?"

"We've always kept a place for you."

"You knew I would come back?"

"Of course."

The camp had swelled like a woman pregnant with twins. It was composed of moveable houses and airships and every other form of traveling housing known to man. Walking into the camp was like walking into a tribe of infinite tongue and texture. Every culture ever studied in The University was present there, spread out under the lush canopy at the center of the great continent.

Salome pulled me through the throngs of people to a tent not too far from Xander's. She pulled back the red flap and showed me inside. The tent was small, but warm. There was a small cot with warm blankets and a heater at the foot of the bed. There was an old red chair with a table beside it. I sat down and looked up at Salome with tear-soaked eyes.

Salome went to the bed and laid fresh clothes out for. "There is a fountain for washing behind your tent in the woods. You should bathe."

I stared at her blankly. She disappeared and reappeared after a few moments with a warm towel.

"Stand up," she said. I obeyed blindly.

She took off my dirty clothes and washed me. I was filthy. It had taken me ten days to walk to the camp, without rest or food, through rain and mud.

She dressed me in a simple white gown and laid me down on the clean sheets. "I'll be back with food," she said.

I laid there for a long time staring up at the top of the tent. I felt dead inside. Salome returned and helped me eat a light broth. "What happened to you, sister?" she asked.

I couldn't answer.

Salome stayed with me. She combed and braided my hair and tucked me in. She turned off the lantern, and when I awoke, she sleeping on the old, red chair next to me. I sat up, and she jumped up. It was dark outside and the camp was silent.

"Are you okay?" she asked.

I nodded.

"What happened?" she asked again.

"So much I can't even begin to explain," I said.

Xander sat on small stool in the center of a great hoard of people.

The people sat at his feet in the grass. All life was farce and all passion and faith was folly, so why not follow the folly that was honest—the folly that was my family and my blood. I was a monster, but even a monster could seek peace.

So I listened to Xander. His words came out like an old song, beautiful and tragic. He said to stop fighting and find peace. All life has meaning, he said. All life is God's work. It is God's art, and we are God's children. Would it not break our hearts if our children killed each other over a crust of bread or a bit of land or a stolen toy?

I lost myself in all of Xander's promises. I liked to pretend that somehow I could be someone else. I couldn't bear the thought of wandering the earth with nothing but a sword and the wind. I had been too long in the company of people.

I was lost there. The landscape was sublime. The mountains rose up to the east and to the west was a soft, rolling meadows. Our camp was in an old forest, thick with undergrowth and heavy with dew. I would sit on the moss and stare at the sky. Every part of me wanted to go back. I wanted to return to my books and my musty apartment.

I felt too old to fight, and I knew too much of the world to think that I could ever go back. So I sat on my rock, beside a stream and watched the Caeimoni. I accepted their gifts and let them put garlands of flowers in my hair. I listened to them ask me to pray for those they had left behind.

Ieya found me sitting beside a stream, staring vacantly into the water. She didn't say anything at first. She just sat with me. I didn't expect her to say anything.

"Forgive me," she said so softly I almost didn't hear her.

"For what?"

"It was me. I let the Verdune into our water treatment plant."

I didn't respond. I just stared at my old friend. Time hadn't been kind to her. She was fifty, but she looked like a little old lady. Her skin was thin and wrinkled. Her hands were bent with arthritis.

"Please," she whispered. "Please." The brook beside us was loader than she was. Tears spilled out of her eyes and down her cheeks.

"Oh, Ieya," I said. "There's nothing to forgive. I've done terrible things too. All we can do is move on and try to be better than we were."

"I destroyed our tribe."

"You did," I answered. "But they killed you first."

I stood up and walked away. I left Ieya to her silent regret. I thought that was the kindest thing I could do.

I had been with them for more than three weeks when Xander called me to his tent. He didn't say anything to me. He only reached out his hand. I took it and sat down next to him. He kissed my forehead and touched my cheek.

I sat with him in the dirt, and he took off my clothes. He looked at me. He looked at the mess that was my body. I felt tears in my eyes as he stared at my mangled legs. His touch was so gentle that I almost didn't recognize it. He laid his hands upon my legs, and my scars disappeared. He laid his hands upon my back and breasts and my tattoos vanished. I was clean and white as I had been before I had ever entered the karash.

I rested my head on his lap and let all the years wash away in an ocean of tears. I sobbed like a baby looking for its mother. I sobbed like that little girl in the mountain of death should have been sobbing. Xander stroked my hair and kissed my forehead. There were not enough tears. I knew then that I was broken. I was as broken as Ieya, and I didn't know how to fix myself, but Xander knew. I lifted up my head and smiled at him.

"Thank you," I said. "Thank you for offering me sanctuary. Thank you for everything. I know I haven't supported your mission. I have not supported your faith, but I've grown to see that what you have made here is a good thing, and I admire the peace you have brought to so many lost souls."

He looked away from me and sorrow spread out over his features. "This can't last," he said.

"What can't last?" I asked.

"Nothing. None of this can last. This place. This camp. It's time for it to end," he said forlornly.

"What do you mean?" I asked in surprise.

"You know. More than any of the others, you know. They are coming. Even as we speak the armies of this world are coming. They'll make us choose between ice and fire."

I pulled his face toward me so I could look in his eyes. They were filled with a gloomy fog. "How close are they?" I asked.

"Very close, and you are all we have. You must stand between us and them. That's why God has brought you back to me." He placed his hand on mine as if he was trying to comfort me.

"I can't. I can't go back to that. You don't know what you are asking. You don't know what I can become," I entreated him.

"I know what you are, and I know what you will be. I know that all

214

peace is fleeting, and that all I can ever really give anyone is hope." He kissed me on the cheek, tears glittering on his face.

"I can't," I whispered.

"I wouldn't ask it of you, but it's not my doing. My time is over now, and my people will need you." He wiped the tears from my cheek and smiled sadly.

"What does that mean?"

"There is an army coming."

"Xander, I can't fight an army alone," I said anxiously.

Xander held me and wept into my hair. I wrapped my arms around him and held him. "I love you," I said to him.

"They're here now," he said. "I'm sorry."

Dania burst through the door covered in sweat. "Xander!" she shrieked. "There's an army here. There are more men than I have ever seen in my life, and they have tanks and missiles."

"What are they doing?" I asked.

"It looks like they are setting up camp," she cried.

"Give us five more minutes. Call a meeting in the main tent. Bring only the disciples," I said.

Dania fled, and Xander and I sat on the dirt looking at each other. "I will die tonight," Xander said.

"Probably," I answered. "We'll all die tonight, unless you can produce a miracle."

We walked to the main tent hand in hand. My moment of peace with Xander had gone. We walked into the main tent and faced the disciples. Xander sat down on a pillow, and I stood in front of the small group of disciples. Dania, Salome, Mark, and a few other men and women, all sat on pillows and stared up at me. They were waiting for me to produce a miracle. They wanted me to erase the army before us as I had erased bands of men before.

"These men," I said. "Are from many tribes. They are all assembled under the banner of the Left Hand of Light with the help of The University to wipe us out. They believe that we will destroy their way of life. They will give us two choices. They will offer us some inhospitable land in the far north beneath a glacier. They will tell us that if we go there and settle and make ourselves into a tribe we may live. If we don't do this, they'll kill us all, without mercy."

Dania stood up and with a high shriek yelled, "Then you will kill them, and we shall drink their blood."

"That's not God's way," Xander said.

"God sent us her," she said, pointing to me. "She's God's way. She's a warrior. God wants us to cleanse the world of its impurities, and now is the time to do so."

"No," Salome said. "No! We are a people of peace. We can't shed the blood of God's children. We must go north. We'll survive. God will see us through."

"We're God's chosen people. God has sent us on a mission to spread his word. We can't back down. Ailive will save us!" Dania yelled.

The room exploded in disagreement. Everyone had an opinion. I waited for Xander. Xander raised his hand and the room was silent.

"We can't go north," he said. "They don't want us to survive. They'll send us someplace it will be impossible for us to survive."

"So Ailive will save us," Dania said triumphantly.

"No," I said. "I can't stop this army. I've been able to stop small groups of soldiers, soldiers that I've taken by surprise. I've stopped small armies of men that were far inferior to myself, and this was with luck. This is an army that's prepared. I can dodge a few bullets, but I can't dodge what waits out there. I can't stop them."

Salome sat down. Her voice dropped to a whisper. "So we are all to go home to our Father?"

"We have time," I said. "They have to send someone with their terms, and then we will be able to ride it out a few days."

So we waited. They sent their emissaries, and their terms were more harsh than I had expected. They wanted us to go to the northeast, where the world ended in black rock, volcanoes, and glaciers. I had been there before. They wanted us to go and live with the rwans. Nothing could survive there. We asked for a few days to decide, and we were granted this time.

We were waiting for Xander to pull thunder out of his hat or for God to rain fire upon our enemies, but there were no more miracles.

I went to bed early the night the emissaries came. I wanted to escape my knowledge of what lay ahead. I was powerless so I turned off my light and drifted away to a better world. I fell asleep listening to the sound of the tent flaps rattling in the wind.

I was dreaming of The University when a small boy awoke me to deliver a note. He woke me up and put the folded paper in my hand. I laid in bed for a while, folding and unfolding the paper. I dressed in white and met Cahir in the woods outside the camp. It hadn't been long since we parted, and I folded myself into his warm familiarity. I wanted him to tell me it was all over. There would be no more fighting. We could go home The University.

I took him back to my tent, and we made love. The dark embraced us, and we hid our sin in the soft shadows of the moonless night. Dania had cast women out as whores for less. When it was over, I realized that I could never really be Caeimoni. I realized that I was not meant for white linen and chastity. I looked back at Cahir sprawled out in my bed.

"What now?" I asked.

"The high council signed a bill that supports any action which results in the decimation of the religious fanatics known as the Caeimoni. You made sure of that. Jacob claimed you were driven mad by your brother's cult."

Cahir shrugged and put his pants on. "Several tribes sit out there. The University has offered them nice packages to help in the elimination of this potential threat. Officially, the bill only states that the IA has received approval in any action that might help in the relocation of the religious fanatics. But the IA hired the Left Hand of Light to facilitate the process, and we found the Critons more than ready to help and there are many others that have been divided by your brother that are all more than happy to help."

"You got what you wanted. Are you back in? Are you part of the IA again?"

"No. I'm with the Light now. I can't go back."

I nodded coldly and hardened my face. "Why are you here?"

"I couldn't leave you to die here."

"Thank you," I said.

"Where is he?" he asked with a hint of anger.

"Who?"

"Xander."

"A few tents over, why?"

"Because he won't even know if you go. He's already dead. Come with me. Save yourself."

"You know I can't," I declared.

"You don't actually believe this, do you?" he asked in incredulity.

"No."

"Then why die for it?"

"Because I believe in Xander, and I believe in the ideal he represents. Because he's my brother, and I love him."

He kissed me again. I missed his touch, or maybe I just missed being touched. I surrendered to his breath. I knew the line that divided us could never be erased. I knew he would kill me if he had to, but I made love to him because I had before, because it was easy and because it felt good. I fell asleep in his arms, and I woke up alone.

I couldn't put the white robes back on, so I put on the black armor I had arrived in. I took only my sword. I made my bed and went to see Xander.

Xander lay in his bed, still, like a sleeping child. I didn't even see it at first. I didn't notice that his white robes were red. I sat down next to him and put my hand on his shoulder and I knew, but there was nothing I could do. I stroked his hair as he had stroked mine. I kissed his face as he had kissed mine, but I was no healer. His art died with him.

I walked out of the tent and screamed. I opened my mouth and screamed some unnatural bellow that didn't belong to any woman or man that had ever been born. What I screamed came out of the depths of all the hatred Jason had ever taught me. I roared like a rwan until the roar became a word and the word was Cahir.

He had used me. He had used me to sneak in and kill my brother. When the roar died, there was only silence. All around me the white clad Caeimoni had gathered. They had tears in their eyes. Salome was clutching Xander's blood soaked blanket.

"I'll kill him," I said as I walked away.

"What happened?" Salome wept.

"I was betrayed!" I yelled. "I was betrayed!" Love and hate blended, and everything I had ever felt for Cahir vanished. I wanted only to see him dead.

I knew exactly where I was going. I walked through the camp and out toward the meadow. Across the meadow, the surreal glare of the army's shield glistened in the moon light like dew on shit. I walked toward it without hesitation until I stood directly in front of the largest airship I had ever seen. I faced this massive encampment and let lose my wretched roar.

He came. He met me outside the shield wall. He was followed by innumerable soldiers of all rank and size, and they made a circle around me, but I didn't care about them. I only wanted him. I wanted Cahir.

"What do you think you can accomplish here? What do you want?" he asked.

"I want to dance," I said as I drew my sword.

Cahir laughed. "I'll kill you. You're better than me. You're an artist, but I'll always have strength and size against you and that will give me all the edge I need."

"Then kill me."

"I did what I had to do," he said. "It had nothing to do with you."

"It had everything to do with me."

Cahir nodded. He stood in front of me and took off his armor and shirt in some ridiculous attempt to intimidate me. He flexed his muscles and stood up to try to emphasize his size. I only laughed at him. I laughed and took off my shirt, showing him my thin arms and soft breasts.

"Xander had to die!" he yelled. A roar of applause exploded from the men around us.

"Why?" I asked.

Cahir drew his sword. "You are my greatest disappointment in life. You've never understood the storm."

"I am the storm," I said.

Cahir and I danced. We dance like we had every night for ten years. Metal hit metal. He would turn, and I would bend to miss his blade. He would swing, and I would block. I jumped and kicked him, making contact, but a kick would not be enough to stun him, so the dance continued.

He still moved like fog. He moved with the wind, and we wrapped ourselves around each other, like we had when we made love. We were physical as we had always been. Nothing had changed. I screamed as his sword tore through the flesh on my shin. I fell and rolled to the right, barely missing his blade as it hit earth.

He moved in behind me and kicked me. His kick knocked me down, and the pain jarred me. I knew he had broken a rib, and I lost my breath. It didn't matter. I put the pain aside and leapt forward. It was such a simple movement, a quick turn and twist and he fell, like a tree. His large body made a heavy thud as it hit the earth. I stood over his body, looking at him. I felt nothing for him but hate. It lodged in the pit of my stomach like a brick of ice. He lay there, unconscious, helpless.

I raised my sword above him. I stood on the brink of killing him, but I hesitated. I looked down at him, and some memory of emotion stopped me. I knew I should have ended it, but I couldn't will myself to make the final stroke.

I dropped the sword he had given me and picked up his curved blade. It was still dripping with my blood. I looked out at the infinite multitude of men that surrounded me and dared them to come forward.

And then the rain came. It wasn't like before. It wasn't a soft purifying rain. It didn't cleanse or sooth. It fell down on the earth in sheets of silver fire mixed with ice. The hail pocked the earth and knocked men from their feet, but it didn't touch me. All around me, men ran for cover. Trees fell and the water flooded the meadow. Lightning painted the sky, and thunder shook the earth.

I turned and walked back home, to bury my brother.

The rain was softer at our camp. It came down gently, covering the mourners in a kind of gray mist. Xander's body had been placed in a cave, and I had to push my way through the throng to get to him. Beside him were many faces, painted with rain and tears, but the only face I saw was Hotem's.

Myhanna was standing over Xander muttering some prayer, but Hotem stood with a face like cast iron. He didn't turn to watch me approach like the others did. His face seemed older and harder, but his eyes were the same. The funeral moved forward. Wailing filled the air, and the faithful fell to their knees begging God for mercy.

But Hotem had no time for prayers, and he pulled me away from the crowd, into the woods where his army waited.

I could hardly hear him over the rain, but his voice was strong. "You saw the camp," he yelled. "What did it look like?"

"I've never seen its equal," I said honestly.

"Did you kill him? Did you kill your traitor lover?"

I didn't answer him, and my silence said more than any words.

"How many men do they have?"

"At least a hundred thousand."

"My men are setting up a shield around the camp. I think we should push all the Caeimoni into that cave. It's huge, and it goes on forever. Even if we lose, some could survive hiding in it. They won't be able to use the airships or missiles with the shield up. When they invade on foot, we'll dress like the Caeimoni and kneel like we are praying, and we'll take them by surprise."

"How many men do you have?" I asked.

"Maybe seventy thousand."

I nodded. "It won't be long before they attack. I think I made them pretty angry when I attacked Cahir."

"Let them come," Hotem said icily.

Hotem yelled orders and men scuttled to and fro and everywhere there was motion and yelling, but the rain poured on. The wind blew, and thunder shook the earth.

Then it stopped. The clouds parted, and the sky turned blue.

"That's strange," he said. The field was soaked. There was at least four feet of standing water in the middle of the meadow and the rest of the field was mud. The sun peeked its lonely head out from behind the fading storm clouds, and an uncanny quiet engulfed us.

I leaned over to Hotem. "How did you know to come?" I asked.

He shook his head. "Do you still think we are nothing but barbarians? An army like that takes time to raise. I have spies everywhere. I came with as many men as I could as quickly as I could. Why are you here? I thought you were one of them," he said as he pointed across the field.

I didn't know what to say, so he and I sat in complete silence staring at the grass and mud. They launched the grenades first. The field erupted with fire and smoke. We all sat patiently waiting for the grenades to stop. The shield held.

We watched with pensive patience as the first tanks started to creep across the field. The tanks struggled a little in the mud and water, but not much and they roared forward, like metal demons portending our death.

"We will die here," Hotem said as he watched them move forward.

"I know."

We both took our swords and stood facing the Light. But we were not alone. Maybe I had never really been alone. The sun dimmed and a shadow spread out over the ground. All eyes tilted upward, and I knew that our time had come.

Jason came with all of his legions, and they descended upon the encroaching army with all the hatred they knew. They had heard my cry and they had come, as they had promised.

I watched in awe as they shredded the tanks with their horrible jaws. Men screamed. Hotem's cavalry mounted their horses and rode forward. I ran into the storm and did what I have always done. I killed everyone and everything that stood in my way.

There were no prisoners that day. The rwans had no mercy. They devoured the wounded and carried off the dead. They fought over corpses, pulling them apart. Long after the smoke had cleared and the battle was over, they covered the field feasting and fighting. Only Jason came to me.

I sat on an empty tank and looked out on the world I had created. Hotem and his men had fled the field, leaving the rwans their spoil. Jason came and sat beside me, and I reached out and touched his back. He was sated. He would stay with me. He would stay with me until the war was won.

I left the field, but the rwans stayed. They slept under the moon on the grass and waited for the inevitable. Before I had left, I had touched them all. I had passed their secrets and kept their promises. Briefly, they were human again. They clung to it for as long as they could, but I knew it would pass and by morning they would be nothing but beasts.

I went back to the camp, and we buried my brother. There were no other dead to bury; the rwans had devoured them all. When Salome heard this, she had whispered, "Our bodies are nothing. The spirit lives on."

Dania had screamed about the rwans being hell-born, but most of us were just glad to have survived. I slept with Jason as I had in my youth. We had defeated a vast army, but that night was filled with tears and lamentation. I felt like my insides had been scraped out and set on fire.

That night the rwan and I were the same. We were empty and soulless, praying for death.

That battle seemed to awaken all the bloodlust in everyone who lived. In the days that followed the battle, hordes of tribeless migrated to our camp, and these tribeless were different. They were raiders and terrorists and mercenaries that had survived through thievery and bloodletting. They came to the camp and pledged allegiance to Xander, falling to their knees and declaring themselves the martyrs' men. They leaned toward Dania, going to her sermons and listened to her prayers.

"Xander has said that this is God's world. He has said that only the faithful will find the city of God. He has said we are his chosen people. It is time for us to fight for what we believe in. He told us to make the world over in God's image. So we must!" she said.

After one of her more impassioned speeches she chased me down and put her hand on my shoulder. "Ailive, The Saint of the Storm," she said softly. "It's time for you to embrace who you are."

I think I must have looked at her like she was the devil, because her smile faded. "You are second only to the prophet himself," she said. "I beg you to come and lead my men on their crusade."

"What crusade?"

"Tonight we are going to invade the Criton city and lay waste to the infidels that started this war."

"I already walked through that waste, and there isn't much left," I said.

"Word has come to me from one of my new followers that those that survived your attack killed all the remaining Caeimoni in the city and have been sheltering the Left Hand of the Light ever since."

"Who survived my attack?"

"Most of their officials were hiding underground."

I shook my head. "I'm sorry to hear that, but I belong here. There's another army amassing. I need to protect this camp."

"God is calling you."

"No. You are calling me, and I will not follow."

That night's conversations blended together in my mind. Everywhere I turned, people were whispering in the dark. The fear was as tangible as the dirt beneath my feet. That same night I found Salome and Myhanna whispering in the shadows by my brother's grave. I didn't know what they were talking about, but I sensed some urgency to their conversation and interrupted them.

"What is it?" I asked.

Salome jumped. "Oh, Ailive, it's you. I thought you were one of Dania's spies."

"Dania has spies?"

"Everyplace," Myhanna said quietly.

"I'm glad you found us," Salome said as she pulled me closer. "Maybe you can help us."

"We need to leave this camp," Myhanna said. "I've spoken with Hotem, and he agrees. These new people that are coming aren't helping us. The world is demonizing us. We're taking in the men and women who have laid waste to entire tribes. We have to leave before things get any worse."

"Understand," Salome said in a whisper. "Xander would take in these people. Xander took in all, but they would have to put down their swords. We are a people of peace, and now armed men are wandering the camp."

"I agree," I said.

"Hotem wants us to move the camp back to the Efferitas' lands," Myhanna said.

"So tell the people to pack," I said.

"Dania has too much power now. Her people believe we should stand our ground. We should fight this out."

"One of you should talk with her," I said.

"I don't think Dania will change her position," Salome said.

"So what should we do?" I asked.

"We're going to try to sneak out with those we can tonight."

"No. You'll be picked off. I've seen the latest intelligence reports. The armies are regrouping. We've got the Left Hand of Light building some kind of encampment to the south of us."

"We have to ask Hotem to bring his troops and go with us," Myhanna whispered.

"He'll do it, but I don't think it was wise. Hotem may not be prepared for that kind of fight," I said. "We may have to wait this out."

"I wish Xander were here," Salome said.

"It wouldn't matter," I said. "There are those that want to kill us and no matter what we do, they'll still want to kill us. I'll go talk to Hotem and see what he says."

It was harder than it should have been to get to Hotem. His tent was elaborate and heavily guarded. None of the guards wanted to let me in to see him. I had to bribe some fat man in a uniform that was too small for him to make it into Hotem's tent. It had only been a little over a week since I had last seen him, but it seemed much longer.

When I finally made it passed the guards, I found Hotem standing over a table reading intelligence reports by candle light.

"You could use an electric lamp," I said softly. "It would be better for your eyes."

"That's not our way," Hotem responded.

"The camp is dividing, and Dania is planning an attack on the Critons."

"I know."

"We're surrounded and outnumbered. We'll be slaughtered," I added.

"I'm aware of the difficulties surrounding us," Hotem said sternly.

"Why wouldn't you let me in to see you?"

"Because you have been with the enemy too long, and you are a distraction."

"I know how they will fight. I'm the best asset you have," I declared.

"That's why you are here now."

"What's your plan?"

"I'm going to let Dania attack. I think she'll do some damage. Her men know what they're doing. We need to eliminate the Critons. I was the one that gave her the information to facilitate the attack."

"If Myhanna knew you had done that…"

"I'm king," he stressed.

"Fair enough."

"Dania will draw their fire onto us, and I think we have a better chance of fortifying our position here and defending it than moving on. We will not survive an extended siege, however, and we must encourage them to attack and hope that we kill enough of them to precipitate negotiations."

"You know what you are doing."

"You're surprised?"

"I haven't seen you in over fifteen years. You were a boy when we parted. I'm surprised at the king you have become."

"You may go now. I'll call you when I need you."

Dania didn't leave, but she did send out her men. They vanished into the evening mist, leaving her alone surrounded by the old Caeimoni. The old Caeimoni, those that have given up safety and tribe to follow Xander, clung even more closely to Salome, whose words of peace seemed more like Xander's own words.

In the midst of this, a new symbol arose, the symbol of dagger. They wore the dagger to remind them of his death, his sacrifice.

He had died so the world would be reborn.

More people came. They flooded the camp. Airships filled the blood-soaked field where our first battle had been fought and all manner of transportation surrounded the camp, forming a new kind of fortification. The newcomers were different; they had tribes. They had converted to Caeimoni and were fleeing persecution.

The more of these people that came, the angrier I knew the world would be, and Dania's attack was all that was necessary to fuel the next major attack.

The next assault was much better coordinated and executed. The attack came at night; we were all asleep, and they killed the guards, but they could not kill Jason and his screams woke the entire camp. I grabbed my sword and rushed outside to see legions of devoted Caeimoni on their knees in the dirt, praying. I cursed at them and ran toward the fire. The camp was on fire, but the faithful didn't seem to notice.

Hotem was already awake. He didn't look like he had ever slept. He was sitting atop a large, black horse yelling orders at men. I couldn't hear him over the din around me but I saw his gestures. He was sending men out to put out the fires, to sneak around behind the troops, to save the women and children. His very gesture sent people running in every direction and in the midst of the chaos. He was as calm as death. He turned and looked at me with his cold, green eyes, and I shuddered. With one kick of his heals, he disappeared into the fray, swinging his sword like a woodsman.

The rwans swarmed above me, carrying off all manner of men. The air was filled with the screams of the dead or dying. I kissed my sword and marched forward.

That night we faced our first real defeat. We were able to drive the soldiers away, but the cost was high, and we were broken. The rain never came and all that was left was dust and blood. I felt like I was in Xender again, staring at the corpses of my tribe. I was unable to save those I fought to protect. I felt defeated.

Our numbers had been cut in half. The soldiers had killed the defenseless without mercy or remorse. They had found people praying and slit their throats. The camp was decorated with sorrow and fear. There were those that wanted to leave. They regretted their decision to join us, but it was too late. There was no escape.

I tried to see Hotem, but he was unreachable, so I worked with Xander's people to bury the dead. We put the camp back together again, but our morale was broken, and our faith was shaken.

Just on the other side of our walls, more troops were coming. They were coming from every corner of the earth to destroy us.

From then on the fighting never stopped. Even when we were able to drive off the armies that besieged us, other armies attacked the outlying Efferitas' colonies so that Hotem was constantly struggling to design new ways to fight off the innumerable armies that seemed to spring up from the dead ones.

We seemed to lose more often than we won. We had few men, and we lacked technology. The rwans were fickle allies, and they came and went as they pleased. The weather was far more reliable than the rwans. I began to shape my emotions to move the clouds. I would think about Cahir and his betrayal, and I would make myself furious and a thunderstorm would come. The angrier I made myself the worse the storm became. I would think about Xander and sorrow would overwhelm me. Gentle rain would fall, bathing the world in soft water. I could control the weather, and I didn't want to know why. I only wanted to use it the best way I could.

Our enemies were beset on all fronts. We attacked one city, only to find it had already been leveled by a hurricane. A large army was lost in the desert while attacking the Efferitas' city when a sandstorm swept down and carried them all away. Hail, rain, thunder, snow, sleet, and tornadoes came and went with diabolical frequency, but even these things I couldn't entirely control, and sometimes our people would be crushed by superior fire power. Hotem and I would flee the field desperately trying to save our wounded.

The best ally we had was the power of fear and myth. Our armies had developed a mythic status. Sometimes armies would approach us, and the men would look up to the sky terrified of the rwans, and with one soft breeze, they would all flee before the battle even began. No one ever knew what would happen from one battle to the next and that fear helped us in more ways than anything else.

I fought, and I sat with Hotem in his war room. I sat with him and watched him plan each battle. He was the only thing holding us together. Within the camp sharp divisions led to fierce debate. I could fight like grim death, but I had no idea where to go no next or how to stop an army. He moved the men and stopped the debates. He gave us purpose. Even Dania did his bidding.

The months ground on, and the camp took on the tone of a death march. The Caeimoni's white had faded to gray, and most of the people hid in their tents or shelter after dinner. We had just fought off yet another besieging army when I decided that I had to see Hotem.

"Sorry, Ailive," the guard said. "Hotem is in conference."

"I just want to speak with him," I said. "I can wait until he is finished."

"Sorry, Ma'am. He left specific orders for you not to be admitted."

"Why?" I asked angrily.

The guard shrugged, and I wandered back to Jason's side to sleep. The next day I was called to Hotem's tent and I went obediently. Hotem was surrounded, as always, by his advisors and generals. Dania sat to his left side watching him work and grimacing.

"You called?" I asked hopefully.

"I need you to make contact with your friends in The University," he said.

"That will be difficult."

"I have a man who can get a note inside. Do you think your friend, the one that came with you to our palace, would still help you if you asked?"

"I'm not sure. If it meets his needs, maybe."

"I need you to send him a note. I need him to find out where the Left Hand of Light keeps its base."

"I don't think he is privy to that kind of information."

"Tell him that if he can bring us that information, we will offer him our aid in moving the Caeimoni out and ending this war."

"I'll write the note, but I don't make any promises."

I walked over to him and stood in his shadow. "I was cast out of The University," I whispered.

"I know that, but I also know that Mia will do anything for you. Send her a note as well. Those that love you, love you well. You inspire a strange fixation in the hearts of those who know you. Send your notes."

I nodded. "Hotem, I need to speak with you tonight," I whispered. The ground beneath us shook. Everyone ran outside to see what was happening. People scattered into the shadows.

"Write the letter!" Hotem yelled. "And give it to my man."

Outside the camp, a group of men blasted into the earth. They were trying to attack from beneath us.

I watched Hotem disappear and closed my eyes. "Let your emotions turn outward," I whispered to myself, and all of my sorrow rose up from me.

I let my soul devour itself. I could fill rooms with my hopeless regret. All the things I should have done lined up before me. I should have tried harder to negotiate with Hotem. I shouldn't have gone with Cahir on that mission. I should have never left The University. But the strangest regret of all filled with immeasurable sorrow, the regret that lingered in all my quiet moments. I should have married Hotem.

All these thoughts filled me up with a divine despair, and the sky turned black. The wind hissed, and the rain came like God himself was weeping. It came it sheets and it drowned the men in their pitiful tunnels.

It was far into the winter when I went out into the snow with a group of Dania's men to find the Left Hand of Light. I met with Jacob in a frozen wasteland that had been abandoned by all but the dead.

Jacob arrived by airship. He was accompanied only by Mia and the pilot.

"Hello," I said.

Jacob looked over my shoulder to Dania's group of savage Caeimoni. They looked like what they had been. They looked like a group of raiders. They were all dressed in black tunics with light leather armor. They carried swords and machine guns. The only thing that had changed since they had begun to follow Dania was that they now wore a huge red symbol on their chests. They wore the symbol of the knife. A symbol which, Dania said, represented the martyrdom of Xander. To me, it only symbolized violence.

"Interesting company you keep now," Jacob said disdainfully.

"Necessity makes all things possible," I responded.

Mia hugged me and kissed my cheek. "I'm glad to find you well," she whispered.

"We haven't much time," Jacob said. "We can't be caught here. Everyone has spies now. I wouldn't have come, but how could I say no?"

"Still fighting for the same cause?" I asked.

"By any means at my disposal."

Something moved in the darkness, and we all jumped. One of Dania's men went to investigate. "Can you tell me where the Left Hand of Light is hiding?" I asked.

"It took some doing. I have an old friend in the IA, but I have what you need. I want you to know that this information came at a terrible cost to my friend."

"It'll be worth it," I said.

"What now?" Jacob asked.

"We'll attack within the week, and then you will have the leverage you need to persuade the council to negotiate. Without the Light, the war will lose its organization, and the council will see that."

"You may not defeat the Light. Even if you do win, there are still a plethora of tribes that will want to fight you."

"But, with the Left Hand of Light gone, they will lack unity, and The University will lack all its influence on the outcome. The council won't like that. You have always been a talker. Convince the council to send ambassadors to negotiate a cease fire. And I can promise you that this is a battle we will win."

"What makes you so sure?"

"Because the alternative is unthinkable."

We left at night. The snow had stopped, briefly, and we headed south. Hotem had agreed to use a few of the airships that had been given to us by some of the fleeing Caeimoni refugees Salome had taken in. He was uncomfortable with the technology, but he cared more about winning than about tradition.

The Left Hand of Light had set up their center of operations on one of the islands of Notua. We were flying close to the ground, trying to hide. It was a beautiful night, crisp and clear, and as we moved further south, the air warmed, and I went outside to watch the world beneath my feet. I found Hotem there. He was uncharacteristically alone. He stood staring out at the world beneath us like he was seeing it for the first time.

"It's beautiful," he said to me. I looked out and saw the landscape Crian, Mia, and I had wandered together. It was stunning and surreal.

"Yes," I agreed. I stood next to him, putting my hand next to his on the rail of the ship. I could almost feel his skin. I wanted to feel his skin. My hand tingled with longing, but I didn't dare reach out for him.

"I've never been north of the Midi River," he said.

"It's an amazing world."

"I would like to see it someday. I would like to see it without the fighting."

"You look tired."

He turned and looked at me. "I'm always tired."

His breath was warm on my hair, and I held my breath, wishing he would move closer. I closed my eyes and tried to mask my desire for his touch. I couldn't let him see how much his presence affected me. I wondered if he still wrote poetry. I wondered if he still read the old philosophers and dreamt of going to The University. I put my hand on the small bird he had given me. It still hung around my neck.

"Tell me about The Left Hand of Light," he said. "What will be facing?"

"They are small in numbers, but amazingly skilled. It's their technology I fear the most. They have cloaking devices that make them difficult to see in hand-to-hand combat, and their armor is almost impenetrable. They are all very well trained in the way of the storm, and they have recently acquired the man who taught me to fight. He is very good. They will have guns that will be small, almost invisible."

"The man who trained you? Cahir? Your lover?"

"Yes."

"You couldn't kill him before." I saw the accusation in his eyes. He was angry at me.

"It was difficult for me."

"Will you be able to kill him now?"

I looked at Hotem. I reached out to touch him, but he backed away from me. "Of course," I said.

Hotem walked away, and I was left alone staring at islands of perpetual sun in the topaz ocean. I pushed my hand against my temple and tried to fight back the wave of disappointment that engulfed me. "He is a king," I told myself. "He will never be yours. You are nothing. You are nothing. A puppet. A pawn."

Suddenly, the air became quite cold, and I watched as my breath froze on the wind. "Let it come," I whispered. "Let vengeance be mine." The water beneath the bow of the ship had frozen, and snow had begun to fall as we landed on the smallest of the Notuan islands.

The island was tiny. It was nothing more than a fallen temple surrounded by a lush orange grove. The topaz water licked the white sands of the pristine beach we landed on. Our men exited the ship and ran toward the temple.

At first glance, the island appeared deserted and as the troops ran from the airships, they were temporarily disoriented by the apparent quietness of the island. The troops were oblivious to what was coming, but I knew what lay ahead in the snow. I saw the footprints in the snow. "It's a trick!" I screamed. "They are cloaked. Draw your weapons!"

Behind me, one of the men screamed, and our invisible adversaries descended on us from all sides. Men fired blindly into the dark and waved their swords at nothing in wild desperation. Hotem stood perfectly still in the center of this and waited. He closed his eyes, as I had once taught him, and listened to the footsteps of his enemies and then he struck out, killing all those that approached him. They died, and as they fell, their blood stained the snow.

I drew Cahir's sword and looked up at the sky. The snow fall came down heavily now and caught on the bodies of the soldiers surrounding us, making the invisible visible. Our boys attacked with a ferocious vigor, and the fight began.

I walked away. I walked backward, to the trees, once heavy with fruit, to a small house with a warm fire. It was a honeymoon house. It had been built for lovers and dreams and the conception of children, but now it was occupied only by Cahir.

"This is where they took Crian," Cahir said as I entered.

"How do you know about that?" I asked.

"The Light knows everything. It's amazing the history they keep in their libraries. Crian was your friend, wasn't she?"

"She was Mia's mother," I answered.

"Do you know why we are here? On this island?"

"No."

"Because we have always been here. The Light has always been on this island. That temple is the temple of Light."

"They have always been sheltered by the Notuans?" I asked. "Ironic. I thought the Notuans were peaceful."

"We all want peace. Crian honeymooned here and the Efferitas, under the orders of Hotem IX, attacked Notua. He knew that the Light hid here. He thought he could dispatch us."

I drew my sword. "And so we have come full circle? Is that your point? Back to the beginning where the old Hotem tried to kill you and failed?"

"I really had no point," Cahir said as he turned to face me. "I just wanted you to know that you are now fighting alongside the very men who killed Mia's father and enslaved her mother."

"I always knew that, Cahir. I know the men I fight with now far better than I ever knew you."

"When you were just a girl, I told you that you didn't love me. You loved an ideal, not me."

"I'm not to blame for your duplicity. I loved the parts of me you showed me. I was young and foolish."

"You aren't young anymore," he said bitterly.

"No. You took my youth," I answered stonily.

"You gave it to me," he said with utter sorrow.

"Gladly," I said with a melancholy smile.

"You were always stupid," he whispered.

"Maybe."

"I want my sword back." His voice turned hard and angry.

Cahir moved toward me and everything seemed to slow down. He seemed large and clumsy. His movements were predictable.

I watched him attack and wondered that he had ever been a challenge to me.

I decapitated him with one quick stroke. He fell onto the same floor where Crian's husband had fallen, and I returned to the snow, to kill the rest of the Light.

The Left Hand of Light's temple was hidden in a grove behind the cabin. It seemed like a lover's chapel, but beneath the surface there was a vast fortress. I opened the door and called to Hotem. He didn't smile. He moved and called his men, and they followed him.

"Is he dead?" he asked.

"Yes," I answered.

"You go first."

I nodded, and we climbed down the winding stairs into the blinding light. There were six or seven guards at the base of the stairs. They fired blindly at me and I fell, pushing my body against the ground. I slid down the stairs on my belly, like a snake. A bullet grazed my shoulder, but I didn't flinch. I moved quickly and was able to crawl beneath two of the men and cut their Achilles tendons. The men fell with two horrible yelps, and I slit their throats before their screams could come to fruition. The rest of the men continued firing at me, and I used the dead men as human shields. I flung one of the corpses at the remaining four soldiers.

The men dodged the corpse, and I slid in between two soldiers and decapitated them. I was too fast for the men. The fired at the air where I had been, and I cut them in half before they even realized I had moved.

Hotem walked behind me like the king he was. He stepped over the puddles of blood and ordered me forward. I held my sword high and went into the pit of vipers. The fight didn't last long. I killed the few remaining soldiers, and Hotem's men killed their women and children as mercilessly as they had dispatched the men.

Hotem's eyes were cold. He moved forward and looked at the papers spread out over Cahir's desk. He looked over everything carefully. He was the eye of the storm. He stared at the papers on the desk quietly, ignoring the bedlam around him. The chaos melted away. The men returned. Their work was done, and they stood at attention awaiting his orders.

"I want one ship to go here," he ordered pointing to one of the neighboring islands. "And one ship to go here." He pointed to another island.

"I want everything on those islands dead. I don't care if they walk on two legs or four. Kill everything and burn them to the ground. This needs to be a message. Those that shelter the Light will die. There will be no mercy."

I looked at Hotem, but he had no time for me. I tried to summon images of the young man who had wept at my feet, of the man who had pledged his undying love, but those images were lost, and I couldn't recognize the king he had become.

The snow continued, and we spread out through the surrounding islands like a plague. It reminded me of my youth. We decimated strangers in the name of faith and honor. I felt Xenderian again, but as the smoke cleared and the snow passed, the charred remains of the island utopia became a reality.

I knew the war ended with our carnage. This kind of total annihilation left an impression on the world. We had wiped out entire cities. The central Notuan islands remained untouched, but the islands we ravaged were nothing but a memory. We killed men, women, and children, and we sowed the soil with salt.

I knew that we would become the name to fear, but I had been that before. I had been fear. I had been karake, and I knew that fear fades with rage and time.

It was a long journey home. The ashes of the dead were infused in my hair. I could still smell the burning flesh. The stench had been so terrible I couldn't get the memory of it from my mind or the lingering smell from my hair. I couldn't sleep. I had lived in peace too long, and war no longer felt like home to me. I walked the long bow of the ship and found my way to Hotem's room. His door was unguarded, and the ship was silent. The men rested, so I pushed the door open and entered uninvited. Hotem lay in his large bed, wrapped in the arms of a pretty girl. Her long, slender limbs were tangled in his. I shook my head and turned to leave.

"Ailive," he said. He pushed the girl off him and rose. I averted my eyes as he put on his robe.

"What are you doing here?" I couldn't translate his tone. His emotion was intangible.

"I," I stammered. "I'm not sure."

"You come into my room in the middle of the night, and you aren't sure?"

"I just wanted to talk to you about something."

"Leave!" he bellowed at the girl, and she gathered her things and vanished.

He handed me a glass of water, and I took it, without drinking. "Why did we burn those islands?" I asked.

He looked surprised. "I thought you were the assassin who killed without question?"

"Time changes us all, Hotem. It's certainly changed you. I wouldn't have known you today." My voice was riddled with bitterness.

He nodded. "Do I seem cruel? I thought you had killed thousands? Killed men in their beds?"

"I haven't been to war in a long time. The gods I once fought for are dead. Now, I need to know why I fight."

"We burned the islands because they were the Left Hand of the Light's suppliers. Those were the Light's families, their sons, and daughters. I know it seems cruel, but you weren't my only teacher. My father told me that if you fight a man, you must kill his children, or they will come back for vengeance, Does this bother you, Saint Ailive? Saint Ailive who tortured me and cut off my thumb?"

I shook my head.

"I will win this war, and I will change this world," Hotem said.

We arrived from the islands still covered in dust and blood, but we weren't given time to think or recover. I left my airship and was confronted by another. I would have recognized it in my sleep. It was lined with gold and painted blue, like the sky. It was Jacob's ship. It was time to negotiate.

Jacob had not changed. He seemed stiff and uncomfortable. He was too formal. Mia came in behind him and settled in comfortably; she smiled warmly at me and barraged me with a long line of questions about my health and the war. She had been a good friend, and I missed her terribly.

Hotem entered the room like a god-king. He was wrapped in purple silk and wore jewels on every finger. He stepped up to his throne, silencing our girlish prattle.

"So," he demanded in his churlish Efferitas. "What do they want?"

I translated to Jacob.

"Well," Jacob said. "I think we all know that the fighting has to stop. The cost of this conflict has become ludicrous."

"I'm sure you have a proposal," I didn't wait for the king to answer. "We know each other, Jacob. Let's not waste our time with pleasantries. Tell me what you want."

"You know we didn't want this war," Jacob said. "The conservatives had absolutely nothing to do with the support that was provided to the Light."

"I know. I know that this is everything you didn't want, Jacob. None of us wanted this."

"Except the IA and Cahir," Jacob said bitterly.

"I'm sorry. I should have left him."

"Regret is not a luxury we have time for. I shouldn't have been so harsh on you for your failure with the Efferitas."

"I shouldn't have gone to Criton."

"What happened there? Do you know what they said? They said you slaughtered the entire city."

"I reacted. I don't know if what I did was right, but lately right and wrong are not as easy to pick out as they used to be. I saw things there that would turn your blood cold, and I killed those responsible for the atrocities I witnessed."

Jacob only nodded. "That night, that single action lit the fire that started all of this. The high council was shocked into an action they would have never condoned otherwise and now they all regret it."

"So how do we end it?"

"I have a proposal, and I don't need to tell you there are those who don't support my proposal."

"Tell me about it."

"You know that only a handful of tribes have really put their troops behind your elimination. Some of those tribes have already been destroyed by civil wars or by your..." Jacob twisted his face in disgust. "Caeimoni raiders. Those that remain are bent on your elimination. Too many have died."

"Jacob, I don't need a history lesson. I know this war."

"Of course," he said. "They won't stop because they believe you are nothing but a group of tribeless and barbarians. They believe you are monsters who have been lucky. You need to prove that you are not."

"So?"

"You have no technology, and you have depleted your resources. Soon, you will weaken and perish."

"And you don't want that."

"You know what I want. Nothing has changed. I'm a patient man. I want peace, and I want my treaty signed."

"And what are you willing to offer?"

"You should pull back. Pull all your people back behind the Midi River. We will give you four nuclear warheads and sixteen war ships loaded with enough missiles to flatten anything that gives you trouble. The tribes that hate you will fling some armies at you, and they will die. If you stay behind the Midi and your threat decreases, they will eventually give up and the war will end."

"I want this field."

"What?"

"I want this field and the land between it and the Midi declared part of the Efferitas' empire. We will pull back, but in the end, when the dust has settled, this will be ours. My brother is buried here, and I want it."

"Done. What about the treaty?"

"Let Hotem and I talk alone."

Jacob and Mia left, and I found myself alone with Hotem for the first time. I walked carefully toward him and sat at his feet. He looked away from me, toward the treaty in my hands.

"You didn't need me for that, did you?" he roared. "I am king. *He was to negotiate with me.* You are a translator!"

"I know his language. It was easier for us to negotiate. He came with a treaty that could stop this war."

"Back to the treaty. You are asking me to sign that damn treaty again.

Did you plan this? Are you that clever? Did you make this entire mess to get me to sign that treaty?"

"No."

"You were born to curse me," he spat.

"I don't understand," I said desperately. I didn't understand why he had become so hostile.

"You left me, for that monster that killed your brother. You left me, and the only reason you would even reduce yourself to look at me is to get me to sign that fucking paper."

My heart was pounding in my ears. My eyes burned. I didn't know what to say. All those nights, I had dreamt of this moment.

I had pressed myself against Jason and regretted every breath I had taken since I had left him, and now the words were gone. I was a courageous person. I had reduced armies to ruble. I terrified men. I had saved the Caeimoni. But I think I began to tremble. I couldn't even look at him. He hated me. How could he hate me?

"You don't have anything to say? No words to defend yourself? You betrayed me. You sold my secrets so you could live with that man," he said.

"No!" I yelled. "I never sold your secrets."

"I'm king. I'm not the boy you left behind. I know what you did. I have spies in The University."

"I didn't," I muttered.

"Get out. I'll take the Caeimoni and my people and retreat, but I will not sign your treaty, and you can go back with your own kind."

I sat there shivering like a child, and I did the only thing I could think to do. My voice was gone. There was nothing I could say.

I took out the bird he had sent me so long ago, and I set it on the arm of his chair.

I stood up to walk away, to beg my way back to The University. I even thought I might go back to the ice with Jason. It didn't matter anymore. Xander was dead, and my stupidity had killed him.

I had driven away the only people that had cared for me, and there was no place left to go.

But Hotem saved me. He put his hand on shoulder. I turned around and looked at him. He smiled. It was the same smile I remembered, warm and full of light.

"You saved it?" he asked.

I nodded stupidly.

"You're crying," he said. "I didn't know you could cry." He wiped my tears away with his hand and looked at them like they were diamonds.

"I'm not what I was. I…" The words eluded me again. I didn't know how to tell him that the world had broken me. How could I have told him that I had grown weak and that all I had left was my sword and my dreams of him?

He wrapped his arms around me and held me so close I couldn't breathe. Surrender. Release. I could have died there and still not have found the words for what I wanted to say. I spoke a thousand languages, but couldn't say anything to him.

Finally the words came out. "I love you," I whimpered.

"What?" he said.

"Don't ask me to say it again." I couldn't stop crying. I felt like some sort of broken faucet, and I hated myself for it.

Hotem sat down and looked at me. "Why are you looking at me?" I asked in strange desperation. I wanted to disappear.

"Is this a trick?"

"Yes. It's all an elaborate ruse." I broke. Not like before. The fury was gone. It was spent. "I spent the last year creeping through every tunnel of underworld to trick you into signing some piece of paper. I studied and learned and worked and fought and struggled and killed in blind rage, and all I have ever accomplished is death. Everyone I ever trusted has used me: my father, Cahir, Jason, Jacob. I have nothing but a bit of blood beneath my nails and mountains of regret, and you ask me if this is a ruse. I have fucked up everything I have touched. How could I be capable of a ruse?"

I fell to me knees on the floor and tried to hide my tear streaked face in my hands. "Hotem, I have tried to do the right thing. I thought it would be better if I left you. I was nothing. I'm not even a real woman. What good could I be to you? You need sons. I thought you would be better off with Myhanna."

Hotem sat down beside me and took me in his arms again. We sat there for a long time. "Since you left," he said. "I have fought everyone in this world to make my kingdom a better place. I've survived rebellions, poisonings, and shootings. I've executed my friends and embraced my enemies. I built a city worth fighting for and through it all you are the only thing I have ever dreamt of."

He lifted my face up so I had to meet his eyes and brushed my hair from my face. "You are the only thing I have ever wanted. You came back, and I thought that God had sent me mercy. But you only returned for the glory of your lover. You have brought me nothing but sorrow."

"That's all I have to offer."

His lips brushed mine, and the depths of my being shivered. He touched me, and everything else was lost. We made love on the ground with the dirt in our hair. The dirt covered our skin and ground itself into us until we were both the same texture and color. I orgasmed, and all the tears stopped. Nothing else really mattered and then he stopped and looked at me and laughed. He kissed my face and laughed.

"I love you," he said and then we began again. I think we could have stayed in that tent forever. Maybe we would have stayed there forever. We drank wine and laughed and had sex on every semi flat surface available.

"You know," he said after a while. "I think Jacob and Mia are waiting outside for us."

"I don't care," I said.

"You care."

"No. I want to be your slave again. Take me back and put me in that little attic and just take me out to use me."

"You are a saint now. You can't be my sex slave."

"You are a priest king. You can't have one." We both laughed, and then we drank more wine until we were both so roaring drunk that we could hardly stand. So we lay together, and he held me.

"Life has not been kind to us," I said.

"It isn't kind to anyone."

"No, but it has been kinder to some than to others. You should sign the treaty. Jacob is a good man. He wants to help you."

Hotem looked at me, and a shadow passed over his eyes. His smile faded. "How will this treaty help?" he asked.

"It will bring teachers to your city. Every child in the city will learn to read. They will build hospitals and provide doctors and vaccinations and The University will be saved. It's a place of shadow and light and if it dies, so does all the knowledge in the world."

"I'll sign your treaty if you marry me."

"You still want me? I'm an old woman. I can't have any children. I couldn't even when I was young."

"You don't look old. You still look like you are twenty, and I definitely look my age. You'll be the one married to an old troll."

I touched his face. I traced the lines and the long scar on his cheek bone. "You are beautiful."

"You don't have to say that," he said.

"How can you marry me? Don't kings need heirs?" I asked with a kiss.

"I don't care about that," he said as he traced the outline of my clavicle with his finger.

"Don't you need an heir?"

"I'll adopt."

"I'll make a terrible queen," I insisted.

"Just say yes."

"Yes."

So we got dressed and tried to sober up and called Jacob and Mia back to the tent. We must have looked ridiculous. Hotem's turban was crooked, and our clothes were dirty. We had dirt on our faces and for some reason I couldn't stop smiling. Outside, the world was on fire, but I couldn't stop smiling. Hotem's hand was in mine. His pulse thrummed against my palm. I was his, and I felt like I was young again. I felt like

I was a girl with flowers in her hair who dreamt of her wedding day.

I handed Jacob the signed treaty, and he smiled. "Thank you," he said to Hotem in his clunky Efferitas.

"Ailive speaks well of you. I would not have signed it if she had not argued your case so persuasively."

"She is an able speaker and an asset to The University. I hope she will consider returning," Jacob said.

"She has already made an agreement with me," Hotem said.

"Do you mind me inquiring as to the nature of the agreement?"

"She and I are to be married."

I think Jacob coughed. "Congratulations," he said stiffly.

Mia smiled. She leaned over and hugged me. "I know that I should not speak this way now, but I want you both to know that I always hoped you would return to each other."

"Thank you," I said, and I kissed Mia on the cheek.

"We'll leave tonight," Hotem said. "As soon as we can break camp."

Jacob looked at me. "May I walk with you before we leave?" he said.

I looked at Hotem for approval, and he nodded.

"Of course," I said.

Hotem called a meeting with Dania, Salome, and the other leaders before I had even left the tent. I took Jacob's arm and led him out of camp into the woods. As we walked by, people looked at me and giggled. At the time, I didn't understand why, but I have long since realized that Hotem and I had been everything but discrete in our activities.

I took Jacob past the shield wall and into the woods to a pretty place where several small steams converged to form a pool. The pool was dark, lined with lily pads and odd amphibians. Jacob stood and looked down into its murky depths. His hands were folded behind his back.

"I regret having been so hard on you before. It was inappropriate of me to ask you to use yourself that way," he said.

"There is no animosity between us, Jacob. You are my mentor, and you have been my friend."

"I don't know what has happened since we parted, but I want you to know I don't expect you to follow this course of action. You may return with me, and we will find some other way to work with King Hotem."

"That's not necessary," I said.

"You are a dedicated woman. I know that whatever drove you to your action in Criton must have been merited. I know you didn't want to be with Hotem to secure our needs. I don't want you to compromise yourself for me."

"I want to marry Hotem."

"Really. I was under the impression that you were very passionate about Cahir and had no interest in any others."

"Cahir was easy, but he was wrong."

"No, Cahir was right. I hated him, but he was right."

"What do you mean?"

"Once in council, he said that when the tribeless outnumbered those in tribes the only possible outcome would be global upheaval. Isn't that what is happening? Isn't that what has happened?"

"Whatever has happened, he instigated it. He wanted war."

Jacob shook his head. "How can we live through such times? I have seen such monstrous things, and I'm weary."

I put my hand on his shoulder. "I know, but you are a great man, and you'll make things better."

"I've never said thank you."

"For what?"

"For all of your help. For staying with me all those years. You're a very admirable woman, and I will always think of you as my friend and peer."

"That means a lot to me."

Jacob and I talked for a long time by that pool. He told me about the web of politics and debates that had led to this moment. He told me the details of the war that I had missed. I enjoyed listening to him talk. I enjoyed the fountain of information that poured out of him. We walked together, and he gave me a few books and by the time we made it back, the camp was already well on its way to being broken down.

It was Salome who called us all together. Things are never simple. Dania was pacing in the tent and waving her arms about. She was ranting about something, and when we entered, she stopped. She waited for everyone to arrive, and then she just yelled.

"This is not what Xander would have wanted! We can't just surrender because The University told us too. We have Ailive. We have the rwans, and we have God. We'll be victorious."

"This isn't surrender," I said. "This is compromise. There's a difference."

"God has called on us to spread his word. If we flee to the desert, they have won."

"We aren't fleeing," Salome said. "The world knows God's message. We've been given fine land on which to build a temple, a great cathedral, and for us to build a city for our people."

"You're a coward. Xander would scoff at your weakness," Dania said.

"Xander hated war," I said. "He hated the warrior in me. Don't use my brothers' name to incite war."

For a few minutes there was silence. Dania hesitated, but she couldn't contain her mouth. "The Efferitas are savages. How can we accept their charity when we know it may turn to cruelty tomorrow?"

Hotem spoke loudly. "We have never shown you anything but hospitality."

"Yes. Tell that to my oldest daughter, whom your soldiers killed and raped."

"Those were my father's soldiers."

"Yes and what will your sons' soldiers do? You guarantee us peace and safety, but you will die some day and then what? Will we be safe then?"

"I'm changing my kingdom. Myhanna is Popess, and she is a Caeimoni. Our land can be yours if you choose to take it."

"I'll not sell out my faith and my people for a scrap of paper signed by tyrants," Dania said.

"We'll die here. I can and have fought many, but I can't fight the entire world. Hotem's soldiers are dying. We're almost out of food. The rwans come and go as they please and your new brand of warrior Caeimoni are nothing but glorified terrorists. This scrap of paper can save us, and Hotem has offered us sanctuary. If you don't see God's hand in this miracle, I doubt you will ever see it anywhere," I said with a wave of my hand.

"I'll leave this place tonight. I can't follow you on your path to sacrilege. All those who have faith in my belief are welcome to take up their swords and follow me. Above all others I beg you, Ailive, to join me. You are the saint of the storm. You alone have saved us."

"No. It took many to save us, and most of them are dead on that field. Your saints have painted the ground with their blood. I will not make any more martyrs. You do what you want, but I'm going with Hotem," I said.

So there was a great schism in the Caeimoni and those that left that night became the Danians and were people of the knife. I watched Dania take her people away in the night and felt like she was tearing my brother in half. If he had been alive, he would have gone to Dania with his sweet words and kind touch. But he was gone, and none of us had Xander's uncanny ability to soothe the angry soul in people.

Dania did not take many. That was what saved us from the schism. She only took a little less than two hundred men and two women. Most of those that followed her were the remnants of the raider armies. Dania was not popular, but the schism affected the way the other Caeimoni saw its leaders and the integrity of the newborn religion as a whole. It was born as a religion deeply divided.

After we watched the Danians leave, we finished our packing and began our slow procession south. Hotem withdrew all of his troops to the south of the Midi and the entire Caeimoni camp, over one million strong, migrated back over the Midi River. It was a long journey, and we were crippled by the elderly and children.

The occasional attack slowed our progress even further. We would have been killed if it had not been for the supplies and support The University provided us. Sulen even came with a large detachment of the IA to help us. We suddenly founded ourselves surrounded by rocket launchers, cannons, and missiles.

Sulen worked relentlessly to aid in our defense, but he avoided me as much as possible.

"Why are you helping us?" I asked him. I caught him with his back turned, and he scowled at me.

"I see Cahir is easily replaced," he said cruelly. "You already look the part of queen."

I was wearing a gilded dress, and Hotem had given me a small diadem to wear. I shifted uncomfortably in my clothes.

"Cahir left me," I answered.

"And his departure obviously left you in mourning," Sulen spat.

"Why are you here? You hate the tribeless. You were Cahir's man."

"Once this rabble is resettled they won't be tribeless anymore, will they? I just want this war to end, and I want to see our city prosper again."

"You aren't here as a spy?"

"Are you kidding? For who? You and yours have killed all of my allies on the outside. All that's left are a handful of half dead legions fighting for hate alone. You've won, Saint—or is it Queen—Ailive?"

It took us three months of walking and dragging to get everyone to the other side of the river. When we finally crossed the Midi, we found University-made warships lined up on the river. Salome took Xander's followers to the soft plains just south of the Midi and began to build her city, and Hotem and I manned the warships and began the lengthy process of learning how to fight a modern war.

Hotem's officers found themselves surrounded by University-trained soldiers and weapons the likes of which they could only imagine. We thwarted every attack so conclusively that the seven tribes that had been our worst adversaries called for a meeting to discuss terms.

Thus the Union of Tribes was born, for Hotem, whose vision is far, sent emissaries to every tribe and had The University send emissaries to every tribe requesting a meeting of all tribes in the interests of peace just outside The University. All the presidents, councilors, dictators, chancellors, prime ministers, kings, emperors, and chiefs met to discuss how best to prevent another Great War.

After fifteen days of labor, the great men and women of the world produced a treaty that bore rules to govern all of mankind and to protect its children from the cruelty of fate. Hotem agreed to open his doors to all tribeless seeking refuge. The tribes agreed that there would be no further attempts to eradicate the tribeless, but that raiders could be detained for trial and punishment according to law. An intertribal court was established, and The University became the very definite center of the world.

Jacob sat as The University's voice to the world, and Mia was at his side. Jacob had acquired the power he longed for. He was the heir apparent to the role of High Councilor of The University.

It was a long year of standing beside Hotem before I could become his queen. We were traveling back to Efferitas and had stopped at the Plain of Blood, where my brother was buried. Salome had named it. It was a place that all tribes feared as haunted or sacred. Hotem and I decided to be married there because it was there that we had first made love.

The night before my wedding, I was shivering in my bed. My stomach was in my throat and my throat was on fire as I left the airship to walk to my brother's grave.

I put my hand on the stones where he rested and wept, begging his forgiveness. I must have fallen asleep there and when I awoke, Jason was there. He was sitting next to me, as he had for so many years, looking down on me.

"We are the same, you and I," I said as I touched his face. "Monsters fighting to be human."

He turned into the morning mist and walked away. I followed him. He led me out of the woods and onto the killing fields, where the mist hung low and heavy. I couldn't see anything but Jason and then he disappeared. I wasn't sure of what I was seeing at first. I thought I was asleep or that the mist was playing tricks on me, but I couldn't deny what I saw.

"Xander?" I said.

He embraced me and kissed my head. "Baby sister," he said.

"Am I dreaming?"

"All life is a dream, but this is real."

I reached out and touched him. I touched the wounds on his chest. "Xander," I said. "I'm so sorry. I brought Cahir into the camp. I told him where you were. Please, forgive me."

"I forgave you before it even happened. God forgives all and so do I. I have come to heal two more wounds and the rest must be left for the next life."

"What?" I stammered stupidly.

"The first are not yours," he said. He raised his hands and the mist cleared. I turned and I saw every rwan that had ever walked the earth standing in concentric circles around us. They stood facing us with their wings open and touching. They stood with their eyes opened wide and filled with fire. "Jason," he said. "Your sins and the sins of your people are forgiven." He leaned forward and touched the beast and all the fire in him faded. His red eyes dimmed, and the blood beneath his black skin became stone. The life in Jason's legion faded with a single breath, and I was left standing in a field of statues. The rwans had died.

And then Xander touched me. He touched my abdomen. He fell to his knees and kissed my stomach. "I held you in my arms when you were still an innocent," Xander said. "You were my beautiful baby sister, and I loved you more than any other. May you have that joy. The joy of holding your beloveds in your arms and watching them grow into all you hoped they could be."

I screamed, and the mist descended. There was a pain in my gut the likes of which I had never known, and when I stood up, my dress was soaked in blood. I thought I must be dying. I was hemorrhaging, and Xander had left me alone to die in a field of statues. I fell down again, staring at the blood on my gown. I screamed and men came. They carried me carefully to the doctors.

The doctors laughed at me. They laughed so hard I blushed and they didn't believe me when I said nothing like this had happened to me before. It didn't matter. I was menstruating. I took my medicine and cleaned myself. I was a woman.

XII
Peace

Hotem took my hand and we stepped off of the airship onto the soft earth of his palace. People bowed as we passed by. I was still in my purple wedding gown. I must have been glowing. It was the same room we had started in: the room I had taught him to fight in.

Hotem undressed me slowly, and then I undressed him. We slid into the bed we had spent so many nights in without ever touching.

"I've waited forever for this," he said.

"I think I have too," I answered happily. "I should have said yes before. I shouldn't have ever left you."

"You did what had to be done. You are part of history now. You can't regret your actions," he said as he kissed my stomach. I laughed as he kissed me.

"You're history. Xander was history. Even Cahir was history. I'm just a side note."

"You are history. You are a goddess." His voice became a caress.

"Be quiet," I said smothering him with my mouth. We didn't leave that room for a week. When we did emerge for our wedding banquet, Myhanna was more than annoyed by our behavior.

Hotem disappeared for a few weeks after the banquet. He had to work, and I was left alone in the palace. I was a bad queen. I did nothing to run the palace and ignored all pleas for help from the servants and politicians. Mostly I sat on the veranda reading and watching the world pass me by. Hotem returned at night and crawled into bed with me.

"I missed you," I said lovingly.

"I missed you," he said.

"Did you save the empire?" I asked.

He smiled. I loved his smile. I loved the way the corners of his eyes wrinkled. "Far from it," he answered.

"I have news." I tried to hide my smile but I couldn't.

"Really."

"I'm pregnant!" I exclaimed.

"What!?" Hotem asked. "Are you joking?"

"I'm not good with jokes."

Hotem grabbed me and pulled me on top of him. He looked at my eyes. "I don't understand. I thought you were…I thought your tribe took that from you."

"They did."

"Then how?"

"It'll sound crazy."

"I'm used to that. I lived with the Caeimoni."

"Xander healed me."

Hotem leaned down and kissed my belly. He rested his head on it. "Thank you," he said.

I bore Hotem two sons. At first, I was afraid of them. I didn't know what to do with them. I had a nurse who would sit with me and hold them for me. I would watch the way she cradled them and the way they leaned into the warmth of her embrace.

They were too beautiful. After my first son was born, I would go to the nursery and just stare at him. I was mesmerized by the smallness of his hands, his tiny feet, and the way he looked at me with wide curious eyes.

I couldn't believe this tiny life had sprung from me. It seemed impossible. Eventually, I gathered enough courage and held him. The nurse sat beside me and told me it was all right. She put her hands on my shoulders and stood behind me.

"Your baby loves you, Milady. You're a natural mother. Don't be afraid," she said. And my little Hotem leaned into my embrace. So I would sit in my chair by the window all day and hold him. I would stare down at his perfect face until he wanted to break free of me and sit on the floor.

Hotem came home and soon, I was pregnant again. He reveled in his son and would place his face on my belly. He spoke to my growing belly like the baby inside was a man already, his heir to be.

Hotem often invited me to join him on his journeys. I always refused, but he wanted me to be part of his new political plan. He had begun to build a senate, in which all of his people and all of the colonies could have a say. He traveled to the colonies incessantly, trying to help them elect senators and officials from amongst their own.

I helped change the land in my own way. I helped with terraforming. I would sit in my room, clinging to my sons and weep. I couldn't say why I was weeping. I think I was haunted. My memories overwhelmed me and clouded my eyes with visions and dark dreams, and the water leaked from them like an old wound that would never heal. When I cried, the rain came. It flooded the desert and forever changed our world.

When Hotem left, he would always leave poems under my pillow. Soft kisses composed of words. I put them in a box beside my bed and read them after the boys were sleeping. Time slid by us and Hotem came and went like the wind. He would crawl into bed with me late at night and make love to me and before he left he would always ask the same question.

"Come with me?" he would ask.

I shivered and wrapped my arms around him. The thought of leaving my little piece of paradise left me cold. In the palace, I had my rooms and my boys and my view of the garden. No one asked anything of me. "I can't," I always said, and he would disappear again to face his angry world.

Finally, he stopped coming at all. I got letters. I heard the news, but almost a year had passed, and he had not come for me.

Myhanna often visited me during the days. She would sit next to me in her long white robes and stare vacantly at the three room nursery the boys and I spent our days in. She said little and for the most part seemed happy that I was a nonentity politically. Her tone changed after my second son had his first birthday.

"The world is changing," Myhanna said to me one day. She was looking out the window at the cherry trees. They were in bloom, and their aroma filled the pale blue room with an intoxicating odor.

"I don't care," I said as I pushed my older boy around in a toy airship.

"Obviously," Myhanna said dismissively.

"You don't need me," I said after a while. "You both ruled together before I was here. Things don't need to change. I'm happy here."

"I see that."

The baby started to cry, and the nurse ran to his side. She picked him up and handed him to me, and I sat down and started to rock him.

"Hotem needs you," Myhanna said firmly.

"Hotem is fine," I answered airily.

"How would you know? When was the last time you saw him?"

"I can't remember," I answered.

"Don't you care that you never see your husband?"

"He has to work. He's a powerful man. The world is changing. I would be a fool if I expected him to sit with me holding my hand and singing me love ballads."

"He needs you, and you should go to him," Myhanna asserted.

"Why?"

"I'm not at liberty to say. You can't hide in these three rooms forever. The Ailive I knew all those years ago, the Ailive that taught me to defy the world, would never be content to lock herself away and fade into a glorified nursemaid."

"I'm happy," I said again.

"Happy? Really? I think you are hiding from the world."

"I am hiding. I'm tired of the world. I don't want to be part of it anymore."

"You're a queen. You're a saint. You're a wife. You can't hide. Your husband needs you."

"He never says so," I answered sadly.

"You never talk to him. How can he say what he needs if you don't talk to him? Men are strange beasts. They may appear hard, but they can't live forever on the memories of love. They need their wives near them."

"He has said he needs me?"

"I know him. I'm his most trusted advisor. I know what he needs."

"What about the boys?"

"They have five nannies. They'll be fine. I will look in on them myself."

I packed my bags quickly and took an airship to see my husband. The city had changed. Electric lights glimmered in windows. Small mopeds navigated the narrow streets. Long roads crossed what had once been desert but had become pastures and fields connecting the colonies. Hotem had been working hard.

We landed in a small village colony by the water. The little village was built mostly of stucco houses and huts, but they had begun building several large brick structures in the center of town. Acres of cropland surrounded the village and construction had begun on some kind of port. I had dressed humbly, as always, in a simple silk sari. My hair was down, and I wore no shoes.

I stood out, because I was small and fair, but no one would have guessed me to be a queen. I left my escort at the airship and carried my own bags into the town.

I saw Hotem's men surrounding a low, ranch-style structure in the middle of town. His men garrisoned the house, and his flag waved high above the building.

"We're sorry but we can't let you in, ma'am," a soldier said as I approached.

"Why not?" I asked.

"The king is here today, and he is holding court."

"Court?" I asked waiting for them to recognize me.

"He's here annexing Byhala as a state of the empire," the man said. "He's giving these people equal rights."

"Really?" I asked haughtily. "Who's he seeing today?"

"That's private."

"I want to go in," I said with irritation. I still expected them to realize who I was.

Another guard drew his gun and the men surrounded me. "Go away, lady," one of the guards said. "We don't want trouble."

"I'm the queen. I'm Ailive. I want to see my husband now, and if you don't let me cross I'll break all your knees."

"You aren't the queen," another guard said.

"Why don't you think I am the queen?"

"She never leaves the palace, and she would not be walking barefoot like an urchin alone in the middle of nowhere."

"I'm glad you're intimate with her enough to know what she would and would not do."

A crowd of people began to gather around us, listening to or argument. A small girl in filthy rags approached me and looked up at me. She smiled and yelled, "It's her! It's Saint Ailive."

For a moment there was silence, and then the crowd surrounded me. They asked for prayers and praised me for all the king had done for them. "What has the king done?" I asked.

"He helped us rebuild our fields and city," an old lady said. I kissed the old lady and gave her a small ring from my finger.

"Can I go in now?" I asked the guard. The dimwitted man relented, and I stepped over the threshold into an air-conditioned, miniature replica of the palace.

It was uncannily quite. I tiptoed through the rooms until I found my husband in the arms of a young, dark haired girl.

For several moments, I watched them. I finally realized what I had given up for safety, watching him with envy and longing.

I had lost what had taken a lifetime to find.

Finally, I pushed back the curtains and entered the room. The girl froze, and Hotem looked up at me with shock.

I walked across the hard, stone floors and threw open the curtains around the windows, revealing a brilliant view of the sea on the other side of the city.

"The people tell me you are doing marvelous work here," I said to Hotem. "They say you are making a senate and giving them the right to hold office in it. They say you are making them equals and Efferitas' citizens."

Behind me I heard the girl shuffling for her clothes in a desperate attempt to flee with dignity.

I walked over to her and put my hand on her shoulder. "Don't leave yet," I said softly. "Go out to the kitchen and get yourself some tea. Pull yourself together. Get dressed. You're in no danger."

Hotem sat naked on the bed. He stood up casually and put on his robe as the girl left. "Myhanna told me to come," I said.

Hotem said nothing.

"Is this why she told me to come?" I asked.

"I don't know why she told you to come, and I don't know why you listened. I've asked you to come with me a thousand times," he said glibly.

"I'm sorry," I said with true repentance.

"Don't be. I'm a weak man." He spoke with a sudden earnestness that sharply juxtaposed his previous tone. He looked sad.

"This is a beautiful place," I said softly as I looked out the window.

"And it will be more beautiful still. We are building a huge port here that will carry our grain all the way to Notua and the northern coastal regions."

"What's her name?"

"What does it matter? She's just one of many." Hotem poured himself a glass of wine and walked toward me.

"Many?" I regretted staying so long from his side. How many women had he left naked and alone while I hid in my tower?

"Why do you care? You haven't been interested in me since the boys were born," he said gruffly.

"How many?" I asked.

He turned on me with accusation in his eyes. "Were you using me?"

"Using you?" I asked in disbelief.

Hotem sat down on the bed again. Without his turban on, his hair was long and curly. It was dark flecked with gray. "For a moment, you were mine. I signed your treaty, and I can't say I regret it, but now you have vanished from me, and I have to know if all those words were just part of an act to get your way."

"I can't act," I said.

I heard wind chimes in the distance. I looked around at the room, beneath the façade of the wealth, it was quite plain. It had once belonged to a poor people.

"You never sit by me before the people. You never go with me to the colonies or on ambassadorial meetings. You hardly even talk to me anymore. I come, we make love and I go."

"Forgive me, Hotem. I told you I would make a poor queen."

"You would make a great queen, if you wanted to. If you wanted me."

"I'm not a poet. That's your place. I wasn't born into a world of romance and fancy. I don't know these things. If I don't tell you I love you in a way that convinces you, it's because I lack the talent, not the will."

"Why don't you want to be with me?"

The wind blew in through the room knocking over a stack of papers on a table. The papers were cast into the air and fell lightly to the ground.

"I want to be with you, but I'm tired, and I just want peace."

Hotem touched my face and smiled. He wasn't young, but his beauty remained. He pulled me too him and held me.

"I'm sorry about the girl," he said.

"What's her name?"

"Hannah." I frowned a little. She had the same name as the slave girl the men used to pass around.

"Be kind to her. Don't just use her up and toss her away. Does she have family?"

"I don't know."

"I'll find out."

"Did you use me to get what you wanted out of me?" he asked again.

This time his tone was softer and sad.

"No. I love you. I'll send for the boys, and I'll go where ever you go. I'm yours."

He reached out and stroked my hair. I leaned into his touch like a cat.

"Mia wants to meet with me. Come with me. Help me negotiate this new treaty The University is offering."

"I'm yours, my love. Until the day I die, I'm yours. I'll go where you send me."

He pulled me down with him, and I lay with him on the bed. "Who are you?" he asked.

"Just Ailive. I was born a killer. I became a scholar and then a soldier and then I was yours. I'm yours."

He fell asleep in my arms, and then I went out to Hannah in the kitchen. I walked her home and apologized to her family. I offered them money and begged their forgiveness.

The mother looked at me like I was mad. "Why aren't you angry?" the woman asked. "Our daughter seduced your husband. She has always been this way. You should have her flogged."

"Your daughter deserves better," I said.

I went with Hotem to the killing fields to meet with Mia. There was an enormous church on the site where our tents had been. The church was a mixture of Efferitas and Xenderian architecture that seemed all wrong. It was made of white marble, but it was built with round domed architecture. To get into the church, you had to walk through the field of dead rwans. There was housing for pilgrims in the church. Hotem and I stayed in a simple room at the back of the church.

Hotem took my arm. We walked out into the woods together, to Xander's grave. We met Mia there.

"Strange place for a meeting," Hotem said as we walked there.

"Mia is a strange girl," I answered.

Mia stood in the mist waiting for us. "You came!" she exclaimed when she saw me. "I was told you wouldn't come." I hugged Mia. She looked wonderful. The elixir had softened her features, giving her the strange immortality of University scholars.

"You've aged," Mia said sadly.

"I'm not one of you anymore. I don't have the serum."

"It gives you a wisdom," Mia said. "You look regal."

"Thank you."

"You have a proposal for me?" Hotem asked.

Mia handed him a thick stack of papers. "It'll take me a week to read this," Hotem said. "Can you sum it up a little for me?"

We all sat down on the stone benches that had been put in the woods around the tomb. "It's simpler than it seems," Mia said. "I propose a complete union between The University and Efferitas' nation. We would like to build a number of large roads between our two nations."

Mia pulled some papers out of her bag and shuffled through them as she spoke. "As part of this proposal, we would build and staff over one hundred schools for varying age groups in the capital and in the colonies. We would build power plants and staff them until your people were competent enough to take over. We'll build hospitals and send doctors and nurses. We will make the elixir available to nobility, including yourself and your queen. We help you with more modern agricultural techniques so your croplands will be more productive."

Mia stopped suddenly and looked at me very intently. "I'm not going to lie," she said. "We need you, and I think what we have to offer will make your empire a better place for all of its people."

"In essence," I said. "We'll become your colony."

"No," she said. "You'll maintain all political autonomy."

"But you will build a culture of dependency. You'll have power over us," Hotem said. "I'm not comfortable with this."

"Don't trust my people. Trust me. I'm a councilman now, and this is my vision of the future and you know that I'm as much Efferitas as anything else. I grew up in your palace."

"Why meet here?" I asked her.

"I wanted you to know that I'm not a University scholar. This treaty is not about power and manipulation. It's about preserving your brother's ideals. We need peace and stability, and this treaty will unify the two most powerful forces in the world. It will work to stabilize us both. Jacob will do everything in his power, and he has a lot of power, to preserve the integrity of this document."

"You've changed. Crian must be proud," I said.

"Crian died," she said. "There was a problem with the artificial atmosphere on the moon. We lost half a million people along with our agricultural land and our uranium mines. We've been in mourning for months." Mia's political façade faded for a moment, and I saw a little of the Mia I used to know. I felt sick. She seemed so sad and lost. I couldn't imagine Mia without her mother. I hadn't realized how long it had been since I'd seen Crian.

"I don't know what to say," I said.

"There's nothing to say," Mia said. "It was a minor miscalculation. A number that someone forgot to carry when predicting the orbit of the moon and its proximity to the sun."

"I'm sorry about your mother," I stuttered. I had always thought I would see her again. I had assumed that time or life would bring us back together.

"Such is life."

"Give me a few days to read this over and think. I need to talk with my advisors," Hotem said. He was a cold man in many ways.

"That's fine," Mia said. "I'll wait for your response. I'm staying in the church."

"No airship?" I asked.

"Not this time. I wanted to stay in the temple. I knew your brother. He was a good man. This is a good place to mourn. I need some time and this gives it to me," Mia said.

"Have breakfast with me then?"

"That would be wonderful."

Hotem nodded to Mia formally and walked away. I followed him into the forest. He was going nowhere. He only wandered. He climbed up over a small hill and stood up at the top looking down. Below us there was the lush woods and green meadow. The meadow was drenched in sunlight and tiny flowers peeked their white heads out from beneath the grass. Bird song filled the air.

I stood beside my husband and put my hand in his. He squeezed my hand slightly and looked to where the meadow ended near the circle of rwans.

"You think we should do this?" Hotem asked.

"I do," I said.

"I don't trust you," he said. "I don't trust her."

"I'm the mother of your children."

"I didn't say I don't love you."

"It will be winter soon," I said as I looked off into the distance. I was bad at politics. I didn't know how to negotiate emotions. I missed the simplicity of my youth. I missed the simplicity of the sword. "The snow will come. In my youth, I used to climb high above my city and sit on top of the great temple, the karash, and watch the world go by. All I wanted was to climb down through the ice and snow and become one of the multitudes of normal people."

I shook my head and turned back to the complexity of my life, back to my tumultuous husband. "You're right not to trust me. I did leave you. I did love Cahir and for a long time, I was his. I wanted this treaty. I wanted to do whatever I had to do to facilitate it. I've been distant since our children were born. I don't talk to you."

"All I have ever wanted is to be normal and in that nursery, with our boys, I'm normal. To them, I'm not a killer or a saint or a queen. Every time I leave the palace people bow. I just want to be Ailive. You don't have to trust me, Hotem, but I love you, and I love our boys, and I love the life you've given me."

Hotem studied me. "I'm sorry about the girl," he said.

"Apologize to her. It was her you wronged."

"I wouldn't know where to find her."

"I hired her. She's my new attendant."

"What's this? Some special torture to remind me of my sins?" he asked angrily.

"Her family was too proud to take my money, so I gave her a job. She loved you. Did you love her?"

"There have been many women since you left, but you have always been the only woman. How could anyone ever touch you? The first moment I saw you on that battlefield I was lost. I thought you were a goddess."

"I'm no goddess."

"Do you know why my father insisted on keeping you in the palace as a slave instead of selling you?"

"Why?"

"Because he knew how I felt about you. He could see it in the way I looked at you. He wanted me to become a man, and he thought you were the one."

"You loved me then? Even after I cut your finger off."

"There has never been anyone but you. But you cloud my eyes. You've loved others. You've followed other leaders. When I'm with you, I don't know if you love me at all, or if you are still loyal to others."

I fell to me knees in front of him. Mud seeped into the soft cotton of my sari, staining it. I pushed my face against his hand and kissed it. "Don't you remember me as I was? Don't you remember when I taught you to fight? I was loyal to none then. There was only you."

He nodded. "I remember."

"That was me. This is me."

Hotem picked me up and threw me down in the grass. He tore through my clothes and bit me. I lay there, submitting to him. He was violent and his weight crushed me, stealing my breath. He pinned me to the earth and pushed me into the mud and when he was done I wrapped my mud stained arms around him and kissed his tears away. He lay on top of me, and I held him, stoking his hair.

The sun set above us, coloring Hotem in violent alizarin crimson, and he propped himself up and looked down at my face. He kissed my cheeks like a mother would kiss a child. "I don't care if you are using me," he said. "I would sell my soul for you."

"Beloved," I whispered. "I would never let you. I love you, and I won't leave you again. I will be by your side for as long as you need me. I promise."

He wrapped me in his cloak, and we walked back to the temple. I bathed, and he and I went to or first official dinner as king and queen. I took my crown out of its velvet box and put it on my head. It felt heavy and uncomfortable. I was still beautiful, but I no longer felt like myself.

I sat with him in front of a room of diplomats and pilgrims. We held hands and greeted people from every nation. We spoke of politics and the changing world. The catastrophe on the moon was still on the tip of everyone's tongue. I smiled and nodded, but had little to say. But Hotem held my hand, and when he looked at me, I knew I had to be there.

Mia and I met in a small restaurant near the temple for pastries and fruit. Mia dressed simply, in pants and a light blouse. She looked plump and pale, like all the other scholars. She looked the part.

"Queen," she said, bowing to me.

"Please, don't do that," I said. "Or I will have to start calling you councilman, and you don't want that."

She sat down next to me and smiled. "Who would have thought that two slaves would end up with such titles?"

"Who would have thought that the great and mighty University would become desperate enough to join hands with a barbarian horde?"

"Strange times we live in," Mia said. "What's it like? Being a queen? I have to tell you, I was mad for a long time. I thought you'd be coming back to The University with Jacob and I."

"I'm a pathetic queen."

"Good to know you're pathetic at something. You've excelled at everything else."

Mia and I laughed. "I guess we all have our weak points," I said. "I'm a horrible wife too, apparently."

"I'll give you some pointers. I'm the perfect wife," Mia said with a blush.

"You're married?" I said in disbelief.

"Yes," she said happily.

"Congratulations. Who?"

"You never met him. He's on the council too. He's a good man. I love him very much."

"So how do you go about being a good wife?" I asked with a smile.

"I think it's mostly sex, all the time, and a lot of compliments," she joked.

We laughed again. "Well if that's all, I better go home and get to work," I said.

We talked for about the smaller things in life for a long time. She told me about her new apartment and her husband. She spoke of trying to get the appropriate approvals to have a baby, and I told her about my sons. Outside, the sun rose high above the verdant mountains. Mia and I held hands and spoke of her mother's death and finally she said the thing that weighed most heavily on her mind.

"Will Hotem sign the treaty?" she asked hesitantly.

"I don't know. He doesn't trust you or I. He's meeting with his advisors today. We'll see."

"He doesn't trust you?" she asked.

I looked out at the mountains. "I haven't seen much of him over the last few years."

"Why not? You and he were meant to be."

"I just wanted to stay with my boys. He had to change the world, build utopia."

"You should have taken the boys and followed him."

"I don't care about politics."

"You have to be joking. You worked tirelessly with Jacob to change the world. Your actions have been the foundations of the new world. You can't just stop caring."

"It isn't that important."

"It hasn't been long," she said, "since you stood on that battlefield defying the world. You were the one that negotiated the treaty between The University and the Efferitas. How can you be quiet now?"

"I'm not like you, Mia. You love your work, and you love designing this new world. I'm a remnant of an old world, and I'm happy to let you build this new one."

"I don't understand," Mia said again. She still looked as young as the first day I had met her. Her face was smooth and clear. I had aged.

"Mia," I said. "I have seen too much. I can't have your hope in life. I don't believe this will last. People never stop fighting. I lack the idealism required to help you create your dream. But I'm queen, and I will help you make your dream feasible within this world."

"We've all seen horror," Mia said. "That doesn't mean we should give up."

I smiled. "You sound like Myhanna." I shook my head and looked down at my hands. "No. Part of me is broken. Don't ask anymore of me than what I have already given."

"You'll lose Hotem and eventually you'll lose your boys. They'll grow up and become kings, and you will become nothing but an old nursemaid."

I smiled at her. It was a faint smile. "Maybe I'll take your advice and go home and be a good wife. Maybe that will be enough."

Mia and I sat in the sanctuary together. The evening light slid in through the stained glass staining our faces with a myriad of color. The entire room had become a cacophony of colored light. The sanctuary's walls were mostly stained glass depictions of the great war and Xander and in the evening and morning sitting in it was like sitting in the inner chamber of a rainbow.

Hotem and his men found us in this chamber. He regarded us coolly. He was dressed as a king should be dressed, wrapped in jewels and crowned. He didn't say anything. He just handed Mia the proposal. She took the document and clutched it to her chest like it was her greatest treasure.

"Your people can start on their road construction whenever they are ready. Let my people know what supplies you need. You can use Ailive as your contact."

Hotem turned and walked away as abruptly as he had come. Mia reached in her bag and gave me a list. "Go," she said. "Chase him before you lose him forever. Everything I need is in that letter. You know where to reach me."

I stood up and ran after Hotem. I left the sanctuary of light and entered the cool stone halls that ran in between the pilgrim's rooms. "I don't have time for this now," he said to me when I opened my mouth to talk.

"Please," I said.

"I have to leave to settle a dispute. Go back to the boys."

"I'm coming with you."

"No."

I grabbed him and kissed him. I held him to me so he couldn't break free and finally he gave in. When I let him go, he could barely breathe.

Hotem's advisors and guards stood around us staring at me like I had just set fire to the church. "Please sir," I said. "I need only a few moments alone with you." I pulled Hotem away from the shocked crowd and down the hall to our room. He stared at me as I undressed. I made love to him with ferocious intensity and when we were done, he stared up at me with wide eyes.

"Stay with me," I said. "Come home with me, and meet your boys and then we can all travel to the ends of the earth together. I love you. I need you. Don't leave me again."

"Okay," he said, and we made love again.

Hotem returned with me. He sent one of his advisors to settle the dispute and he stayed the boys and me for a long time. He supervised the empire from afar, and the new improvements in communication facilitated his ability to rule from a distance. The boys grew. Our world flourished. I helped Mia initiating her proposal, and when I wasn't working with Mia or with Hotem, I was with my boys.

Every morning I taught them the dance. They learned to fight the old way with the wind and a blade. They had a plethora of teachers, but I taught them what I thought they should know. I took them down into the city and made them walk and live with the people. We went to Salome's city and helped her give medicine to the throngs of sick tribeless that flocked to her sanctuary in the unending aftermath of the Great War. Five years had passed, and it felt like the world was still healing.

I taught my boys to walk and to travel on foot. I taught them to survive, but mostly I loved them. I bathed them in my silent adoration, because they were the only miracle that mattered to me. They were my heart and my soul, a piece of mercy, my little Hotem and Hotus.

Despite my love for our children, Hotem remained the fire of my life. I was determined not to lose him again. After ten years, he gave me a third child.

Before I knew I was pregnant with Aeila, I had a wretched dream. I was holding one of my babies, but it was possessed by a demon of the old world. I clutched my baby and fought the demon. Salome, Myhanna, Hotem, and even Xander stood with me and together we all laid our hands on the baby and called on all the power of heaven to save it, but I was weak and I fell and when I fell, the baby was lost to the demon and so was I.

Once I felt Aeila growing in my womb, I knew the dream had been about her. I sang to her every night and during the day, despite my complete lack of faith, I would let Myhanna pray over my belly and anoint it with oil. But my fear was not assuaged, and I knew I could not rest until I had found out the meaning of my dream.

Jacob came when I was still in the early months of my pregnancy. He had been high councilman for six years when he came for the inauguration of Mia's train. Jacob came and stood beside Hotem and me on the platform and kissed us both. Age had finally caught up with him. No one lives forever. He was gray and hunched, and he walked with a cane.

We were the first people to ride the express. It was wonderful. The journey that had taken me years, was done in less than a day. We stopped at many places along the way: Salome's city, a few tribal allies that were in the direct line between The University and Efferitas.

The only place I remember is the killing field. The train stopped there, and we all climbed up to the green field into the center of the ring of rwans. Their stone eyes stared out at me through their eerie tomb. I took one last pilgrimage to the edge of the field where there was nothing to mark the place I had almost killed Cahir. I put my hand on the earth and tried to remember his face, but his memory had faded like the bloodstains on the ground.

Hotem and I spent the week at The University with the boys. The boys loved The University. They stared up at it in complete awe and wonder. The University had changed. It had grown, and there were more students. The Efferitas' students alone had more than doubled the student population at The University. Students gathered everyplace and all the classes were filled beyond capacity. Everyone was rich and apparently happy.

I knew that The University was a deep pool, and I wanted to know was lurked beneath the surface. I couldn't believe that one thing could spare a world of all troubles, so I went to see Sulen. He still sat on the security council, despite all the recent changes. He saw me reluctantly. He met me at a dank little bar at the edge of the city.

"Things look like they've improved here," I said blandly.

"What do you want?" Sulen said with an irritated grimace. "You aren't a queen here, and I'm busy."

I shook my head. "I'm not entirely sure. I just wanted to know how things were. I just wanted you to tell me about the things that can't be seen."

"You want me to say that you and Jacob saved The University? Right? I'm not going to say that, so you should just go home to your savages."

"I want the truth."

"The truth?" he asked in disbelief. "The IA and the security council is now tightly regulated by a wonderful new bureaucracy call the Department of the Interior. The DI. They spy on us constantly and report everything we do. People are arrested for nothing. People lose their jobs for nothing. They built a new base on the third moon. They named it Anon. Anyone who violates the new Peace Act is sent there.It isn't a prison, just a desolate place composed mostly of red rock and dirt. Terraforming there is a nightmare. We have become a paranoid people, and for what?"

He threw his hands in the air and shook his head in impotent rage. "Another Cahir? He wanted the scholars brought down a notch and for ordinary people, like myself, to move out of the dark parts of town and have real lives. If the tribeless had been resettled earlier, the Great War never would have happened. He was right."

Sarcasm dripped from his tongue as he spoke his next words. "So now everything here is pretty. The students and the professors live in their pretty painted world and the rest of us? We live off their scraps. We eat when they tell us to eat and have babies when they say we can; one baby per couple when they turn thirty and if you miss that window, if you are sick or unable, you lose your chance. We get sick. We grow old. We die, while they live forever. More and more people go to the moons, seeking a better life. And maybe there is something better up there, but I don't think this place is better. Is that what you want to hear?"

"I'm sorry, Sulen."

"No you are not. You never loved him. You just used him up and spat him out at your leisure."

"He used me, too."

Sulen didn't answer this. He seemed very old, and he was tired. He leaned back and stared at me for a long time. "I understand what you did. There are no easy answers." He shook his head, and suddenly, he seemed so sad that I wanted to embrace him. "We all have our own battles to fight, and you saved your own."

"He killed my brother," I said.

"I know. The prophet."

Sulen and I shook hands and parted in poorer spirits than we had started. He told me the truth I knew was there. I saw the citizens of The University wearing their gray robes, hidden behind all the glory. They couldn't travel with the students, and they couldn't eat with them. They cooked their food and built their houses, but they were the part of The University that was not supposed to be known.

I told my boys about my meeting with Sulen. I told them about Cahir. They were twelve and thirteen, and I wanted them to understand the world. I told them that every freedom comes at a price. I took them to the dark parts of the city, and we walked amongst the citizens. We ate at their diners and sat in their chairs. Little Hotem watched with wide eyes, but

Hotus only glared with disgust.

I took them to every alley of The University. I needed them to understand that the world was not a utopia and that the battles we fought often brought pyrrhic victories. "We could travel the world and see that the glory of one people is built on the back of others," I said. "You boys are my heart, and we shelter you from such things, but you will be kings, and you must understand the cost of your decisions."

I pointed to the dark alley behind me. "This is the cost of my decision to fight against Cahir. These people will never be free. They will never be called this, but they are slaves here. They are always watched, and they can't even choose when to have children or marry. This is the price that was paid for our freedom."

"They could leave," Hotus said. "They aren't slaves."

"And go where?" I asked.

"They could come to us."

"This is all they've ever known."

"There are worse existences."

"Yes," I said. And so I was inspired to take my boys around the world. We went on several ambassadorial missions and the boys and I crept through the slums of every city that would have us to learn the nature of the world. It was on these journeys that I had an exciting revelation. My boys had inherited my ability to speak in tongues. I got bigger and rounder, and my boys relished the world they saw before them. Little Hotem seemed the most impressed by our journeys. But our voyages were cut short by my impending labor, and we returned home for the birth of Aeila.

Aeila was born in the midst of the gnawing, and she was perfect. My last child was as beautiful as all the stars in heaven, and everyone rejoiced in her beauty. The boys loved her and for that first year after her birth, Hotem gave up his travels and our family became inseparable.

Hotem was able to rest. The colonies had been completely annexed into the government and had given themselves names and became cities in a nation connected by common coin, education, and free trade. These cities had self-sustaining governments, and the senate did more and more of the work, so that Hotem, who was becoming an old man, could just sit and be with us. That was our year. It was blissful and perfect. Hotem spent untold hours with the boys, explaining government and the duties of the king. I held my girl, and all my bad dreams faded away.

Thus on my sixtieth birthday, Hotem and I settled down to enjoy the fruits of our labor. We had a grand part, to celebrate our anniversary and everyone was invited. I still looked younger, having been falsely preserved, but my king looked faded and tired in his regal brocade. We entered the party hand-in-hand. He was my best friend as he had been all those years ago when I was a slave. I still called him my beloved, and he still kissed my hand at every greeting. So we entered our great hall with our boys at our side and were greeted by adoring subjects and yells of triumphant.

It was at this moment that Kirtach, and a small army of deposed nobles and their children emerged from the crowd. They all had guns and a few had grenades and rocket launchers. One man had a flamethrower.

The music stopped, and the smiles faded. My son, Hotem XI, lifted Aeila into his arms. Where there had been joy, there was fear. The room was crowded with children and unarmed women. The men and the guards had been killed. Some woman wept in the distance, praying that they spare her children. Myhanna dropped to her knees and began to whisper some strange prayer and so did the other priests and priestesses in the room.

I was tired, and my rage was spent. That night I did what I had to do, but it was different than it had before. The storm came like a breeze in a stagnant swamp, hot and full of humidity. I moved quickly, but each movement was planned and heavy. I slid behind the man in front of me, snapped his neck and took his sword. I switched off the lights and moved in the darkness. With my sword, killing the rest was easy. They fell quickly, and when the lights went on, their mutilated remains lay in pools of blood.

The hall was silent. No one had been prepared for the violence. No one knew what to say or do. My boys ran to me and embraced me, but Aeila stayed back.

The doctor was a crabby, old University scholar. He was brilliant, and we accepted his harsh demeanor because we knew he was the best.

"I can sedate her," the doctor said. "Or I can give her mood elevators, but that's all I can do."

"What's wrong with her?" I asked. I was still clutching Aeila to my chest. The night after the assassination attempt she started crying, and I couldn't get her to stop. Her wailing filled our halls with foreboding, and no one could explain the crying.

"She's obviously been through a trauma," the doctor said. "You should try taking her to a child psychologist."

"She hasn't talked in days. What are they going to do?"

"You could take her to The University. There is a hospital there that specializes in posttraumatic stress, maybe they could help. Psychiatry is not my specialty."

"Just give me the information."

The doctor left, and I reluctantly passed Aeila off to one of the nannies to hold. I knew what I had to do, but I couldn't bear the thought of telling Hotem or my boys. Hotem and the boys were sitting together in the library playing cards when I found them. They were all worried and recent events had left them tired.

"What did he say?" Hotem asked nervously.

"I have to take her to The University," I said.

"You can't leave," Hotem said.

"I have no choice. There is no help for her here."

"Send one of the nannies with her."

"Hotem, you know I have to go."

Hotem swung wildly, knocking an old statue onto the floor. Silence filled the room. "I won't let you go," he yelled.

"Come with me then."

"You know that I can't leave after the assassination attempt. I have to attempt to find out what instigated this."

"It will only be for a few weeks. We're apart all the time."

"This is different," he said angrily.

"How?"

"It just is," he snarled.

"You won't go." Hotem left the room and slammed the door behind him. The boys looked up at me with concern, and in the distance, all we could here was Aeila's screaming.

The boys left first. They were young, but they needed to go to The University early. Hotem was feeling his age and was afraid he would die before the boys got a University education, so he sent them off at fifteen and fourteen to go and learn the secrets of the Universe.

I left the day after the boys did. My dreams had become more and more vivid, and I knew where I had to go. Aeila's wailing rarely ceased.

She sat in her room weeping. I couldn't bear it anymore.

XIII
The Plebian

I didn't tell Hotem I was going. I merely pulled Aeila's sleeping body into my arms in the middle of the night and snuck to the train station. Everything was quiet and dark, and I put on the gray suit of a University professor. I wrapped Aeila in warm clothes and carried only her bag and the things I needed for her. I had sedated her to stop her crying.

The train station was crowded, even in the middle of the night. It was filled with people trying to go one way or another and beat the daytime rush. I sat on a stone bench deep underground surrounded by glowing neon lights preparing to leave behind the only real family I had ever had.

It was a strange feeling. I had been in the same place for sixteen years. I liked my life. I looked down at Aeila. She was a pretty girl, small for her age with dark, curly hair like her father's. Her eyes were mine, but her coloring was his. I knew when she woke up she would begin to cry again, and there would be nothing I could do to soothe her. The people around me seemed half-asleep. They yawned and fidgeted, and I knew as soon as we boarded the train everyone would drift into an uncomfortable slumber.

The train arrived, and we boarded silently. Everyone was wearing gray. It looked like a train to the underworld, occupied by gray clad dreamers.

When I got to The University, I found Mia, who gladly offered me a place to stay.

Mia took care of Aeila while I went to find what I needed. I spent all day in the library, and when I was done I wandered back and sat down next to Mia. I wandered through the old university to Mia's new apartment amongst the immortals. I rode the lift to her place in the clouds and when I sat down Mia took my hand.

"Thank you," I said to my old friend.

"I'll pray for your girl," Mia said softly.

"I think I'm going mad," I said suddenly.

"Why?"

"I've been having waking dreams."

"Hallucinations?"

"Maybe."

"What happens in them?"

"I see her. I see Aeila, and she's possessed. She stands in front of me drenched in blood, and there's nothing I can do to save her."

"It's just a dream."

"It's more than a dream. It's like I'm looking through a window and on the other side of the window is our future. She's become a monster, a blood-soaked queen."

"It's just the fatigue. It will pass. We have the best hospital in the world. They'll save her. It will get better."

"Thank you," I said. "I'm not taking her to the hospital. I have to take her away. I have to take her to an island that the world doesn't touch."

"I don't think that place exists."

"It does exist. I found it at the library. There is a place that The University is forbidden to go. It's at the edge of the world where no one goes. I'll take her there. She'll know nothing of this world. She'll be safe. She'll never know who she is, and the demon in her will sleep."

"What about Hotem?" Mia asked in utter incredulity.

"Don't tell Hotem where I'm going, please. He'll force me to return," I begged. Tears rose in my eyes. I didn't hid them anymore. I just let them pour out of my eyes. I couldn't imagine a life without Hotem, but I knew that there were more important things in life than the romantic dreams of one woman.

"I'll be silent as the grave," Mia answered.

It was a long flight to the Islands of the Golden Butterfly. It took several days. The weather was horrible, and we were forced to land several times. We landed on the largest island, in the center of a town composed of long, interconnected brick homes. No one came out to greet us, so I left Aeila asleep and crept out into the cold to beat on doors.

I was met by an elderly woman who thought I was insane. She called several other people who also seemed to think I was crazy. Finally, a young man in a heavy fur coat led me through a labyrinth of dimly lit halls that connected the houses and buildings until I came to a cozy room filled with heavy tapestries and thick furs. Couches surrounded a warm fire and paintings hung in between large bookshelves. An old man sat in front of the fire holding a book.

He smiled warmly at me. "I have been told that a crazy woman won't go away. I guess you are that crazy woman?" He spoke in thickly accented Etrusan. He seemed uncommonly friendly, wrapped in blankets and heavily bearded.

"I may be," I said in his language. It was a beautiful language, melodic and sweet.

"So what can I do to help a crazy woman?" he asked.

"I don't know. I guess that's the nature of madness."

"Why don't we start with who you are?"

"I don't really know anymore."

"You don't have a name."

"Ailive."

"And where do you come from, Ailive?"

"I don't know."

"Ahh," the man said, setting down his book. "You are a mystery then, a woman from nowhere who arrives in a very expensive airship in the middle of winter. No one comes here in winter, you know. Fate must have been watching you to grant you mercy from the weather that kills most that travel in the winter."

"I need help," I asked desperately.

"Most who come here do. How can I help you?"

"I have a little girl. She's my last. I had a dream, before she was born, that something terrible would happen to her, and I think this place may save her."

"So dreams brought you here?" the plebian asked calmly. He seemed to know the answer to his question even as he asked it. There was a wisdom in his eyes.

"Nightmares."

"You speak our language well. How is that possible?"

"I have a gift with languages," I said softly.

The man nodded and got up to pour himself a drink. He brought me some. It was a sticky sweet, warm concoction that overwhelmed my senses with an instant euphoria and profound sense of peace.

"I know you," he said. "Even here, we are not shut off from the world. I will do everything I can to help you and your daughter, and I consider it a profound honor that you came to us."

A sudden fear grasped my heart. "Are you Caeimoni?" I said. I didn't want to be worshipped or praised. I just wanted help and quiet.

"No. We are an old people, and we are set in our ways. We have our own faith, but your story has always filled me with sorrow."

"You know my story?"

"Bits of it. Just what everyone knows."

"Oh," I said. "Who are you?"

"I'm Illom. I'm the plebian."

"What is that?"

"Long ago my people decided not to have kings, but we failed at democracy and republic and communism and all other forms of group ruled government as well, so we decided to choose the smartest child from among the poor or lower class and make him the plebian, the ruler.

After we are chosen, we spend our lives studying and meditating until the last plebian dies. I'm the current plebian."

"So you are like a king?"

"No. I have no power that isn't given to me and cannot be taken away.

I'm a servant of the people and not vice versa."

"Oh," I said.

"Let's get your daughter." He and a few of his people went with me to get Aeila. He carried her. He held her tiny frame and commented on her beauty. He took her to a place at the end of the maze of houses, maybe in the center, built entirely of ice.

It was elaborate and ornate, filled with sculptures of all manner of enormous sea beasts and intricate butterflies. There were many rooms that were all frigid and uninhabitable, but at the center was a warm room, with a large fire suspended over a place where the ice opened up to water. The water was deep and the ice was thick so that you had to look down over the edge of fifteen feet of ice before you saw the black pool beneath.

The room was filled with the most amazing candles that spun upward and were inlayed with gold and rocks.

"What is this place?" I asked.

"The winter castle," Illom said. He laid my daughter down on a fur on top of the ice and pulled something out of the dark pool. It was a net filled with black, snake-like fish. He cut one open and filled Aeila's mouth with its blood. She gagged and fought, but then he gave her the warm drink he had given me, and she stopped crying. He looked up at me and smiled.

"She'll be fine here," he said.

"What did you do?" I asked.

"The fish oil is the essential oil used in The University's serum. It has an infinite number of healing properties that The University has yet to entirely understand."

"Really?"

"Your brother came here once," Illom said.

"Xander?"

"His second year at The University he came here to learn about the serum. He was a great man. He spoke of you. He worried about you. I admire what he did with his talents."

"What did he learn here?"

"I told him all of our secrets."

"What secrets?"

"The secrets to eternal life. The secrets we have learned beneath the ice, beneath the sea. The secrets of the old nations still live beneath the ice here, and we keep those secrets. This is the reason The University doesn't allow us to have visitors. I told your brother how to heal even the deepest wounds and use the secrets of the old world."

Aeila looked around and then ran to me saying my name. I embraced her and pulled her into my arms. She kissed my cheek and seemed better.

"I think I need to stay here," I said.

Illom only nodded, and we stayed. We settled into a little house hidden in the ice. We fished and separated the oil from fat of the great sea beasts to make candles and oils. We helped them build their ice castles and harvest the black fish to send to The University and then we watched the castle melt and the fish swim away.

Every year they did this. They built their castle and watched it fade away and every year their castle changed. In the summer, we all went outside and wandered the fields looking for berries and watching the butterflies. In the winter, we descended into our homes to build our castle and fish for sea beasts and the black fish. In the summer, there was only sun and light. In the winter there was only darkness.

Aeila studied and learned. She was a quiet girl who liked books and dolls. She was what I had wished I could have been in another life. She never held a sword or saw a battle. She lived in quiet warmth surrounded by quiet people who worked and read.

Life can be cruel, but it can also provide the most sublime mercies. I had been on The Island of the Golden Butterfly for two years, and I had found peace there, but little joy.

In the autumn of our third year, Hotem found me. He arrived in a tiny airship accompanied only by his pilot. I was working with the other islanders when he arrived. We had already dug in for the winter and had begun construction of the winter castle. I was wrapped in furs and heavy wools and was standing in the snow chiseling a giant serpent out of ice.

Aeila was inside, studying with the other children.

I saw the ship land in the snow, and I watched with intense joy as my husband waded through the snow to find me. He didn't recognize me, but I ran to him and embraced him. He almost fell over when I tackled him, covering him with kisses. He pulled the wool away from my face to look at me.

"I missed you," he said as he kissed me.

"Thank you," I said over and over again.

I took him inside and sat him at my little wooden table. He looked so ordinary by the dim flickering of the fire. His face was creased with age, and he wore a full beard that was filled with gray. He still wore his turban, but it was black and plain. He was wrapped in a heavy coat and thick boots. He ate the fish gruel I gave him gratefully and stared at me for an eternity. I must have looked different to him as well. The cold wind had aged me. Only my face showed from beneath all my bundling, and it too was wrinkled.

"How did you find me?" I asked finally.

He smiled. "I'm a king. I have known where you were for a long time."

"Why did you not come to me sooner?"

"Why did you go?"

I looked down at my hands. They were cracked and bleeding from working in the ice. I shook my head, stifling my emotions. "Don't you know?" I whispered.

"You didn't want her to become like you," he said.

I nodded.

"I knew. I knew when you told me you wanted to leave that night. I knew and that's why I didn't want you to go then and that's why I didn't come sooner. I didn't want to frighten you. I didn't want you to think I would make you come back."

I ran to him and buried my face in his lap. With the softness of a mother caressing her infant, he undid the wool around my hair. He set his hands on my hair and stroked it like he would a baby he was lulling to sleep.

"Did you know that Xander and I once traveled together?"

"No," I said.

"When he was in Efferitas, he came to me and asked me to walk with him to the ocean. We walked together, and he said very little. The only thing he said was this, 'One day, my sister will be your queen,' he said. 'You must take care of her. God has asked too much of her, and she has broken. Always give her any solace she seeks.'"

The sun faded outside, and the room dimmed. We made love as we always had in my tiny bed in a darkened corner. We were old, and the passion had faded. We were not seeking fire but solace. I didn't ask him about politics or the kingdom. I didn't care about the world.

"How are the boys?" I asked.

"They will be coming back from The University this spring," he answered. "They have done very well. I have been told that they are brilliant. They both studied warcraft and sociology. I haven't told them you left. I just told them that you were too sick to come and visit them."

"Thank you for that."

"They'll be angry when they come back. They ask about you all the time."

"Just tell them the wind called me home. They'll understand that."

"They'll understand, but they'll still be angry."

"I know."

Before he left he went and watched Aeila in school. He stood for over an hour watching her write her letters and paint pictures of sunsets. He left pretty dolls and stuffed toys and then he disappeared, leaving me with my silence.

Every autumn he came, and every autumn it was the same. The boys missed me. The boys were angry, and I saw in his eyes that the world was changing, but I couldn't return with him. I had become part of the ice.

I had grown old by the time I spoke to anyone from the outside besides Hotem. Dania found me. Aeila was almost thirteen when she saw an army of airships drifting in over the glaciers. It was spring, and the winter palace had melted, leaving an enormous fishing hole in its place. Aeila had been gathering berries, and she dropped her basket to run home tell me. The entire village wandered out of their houses at the sound of Aeila's yelling. We were a quiet people who spoke little and read much.

The ships landed, and Dania emerged in all her glory. She was wrapped in gold and surrounded by white clad bishops with ornate robes and intricate scepters. The island people were unimpressed, and Illom greeted Dania in the same pleasant manner he would have greeted a wondering tribeless.

I sent Aeila away. I didn't want her to know the outside world. She was a creature of books and long winters. She studied and painted. She was surrounded by doting islanders and gentle playmates. I didn't want her to see Dania and her web of glorious violence.

I would not go onto Dania's airship, so she came with me into my tiny house. It was only one room with two beds and a pleasant sofa. It connected to the rest of the village, like all the other houses. Dania wrinkled her nose with disgust when she walked in, but she masked her disdain quickly.

She bowed to me. "Saint Ailive," she said loudly. "Our people have found great need of you. We have come to implore you to return with us to your home. We have rebuilt your great churches and temples and returned your city to its former glory. I have come here, with more than six thousand, five hundred pilgrims, to sit at your feet and learn your wisdom."

I looked outside, through my tiny window and saw the large airships. Pilgrims were already beginning to pour of the airship and wander through the tundra.

"I'm no saint," I said.

"Saint Ailive," she said more quietly. "You're the patron saint of our city. I have spent my life writing the books of your life. Times have become difficult for us. We're beset on all sides by enemies. Your people could use your wisdom."

"I have no wisdom to offer, and I ask only that you leave."

Aeila was peeking into the room from the doorway. She was a curious girl with a mischievous side.

Dania put her arm on my shoulder. "Please," she said in a whisper. "We only want to honor you. Please come and help us. We're surrounded by followers of the new prophet and heretics besiege us. You've saved us before."

"I have said no. Look at me, I'm an old woman. I can't fight any longer and even if I could, I gave up the sword years ago."

Dania nodded sadly. "At least say a few words to the pilgrims."

I walked outside with her and spoke to her legion of followers. I didn't say much, but I decided to tell them a story. I told them Jason's story. For some reason, it seemed appropriate.

I know I'm dying now. My Aeila stands by me as she always has.

Time has worn me thin. She strokes my hair and feeds me broth and her eyes speak a thousand words her lips will never utter. She's afraid, and she's alone, but at least she has known peace. That was the only gift I could give her. She'll never hold a sword.

Sometimes I regret my decision. I see Hotem in my dreams. I hear him calling my name. I hear my boys.

Sometimes I even hear Xander calling to me from the longhouse. I can hear him calling to me to come and follow him to his God.

But for me, through this long life, there is only one thing I have really learned. There is no God.

I have watched all manner of people lost in their lives. They fight and bicker and struggle and the fighting never ends. In truth, we all walk the way of the storm. This is the only god I'll ever know.

About the Author

I am a therapist and writer who lives in Alabama with my three corgis, children, husband, and other strange creatures.

Website: http://www.jessicapenot.net

Blog: http://www.ghoststoriesandhauntedplaces.blogspot.com